T...
...RT

*These a... ...y the men and women who made bo... ...s their home and their future. It is the story of America itself.*

## CRIPPLE CREEK

When a cave-in at the Rattlesnake mine kills six workers, one man is to blame—Philip LaFarge, the mine's greedy owner. But he'll be damned if he's going to take the fall . . .

## DEADWOOD

Nathaniel Jones is a newspaper reporter, not a soldier. But he'll need all of his meager survival skills when he becomes a correspondent for General Custer's mapping expedition . . .

*Berkley Books by Douglas Hirt*

**CRIPPLE CREEK**
**DEADWOOD**

# DEADWOOD

## Douglas Hirt

BERKLEY BOOKS, NEW YORK

DEADWOOD

A Berkley Book / published by arrangement with
Siegel & Siegel, Ltd.

PRINTING HISTORY
Berkley edition / January 1998

The Putnam Berkley World Wide Web site address is
http://www.berkley.com

ISBN: 0-425-16152-8

BERKLEY®
Berkley Books are published by The Berkley Publishing Group,
a member of Penguin Putnam Inc.,
200 Madison Avenue, New York, New York 10016.
BERKLEY and the ''B'' design
are trademarks belonging to Berkley Publishing Corporation.

PRINTED IN THE UNITED STATES OF AMERICA

10  9  8  7  6  5  4  3  2  1

For Tom Hirt

# THE BLACK HILLS

*There are whole mountain ranges of granite. Some of it is hard and fine and variable in color; other portions exceedingly coarse and friable, containing great sheets of mica and large crystals of tourmaline, and occasionally large masses of feldspar or quartz.*

*A large part of the rock formation is carbonate of lime (marble), of various degrees in hardness and fineness. It is sometimes all one color, white or dark, sometimes as veined and mottled as the Egyptian. Of that which is good, there is sufficient quantity to supply the sculptors of the world and all the cemeteries. . . .*

Aris B. Donaldson
*St. Paul Pioneer*
**August 15, 1874**

# PROLOGUE

*1842—Somewhere in the northern Black Hills*

The arrow whizzed past Carson Grove's ear like an angry hornet and thumped into the trunk of the ponderosa pine just ahead of him. Grove winced, ducked his head, and threw himself into the bramble of raspberry bushes off the side of the trail. It had been a gut reaction. He had no more control over it than he would have a sneeze.

The next instant Jim Bridger was grabbing him out of the pincushion underbrush. "You hit?"

"Hell no—least I don't think so," Grove gasped, crushing the black felt hat back on his head. On top of feeling foolish, he now itched in two dozen places.

Pierre Fontenelle, the one they called Frenchie, drew up alongside them, puffing like he had run a mile, which was near enough the truth. "Run, men! These red devils, they're breathing up our asses. Come! Run, run!" He wheeled, threw his rifle to his shoulder, and fired at something that moved in the thick forest behind them.

Through the gray smoke of the rifle shot, Bill Waller came charging past, not even bothering to slow for them, his legs and arms pumping like the piston of a riverboat's engine.

Bridger pushed Grove on ahead of him. "Get moving!"

The four men charged along the forest trail, dodging thick timber, crashing through brambles and splashing across the swift, cold streams. Now and again an arrow would sing past them or the sound of a rifle's shot would make them duck their heads. But nothing could make them stop their headlong plunge through the forest—not their burning lungs, not their cramping leg muscles. Nothing until their frantic rush took them to the edge of a precipice and they all halted.

Fontenelle leaped behind a tree and sighted along the barrel of his J. Henry Lancaster rifle. It barked, then punched his shoulder, and somewhere back among the trees a man howled. Fontenelle grinned. "Aha! That one is singing a new tune!"

"What did we ever do to them?" Waller managed to gasp, doubled over.

"We come a trapping on their sacred *Paha Sapa* . . . the Black Hills, hunting grounds of the Great Spirit," Carson Grove answered, anxiously studying the desolate gulch that fell away below them, barring their way. The rugged sides dove steeply to a swift creek below, and then rose even more steeply to a bare hill where a pile of brown stones caught the morning sunlight. A fire had raged through this place recently, leaving behind a charred valley filled with dead wood. "I don't know . . . about you . . . Bill," Grove panted, his lungs burning, saliva streaking his black beard, "but I lost fifty dollars' worth of traps back there. This *Paha Sapa* place is about the most unhealthy and unprofitable place I ever did trap!"

Bridger said, "We lost it all today, boys, but we still got our scalps, and our rifles. We either take a stand here or try to get across this gulch."

"Across that?" Fontenelle said as he rammed a ball down the barrel of his rifle and fitted a cap to the nipple. "You must be crazy in the head, Gabe!"

Just then a chunk of bark exploded from the tree near his head. "*Oui!* Across that!" Fontenelle didn't wait to be asked again.

"Oh, shit!" Waller cried, scrambling over the dead timber and plunging down the gulch after the Frenchman.

Grove took aim and fired through the trees. An Indian spun around with a knuckle-size hole in his breast. Pulling back and spilling another charge of powder down the barrel, Grove glanced at Bridger. "We stand or run?"

Already a dozen more Sioux were fanning out through the trees. At the head of the war party was a strong young chief named One Stab. Grove had met One Stab once or twice, under friendlier circumstances—a marriage, to be exact.

Bridger finished reloading and drew back the hammer of his brand-new Hawken rifle. "I can buy me another set of traps easier than I can replace this scalp of mine, Grove. I say Waller and Frenchie have the right idea—we run."

Grove grinned. "You got a good head on those shoulders, Gabe."

"And that's where I'd like to keep it."

They swung out from behind their cover, fired together, and then, leaping over the edge of the gulch, bound down the steep incline, jumping and dodging dead wood where they could, tumbling over it where they could not. New-growth pines rose knee-high, covering the steep descent and further impeding their mad rush toward the winding creek far below.

Fontenelle and Waller had already reached the creek. From behind blackened timbers, they fired up the side of the gulch to keep the Sioux back from its edge while Bridger and Grove high-stepped over the fallen wood, arms and rifles waving wildly in the air.

When they finally dove to cover, Fontenelle grinned over at them and said, "So, you decided to join us?"

Swiftly Grove and Bridger reloaded their rifles.

"Don't get the idea we actually missed your company, Frenchie," Grove said, rising above the blackened tree trunk just long enough to squeeze off a shot. Of the four of them, Pierre Fontenelle was the youngest, just twenty-two. He was also the least experienced. He had bright blue eyes, sandy hair, and handsome features, but his attempts at cultivating a proper beard and mustache had been an utter failure and a never-ending source of embarrassment. Just the same, Fontenelle's disposition was usually sunny—one of his winning traits—and he had the ability to find humor in the most harrowing of circumstances. Although Grove generally treated him gruffly—Grove treated everyone gruffly—he liked the young man.

Bridger fired next and pulled back. "We are in a fix here, boys. Them Sioux outnumber us five to one."

"I say we skedaddle down this here creek. It's got to open out somewhere." Waller glanced at the swift water tumbling down the gulch.

"*Oui*, it opens into their arms," Fontenelle observed dryly, pointing at the six or eight Sioux who had closed off their avenue of retreat in that direction. The Indians were moving slowly up the creek, almost within range of the trappers' rifles.

Grove swung around and shouldered his rifle.

"Save your bullets and powder," Bridger warned.

Grove ignored him and rested the long barrel of his New English pattern rifle upon a log. Steadying it, he caught his breath and his finger tightened upon the trigger. The 32-gauge rifle thundered, leaped off the log, and two hundred and fifty yards down the gulch a sledgehammer blow flipped an Indian backward off his feet.

Fontenelle gave a whistle of approval.

Bridger glanced up the gulch. "That way is cut off too."

"Holy Mary Mother of God," Fontenelle said, crossing himself twice.

"Whose wonderful idea was it to string our traps in these hills?" Waller carped.

Three heads turned toward Carson Grove.

Grove grinned and his shoulders shrugged beneath dirty buckskins as he rammed another ball down the barrel of his rifle. "I didn't hear no objections from no one when I suggested it."

"You said it was your wife's people who hunted these hills," Bridger shot back.

A bullet splintered wood chips in their faces. They ducked down lower.

"It is, usually. One Stab, though, he ain't but distantly related. I reckon some Indians just don't hold to family ties like others."

"So, now where do we go?" Fontenelle asked.

Bridger looked over his shoulder at the steep wall on the far side of the gulch, across the creek. "Looks like we got but two choices. Either we hunker down here and fight till lead and powder run out, or we take to that thar hill like men with a bear on our tails."

"Our chances hunkering?" Fontenelle insisted.

"Good enough, I reckon, to guarantee that your scalp will be hanging on some buck's lodgepole tonight."

"Then I think we ought to start climbing—now!"

Hunched over, they charged across the creek. In a moment they were clawing over the fallen trees, clambering up the far side of the gulch. Grove stole a look over his shoulder and counted nine Sioux. His lungs were afire and his legs weighed a hundred pounds each, but he pushed on, carried up the side of the deep valley on sheer fear alone.

Leading the warriors, One Stab whooped and waved his bow over his head to encourage his men toward more speed. As the chief fitted an arrow to the bow, Grove called out a warning. The four men dove behind a scorched log, and a heartbeat later the arrow sang overhead.

"Damn close," Bridger hissed, swinging his Hawken rifle around and putting a bullet through the leg of one of the warriors below. The four mountain men were up and running again, slogging their way toward the crest of the valley. Their labored breathing had been reduced to ragged gasps, and sweat and saliva streamed down their eyes and cheeks.

"We're almost there, boys," Bridger rasped. The pile of brown rocks that they had spied from the other side suddenly loomed in sight overhead. The men groped up the last few dozen feet of hillside. Their only consolation was that the Sioux seemed as completely done in as they were.

The last few feet were like torture in hell, then they scrambled around the rocks, drawing oxygen like red coals into their lungs. Grove leaned over the top of one of the rocks and fired. An Indian cartwheeled backward, taking another man with him halfway down the timber-clogged slope.

Reloading automatically, Grove blinked the stinging sweat from his eyes and heard Waller's rifle boom to his right. Bridger took the next shot.

Fontenelle was feeling the exertion worse than the others. This was his first trip into the mountains, and the men sometimes poked fun at his innocence and called him a willow sapling. Now he fell to the ground, panting, his fingers clawing at the dirt as he tried to recoup his strength, and no one was laughing.

"We got to keep going," Bridger managed, looking up at the more gently climbing ground that faced them.

"A moment, please," Fontenelle gasped.

"Ain't got a moment, Frenchie," Grove said. The men rose wearily. Waller, Grove, and Bridger fired another volley down into the gulch to keep the savages' heads down.

"I have heard it said," Fontenelle wheezed, his words clipped short by the ragged meter of his breathing, "that no white man . . . has ever come . . . out of this place alive."

"That ain't true. I've been in and out of the *Paha Sapa*—more'n five or six times," Grove said.

Fontenelle managed a grin. "But your wife's people run the place, *mon ami*."

"Let's git," Bridger ordered.

Fontenelle pushed to his knees, his fist clutching a handful of grass and dirt as he sat up against the rocks. The three other men had already started up the rising land.

Grove turned back. "Frenchie! Get a-moving!"

"Mother in heaven!" Fontenelle cried.

They stopped and looked back. Fontenelle was still sitting there, but now he was staring with huge eyes at something in his hand .

"Frenchie!" Grove ordered.

The Frenchman continued staring at his hand, transfixed. A Sioux came up over the edge at that moment and Grove swung his rifle, firing from the hip. He rushed back to Fontenelle to get him moving. Fontenelle shoved his hand under Grove's nose and said, "Look! Look what I have pulled up out of the grass!"

It was a gold nugget, bigger than any Grove had ever heard tell of! It was the size of a walnut, and shaped like a horseshoe, almost perfectly formed. At the apex of the horseshoe, as if purposefully set there by a jeweler, glinted a diamond-shaped chunk of white quartz.

"Look at it, Carson. It's gold. Gold! A golden horseshoe! My lucky horseshoe, no?"

"We ain't got time for this, Frenchie. Let's get moving!"

"We can't leave now! There might be more lying around! We will be rich men!"

"We will be dead men if we don't hightail it out of here!"

That seemed to sink in a little, but just the same, Fontenelle hesitated.

"Pierre, come to your senses," Grove hissed.

The sound of his name seemed to shake Fontenelle from his trance.

Ahead, Bridger brought his rifle's barrel down and fired. The Sioux that had appeared atop the brown rocks disappeared behind them.

"*Oui,*" Fontenelle said, remembering the danger. Clutching the nugget in his fist, he struggled to his feet. The two men had only just started up the rise when Grove heard the whizzing of an arrow. He ducked his head as it thudded into something behind him. Grove turned as a wide, startled look suddenly contorted his friend's face.

The arrow had pierced Fontenelle's heart and had come through his chest, the point of it protruding the length of a hand.

Grove broke stride, uncertain if he should go back, but the Frenchman was dead before he hit the ground, and Sioux were now swarming up from the gulch.

Life was always tenuous at best on the frontier, and men like Grove, Bridger, and Waller had come to accept death as a natural part of it. Just the same, Frenchie had been a good and trustworthy companion, a valiant fighter, a man who would not desert a friend—a man who would be greatly missed.

As Grove fled with the others his heart sank, and the stinging that moistened his eyes was more than just the sweat flowing freely down his body.

He would never forget Frenchie, nor would he forget that gold nugget—that "lucky horseshoe"—or what the sight of it had cost Fontenelle. . . .

Bent over, exhausted, and fighting for breath, Chief One Stab stopped upon the crest of the gulch. Slowly he straightened up, his chest heaving, the air stinging his lungs. The white men had given them a good chase. They had run them through some of the deepest woods of the *Paha Sapa,* and they had managed to elude his braves. All but one of them, that is.

Drawing great drafts of air into his lungs, One Stab called an end to the contest. Sweat glistened upon his naked chest, and the scars from the sacred Sun Dance, still new and pink, stood out like two thick cords across his breast. He approached the brown rocks where the body lay facedown, One Stab's arrow protruding from its back. The other braves gathered around as One Stab drew his sharp knife and cut the top scalp away from the skull and held the prize high overhead.

Turning the dead man over, One Stab claimed the hunting bag, powder horn, and the supreme prize of all, the long caplock rifle. With a cry of victory, he thrust the rifle to the sky, then returned to stripping the white man of anything he perceived as being valuable. In his search, One Stab opened the fingers that had balled into a fist, curious at what the hand clutched. It was one of the yellow rocks that the white man valued. One Stab frowned, and he was about to throw it away when a thought struck him. He stopped. This rock was shaped differently from others that he had found in the *Paha Sapa*. Turning it over in his hand, One Stab decided that it looked vaguely like the sky symbol, with the eye of the Great Spirit of the *Paha Sapa, Wakan Tanka*, embedded at its apex. Yes, that was definitely what it was. It had to be a good omen, and he dropped it into the buffalo scrotum pouch at his waist.

Later, when the warriors returned to their lodges, Chief One Stab showed the yellow rock to his wife, Spotted Doe Woman. She declared that it was a *Tukan* from the Great Spirit and that it would bring good fortune to the family. It must stay with the family, she decided. "I will give it to our son when he becomes a warrior and has a family," she said, and she placed the rock with her other fetishes.

One Stab forgot the yellow stone almost immediately, but Spotted Doe Woman cherished it, and when their son took a wife, she passed it to him so that his family would profit from possessing it, even as her family had.

And so the nugget's journey began.

# ONE

*July 1874—The plains north of the Black Hills*

When a horse wandered into the ring of their firelight one of the startled soldiers lifted the frayed end of its picket, took one look, and shouted, "Indians!"

In an instant the troops of the Seventh Cavalry leaped to their feet, grabbing up rifles and hitching their galluses up over their shoulders as they fanned out through the camp. Over a thousand cavalry, infantry, and civilian personnel, squatting around campfires or stretched out on bedrolls after a long day's march, came suddenly alert.

Nathaniel Jones dropped his plate of beans and antelope meat and was about to rush to his tent for his revolver when the gray-haired old man sitting at his side grabbed his arm and stopped him. "Let the soldier boys handle it, Nate," he said in an easy, laconic voice.

"But the Indians! They've tried to scatter our mounts. There may be an attack any moment—" Suddenly Jones noticed the tight grin that had moved across the old man's weathered face.

No one knew for sure how old Carson Grove was, only that he'd been forty years in the mountains, trapping beaver in the early days, guiding Oregon- and California-bound pilgrims in the fifties, hunting meat for the railroads in the sixties. Now, in 1874, Grove was hunting meat again, this time for Lieutenant Colonel Custer's expedition into the Black Hills.

Soldiers dashed past them, their rifles and sabers rattling as the captains ordered them to different points on the perimeter of the camp. Jones sat back down uneasily and said, "No Indians?"

Grove bit a square of antelope meat from the point of his knife. It disappeared behind the tangle of his gray beard. As he chewed he said, "Custer has ten companies of cavalry and two of infantry under his command. Now you tell me, do the Sioux got turkey feathers for brains?"

"Well, then who cut the picket ropes?"

Grove set his tin plate aside and caught the dangling rope of a nearby horse. He studied the frayed end a moment, returned to his place by the fire, and with the ghost of a grin hidden behind his beard, resumed eating, using the edge of his skinning knife like a spoon, licking the brown beans from the razor-sharp blade that only a few hours earlier had cleaned the half dozen antelope he had brought into camp. "It weren't no Injun, Nate" is all he said.

Across the encampment Lt. Col. George Custer stepped from his big, rectangular wall tent, a gift to him from the Northern Pacific Railroad. He stood before the open wind-flap, peering out into the darkness as soldiers hurried past. Yellow lantern light from inside the tent reflected off his hair and brightened the back of the fringed buckskin shirt he sometimes wore when he went hunting. At his heels yapped two of the hunting hounds that he had brought along on this expedition. Major Forsyth stepped out of the shadows and the two officers conferred as Major Sanger's infantry formed up and took their positions. The guards on picket duty had started collecting the stray horses and staking them down again while a company of Custer's cavalry prepared to mount up.

Jones gave Grove a confused look. "If not the Sioux, then who cut those picket ropes?"

"Let's see if them soldier boys can figure it out on their own" was all Grove would allow just then.

Aris Donaldson came across the camp and hunkered down by Jones's fire. Donaldson was actually the expedition's botanist, but the *St. Paul Pioneer* had hired him to send back accounts of Custer's grand march through the Black Hills, and in turn, Donaldson had conscripted Jones to help with the writing while he collected and pressed the plants of the area. In real life, Donaldson taught English literature at the University of Minnesota. Everyone on the expedition just called him "Professor." Donaldson was a large, friendly man, as reserved as he was rotund, in his mid-forties, with a full black beard that came nearly down to his chest and black hair thinning at the temples.

"What do you think, Mr. Jones? It looks like what everyone has feared is finally coming about. You didn't hear anything, did you?"

"No, nothing."

The camp was a jumble of activity, with men scurrying every which way—everyone, that is, except the Arikara and Santee scouts sitting around their fires at the edge of camp. They, like Carson Grove, appeared unconcerned, even amused. Across the trampled grass of the bivouac, Custer retreated to his tent. Forsyth set off in another direction. The cavalry departed through the line of infantry and disappeared into the night.

"The Indian scouts seem to be enjoying it," Donaldson pointed out.

Grove gave a short laugh, scrapped the remains of his dinner into the fire, where they sizzled upon the coals, and stood, taking up the long Sharps rifle that he had affectionately named Big 50. "I think I'll just find me a tree to water, boys."

Jones hadn't seen a single tree all day, but since coming to know Carson Grove these last couple weeks on march, and the weeks before that while waiting for the new

Springfield rifles to arrive at Fort Abraham Lincoln before the expedition could get under way, he knew the old mountain man could find virtue in a bawdy house if he wanted to. Locating a tree somewhere upon these flat, empty, gumbo prairies, Jones mused, should be a simple matter for him.

Donaldson watched Grove stroll off into the darkness. "That old man doesn't seem much concerned either."

"He says it isn't Indians at all."

In the flickering firelight Donaldson's view came back to Jones's face and his dark eyebrows hitched down. "How would he know that?"

Jones shrugged his shoulders. "How does he know half the things he does? He just knows."

Carson Grove stood in deep shadows behind one of the supply wagons, staring up at the dark, frosted sky, listening to the patter of urine upon the ground at his feet. When he finished, he buttoned his fly and, grabbing up Big 50, started back into camp. Not everyone had taken the alarm to heart. After the first ripples of the impending attack had made their way through the camp, most of the bullwhackers, mule skinners, and cowboys had settled back down to what they'd been doing. After all, Custer was here, and he had most of his Seventh Cavalry with him. Indians were his problem, not theirs.

Grove heard low laughing coming from the other side of a canvas-covered supply wagon. When he stepped up alongside it he saw the faces of four men sitting near a fire, playing cards. He knew two of the men there. One was a supply wagon driver, a young bullwhacker with a reputation for winning at cards by the name of Roman Kinsey, but if you ever called him "Roman" to his face you'd likely feel the keen edge of his bowie pressed up against your throat faster than cracked corn disappears down a chicken's gullet. His friends, what few he had, just called him Ro. The only friend that Grove knew Kinsey palled around with was a fellow named Bradley Sink. Sink was sitting across from Ro, wearing a battered slouch hat and holding a handful of playing cards close to his vest. Both men were trouble, and in his old age, Grove preferred to avoid trouble where he could.

They hadn't heard him come up, nor had they noticed him standing there, quietly watching. He was about to move on when all at once Ro said, "Say, ain't that General Custer coming this way?" pointing across the encampment, where a hundred small fires like their own flickered, illuminating the trampled grass.

As the men turned to look, Ro swiftly reached behind his back, slipped three cards up under his vest, and in the next instant was fitting three new cards into his hand. The maneuver took less than two seconds, and from Grove's position he could see that the new cards were a trio of aces. Bradley Sink was the first to look back. Bradley's and Ro's eyes met and Ro gave him a slight nod. Sink laughed and said, "You need to get your eyes looked at, Ro. That wasn't the general, was it, fellows?" He glanced at the two suckers. One said he had seen nothing. The other thought he'd seen a man who looked like Custer.

"I reckon I must have been mistaken, boys," Ro confessed, sounding embarrassed.

Everyone shrugged the incident off and the game went on, the only difference being that now Kinsey was holding a winning hand.

Grove backed off quietly and made a note never to sit in on a card game with Ro Kinsey.

A few minutes after the troops of Company M had ridden out, two soldiers entered Custer's tent. A moment later they emerged with the lieutenant colonel and went to the picket line, where Custer examined one of the cut ropes. He said something, pointed, and one of the soldiers jogged over to the scouts, bringing back an Arikara by the name of Bare Arm. The scout and Custer spoke, then both laughed and Custer ordered the bugler to sound recall.

As the troops rode back into camp and dismounted, Nathan Knappen of the *Bismarck Tribune* and Bill Curtis of the *Chicago Inter-Ocean* came to the campfire by the correspondents' tents.

"What was it all about?" Donaldson asked.

Knappen said, "The boys in blue rode out to chase down poor Lo, but lo, Lo was nowhere to be found— boohoo." He laughed.

Jones was more interested in the cut picket lines than in Knappen's sorry poetry.

"They weren't cut at all," Curtis explained. "Seems everyone but the military knew that. Well, almost everyone. When Custer examined them he knew right off they hadn't been cut. Then that Ree scout told him about the prairie swift foxes hereabouts. Seems they have a penchant for chewing things, picket ropes being one of their favorites." Curtis grinned. "They will steal you blind if they get a chance."

Jones laughed. "The cavalry chases foxes!" He glanced at Donaldson. "This will make interesting reading for the folks back in St. Paul."

Someone cleared his throat behind them. Sam Barrows of the *New York Tribune* joined the circle of correspondents and poured himself a cup of coffee. He set the pot back on the banked coals and said, "I just had a little talk with the general. He requested that we not make too much of this incident. He didn't come right out and tell me not to print it, but I got the feeling he would consider it an embarrassment if we did."

"Censorship of the press," Knappen declared. At nineteen, Nathan Knappen was only two years younger than Jones, and the most outspoken and impetuous of the group.

Barrows grunted. "Perhaps. But you know how Custer is. Treat him right in the press and he treats you like royalty. Cross him, and you can bet it's the last time you'll ever be invited along on one of his forays. And the folks back home do love to read about Custer's expeditions."

Barrows understood the truth of that firsthand. The year before he had accompanied Stanley and Custer on their

Yellowstone Expedition, and it was because of Barrows's friendship with Custer, and his friendly pen toward the brevetted general, that Custer had invited him along on this Black Hills reconnaissance.

Later that night, sitting on the edge of his cot and bent over the wavering flame of a candle lantern, Jones wrote in his journal:

*July 17th, 1874. It has been a hard push since marching away from Fort Abraham Lincoln on July 2nd. Inside my head I still hear the tune Custer's brass band played as the fort receded from our view: "The Girl I Left Behind Me." It was glorious to finally be on our way after our long delay . . . especially because once we left the muddy Missouri River behind, we also left behind the hordes of voracious mosquitoes that for weeks had made our lives miserable.*

*Today we entered a land devoid of all beauty which Ludlow, the engineer, calls "Badlands." Yesterday we marched thirty miles, and tomorrow it is expected we shall get our first view of the Black Hills. It is after eleven and I am about to turn in for the night. Knappen is already snoring away in the next tent over; I can hear him plainly now that the camp has quieted down. Above his loud purring I hear the yapping coyotes and the small scuffling sounds that one tries to identify but fails utterly to do—that is, of course, unless you happen to belong to that hardy breed of men who live out their lives on these harsh plains.*

*Carson Grove happens to be such a man. To illustrate, a small incident occurred tonight that will find itself recorded only here, in my private musings, for the Gen.—well, officially Custer is a Lieut. Col., but it is customary to call him by that elevated rank which he earned during the War of the Rebellion— has requested the event be kept from the public record as it might prove a slight embarrassment to the*

*Seventh, of which the general is so justly proud. Around eight-thirty o'clock several horses wandered into camp, their picket lines cut, or so it appeared to the soldier who first sounded the alarm.*

*Upon the sound of an alarm, our soldiers rushed to the perimeter while a company of cavalry mounted and rode out. Mr. Grove, sitting at my elbow when all this came about, flinched not an eye at the perceived danger. He knew very well, as apparently did the Ree and Santee scouts, that there were no lurking savages in the dark. In fact, he knew all along that the ropes were cut not by the blade of a savage's knife, but by the sharp, gnawing teeth of swift foxes, which later were identified as the species* Vulpes velox.

*Custer's troops returned a few minutes after the mistake had been discovered, looking quite embarrassed at being fooled by the wiles of mother nature. . . .*

*Mr. Donaldson, with whom I share this tent, has just arrived, his arms filled with the botanical specimens he has collected these last few days, ready for one of the plant presses he keeps beneath his cot. I shall end this narrative now, the point of it being to record these singular events in order to fix firmly in my memory the characteristics of the men who inhabit this region—be them red-skinned or white.*

# TWO

Western Dakota Territory's barren, windswept plains seem even bleaker viewed through a pair of army field glasses from the rocking bed of a covered wagon. For Nathaniel Jones, the adventure was wearing thin. Instead of the excitement he had hoped for when Donaldson had offered him the opportunity to come along, he was discovering that military expeditions consisted largely of hard marches and hastily erected camps. At least here, far from the banks of the Missouri River where the expedition had been stymied while waiting for the arrival of the new rifles, there were not the voracious clouds of mosquitoes.

Jones was ready for most any diversion that next morning when Carson Grove rode up alongside the supply wagon leading an extra saddle horse with one of the new Springfield carbines hanging off its side.

"Gonna do some huntin', Nate. Care to ride along?"

"I'd be pleased to, Mr. Grove. The back of a good horse is far superior to the bed of a heavily sprung army supply wagon any day." He slid the glasses back into their leather case, belted his revolver around his waist, and leaped off the end of the wagon. Grove drew up long enough for Jones to shove his boot into the stirrup and swing onto the saddle. They rode forward through the ranks of covered wagons that rolled four abreast, stretching back nearly a half mile, past the blue ambulances, past the artillery, past the brass band mounted on white horses, to the front of the column where Custer was watching his hounds ranging far ahead.

"The general's permission to do a bit o' hunting," Grove said.

Custer looked over. The freshly cropped curls of his hair sticking out from beneath his black slouch hat shone reddish-gold in the morning sunlight. His fair, youthful skin was burnt to a ruddy blush, and his bright blue eyes glinted effervescently. He obviously enjoyed expedition life . . . and watching his hounds romping through the line of troops. Jones had only met the "Boy General" two or three times, and then only briefly. Today he was struck by the lieutenant colonel's dimpled chin, which receded, he mused, in a manner some might consider unmasculine for a man of Custer's vigorous reputation. Jones thought that perhaps the hugely flowing mustache might be Custer's way of compensating for the lack of chin. Custer, in his fringed buckskin hunting shirt over the sky blue trousers, looked rather dashing.

"It is a wonderful day for a hunt, Mr. Grove. I was thinking of doing a little of that myself later in the day."

"I'm taking Mr. Jones with me."

"Very well. Have one of the wagons accompany you, and try not to let our party get out of sight. I'll send a couple of the Rees with you." Custer passed an order back to Lieutenant Wallace, who was in command of the scouts, and a few minutes later Jones and Grove were riding beyond the safety of the convoy and up a rise of land in the company of four Arikara. From the top of the ridge, the caravan below appeared to stretch on for miles, a sea of white canvas flanked by columns of blue.

"That's a sight to gladden the heart," Jones said.

Grove looked over. "How so?"

"Well, I mean, we are in the middle of hostile Indian country. If the Sioux decide to attack, it's heartening to have so many troops nearby, and Custer in command of them.''

"Hmm. They make you feel safe, do they?''

"Well, yes. Don't you think so?''

Grove frowned and turned his horse away, angling down the hill toward a distant heard of antelope. "Sure do, Nate—about as safe as standing under a tree in a lightning storm.''

Jones urged his horse after him. "You don't agree?''

Grove was making for a ridge of high ground overlooking the grazing herd. Behind them, the supply wagon clattered noisily as it followed over the steep and rocky ground. The scouts had moved into a line about two hundred yards off to one side of them. "In '68 all this land was given over to the Sioux by the 'Father' in Washington City. Today there are almost two thousand soldiers and civilians marching into what the Sioux consider sacred ground—the hunting grounds of the Great Spirit, *Wakan Tanka*. And why do you think that is?''

"This is a scientific expedition. We are here to assess the geology and biology of the area, and to make reliable maps. Custer sent word to all the chiefs that this was only a survey mission and that the government meant the Indians no harm.''

Grove grinned. "And you believe that?''

"Well . . . why do *you* think Custer is here?''

"I'll tell you why he's here.'' Grove reined in suddenly and peered intensely at Jones. "It's because of the rumor of gold. Your Unky Sam wants to know if it is true or not. That's why among the scholars and soldier boys, you got them two mining professionals, McKay and Ross. You pay attention now—more good men have gotten themselves kilt over gold than over bad women or bad whiskey. If'n it's true and they do find gold in the Black Hills, sure as a polecat has got perfume, the gover'ment's gonna find a way to take these hills back from the Sioux. And if that happens, white men are gonna attract trouble like old Ben Franky's kite pulled down lightning.'' He heeled his horse and got moving again.

At the ridge they dismounted and studied the animals below. The antelope were wary of the hunting party, every head turned now, but since the distance between them was considerable, they held their ground. The wagon continued forward, creaking and rattling. Grove motioned impatiently to the thoughtless driver to stop. It was then that he saw that the man on the high seat was Ro Kinsey. Kinsey gave the old man a scowl and brought the wagon to a halt about a hundred yards back. The Rees swung to the ground and led their mounts slowly toward the site where Grove was preparing his hunt.

"A damn nuisance, that one."

"Who?"

"That driver. He would have drove right into the middle of that herd."

Jones glanced over his shoulder at the driver. He did not know the man, and turned his attention back to the hunt at hand. He shoved a .45-55 cartridge into the Springfield carbine, shut the breech block, crawled to the edge of the ridge, and squinted down the barrel. He put the carbine down and looked over. "This is a mighty long shot, Mr. Grove. Maybe we should move in a little closer."

Carson Grove had removed a two-legged wood and leather cross-tree from a leather pouch and was setting it up on the hard ground. He laid out a canvas buffalo belt that held thirty-five of the huge .50-90 cartridges and removed three of them, setting them up on their ends. "Antelope got sharp eyes and are skittish as a bride on her weddin' night, but they're curious critters too. They'll stand still and watch you and me so long as we don't appear a threat to them, but as soon as we move in too close, they'll scatter to the wind. In fact," he went on, snapping the vernier sight into its upright position and fiddling with the knurled thumbscrew on top, "they ain't like buffalo either. After the first shot they won't wait around to think about it but will all head for the hills. If we are lucky we might pick off one or two on the fly."

He glanced at Jones's cavalry carbine and said, "Better set the sight on that piece a mite higher."

Jones elevated the rear sight up one more notch to the 300-yard mark and squinted along the short barrel again.

"Pick one out and line him up. I'll shoot first, then you. You won't have time for a second shot so make your first one count."

That rankled Jones a bit. He had hunted all his life and figured he could bring down at least two antelope before they moved out of range, although he had to admit he did not know what the range of these new Springfield carbines was. The infantry carried the longer, rifle version of this arm, and with it a more potent .45-70 cartridge. Jones wished that he had a few of those heavier cartridges now, and perhaps one of the longer barrels as well. The thirty-inch tube on Grove's Sharps gave him a definite advantage. Still, Jones was determined to show the old mountain man that he could shoot as well as anybody.

The scouts stopped some distance back, watching them. That made Jones even more determined to prove his mettle. He stretched out on his belly, fixed his elbows upon the ground, and shoved the carbine against his shoulder. Alongside him, Grove wedged a small leather sandbag in the crouch of his cross-tree and sat down behind it, resting the heavy barrel of his rifle on the bag. At the sound of the Sharps hammer clicking back into place, Jones cocked his piece as well.

"Ready, Nate?"

"Whenever you are." He tried to sound confident, but at this great distance the front sight of his carbine was bouncing wildly over its target with every beat of his heart.

For a long moment Jones waited, holding his breath. Then Grove's big Sharps boomed to his right. Jones flinched at the sound of it, blinked, and by time he found his target again the antelope had begun to move. The Springfield leaped in his hands and he immediately thumbed the cam latch, ejecting the smoking shell and shoving a fresh one in its place. Grove's rifle boomed again, rattling Jones's teeth. The antelope were running now. Jones picked up one of the fleeing animals in his sights, led it by a full length, and squeezed the trigger. The carbine bucked against his shoulder, but he had no time to determine if his shot had met its mark. He broke open the action for a second time and fed in another round. Grove's third shot exploded near his right ear. Jones fired again, and once more the barrel leaped, hiding the results of his shot from him. He reloaded and took a final shot at the receding rumps, and then the animals were only tan and black dots on the vast landscape, disappearing down a ravine.

Grove grinned as he wrapped a hand around the barrel of his rifle. "That warmed Big 50 up a bit." He worked the lever, ejected the spent shell, and blew into the breech, forcing a small cloud of gray smoke out the muzzle. The scouts came forward, laughing and chattering and nodding their heads. Jones wiped sweat from his eyes and looked back at the killing grounds. Three antelope lay below. He wondered which one was his as Grove collected the spent shells and dropped them into a pouch.

When they examined the three antelope everyone agreed that the bullet holes had all come from Grove's Sharps. "Well, it was stretching it a mite for that stubby rifle, Nate," the old man said, but that didn't make Jones feel any better. As the wagon made its way down into the valley, Grove gutted one of the animals, recovered the smashed ball of lead, and held it up as a prize while the scouts tackled the other two antelope. They had the three animals opened up and cooling by time Kinsey had worked the wagon down over the shelf of rock into the valley. The Indians loaded them aboard.

Kinsey stayed on the seat; apparently, Jones reflected, hauling meat was Indian work. The driver looked at him and said, "I seen it all from that higher ground. Mighty fancy shooting, Deadeye!" Kinsey laughed, then said, "You'd be real handy in an Injun fight—as cover to shoot from."

Jones dropped his rifle and started for Kinsey with his

fists balled. Grove stopped him. "Don't waste your time on him, Nate. All hot air does is dry out a good seep, and that one has got so much in him, he'd turn all of the Salt Lake into a sandy beach in about ten minutes."

Ro glared at Grove. "You watch yourself, old man. I eat codgers like you for breakfast."

Grove whooped and slapped his leg. "The day I got to worry about wet-nose kids like you is the day they lay me six feet under. Now, you take that meat back to Custer, and I'll send these Rees along with you . . . just to make sure you don't take a fancy to one of them does back there. Nate and me will be along directly."

The Ree caught the drift of Grove's words and laughed.

Ro's scowl deepened into a hateful snarl, then he yanked the reins around and started the wagon moving out of the valley.

When the wagon and scouts had left them, Jones said, "Is it safe to be out here alone, Mr. Grove?"

"Alone? We ain't alone. There is the two of us. Anyway, I want to show you something, Nate." He turned his horse to the south.

"Shouldn't we stay close to Custer's troops?"

"Custer ain't far away," Grove said, unconcerned.

They rode toward a high hill in the distance that shimmered beneath the summer sun. The ground rose and Jones caught a glimpse of the long column of soldiers, supply wagons, and cattle snaking through the valley to the east, the whole convoy headed up by Custer's brass band mounted on white horses. As Grove had indicated, Custer was only about a mile off, and that made Jones feel a little easier. The ground climbed, giving him a wider view of the desolate land, which faded to an indistinct dusty yellow line at the horizon, broken here and there by a lonely, pine-covered butte.

"Where are we going?"

"Just ahead," Grove said, pointing at a tabletop hill where grass and stunted pines grew. They picked up a game trail and followed it to the summit. Grove reined in and swept his wide hat from his head, sleeving the sweat from his brow. He held the hat toward the sun, shading his eyes as he stared ahead. "Take a looky there, Nate."

Jones squinted, but all he could make out was a smudge in the dim distance, as if a cloud had cast a shadow upon the land—except that there were no clouds. "What is it?"

"Them's the whole reason you and me and a thousand of Unky Sam's finest are out here, Nate. Them's the Black Hills."

Jones looked again. From this distance they didn't appear very impressive. "How far are they?"

"I reckon forty, maybe forty-five miles."

"You know this country?"

"I knew it pretty good once, a lot of years ago. Over there to the east, that's Slave Butte, and over that way is Deer's Ears Butte. If you look real hard thataway you can just make out Bear Butte. It's a landmark to keep an eye out for if'n you're coming to the hills from the east"— he paused as a frown worked its way across his face, almost hidden behind the forest of whiskers there—"as I reckon many a man will be in not too many years."

"You don't approve of Custer being here, do you?"

"Since when does the gover'ment need my approval for anything they do?"

"But it's true, isn't it?"

Carson Grove rocked back in his saddle and screwed his lips into a thoughtful frown. "There is a kind of man who needs more elbowroom than most others, and them soldier boys being here has just made the room a whole lot smaller."

"You're talking about the Indians."

Grove laughed. "No. I'm talking about me! Me and folks like me: old Joe Meek over in Oregon, Jim Clyman in Calee-fornee, or old Gabe"—Grove's voice cracked— "nearly blind now and crippled up, he is." Grove thought a moment, then added more somberly, "Men like Frenchie Fontenelle." He studied Jones's face a moment.

"What are you looking at?"

"You've got his eyes. And some of his features as well."

"Whose eyes?"

"Fontenelle, that's who. I look at you and see a little bit of him, just the way he was more than thirty years ago."

"Fontenelle? Lucien Fontenelle?"

"That's a different one. This fellow was named Pierre, and he warn't but a year or two older than you are now."

"What're you getting at?"

Grove looked away. "Well, it's like this. The soldiers come, take a look around, like what they see, and hurry on home to tell President Grant back in Washington City. Next thing you know, the Injuns are out of the Black Hills, and the white men are in. Of course, when that happens the Sioux taste bile, lots of blood gets spilled, and me, well, I have to move a little farther west. Only problem is, there ain't many open places left."

"Then why are you working for Custer?"

Grove winced and glanced away. "I ain't a rich man and never plan to be. They pay me to hunt meat for them, and I'm good at that line of work, and too old and too dirt poor to turn down hard cash."

"Then I don't suppose you can blame it all on Custer and the government."

"No, I can't. It's part my doing as well, and that's what leaves the bitter taste. Because when you get right down to the bottom of the jug, Nate, I'm no better than Custer or any of his soldier boys—maybe even a little worse, because I know better, or ought to."

They sat there a moment while their horses tugged the short grass from the rocky soil. Then Grove looked at Jones and grinned. "Say, you got grit, Nate. You was about to give that bigmouth Ro Kinsey a dressing-down, warn't you?"

"I suppose I should let water roll off my back, but sometimes my temper gets the best of me."

"Folks like him need a good dressing-down now and again. He's bad medicine. I'd steer clear of him."

"I can handle Ro Kinsey."

"Maybe you can, and maybe you can't."

"I've done a bit of boxing in my day, Mr. Grove."

"That don't mean beans out here, Nate. Kinsey cheats at cards. I seen it. A man like that ain't to be trusted to fight fair—or anything else. Keep it in mind if it ever comes to that."

They turned their horses away and started back down the side of the mesa. Grove took the lead and hadn't gone but a little ways when Jones saw something move on the ground. Grove's horse saw it too and reared back, spinning away. Grove had been studying a far-off ridge and before he knew it, he was tumbling off the horse's back, his rifle flying into some scrubby bushes nearby.

The old man landed hard and his horse bolted, taking off like the wind down the hillside. Jones drew his revolver and fired three times into the ground. He leaped out of the saddle, mirror-steel glinting in the sunlight as his knife came from its sheath. He crushed the still writhing rattlesnake with his boot, cut its body free, and ground its head into the gravel beneath his sole. Only then did he turn back to check on Grove.

"Are you all right?" he asked, kneeling by the old man's side.

Grove groaned as Jones eased him over and sat him next to a rock. "It's my leg. I think it's busted."

Jones examined the leg and agreed that it felt broken.

"Reckon you better get me back to the surgeon."

"Your horse spooked. If you think you can ride, I'll help you onto mine."

"Hell, Nate, you'd think at my age I'd have sense enough not to woolgather. That gets a man dead faster than anything else in these hard lands, and don't you go forgetting it."

"I won't," Jones said, helping Grove onto his good leg and hobbling him over to his horse. After some groaning and cussing, Grove managed to settle himself on the saddle. He looked down at his buckskin-covered leg. "At least the bone didn't come through the skin."

If Jones hadn't been so concerned, he would have laughed at Grove's pragmatism. He gathered up the reins and started the animal back to Custer's convoy. But Grove stopped him. "Go fetch my rifle, will ya, Nate. It cost me twenty-eight dollars C.O.D. out of the Meacham catalog."

Jones fished it from the bush and looked it over. The rifle didn't appear to be damaged, and Grove seemed mighty glad to have it back.

Grove tried to stifle his low groans as they made their way back to the convoy of soldiers. After a few minutes he said, "Me and Jim Clyman was hunting the Napa Valley about ten, twelve years ago. It was a glorious day. We'd gotten out before daylight, and by noon had us three deer. We was cooking some of the meat for a meal when Jim thought he heard something back in the trees. We took our rifles and circled around, him to one side, me to the other, but we didn't find what it was that had been scuffling around. We started back to our roasting venison and about a dozen rods or so we discovered the tracks of Old Ephraim. Sure enough, they went straight down into our camp. We arrived back to discover the biggest griz I ever did see, making himself a meal out of *our* venison!

"Now, Jim has always been right free about sharing his victuals, but he never did cotton much to a thief, and we both figured that was exactly what that bear was, so we drew a bead on him. We fired off two volleys and reloaded faster than two white men at a Blackfoot hoe-down. I scrambled off one way and Jim took off the other. By the time Ol' Ephraim decided which one of us he was madder at, Jim had his rifle reloaded and capped, and fired again. I gave it to him next, and for about five minutes we kept his head turning left to right. Then I got my foot caught in a crevice and went over backward, busting this very same leg. The bone come through my hide that time.

"That bear was about nine-tenths dead, but when he saw me go down he mustered his remaining strength and took his advantage. If it wasn't that Jim's next shot busted its spine, I'd not be here today to tell you about it."

"I've never seen a grizzly bear."

In spite of his pain, Grove managed a laugh. "And hope you never do, at least not close up. If you ever have the pleasure, pray you've got a big-bore rifle, like Big 50 here."

Grove patted the heavy Sharps rifle that lay across his saddle. "Anything less will only stir its wrath and—" Grove's words suddenly cut off.

Jones looked back and saw the old man stiffen in the saddle, his broken leg dangling at an impossible angle and his sharp brown eyes wide and alert. "Hold up, Nate," he said all at once.

Jones brought the horse to a halt and followed the old man's gaze, squinting hard against the sun. Upon a ridge of higher ground he spied what had riveted Grove's attention and instinctively his hand reached for his revolver.

"Don't even think about that, Nate," Grove warned sharply.

Jones's hand halted, his heart leaping in his chest as the crest of the ridge filled with half-naked horsemen.

# THREE

They rode forward, hands bristling with rifles and war lances. There were seven of them, and at the head of the band was a scowling warrior carrying a '73 Winchester carbine. His long, unfettered black hair glistened in the sunlight, and on the side of his sorrel pony hung a buffalo hide shield. As he drew nearer Jones saw the ugly scars that marked the muscles of his powerful chest. The man continued forward while his braves fanned out in a circle. At his side rode another man, naked except for a breechclout and three eagle feathers in his coal black braids.

The first Indian wore two eagle feathers in his hair. He was a short man, with a rather fair complexion for a savage, Jones thought. Around his neck was a tong threaded through a thin bone of some sort, and a bag that Jones suspected was where he kept his superstitions. His black eyes lingered upon him a moment, shifted to the revolver at his side, then moved directly to Grove, who had yet to speak.

"Grove," he grunted. To Jones's surprise, the two men clasped each other by the forearms.

"Tasunca-uitc," Grove replied. They traded tonal grunts and hand signs, and Jones might as well have been in Arabia instead of Dakota Territory, for all that he understood of it. But two things were repeated thoughout the conversation. *Paha Sapa* was one, and always the Indian would point to the south when he said it. But the word that riveted Jones's attention was his own name. At its mention the Sioux's dark eyes settled upon Jones's face and lingered there a long moment, as if imprinting his features upon his savage brain. While they were looking at each other squarely like that, an arm's length apart, Jones suddenly realized how young this warrior was—perhaps in his mid-twenties, and certainly no more than a few years older than he himself.

The warrior looked back at Grove, pointed at the broken leg, and grunted a question. When Grove answered him, grins and low chuckles rippled through the circle of Indians. Grove managed a chuckle too, although Jones saw the grimace of pain behind it.

All at once another Indian rode down from the ridge into the middle of the powwow and made some urgent grunts as he pointed back toward the ridge. The leader nodded his head, said something in parting to Grove, and the next moment he and his warriors had scattered into a ravine and vanished with only the faint haze of settling dust hanging in the air to mark their passing.

Jones let out a long breath. "What was that all about?"

"The Sioux are worried about the white soldiers going into the sacred hunting grounds of *Wakan Tanka*. They are keeping a close eye on Custer and his boys."

"*Wakan Tanka*?"

"The Great Spirit."

"Was that a Sioux medicine man?"

Although the pain of the broken leg was great, and etched deeply on his face, Grove still managed a laugh. "Hell no, Nate. He's no shaman. That there was one of their war chiefs. His name is Crazy Horse, and the fellow next to him is what you might call his right-hand man, a warrior by the name of Little Big Man."

"Crazy Horse! The savage that decoyed Fetterman's troops into Red Cloud's ambush? One of the Sioux that refused to sign the Laramie Treaty? You know Crazy Horse—personally?''

''Know him? Well, I should say I do, considerin' I married his ma's cousin. You might say we are kin, him being a distant nephew, or second cousin, or something.'' Grove gave a short laugh. ''I know that Injun, all right. He's a right dangerous fellow. If he says he'll fight to his last warrior to keep the *Paha Sapa* from the white man, you best believe he means every word of it.''

Jones was momentarily stunned. He'd heard of Crazy Horse, of his hatred for the white man, and here just minutes before he had looked the man in the eye without four feet separating them. And on top of that, he was related to Carson Grove! A nephew! ''What is *Paha Sapa*? I heard him say it several times.''

''It's what they call the Black Hills. And by the way, I told Crazy Horse that you were my adopted son. In his eyes, that makes you kin as well. To *some* Injuns, family ties are important. I know they are to Crazy Horse.''

''You did what!''

''He was measuring up your scalp, Nate. I had to come up with something quick.''

Jones gulped.

Grove's eyes compressed and his expression turned suddenly intense. ''Listen now. Custer and a bunch of his boys are going to be riding up over that ridge in about a minute. Not a word about this to him, okay? We wouldn't want to give the general any cause for alarm, now would we?''

Jones nodded his head, still not quite recovered from the episode. ''All right, if you think it's best not to say anything.''

''I do.''

Just then, as if in answer to Grove's prediction, Custer and about sixty men of his Seventh Cavalry came bounding over the ridge. Custer spied the two of them standing there and brought his troops to a halt.

''Afternoon, General,'' Grove said cordially when Custer reined to a halt.

"Mr. Grove. I'm relieved to find you still in one piece, and with your hair intact."

Charley Reynolds, Custer's chief scout, turned an eye to the ground and began riding slow circles across the area where only a minute before Crazy Horse and his warriors had stood.

Grove masked his pain with a grin. "Whatever would give you the idea I was in any danger of losing this old gray mop of mine, General?"

"We heard gunshots, and then a few minutes later your horse came charging through the flankers."

"Well, let me tell you about that," Grove said, his easy voice edged with pain. "Me and Nate here had just been up that thar hill a-sightseeing when this son of Satan strikes out at my horse's fetlock. I admit I might have been doing some woolgathering when the serpent struck, for the next thing I know, I'm laying on the ground with a busted leg and old Nate here is sending that no-good rattler on to perdition. The horse, he just naturally did the sensible thing and lit out of there faster than cayenne peppers through a greenhorn's gut, leaving me afoot."

Charley Reynolds urged his horse forward. He was a short, stocky man about thirty years old with brown locks kept cropped at his ears with the uneven barbering of a bowie knife's blade. He had a broad, intelligent forehead, wary eyes, and a soft-spoken voice. He was not known to drink, smoke, or cuss. He'd been a meat hunter in the Black Hills area for years, and most everyone who knew him just called him "Lonesome," although Custer always referred to him as Mr. Reynolds.

"You didn't happen to see any Sioux, did you, Mr. Grove?" Charley asked with a note of suspicion in his soft voice.

"Sioux? Whatever makes you think we run into any Sioux, Lonesome?"

Jones watched a grin that came to Charley's face. If Grove didn't want to admit that there had been seven Indian ponies standing on this very spot only a few moments earlier, well, that was his business. Lonesome wasn't the sort of man to push such matters, which was one reason he was generally admired by most of the men on the expedition. "I reckon it's time for me to do some woolgathering myself, Mr. Grove," he said, and reined around and rode up to the ridge line to have a look about.

Custer said, "I'm pleased to find it is nothing more serious than a broken leg, Mr. Grove. I am a little disappointed, however, that we have but only distantly spied the signs of the citizens of this county, and then without a shred of hostility. A bit of a chase would do the men some good, and it would give me something more exciting to fill my letters to Libbie with than accounts of my hunting trips."

Jones said, "You did send messages to all the chiefs explaining the peaceful nature of this expedition, General." Jones, like most of the men on the trip, addressed Custer by his brevetted rank. With the recent reduction in the size of the military, and rank being so hard to come by, most officers who had earned higher rank during the War of the Rebellion used their war-earned titles whenever possible. "Perhaps they see no point in being antagonistic. After all, you do have almost the entire Seventh Cavalry with you, certainly a formidable force in the eyes of these savages."

Custer threw back his head and laughed, his blue eyes glinting, the golden curls of his shorn hair shining in the sunlight. "Yes, indeed, my good man. We have routed the noble savage without a single shot. So be it—I have no desire to spill Indian blood on this trip, nor to have any of ours spilt either." Custer turned to one of his men. "Corporal Flanders, return to the column and bring up an ambulance"; then, to Grove, "Let's get you down off of that horse. Traveling that way must be most painful."

"Yes, sir, General, mighty painful," Grove admitted. His face had paled and was prickled with sweat. Three troopers came to his aid, giving him a hand off the horse and a sip of water from a canteen, and everyone waited until the ambulance arrived.

•    •    •

The company pushed hard the next day, ever south, with glimpses of the Black Hills growing nearer as the hours rolled by. Carson Grove spent most of those hours in the back of an ambulance, his leg newly encased in a shell of white plaster. Jones had retained the cavalry horse he'd ridden the day before, and it was a good animal, for although Custer had few vices in life—like "Lonesome" Charley Reynolds, he did not cuss, smoke, or drink—he did indulge himself in one area: his livestock. He owned a pack of superb hunting dogs, and he always procured the finest saddle horses that could be found for his men of the Seventh Cavalry.

Jones spent most of the day moving through the lines of wagons and cavalry as the bleak landscape became less and less arid. He visited with Grove for a while, then spent an hour or so with an old mule skinner named Buckskin Joe. Joe was the self-proclaimed oldest man on the expedition, although Jones figured he'd be in a tight race with Grove on that. Like many men who had spent many years on the frontier—forty-one, according to Joe—he was soft-spoken and reserved, as if talking was something he had not practiced often enough.

Afterward, Jones rode toward the head of the column, where he spent some time admiring the fine white horses upon which Custer had mounted his brass band.

About three that afternoon they crossed an old trail. Custer brought the expedition to a halt while he and his interpreter, Louis Agard, examined the trace left in the ground.

Jones moved in closer as Agard was saying, "This is General Raynolds's trail, all right, General." He studied the terrain around them and nodded his head. "Yep, that's it all right. It's all looking familiar now, General. It's hard to believe, but them tracks was made fifteen years ago." Then Agard shook his head. "I remember that trip like it was only last year."

"We will follow it a little way before crossing over the river," Custer said, looking across the Belle Fourche, which was a branch of the Cheyenne River, and studying the Black Hills beyond, which had grown much closer now.

Yesterday, when Jones had spied them from the top of that mesa, they'd appeared only a distant smudge upon the land. Now they were taking on a shape and size. It got his blood moving. What secrets were held inside those closely guarded hills that would make the Sioux so jealous of them? By tomorrow the expedition would be well within them, and then he'd know . . . and shortly after that, so would the whole nation.

That evening Jones met Grove hobbling around on a pair of government crutches. Grove seemed in a hurry to be somewhere.

"How are you feeling?" Jones asked.

"Like a damned fool," Grove answered, rowing his way toward Custer's tent. "Big powwow going on, Nate. Don't know what it's about. Come along and let's peek in on it."

Jones grabbed up a pencil and a pad of paper and a few moments later was one of seven men crowded into Custer's wall tent. In the center was a table, and surrounding the table was Custer; Bloody Knife, who was chief of the Santee; and another Indian by the name of Goose. Curtis, the correspondent from the *Chicago Inter-Ocean,* was there as well, pencil and pad in hand.

Jones inched over and said, "What's going on here, Bill?"

Curtis whispered, "The general is trying to verify the landmarks on Raynolds's map. We crossed the old trail today, the one he'd made when he went to explore the Yellowstone region."

"Yes, I know."

Custer removed a roll of paper from a leather tube and spread it out on the table in front of the Indians. They gave it a glance, but seemed unimpressed.

"This map was drawn fifteen years ago," Custer said, and Agard translated.

Goose yawned and glanced out the door-flap. "You get

for me whiskey from sutler?'' Goose asked in broken English.

"Perhaps later. Look at this, Goose, and tell me what you know of the land.''

Goose glanced at the map as a three-year-old might glance at the scribblings of a mathematics professor. Custer pointed to a line drawn along one edge. "This is the Heart River.'' He drew two circles with a pencil. "This is where Fort Abraham Lincoln stands today, and here on the other side of the river is Bismarck.''

Goose's eyes narrowed slightly as if a bit of understanding was coming to him.

Custer pointed to another squiggle line. "The Missouri River.''

Goose suddenly grabbed up the paper. He rotated it until he had it agreeing with the compass points, and said, "This is wrong.'' Then, taking Custer's pencil, he altered the line of the Cannonball River and two or three other landmarks. After a few minutes of grunting and moving buttes and rivers around, he threw the map aside in disgust. "It is all wrong!''

A small chuckle rippled through the tent. Custer patiently retrieved the map from the ground and said, "Perhaps it is wrong. That is one reason why we're here—to correct the mistakes. This map was drawn before any white men were here. It was drawn from what the Indians had told the white man.''

Goose sneered. "Then the Indians were white Indians.''

Custer grinned. "We intend to draw new maps . . . with your help.''

"I help you make better map. Get Goose whiskey from sutler now?''

"When we have finished our job, I will give you one of the new maps, if you wish.''

Goose laughed and pointed to his head. "I keep my map here.''

Goose and Bloody Knife pushed through the crowd and made straight for the supply wagon. Custer dismissed the gathering in his tent, and as Jones and Grove stepped back out into the night they saw that the two Indians had gotten their bottle of whiskey and were taking it back to their encampment at the edge of the bivouac.

"They'll get drunk tonight and have another one of their war dances," Grove said disgustedly, swinging the crutches ahead of him, aiming toward his tent. "Drums, howling, and chanting until three in the morning—and no sleep for the rest of the camp either." He paused, then said, "I don't trust that Injun Goose. There's talk he'll betray the expedition to Sitting Bull before we are done with it."

"You think he will?"

"I think he would . . . if it wasn't for Bloody Knife. Bloody Knife won't permit it—leastwise, I hope not."

The following day the expedition penetrated the Black Hills. The change from blistering sun, harsh, dry plains, and eye-stinging alkali dust to this place of tall, cool pine trees and deep valleys was like stepping into a little corner of heaven. The beauty of it alone was enough for the Indians to treat it as a treasure. But Jones knew there was more to it than that. These hills, rising like a 150-by-75-mile oasis in the middle of a grass desert, were a shelter from the cutting winter winds, a hiding place from attackers, a never-ending larder of deer, bear, and fish, and perhaps most important, a natural barrier that diverted the great herds of buffalo north and south onto well-known trails where the Sioux could easily hunt them. Of course, that was back when there had been great herds of buffalo. The coming of the railroad had changed all of that, driving the woolly animals farther north. Few ever came this far south anymore.

Custer encamped near a mountain the Sioux called *Inyan Kara,* the Masked Mountain, up until that time thought to be the highest peak in the Black Hills. The first casualty of the expedition came the next morning before daylight when the camp was startled awake by gunfire. A long-standing feud between two soldiers had finally come to a head during the wee hours, and had ended with one of the men, George Turner, on the ground with a bullet in his chest and the other, William Roller, under arrest. Jones just managed to tug on his trousers and boots and make his way to the scene of the crime in time to see Turner lifted upon a litter and carried to the surgeon's ambulance. He died a few hours after sunup, bequeathing with his last breath all his earthly possessions to a man named Hughes in Jeffersonville, Indiana.

Turner's was the first death that day would see.

Jones spent all morning in camp writing his newspaper article from the notes he had taken. Donaldson would proofread it, of course, and alter it some, as was their agreement, and that was all right. Jones had his notebook and someday he planned to fashion an account of the expedition from the reminiscences he had jotted down.

The scientific folks went about the area collecting, weighing, and measuring. Captain Ludlow came back that afternoon after taking his barometric readings and declared *Inyan Kara* to be 6,600 feet above sea level. Donaldson, too busy collecting to bother with writing, brought his horse, Dobbin, by their tent to drop off a sackful of twigs, leaves, and flowers to be pressed later. Jones turned the article over to Donaldson, who quickly edited it, then packaged it up with the other press releases that would be sent back to Bismarck by a dispatch rider on a fast horse the next morning. Afterward, with time on his hands, Jones searched out Carson Grove and found him with the surgeon.

"Damn thing itches worse than sleepin' with a flea-bitten dog," Grove carped, trying to reach the affected area with a long twig.

The surgeon had little sympathy for Grove. A broken leg was not a particularly critical matter, and the surgeon had more immediate concerns. Several of the men had come down with dysentery, and one in particular, a soldier named Cunningham, was in a bad way. Until today Jones had never seen a dying man. He'd looked over a few that had already made the trip across that great divide, all dressed up in their Sunday best and looking unnaturally serene in a silk-lined box, but never one with one foot on the platform and the other on the step of that fearsome train to eternity.

He'd seen two today.

Cunningham was only vaguely conscious. Jones didn't know if he understood he was dying, or if he was even aware that one of the surgeon's aides was trying to get him to swallow water. He was burning with fever, and the whites of his eyes, when they would blink open for a moment, had a sickly yellow pallor to them.

"Does he have kin to be notified?" Jones asked softly of the doctor.

"None that I know of. But this army is full of men with no past. He's bound to have kin somewhere back in the States. Whether Cunningham is their name, or if it is one that he assumed when he enlisted, there is no way to know."

"A man's got the right to keep his past from prying eyes," Grove gruffed as he sawed away with a twig between the plaster and his leg.

Nearby lay that morning's victim. Turner's body was wrapped up in his blanket, a frowning soldier working over it, methodically stitching the dead soldier's tent around the blanketed body, encasing the man in a cocoon of government canvas.

That night there was a double funeral, held after dark to keep it from the eyes of any curious Indians who might want to disturb the site later. The two men were buried in the same hole. Sergeant O'Tool read the service from Colonel Hale's prayer book, and Custer's brass band played taps beneath the starry sky. Jones didn't see one dry eye among the battle-hardened soldiers as the sorrowful music drifted through the shadowy valleys of the Black Hills.

# FOUR

Upon entering a new valley, or discovering a geological feature, it was common for the officers and scientists to give it a name. That next morning, when the valley opened before them, the entire expedition came to a halt and the men stood in silent wonderment as they gazed at what lay before them. It was immediately named "Floral Valley," and as the expedition entered it soldiers stopped to gawk at its beauty and to gather handfuls of flowers while cavalrymen and teamsters bedecked their horses' bridles and harnesses in caparisons of red, yellow, and blue nosegays. Camp was immediately set up and Custer sent his brass band up on a ledge of rock and had them play "Trovatore," "Mockingbird," "The Little German Band," and a whole afternoon worth of other tunes.

In his tent, Donaldson sat on his cot collecting new species of flowers from the ground beneath his boots, squealing delightedly, as if he'd just plucked a half-ounce golden nugget from the trampled grass. The two miners that Custer had brought along were not so enthusiastic. Ross and McKay burrowed five feet down before hitting bedrock, but no yellow metal. Jones rolled up his sleeves and fell in with several other soldiers and civilians in lending a hand with the digging. Afterward, McKay, a man of about forty with a thin face, sunken cheeks, and a crooked nose, gave Jones a lesson in panning gold and a gift of an old pan that he had among his belongings.

When the day was over it was hard to tell who was more disappointed, the miners or those gold-fevered men who had plunged enthusiastically into the endeavor. Some were grumbling that the stories of gold in the Black Hills were the wishful thinking of a country gripped in the stranglehold of hard economic times. There were vast layers of yellow gypsum throughout this country, and it was this, some were saying, that was the source of the rumors.

With shadows lengthening across the camp, Ro Kinsey bought a bottle of whiskey from the sutler's wagon and went off through the scattered campfires and rows of tents to find some excitement.

"I've seen that look on your face before," Bradley Sink said softly as he found his friend lingering in the shadow of a covered supply wagon, watching three men sitting around a campfire not far away.

Ro glanced over. "What look is that?" he asked, chasing his words with a swallow of whiskey.

Sink borrowed the bottle and took a long pull at it, sleeving the dribble that made its way down his unshaven chin. "You know, like the fox eyeing the chicken coop."

"You mean, predatory?" Ro lifted an eyebrow questioningly.

"Yeah, I suppose." He gave the bottle back to his partner. "So, what are you scheming now?"

"What else?"

"Quick scratch?"

Ro nodded his head at the three men. "Now there's a sleepy bunch if I ever saw one. I'd judge they'd welcome a bit of entertainment if it came their way, wouldn't you?" Ro took a deck of cards from his pocket and grinned wolfishly at Sink.

"You know them?"

"Them two with the firelight on their faces, they're a

couple of the camp scribblers. The one on the right is Donaldson; the one to the left, he's Knappen.''

''And the gent with his back toward us?''

''I don't know. He hasn't turned his head. I reckon it's time we go over and introduce ourselves, don't you think?'' Ro pushed away from the wagon and Sink followed him.

''Evening, gentlemen,'' Ro said, stepping into their firelight. ''Anyone up for a friendly game of poker?'' He grinned, looking at their faces. Then his view came to a halt on the man whose back had been toward him. ''Well, if it ain't Mr. Deadeye. I don't think I caught your name out there, mister.''

''Jones. Nathaniel Jones'' was the curt reply.

Ro laughed, then a sly smile moved across his rough face. Kinsey had learned long ago that it was never profitable to stir the wrath of a sucker you planned to fleece. ''Say, I didn't mean nothing back there. I was just funning you about missing them antelope. Hell, that old codger had you outgunned six ways to Sunday with that heavy Sharps of his. Heard he busted a leg or something.''

''He did.''

''Hope he's all right. They say old men's bones never knit back the way they was.''

''I am sure Mr. Grove will be just fine.''

Ro glanced at the other two men. ''My name is Ro Kinsey.''

''Aris Donaldson.''

''You're one of the newspapermen, ain't you?''

''I am officially the expedition's botanist; however, with the aid of my friend here''—he indicated Jones—''I do file reports back to the *St. Paul Pioneer*. Mr. Knappen over there writes for the *Bismarck Tribune*.''

''Pleased to meet you both. Me and my friend, Mr. Sink, was wondering if you gents would be interested in passing some time with Lady Luck.'' He sat on the ground and removed the cards from their pasteboard sleeve. Donaldson and Knappen were interested. Jones's face remained set in stone.

"I'll play some," Knappen said. "We weren't doing anything but pitching twigs into the fire anyway."

Ro glanced at Donaldson. "You look like a man who has handled a deck of cards before."

Donaldson grinned behind his thick black beard, and he gave a low chuckle. "It is not something I enjoy often, but tonight I'm feeling lucky."

Jones stood. "I'm going back to our tent,"

"What, you're not going to join us?" Ro said.

"No." He glanced at his friends. "I can't tell you what to do, but I'd advise you to be careful." He started away.

"I'll take that to mean I'm just a good cardplayer, and that you meant nothing personal by it."

Jones turned. "Take it any way you like, Kinsey." He wheeled back toward his tent.

"Hey, Deadeye."

When Jones looked again, Ro Kinsey pointed a finger at him, sighted along it, cocked his thumb back, and let it fall. "I got you in my sights, Deadeye." He laughed, then passed his bottle of whiskey to the men seated around the fire. Donaldson sniffed at it, wrinkled his nose, took a small sip, and passed it on to Sink, who had taken Jones's spot.

"Let's liven the evening up some, gentlemen. What will it be tonight? Five-card stud? And what do you say we make it interesting?" He fished a small pouch of coins out of his vest pocket and set it in the ground.

The bottle came back around to him and he pretended to drink, then started it on its way again. When playing cards, Ro Kinsey preferred to remain sober while his opponents got drunk.

No one wanted to leave Floral Valley, but the next morning Custer pushed on anyway, following a stream up the valley. The deeper they penetrated the Black Hills, the more beautiful and compelling the place became. Talk began circulating among the men that it was just too beautiful to leave off limits to the white man—even if there should turn out to be not an ounce of gold in the whole place.

Jones sought out Carson Grove that afternoon and found the old mountain man on the seat of one of the supply wagons with a glazed look in his eyes and a frown dragging down the corners of his mouth behind that forest of gray whiskers.

"How's the leg?"

"Still itches," Grove gruffed.

"What's got you in such a foul mood, Mr. Grove?"

The old man looked over and was about to speak, then stopped and seemed to reconsider. "Have you noticed the Ree scouts?"

Jones had the impression this was only a secondary thought to Grove, and not the real cause of the scowl. But he looked ahead anyway to where the scouts were riding. The Ree had stripped off their shirts and rubbed vermilion on their faces. They had wrapped their heads in colorful cloths and were fixing feathers to their hair as they rode.

"What does it mean?"

"It means they are itching to spill some Sioux blood. All morning we've been passing signs that Indians have recently been through here. The Ree are looking forward to gettin' some revenge."

"Revenge? For what?" Jones knew there was no love between the Arikara-Ree and Sioux. That these Ree had kept peace with the Santee Sioux who made up a greater part of the group of scouts was a supreme feat of diplomacy for Custer. But there was no such arrangement with the other Sioux they might encounter. Still, Jones was not aware of any particular grievance for which they should be seeking revenge now. The Ree and Sioux just sort of hated each other in a general way.

"A few weeks before we left Fort Lincoln," Grove said, "a bunch of Sioux attacked a Ree village near Fort Berthold."

"I didn't know."

"Bloody Knife's son was killed in that attack."

"So now they're putting on war paint expecting to run across some Sioux here?"

"It will be curious to see just how much control Custer has over the scouts if we do."

As they talked, Jones watched Bloody Knife angle his horse in the direction of Custer. The lieutenant colonel gave the old Indian a nod and Bloody Knife turned toward the head of the column of Ree scouts.

"What will happen if the Ree do find Sioux, and Custer can't keep them from attacking?"

Grove shoved a wedge of tobacco in his cheek and started chewing. "Sitting Bull has got about five thousand braves up in these hills, probably watching us right this minute. If Custer can't keep his scouts in line, likely one of these pretty valleys will run red with blood, and you and me will find our scalps hanging from some buck warrior's lodgepole." All at once he stopped.

"What is it?" Jones asked, sensing the old man's apprehension.

Grove pointed. "There is a haze of smoke hanging in the air over that next valley. See it?"

Jones could not, but apparently the Ree had. Bloody Knife glanced at Custer, who in turn motioned the Indian chief ahead, and at once the Ree burst into a run, leaving the column behind. They charged up the hill and reined in, leaping from their horses and skulking up over the ridgeline.

It seemed as if they had only just disappeared over that ridge when suddenly a Ree reappeared, swung up onto his horse, and came galloping back.

"I'm going to see what has happened." Jones rode ahead through the ranks and nudged his horse up to Custer's side. Custer was not the sort of man to snub the press—Jones had come to understand this early on in the expedition—which gave the members of the correspondents corps an advantage that enlisted men and even some of the officers lacked when it came to approaching the famous Boy General.

"What's happening, General?" Jones said. He'd also

learned early on that if you wanted favor with Custer, the frequent use of "General" was as good as an open door.

"We are investigating signs of Sioux inhabitation, Mr. Jones."

"Are you expecting trouble? And is it true that Chief Sitting Bull has five thousand warriors in these hills?"

Custer looked over at Jones and smiled. "Are you making notes for your next dispatch?"

"Yes, sir. News is my business."

Custer's blue eyes were the color of the Dakota sky above, and not the least alarmed. "I am not expecting trouble, Mr. Jones, but I am prepared for it. And as far as Sitting Bull is concerned, he may have five thousand warriors at his command as it is rumored, but he has not enough rifles to arm five hundred, nor have I ever known of that many Indians together without a hundred different battles raging within their own ranks. The Indians can't get along with each other long enough to mount any kind of successful attack against my Seventh." He grinned and his white teeth, which had never endured the yellowing stain of tobacco, seemed to gleam in the sunlight. "You can print that for your readers, sir. Ah, it looks like Bloody Knife has sent back a rider," he said as the Indian came through the flankers. "We will shortly know now what is ahead."

Custer's interpreter, Agard, rode up as Custer brought the column to a halt. The rider was an eighteen-year-old buck named Young Hawk. He told Custer that they had found a recently abandoned Sioux encampment, and that the Ree were anxious to pursue them. Custer flatly forbid any pursuit until he had a chance to reconnoiter the abandoned campsite, and sent orders for Bloody Knife to bring all his scouts back to the column.

Bloody Knife returned with his men to argue the order, but Custer remained firm. He did agree, however, to allow two of the Ree to scout ahead, but with strict orders that any Indians found were not to be molested.

•   •   •

Custer made camp for the day a short time later, and Jones and Donaldson dragged out the tent and pole and began setting up home for the night.

"You've been down in the mouth about something all day, Mr. Donaldson," Jones observed as the rotund botanist drove a stake into the ground with a hammer.

"A man is never too old, I suppose, to learn that he's a fool."

"How so?"

"You were smart to walk away from that man, Kinsey. He plays a wicked hand of poker."

Jones had been asleep when Donaldson had come in the night before. He had awakened only momentarily at the sound of the big man stumbling in and grunting softly as he sat upon the edge of his cot removing his boots, then he was asleep again. This was the first he had heard of the outcome of the game.

"You lost your money, did you?"

Donaldson nodded his head. "I don't think poker is my game, after all. I thought I had a hand that would knock the socks off all comers, but somehow Mr. Kinsey managed to come up with a pair of aces." Donaldson shook his head. "Twenty dollars. Nearly a month's wages. Gone like that!" He snapped his fingers, then drew in a deep sigh.

"He cheats, you know."

Donaldson's large head snapped up. "How could you know that?"

"Mr. Grove told me so. Just before his accident."

"How would he know?"

Jones laughed. "I've stopped asking 'how.' He just knows."

Donaldson's broad brow wrinkled as he frowned.

A rider coming into camp took their attention away from the task of setting up the tent. Two Ree had returned with news that a camp of five lodges had been discovered not far away. Custer, Agard, and a company of cavalry prepared to ride out to talk with them.

"I'm going with them," Jones said, grabbing up the reins of his cavalry horse. "Want to come along?"

Donaldson shook his head and pointed at his horse Dobbin and the sack of specimens tied to its saddle. "I've got to get those into the presses before they dry out. You take good notes. You're the one doing most of the writing anyway."

Securing Custer's permission to accompany the others, Jones joined the small party. The Sioux encampment was only a mile off. Custer's Arikara scouts were strung along the brow of a hill with their Springfield rifles cocked and a look of pained anxiety on their painted faces. They plainly wanted nothing more than to be allowed to charge down upon the peaceful little village and avenge their people for the attack at Fort Berthold—even though it was doubtful that this isolated group had played any part in the raid.

Custer, however, intended a peaceful meeting, and recalling the scouts, he sent Agard and two Ree down into the camp under a flag of truce. At the same time, he put his troops in a circle around the encampment, moving everyone into position so quickly that the Sioux were taken completely by surprise.

The appearance of Agard and the Ree were the first indication to the Sioux that they were not alone in this wilderness. Instantly the children ran for the protection of their mothers' dresses while older children dashed into the trees and the few young men in camp grabbed up arms, preparing to fight if need be.

Agard reined to a stop. A warrior stepped from one of the tipis and came over. Jones could not hear what was being said, and it would have done him little good if he had, for Agard was speaking the Sioux language. Agard pointed back toward the rise, where the troops had spread out in a line, and at that moment Custer rode in and threw up his hand in a gesture of peace while Agard quickly explained his group's reason for being there. All the while the Sioux eyed the Arikara with deadly fear.

From his position atop the ridge, Jones could not see all that transpired down in the camp. But knowing what he did of human nature, he was certain the Ree were working the fear angle for all it was worth. If they could not shoot these peaceful but hated Indians, they were going to try and pummel them to death with their fierce demeanor.

There were five tipis in a circle. Within the circle burned several fires. Nearby grazed about thirty or forty ponies. The carcasses of six deer hung cooling, and great quantities of butchered venison hung on poles to dry. Two or three women were sitting in the doorways of their tipis holding babies on their laps. Three other women had been scraping hides; they cowered now, clutching their little children tightly as men with old caplock rifles came forward.

Jones moved in closer, leading his horse. By this time, Custer was walking among the people, shaking hands with the leaders, reassuring them that he meant them no harm. Jones counted twenty-three natives; however, their chief, One Stab, and a small hunting party were due back any minute.

Jones worked his way within the circle of tipis, not a half dozen feet from Custer and Agard. The warrior who had first come forward was named Slow Bull. Jones scribbled this on his small writing tablet. Barrows of the *New York Tribune* was there, along with Curtis and Knappen, all of them crowding near enough to hear what was transpiring between these two men.

Slow Bull was speaking, and from Agard's translation, Jones gathered that the Sioux were more concerned about the Ree than about the soldiers.

"I will protect you and your people, Slow Bull," Custer reassured them. "And I will give you gifts, too."

After a few minutes the camp settled down, and the children who had dashed off into the bushes began reappearing. Slow Bull sent a couple of boys out to bring back One Stab, then led Custer, Agard, and the company of correspondents to his tipi. By this time Agard was busier than a one-handed juggler, translating questions that were coming in from every direction. Jones was surprised by the neatness of Slow Bull's lodge, and by the friendliness of his wife, an attractive woman with braided black hair, a wide, flat face, and a straight nose. She was a daughter of Red Cloud, it turned out, and the men immediately called her Mrs. R. C. Slow Bull.

Around the inside perimeter of the tipi were the family's belongings, neatly rolled up in clean skins. The floor was covered with skins as well. As the guests seated themselves on the floor, Slow Bull prepared a pipe to be smoked. A dog wandered in, sniffed each man, then curled up and went to sleep in the middle of the floor.

"Where are your people from?" Custer inquired.

"We are from the Red Cloud Agency," Slow Bull told him. "We are hunting for the coming winter. Soon we will go back to the agency for our rations."

"Are you Oglala?"

"Some Oglala. Most Hunkpapas," Slow Bull said.

The pipe went around the circle and then Slow Bull took Custer on a tour of the camp, with the correspondents trailing close behind. Jones noted everything he saw on his tablet. These Indians were an extended family group on a hunting expedition. Slow Bull told them that they had no idea that Custer and well over a thousand men had even entered the Black Hills, for they had been away from the agency for several months.

After the tour, Slow Bull returned the guests to his tent and went out to wait for One Stab. Mrs. R. C. was a splendid hostess. She had four children ranging in age from a suckling at her breast to a boy perhaps six or seven years old. Once her guests were comfortable, she called to a girl passing outside to bring in a pitcher of water, then informed Custer that, regrettably, she had no coffee or sugar to offer him.

Jones saw through this ploy at once. Custer said that he would be happy to supply the Sioux with what they lacked.

After a bit of friendly conversation, Mrs. R. C. became

distracted by something in her baby's hair and spent the next few minutes sorting through it strand by strand in a concentrated fashion. The girl returned with the water that Mrs. R. C. Slow Bull had requested. She was a tall, slender young lady of perhaps sixteen, and when Jones looked at her his breath caught in his throat. She was beautiful! Her hair was long and braided in the fashion of the other women of the camp. She wore a beaded doeskin dress, and moved with the gracefulness of a cat. The sunlight from the doorway behind her highlighted her high cheekbones and showed the perfect oval of her face. Her smile instantly melted Jones's heart.

He was staring, but couldn't help himself.

She set the gourd pitcher of water down on a wolf skin in the center of the tipi and Custer thanked her in her own language.

"You are welcome," she said in faltering English, as if she had only recently learned the words and had not had much practice with them. As she turned to leave, her dark eyes swept over the other visitors. They caught Jones's stare and halted briefly. Then, to his complete surprise, she smiled at him before turning away and disappearing outside.

Jones's heart skipped two or three beats for a moment, oblivious to everything around him, his mind's eye reveling in that brief but open, friendly smile, given as if it had been the most natural thing in the world for her to do. He was still swept up in the memory of it when a few minutes later Chief One Stab and Slow Bull entered the tent.

# FIVE

He was an old man, and he walked with a limp, but his eyes were sharp and quick, and he wore a wary look upon his wrinkled face as he stepped in and immediately picked out Custer as the commander. He was an odd character, and whereas the girl a few moments before might have been a perfect model for the pen and brush of one of those Eastern artists who immortalized the "Noble Indian" on flour and tobacco advertisements, One Stab could have very well posed for a portrait of a penniless tramp.

He wore dirty moccasins on his feet, absolutely nothing on his sunbaked, knobby-kneed legs, a breechclout about his waist, a red and blue agency shirt across his scrawny chest, and a black slouch hat that looked as if the entire Seventh Cavalry had used it for target practice . . . and considering the way Washington was rationing practice ammunition in these tight economic times, Jones figured they just might have.

After introductions all around, One Stab settled down and solemnly packed a pipe with tobacco, and once again a pipe made its way around the little circle of soldiers, civilians, and Indians.

Jones was curious as to what Custer would tell this chief, and what he would learn in return, but his attention, and his view, kept wandering to the tipi's door-flap in the hope that he might catch another glimpse of the lovely Indian girl. He wondered what her name was, and whether she was the wife of one of the braves outside or still unmarried. He had no idea at what age a Sioux girl got hitched, but in the white world she'd have been old enough to keep a father busy full-time holding the suitors back—and looking as pretty as she did, he'd have needed a two-shoot gun to do the job.

Custer said, "We are here on a friendly visit, Chief One Stab. We wish to look the land over, to see the place where *Wakan Tanka* hunts, to see the animals and streams; then we will go back home and leave the Sioux in peace. We do not want to make war."

One Stab listened to Agard's translation, his face immovable, as if etched in stone, then said, "The Long-Haired Chief brings many soldiers." Though the remark was delivered through the interrupter, Jones thought he had detected a note of sarcasm in it.

"There are many Sioux who would make war. Chief Sitting Bull and Crazy Horse are not friendly Indians. I bring soldiers so the Sioux will not attack us."

One Stab grunted. "We took the White Father's peace. We do not make war. Now we get rations at Red Cloud's agency."

"That is very good," Custer said. "Would you help us?"

"What help can an old man give?"

"You have lived long, Chief One Stab. You know the way of the streams, the bends in the hills, the Indian roads through *Paha Sapa*. I would like you and your people to come with us and show us the ways you have learned. We will make short marches, no more than you make moving all your lodges in a single day. If you come, I will give you a ration of food, coffee, and sugar every day, and blankets to take away with you. If all your people do not want to come, maybe a few of your young men will.''

One Stab thought this over, then shook his head. ''We have only twelve men and women, and fifteen children. We want to go back to the agency tomorrow for our rations. We are to leave in the morning. But I can send one of my young men today with you and show you the way up the stream. After that you go by yourself.''

''We already know that way. It will be very helpful if you could delay a week and show us all the ways; then we will leave the *Paha Sapa* and go back to our home.''

''No. Tomorrow we go back to the agency.''

His mind seemed made up, but then Mrs. R. C. Slow Bull leaned near and said, ''If the Long-Haired Chief wishes our help, can we not stay another few days, One Stab? We will get back to the agency in time for the rations.''

One Stab hemmed and hawed. He did not want to do it, but it was apparent that in her own gentle way, Mrs. R. C. Slow Bull wielded considerable power among the people. Finally the old man frowned and nodded his head. ''We will stay one week and show the ways of the hills to the Long-Haired Chief.''

''Splendid!'' Custer slapped his leg with gusto, grinning boyishly. ''You will send some of your men over to our encampment later and we will give them flour, sugar, and coffee to bring back.''

One Stab nodded his head and began cleaning his pipe, signaling that the powwow was at an end.

Custer sent the Ree scouts away, which eased some of the tension in the Sioux camp, and the little party of white men was allowed to look the village over. Illingworth, the expedition's photographer, set up his camera and fought off a band of curious children while he exposed three glass plates. It was a pleasant summer afternoon, the air scented by ponderosa pine and wood smoke, and Jones set off exploring on his own—looking around the back sides of the tipis, smiling and nodding at the owners as they sat in their doorways, and petting the mangy dogs that romped up to sniff his boots and britches.

He finally spied the object of his quest. She was working by a fire with two women who were older than she. He floundered a bit, not knowing what to do next, and then, pretending he was only curious about what they were doing, ambled over.

"Hello," he said as the women looked up. He pretended to be surprised to see the young maiden there. "Oh, it's you. Thank you for the water. It was very good." He smiled.

She returned his smile, and it was apparent she had not completely understood all that he had said. Jones glanced at her left hand, then realized the folly of that. Certainly the Sioux did not exchange rings like white folk did. And besides, he chided himself, what difference should it make anyway? They were from two different worlds, and in a few weeks he'd be leaving hers. Just the same, he felt strangely drawn to the savage beauty.

"Hello," she replied, and quickly said something to the two women with her. They nodded their heads and said, "Hello, hello."

"What are you doing?" He pointed at the fire.

She thought a moment, then said, "Work. Food." Her vocabulary was small, but she seemed to understand more English than she could speak.

Jones managed to take his eyes off her long enough to study what the women were doing. They had rigged up a frame of four sturdy saplings, each about four feet long, tied together at the top and spread out at the bottom to form a sort of tripod—well, "quadpod," Jones figured it might be called. About midway between the four legs the women had tied a leather sack of some sort. The sack held a dark brown, steaming liquid with bits and pieces of meat and vegetables floating on top in a fine, grayish scum. The fire they were tending had been allowed to burn down to a thick bed of glowing coals. In these coals was a pile of smooth river rocks about the size of his fist. The sack was not suspended over the heat of the fire, he noted, but off to one side of it.

"Show me how this is done." Out of the corner of his eye, Jones noted the glances that passed between the two older women, and the guarded grins which he was not supposed to see. But the girl seemed delighted to explain the process, and with her limited vocabulary, and a demonstration, she managed to convey to him the theory behind Indian stew making.

The leather sack, she explained, was the stomach of a buffalo. It was filled with water, meat, wild turnips which she called *pomme blanche,* peas, and various other roots which she could only identify by their Sioux name. She said something to one of the women, who studied the stones, chose one, and with a forked stick quickly plucked it from the bed of coals. The third woman swished most of the ash from it with a fringed, leather "duster," and the stone was gently dropped into the sack of stew. A cloud of steam burst forth as the heated stone sizzled to the bottom and clunked softly against the stones already there.

"Ingenious!" he proclaimed.

The girl was delighted that the demonstration had pleased him, and he was delighted at her wide, lovely smile and shining black eyes.

Suddenly he remembered his manners and swept his hat off his head. The women giggled. Jones felt a blush coming on. "Er, my name is Nathaniel. Nathaniel Jones," he said. "What is your name?"

She spoke a long word that slipped past him like water through his fingers. Then she laughed at the blank look on his face and said much more slowly, in her uncertain English, "My name Morning Snow Woman."

"Morning Snow Woman. That is very pretty."

"Grandfather give me name."

"Do the grandparents always name the children?"

She had to sort through this question. "Yes, grandfather, or father older brother. Or sister."

"You speak English quite well."

"Learn words of the white man at Red Cloud Agency," she said with obvious pride.

Emboldened by her friendly inclination toward him, Jones said, "Would you show me around your village?"

The nod of her head gladdened his heart. When she stood, she was almost as tall as he, and her long braids, wrapped in buckskin and bead laces, fell nearly to her waist. They'd started to leave when a man's voice barked out. The language was Sioux, but the pitch was clearly that of a reprimand, recognizable in any language.

Morning Snow Woman stiffened and turned toward a young brave who was glaring at her from across the encampment. As the man strode forward Jones could see he was more than just a little irritated. Morning Snow Woman leaned near his ear and whispered, "Oh-tah-kee-toka-wee-chakta," then translated, "One That Kills in a Hard Place."

That was an ominous enough name, but not near as fearsome as the look upon the warrior's face as he stopped and glared at Jones.

"Good afternoon," Jones said cordially.

One That Kills in a Hard Place growled and glared more fiercely as he moved possessively alongside Morning Snow Woman. She turned her eyes toward the ground. Jones, not familiar with the customs of the Sioux, figured that this must be her husband. One That Kills in a Hard Place put his buffalo robe over her shoulders, but she stepped out from under it, letting it fall to the ground. His face turned murderous and he wheeled back toward Jones.

Barking a command, he thrust out his finger in an unmistakable gesture, ordering Jones to leave at once. Jones's back stiffened. He had no intentions of being thrown out by this savage, even if it was *his* village, and his woman whom Jones had entreated to take a walk with him. As far as Jones could tell, he had done nothing wrong. If a trespass had been made, the error had been an innocent one.

The warrior made another impatient stab and ground his teeth menacingly.

Jones's knees quivered in the face of this savage warrior, but he stood his ground and firmly shook his head.

That was apparently the wrong response, for One That Kills in a Hard Place suddenly reached for the long knife in his belt. So swiftly did it come from the leather sheath that Jones didn't have time to think about the revolver at his side. His breath caught, and in that instant his body crouched instinctively into a familiar but long-unused stance, his fists balling, his shoulders hunching forward. . . .

Suddenly Chief One Stab was standing between them, with Custer and Agard only a step behind him.

The old chief barked something to One That Kills in a Hard Place. The warrior growled and shot a word back, and then, giving Jones a deadly glare, shoved the knife back into its sheath, snatched his buffalo robe from the ground where Morning Snow Woman had let it fall, and strode angrily away.

"What happened here, Mr. Jones?" Custer demanded with a pinched, impatient look in his pale eyes. Jones did not know if Custer was merely concerned or peeved. He was, after all, in the midst of negotiations with these Sioux for a guide, and this incident just might have jeopardized those talks.

Jones straightened out of his fighting stance, still quivering from the encounter, though he did not let it show. "I'm not certain, General. I merely asked Morning Snow Woman if she would show me around the camp. Suddenly that man came out of nowhere and threatened to impale me with his bowie."

Morning Snow Woman moved to One Stab's side and softly spoke to him. In Jones's agitated state, the sound of her lyrical voice soothed him like gentle music. *But how foolish he had been to seek her out in the first place!*

One Stab heard her out, a small smile slowly moving across his leathery face.

Agard grinned too and glanced at Jones. "Don't take up with another man's woman unless you intend to fight for her, Mr. Jones."

"I didn't take his woman. I didn't even know that she was married."

"She's not . . . yet. But apparently that buck has got his eye on her."

"She's not married?"

"Not yet."

One Stab spoke to Agard. The two men laughed and Agard said to Custer, "We'd best be getting Mr. Jones away from here before One That Kills in a Hard Place decides to challenge him for her. He has already presented her family with five horses."

"Did she accept them?" Custer asked.

"No, but the fellow is determined," Agard said after consulting with the old chief.

Custer put an arm over Jones's shoulder and turned him away. "Rutting season is over, Mr. Jones. Let's get back to our camp."

"I wasn't 'rutting,' General," Jones said, irritated.

Custer laughed, but firmly escorted him to their horses. As they mounted up, Morning Snow Woman watched from One Stab's side. Then One Stab took Morning Snow Woman's hand and the two of them walked away.

"What is Chief One Stab to Morning Snow Woman, Mr. Agard?"

"What do you mean?"

"Well, they seem rather . . . close."

"They are. He's her grandfather."

Jones looked over his shoulder as they rode away, but Morning Snow Woman and One Stab had already disappeared behind the circle of tipis.

# SIX

"The three dearest things to a Sioux warrior are his horse, his rifle, and his woman . . . in that order. If you go taking an interest in any one of them, you best be willing to butt heads with the owner."

Jones stopped scribbling in his journal and looked up. Carson Grove had arranged himself on the Professor's cot, his plastered leg propped on a green canvas folding chair, his army crutches leaning against the wall of the tent. The late afternoon sun showed through the canvas, warming the back of the old mountain man's buckskin shirt, bringing out the smoky odor of years spent around a campfire.

"I was just trying to be friendly."

Grove's bushy gray eyebrows took a suspicion-filled dive. "I saw the look in your eyes when you were tellin' me about her. If I can see that you was smitten with her, it sure would have been plain to old . . . what's his name?"

"One That Kills in a Hard Place. The name alone is enough to scare off prospective suitors." Jones couldn't concentrate. He put his pen down and screwed the lid back on the inkwell. "It's not exactly like I asked her to Saturday night's dance."

"A man could do worse than to have himself an Indian woman for a wife—"

"I wasn't looking for a wife."

"A good Injun woman is loyal as a coon dog—she'll stick with her man through storm and blaze, follow him to hell and back with nary a word of complaint, defend him and his ownings to the death. She will keep him warm and satisfied in bed, mother his young'uns, cook, sew, clean . . . in fact, there ain't a creature on God's green earth that's more industrious than an Indian woman with a job to do. And I ought to know."

"I know, you married one."

"One?" Grove grinned. "I married three of 'em."

"Three? You have Mormon blood in you?"

Grove smirked. "I used to move around a lot, Nate," he said unabashedly.

"Well, anyway, I said I wasn't looking for a wife. I was just being friendly."

"Uh-huh. And Gen'rl Custer is just scouting out these Black Hills outta purely scientific curiosity."

"I don't know as I've ever met a more cynical sonuva—" The sound of hoofbeats outside changed the course of Jones's conversation. "That must be the Sioux coming for the rations Custer promised them."

Grove grabbed up his crutches and followed Jones out. He gave a hoot and said, "Well, looky there, that's One Stab. I ain't seen that old Injun in fifteen years. You know, him and a bunch of his boys once run me and old Gabe—Jim Bridger to you—out of these hills. Yep, very nearly lost my scalp that time to old One Stab."

"How can you take that so lightly, Mr. Grove?"

"It was a long time past, Nate. We was where we shouldn't have been. I know'd better; so did the others. There was beaver to trap and we was young and full of vinegar! One Stab was a strong warrior back then, but we run faster than he did." Grove's grin faltered a bit at that. "Well, old Frenchie, he warn't as lucky, but we all know'd the dangers of what we was doing. Me an' One Stab, we've come to peace over it. I smoked the pipe in his lodge with him—buried the hatchet, so to speak. Then I up and married one of his sisters.''

Slow Bull was with One Stab, and to Jones's dismay, so was One That Kills in a Hard Place. ''That's him—the young one on the spotted pony,'' Jones said.

''Looks like a mean one,'' Grove huffed as he swung the crutches to keep up. ''I don't know the other fellow.''

''He's named Slow Bull. He seems to be high up there in rank, with almost as much authority as One Stab. Married to a daughter of Red Cloud.''

Jones fished a notebook and pencil from his pocket.

Grove glanced over and said, ''Next to Jim Clyman, you're the writingest person I ever did meet, Nate.''

''It's my job to make a record of the expedition.''

Custer took command of the meeting, grinning, shaking hands, pretending that everyone was friendly and happy to be there. Jones, with a writer's eye to detail, noted that the Sioux did not share Custer's enthusiasm. They were wary of Custer and his Seventh Cavalry, of all the white men, and especially of the Ree hovering ominously nearby and making it clear they'd like nothing better than to slit the visitors' throats and separate them from their hair. So far, however, to everyone's relief, Custer's restraining order was holding up. Just the same, tension ran heavy just beneath the surface.

Custer led the three Sioux toward a supply wagon. As they passed by, Jones heard the lieutenant colonel reassuring One Stab that the Ree would cause them no trouble and that he would send a company of soldiers to protect One Stab's village.

One That Kills in a Hard Place spied Jones and gave him a snarl.

Carson Grove chuckled. ''I don't know what you said to that gal, Nate, but you sure put her boyfriend's feet to the coals. He considers you a real challenger.''

''I didn't say anything. I just asked her what she was doing and if she would show me around her camp.'' On the surface, that was the plain truth of the matter, but Jones stopped short of revealing the unexplainable attraction he had instantly felt for the Indian girl, or the fact that he was certain she had felt it for him as well.

"Well, if you got your cap set for that gal, you best get some lessons in courting, Injun style."

"Mr. Grove," Jones said, exasperated, "I have not 'set my cap' for anyone."

Grove considered him narrowly. "Maybe yes, maybe no. One thing is certain—that Mr. One That Kills in a Hard Place thinks you have."

"Perhaps." Jones sighed. "But I can't see where it will matter much now. In a few weeks we will be leaving these Black Hills—I to Bismarck, then back to Minnesota, and Mr. One That Kills in a Hard Place back to the Red Cloud Agency. Let him growl and grind his teeth if he wants to. He'll get over it."

"He will in time. Meanwhile, if I was you I'd keep an eye over my shoulder while he's nearby. Well, I think I'll go on over there and howdy old One Stab."

Grove rowed his sticks toward the supply wagon, where the Indians were busy loading their ponies with coffee, sugar, hardtack, pork, and various iron cooking utensils.

Jones put his pencil and pad away. His fire for a newsworthy story had cooled and his spirit was strangely heavy. All at once Minnesota looked less attractive than these Black Hills, and inscrutably, the thought of leaving them felt like a dark cloud sitting over his head.

As he started back for his tent Nathan Knappen of the *Bismarck Tribune* veered off his fast-paced course and fell in step with him. "McKay and Ross are trying a new hole down by the stream. I was just on my way to see if the prospects of gold are any better here. Want to come along?"

That sounded like an attractive diversion for his gloomy mood. The notion of washing gold from a shovelful of dirt sparked an interest in him that he'd never known existed until just a couple days ago.

The two men stopped off at Jones's tent, where they found Donaldson happily pressing flowers. Jones picked up his battered gold pan and he and Knappen strolled

down to the gulch. There, a swift stream tumbled past a
couple dozen soldiers and civilians hunkered down, busily
swirling muddy water.

McKay was marching up and down the bank, his
crooked hawk nose dipping to inspect each man's pan. A
little distance away Ross had enlisted the aid of three soldiers to help him excavate a pit near a ledge of white
quartz.

"Mr. Jones," Ross called, motioning to him with his
arm, "come get a panful of this and wash it out for me,
will you?"

One of the soldiers dumped a shovelful of dirt onto
Jones's pan. At the stream he filled it with water and
began swirling it like McKay had showed him a couple
days before. Quickly the lighter humus washed away and
as he worked the material down with an edge of the pan
dipped into the flowing water, the bottom began accu-
mulating the heavier chunks and gravel.

McKay came over and bent down for a closer look.
"That's right, just a gentle motion like you got there."
He poked a long, thin finger into the gravel, plucking out
heavier stones and tossing them aside.

Jones's excitement grew as the particles became smaller
and smaller and a fine black residue started to accumulate
at the bottom of his pan.

"See any gold in it?" he asked.

McKay and Knappen had their heads cocked over his
shoulders. "Not yet," McKay said.

Finally Jones had the pan of dirt worked down as far
as he dared—any more and he feared the swift water
would wash away whatever fine flecks of gold might be
there. He handed the pan up to McKay and the mining
expert sorted through the black sand with a pair of tweezers. The passage of those few galvanizing moments was
marked by the slow frown that worked its way across
McKay's gaunt face.

"Nothing," he finally announced, giving the pan back.
"Well, try another panful and maybe you'll have better
luck." He went off to check another man's progress.

Knappen borrowed a pan from a fellow who had given up on trying to find gold, and after studying the method Jones was employing, he worked a shovelful of soil down to black sand, with the same disappointing results.

An hour passed. Not a flake of yellow showed up in anyone's pan, but the time seemed to fly past for Jones. He might have spent another hour hunkered down there, swirling that pan in the cold, finger-numbing stream, without ever realizing that a commotion had arisen in camp. Before word of what had happened reached the men panning for gold, a far-off rifle shot echoed through the pine-covered valley.

"Them sneaking bastards come in for their supplies, then tried to weasel out of their agreement to guide the general." This was Buckskin Joe, leaning against the tall wheel of one of the nearby supply wagons, disgusted with the whole matter. He spat a stream of tobacco juice that left a brown trickle on his full gray beard.

Jones hurried on and found Custer discussing the event with some of his captains. The other correspondents had gathered around too, and Custer took advantage of this assemblage of the press to inform them that the Indians had slipped away, but that he had sent a guard of his Santee scouts out to bring them back. "Some sort of mis-understanding is all."

"What was the gunshot, General?" Curtis of the *Chicago Inter-Ocean* asked.

Custer smiled easily, as if the matter was nothing to be concerned over. "I don't know yet, sir, but I can assure you my scouts will handle it and be back with word in a few minutes."

"Could this incident precipitate an armed encounter between your troops and the Oglala, General?" Jones asked. His concern was suddenly for the Indians' safety, and in particular, for the safety of Morning Snow Woman, although he was not yet fully aware of this fact himself.

"I have given the Sioux my word that they will be protected. That certainly includes my not attacking them,

Mr. Jones," Custer replied cordially. "In fact, I have ordered a company to prepare to leave within the hour.
There has been some misunderstanding, that's all," he
repeated, "and I intend to clear it up."

Carson Grove had propelled himself into the little circle
of correspondents and was leaning forward on his
crutches. "It's the Ree, General. That little village is
scared to death of them."

"I am well aware of that," Custer replied.

Just then Barrows of the *New York Tribune* looked past
Custer's left shoulder and pointed. "Here they come
now."

The Santee scouts rode into camp escorting only the
old chief, One Stab. Agard gave a rapid-fire translation to
Custer, and from it Jones learned that one of the Sioux,
Slim Bear, had grabbed for the carbine that the scout Red
Bird was carrying, jerking the Santee off his horse. Slim
Bear then fled without securing the rifle, and as he'd raced
away Red Bird had fired a shot. It was not known if the
Indian had been hit. The Sioux had all managed to escape,
except for One Stab.

Custer ordered the chief from his horse. "What is this
all about, One Stab? We approached you with friendship
and goodwill, and have given you food and other supplies.
You agreed to guide us through the Black Hills."

The old chief shrugged his narrow shoulders. He had
discarded his shirt and was wearing only a breechclout.
Jones noticed the scarring on his breast—the same heavy
scarring he had observed on Crazy Horse's chest. One
Stab told Custer that he was only concerned for the safety
of their village, and that was why he had left.

Custer was exasperated with this worn-out line and
commanded a company of his soldiers and scouts to the
village to secure it. The correspondents asked to accompany them but in a rare show of vexation toward the press,
Custer refused the request and ordered a sergeant to keep
One Stab under friendly house arrest. Custer returned to
his tent, permitting only two of his dozen or so hunting
hounds to follow him inside.

The gathering broke up and Jones fell in step with Carson Grove, matching his pace to the meat hunter's hobbled gait. "Was One Stab only worried about the Ree and his village?"

"I reckon that was part of it, Nate."

"You think there is another reason?"

"I suspect the other side of the coin is simple: The Indians just didn't want to show Custer the secrets of this place."

"But they took his presents."

Grove grinned. "Course they did. It's what the white man has been teaching the Sioux to do for the last fifty years."

Jones shook his head as if trying to straighten up a thought that had got stuck crossways. "You do that on purpose, don't you? I know that you have a perfectly rational reason for saying what you do, but you must enjoy seeing me confused."

Grove laughed. "You just ponder it a while, Nate."

Carson Grove had played this game before and Jones was determined that this time he wasn't going to beg for an explanation. He remembered something else, though, and said, "Okay, how about answering another question."

"Shoot."

"That man, One Stab. He had these very pronounced and ugly scars on his chest. I'm sure you noticed them. Well, your *other* distant kin, Crazy Horse, had a pair of scars that matched exactly."

"I know 'em."

"Where do they come from?"

"Them scars are big medicine, Nate. To the Sioux they are about as important as a medal is to a soldier, or a sheepskin to a college gra'ge'ate."

"Are they marks from battle?"

"Not exactly, but they're just as dearly won. They come from the Sioux's Sun Dance. You want something to keep that pen of yours busy, Nate, you sit in on one of their Sun Dances—that is, if you ever get invited. It ain't something they do just for show, you understand. It's probably one of their most sacred dances, and not one for the faint of heart. They usually hold the dance in late summer or early autumn when there has been a successful hunt or big harvest. The dance is done by young warriors. A tall pole is erected and the dancers stand before it, staring up into the sun. The medicine man cuts a hole in the muscles of their chests and drives a stick through them. Two sticks, one in each breast. Then the sticks are tied to thongs which are suspended from the top of the pole.''

Jones winced as Grove described how the warriors dance around the pole for hours and even days, staring up at the blinding sun, straining back against the skewer driven through their chests. Dancing so violently that the sticks rip through the muscle. And if they can't tear themselves free, the medicine man cuts the muscle so that they can manage it. ''It's a sign of their devotion to the sun. You see, the Sioux believe that their body is theirs alone, and therefore, this is their way of giving up the only real thing they own.''

Jones could not imagine such an ordeal, yet he knew such practices existed among the aborigines of other countries. At the sound of horses, he and Grove stopped and watched a company of cavalry and scouts ride away from the camp.

Grove said, ''Custer is keeping his word to the chief.''

''Would the Ree really attack One Stab's village against Custer's orders?''

''They would, if they thought they could get away with it.''

The scouts and soldiers returned a couple hours later with word that the entire Oglala village had been taken down and moved. There was not a person left by the time they'd arrived. They did find some blood on the ground near where Red Bird had shot at the fleeing Slim Bear, but whether the blood was from the horse or from the Indian, no one could tell.

That evening Nathaniel Jones opened his journal and inscribed his notes.

*Tuesday, the 28th. inst. Today we had our first encounter with the natives of this beautiful land. A peaceful tribe of Sioux hunters from the Red Cloud Agency, numbering about twenty-five souls, was discovered camped in a small valley. They had been there for quite some time, it appeared, for skins of antelope, deer, and bear were staked upon the ground everywhere and from poles strung around the camp hung drying meat. Our appearance surprised them and for a while they feared for their lives, not so much from Gen. Custer's 7th, but from the Arikara scouts, whom it turns out are mortal enemies. The people were most cordial, especially the wife of one of the camp's leaders and a daughter of Red Cloud, a woman we called Mrs. R. C. Slow Bull. Gen. Custer and the chief, a dried-up old man known as One Stab, came to an agreement: One Stab would assign a brave or two to guide us through these mysterious hills in return for supplies of food and cooking utensils.*

*The meeting went well and all seemed satisfactory and aboveboard, but later it was learned that deception was afoot. The villagers had pulled up tipi, pole, and winter stores and had secretly left for parts unknown while One Stab and a handful of his braves came into our encampment for the promised supplies. It was only through the keen observation of some of the men and Custer's quick action that the ruse was discovered. The Indians fled, with Custer in pursuit, but the Gen. did manage to bring back One Stab, and has impelled the man to keep up his end of the bargain by putting him under arrest. One Stab has reluctantly agreed to guide us himself, although his concern now is with his family and he is anxious to be allowed to return to them. And so he shall—in three or four days. Custer has promised him this, and that is a promise that can be taken to the bank, for the general is an honest and shrewd commander, and a gentleman of the first order.*

Jones scribbled down a few of his impressions of the Sioux and their way of life, but he ended his narrative when the matter came to Morning Snow Woman. Once again his heart was suddenly heavy, and he did not know what to make of the feeling. He wished that he had spoken with her one more time before she had left with the village, and he wondered what would become of her. Would she marry One That Kills in a Hard Place? Even though Jones and she had met only briefly, he knew that she did not love the fierce warrior. But did love play a part in Sioux marriages? He didn't yet know the answer to that. All he did know was that now there was an ache in his heart, a wound to his spirit, and that it was going to take some time to get over it. Their two worlds, so very different, had briefly touched and then parted. Although Jones knew that they would never meet again, he knew just as certainly that he would never forget the lovely Indian maiden.

# SEVEN

Expedition life mainly involved pushing on to the next campsite, pitching a tent, cooking your meals, and then going to bed exhausted, only to repeat the whole procedure all over again the next morning. But expedition life had its exciting moments as well. There were always new expectations, the wonderment of what sight would greet them just around the next hill, or the ever-present fear that at any moment Crazy Horse or Sitting Bull might come charging down from the hilltops with the reported five thousand warriors.

And beyond all that, just the thrill of being among the first white men to pierce the heart of the Black Hills, the *Paha Sapa*, soon put Nathaniel Jones's spirits back in good order. Although he did not forget Morning Snow Woman, at least her face, her smile, her musical laugh were not constantly at the fore of his thoughts.

One Stab fell into the spirit of the adventure as well, guiding Custer southward. The old Indian had resigned himself to the job at hand and accepted the task without further complaint, residing with a couple of Santee guards whenever he was not atop a pony leading the vanguard of Custer's troops.

The travel was difficult through the twisting valleys, some clogged with fallen timber, others so steep that Ludlow's engineers had to construct bridges to move the convoy across them. Jones and the other correspondents rode on ahead of the main group with Custer, the scouts, and two company of cavalry, marking trails and setting up the campsites in advance of the main body, which often arrived hours later.

There was a general feeling of goodwill and expectation among the company of explorers as green valleys opened before them, only to funnel them again into deep, pine-scented ravines. The whole expedition had taken on a festive quality, with men singing company songs and Custer laughing at his hounds up ahead, darting back and forth after a flushed rabbit or startled deer. As they rode along, men plucked handfuls of raspberries from bushes so heavily laden that the boughs bent nearly to the ground. And at their horses' hooves lay a carpet of bouquets so thick and fragrant it was almost as if nature herself was welcoming them into this once secret land.

Jones half imagined that around the next bend in the trail, or upon the floor of the next valley that opened before them, there would be a company of gaily dressed ladies waiting with picnic lunches spread out on bright tablecloths—wicker hampers of fried chicken and magnums of champagne cooling in bowls of ice. This fantasy replayed itself over and over in his head, and once he was startled from this daydream when among the socialites he spied a raven-haired Indian maiden in a buckskin dress happily dropping hot stones into a buffalo's stomach filled with steaming stew. So out of place was this vision that Jones laughed aloud.

Custer, riding off to his right and a little ahead of Jones, looked back over his shoulder and grinned. "It pleases me to no end when I know the press is enjoying itself, Mr. Jones."

"I was just thinking of a picnic that I should like to attend someday, General. You don't suppose we could round up all the single young ladies from Fort Abraham

Lincoln and Bismarck and escort them here, do you?''

It was Custer's turn to laugh now. ''I fear the eye of man was not so designed by its Creator to behold so much beauty in one place if that should ever happen.'' Custer was in a particularly fine mood. He called for music, and in a moment the brass band upon their white mounts broke into a stirring rendition of ''The Little German Band,'' one of Custer's favorite tunes.

Nearby, atop Dobbin, Donaldson moaned softly and whispered out of the side of his mouth, ''I think if I hear that piece of music one more time I'm going to prostrate myself at the foot of the nearest unrepentant Sioux and give up my hair to him.''

Jones grinned. ''The poor fellow will be hard put to get more than half a fistful, Aris.''

Donaldson frowned and, doffing the straw hat from his head, wiped the sweat from his sharply receded hairline and said, ''I'm afraid it is all that I have to offer the noble savage.''

Luckily, they spied no hostile Sioux, and all that afternoon the music echoed through the Black Hills. Perhaps, Jones mused, Custer's penchant for martial music was the very reason the Indians had left them alone all these days.

Around noon on Thursday, the thirtieth of July, they came into a stunningly picturesque valley near Harney's Peak and set up a camp on what many supposed to be French Creek—the maps they were following were not clear on this point.

By unanimous decision, the valley was dubbed Custer Park, and hardly had the puffed-up general had an opportunity to pitch his tent upon the grassy bowl of his namesake when Mr. McKay plucked a nugget from the black sand at the bottom of his pan and cried, ''Gold!'' This long-awaited news raced through the camp like fire through a tar-paper shack, and started a stampede that instantly had both sides of the creek lined with men.

Jones scouted up his panning partner, Knappen, and they rushed down to the stream and shouldered in alongside soldiers and mule skinners, working their pans as

clumsily as the next man there. Every now and again
someone would cry out, "Found one!" and immediately
all the men would shuffle their positions a few feet nearer
the lucky location and add a burst of steam to their swirling.

When the main body of the expedition finally arrived
in camp some four hours later, Carson Grove scooted off
the back of an ambulance and steered his crutches toward
the activity along French Creek.

He eyed their enthusiasm with a heavy frown tugging
at the corners of his lips. "Ain't seen so much ambitious
energy being expended in such cold water since me an'
old Gabe trapped for beaver over on the White Clay
River." He grinned. "The reason being, it turned out,
there warn't much beaver on the White Clay."

Someone held up a nugget the size of a grain of rice.
That immediately wiped the smirk from Grove's face, and
his eyebrows plunged with suspicion. "Say, what you got
there?"

"Gold, Carson. Real, gen-u-wine gold," the man proclaimed. "Reckon this ain't the White Clay after all!"

Grove took the nugget gingerly in his rough fingers and
studied it without breathing a word. When he handed it
back his expression had gone blank.

Jones noted this subtle change. "Want me to show you
how it's done, Mr. Grove?"

"No I don't," Grove barked, glaring over at him. "I
got better things to do with my life than spend it up to
my knees in cold water. I done that before, and don't
intend to do it no more. Besides, with twelve pounds of
plaster on my leg, how do you expect me to hunker down
there?" He wheeled around and rowed himself back into
the camp.

"What's got into him?" Knappen asked.

"I have no idea."

"Getting crotchety must come naturally with getting
old," Knappen observed sagely.

Jones figured that Knappen really didn't know very
much about people, or life. Not that at twenty-one, Jones

was any great fount of wisdom himself. But Grove was his friend, and Jones stuck up for friends.

"Grove is about the most even-tempered man I know. Whatever is bothering him has nothing to do with his age, that I can say for certain." A note of anger had entered his voice, and Knappen was staring at him. Jones gave a small, apologetic smile and said, "Maybe it's being hobbled by that broken leg. He's a man who likes to be on the move all the time. He's spent his whole life wandering free. Being weighted down with that plaster anchor would be likely to put any man on edge—especially a man like Carson Grove."

Wearing a fringed buckskin shirt and leading a pack of sleek gray hunting hounds, Custer came by to check out the finds. By this time Ross and McKay had pulled up clumps of grass and discovered tiny flakes of gold caught in the roots. Custer said it was hardly a strike, but that he would make a report of it and send it off to Fort Laramie by special messenger in a day or two.

Jones panned the creek a while longer, finding a few flakes of gold. But afterward, when he tallied up all the time he'd put in at that stream, he concluded that the reward was hardly worth the effort. McKay and Ross, however, were about as exhilarated as Custer's hounds when on the scent of game. They scurried from one panning site to another, then ambitiously poked around a quartz outcropping and anxiously punched holes in the green sod with their shovels.

"You finally give it up, Nate?" Grove said some hours later. Jones had found his friend with Buckskin Joe at one of the ambulances. The two men were sitting against a tall wheel of the blue thorough-brace wagon, watching the sun lowering toward the sharp spine of mountain peaks to the west, sharing a bottle of whiskey. Grove was using his rolled-up blanket for a bench and the curve of his saddle seat as a rest for his leg.

"Panning for gold is more work than I imagined."

"And are you a rich man now?" Grove asked.

There was sarcasm in that, but Jones chose to ignore it.

"Sit yourself down, young feller, and have a swig," Joe said, offering up his bottle.

"No thank you. I have to write up my report. General Custer is sending a dispatch rider to Fort Laramie to report the discovery."

Grove gave a disgusted grunt and snatched the bottle away for his own use. After a long pull at it, he said, "Custer's gonna have himself a helluva time of it keeping all those gold-crazed pilgrims outta these hills."

"Even harder time keeping the Sioux from collecting a few scalps," Joe observed dryly.

"I'll put my money on the Sioux."

"Till the government decides to stick its nose into it."

Grove frowned. "This is the start of big trouble, and Custer will be sorry for it in the end, you mark my words. There is gonna be blood paid for what you see happening here today."

"You two are both in fine spirits," Jones said.

Buckskin Joe retrieved his bottle, squinted at the label, then grinned up at him. "Nope. Just cheap Red Feather Rye."

Jones groaned, shook his head, and went to his tent where he carefully unfolded his pocket handkerchief and put the few flecks of gold he'd recovered into a glass vial that had once held a nib for his pen. Afterward, he opened the ledger in which he kept his notes and composed a four-page review of the last several days and set it upon Donaldson's cot to await his editing.

In the darkness he lay like a vast, hulking heap, a slumbering bear beneath his blankets with the top of his head covered in a knitted cap and his fingers clutching the blanket tightly against his chin beneath the long black beard. With every slow, serene breath, the tent walls would tremble slightly and the beard flutter gently as a great rolling snore issued forth and broke upon the sleepless shore of Nathaniel Jones's brain. Hour after hour the rumbling kept him teetering just on the brink of sleep as he lay on his cot.

But the barrage of A. B. Donaldson's unceasing snoring held the slumber at arm's length. Every time his eyes would close and he'd feel his body begin to drift into the welcomed land of dreams, along would come another rumbling wave, a snort and a gulp in its wake, and Jones's eyes would pop wide open and he'd be fully awake again. Finally, knowing defeat when he stared it squarely in the eye, Jones threw off the blanket, pulled on his clothes, and went outside. In the darkness the sky was so filled up with stars that it gave the impression that dawn was just below the horizon.

Jones opened his watch and turned the dial to the sky. Only three o'clock. He sighed and pushed the watch back into his pocket. In all honesty, he had to admit that his insomnia was not entirely caused by the Professor's sawing. Part of the blame lay in the fever he had come down with, that same virulent affliction that affects so many men who get a glimpse of gold straight out of the ground. Although he knew that only one man in five hundred ever makes a big strike, he couldn't help but dream of what life might be like with a fat poke of gold nuggets in his pocket. A nice house in the city with a flower garden along the front porch? A shiny, black Studebaker in the carriage house with a brace of matched horses to pull it? How about a wife busily baking in the kitchen and half a dozen kids playing in a big tree out back behind the house?

Once again, his thoughts screeched to a halt and he had to quietly laugh at himself when he closed his eyes and envisioned a stick and buffalo stomach contraption sitting in the middle of his kitchen floor. He was amazed that the wild, savage beauty of Morning Snow Woman had made such a lasting impression on him. He shook his head and told himself to get such notions out of his brain. He was a product of modern nineteenth-century civilization, and he liked that. Morning Snow Woman was a daughter of the wilderness, and never would the two worlds blend.

Jones looked around the sleeping camp, past darkened tents and the campfires burned down to just a few glowing coals kept alive by a cool breeze coming across the valley. It was peaceful and quiet except for muted, desultory snores. A wolf howled in the distance, a nicker surfaced from the restless horses picketed together. Here and there along the perimeter of the camp he saw the movement of a solitary soldier, or two or three soldiers in a cluster, as they stood on guard duty.

Jones started toward one of the guards. If he couldn't sleep, at least he could pass the time in some friendly conversation. As he was strolling near the camp of the Indian scouts, he stopped at a sound and listened. It was an elk bellowing somewhere out in the forest that rimmed the valley. Jones waited to hear if the lonesome call would be answered by another. It was. This time the call echoed from far down the valley. He stood there listening, and over the next few minutes he identified at least five animals, each bugling from a different direction. Jones thought the season was too early for elk to be calling to one another. He decided to ask Carson Grove about it in the morning, and was about to move off once again when another sound reached his ears—and this one froze his feet to the spot.

It was much closer . . . just inside one of the nearby Indian tents. At first it was only the hushed murmuring of two men talking. The words were not English, but just the same, there was no hiding the conspiratorial nature of them. The whispers lasted only a moment, then fell silent. There was some rustling inside the tent, followed by footsteps.

Jones held his position against the deeper shadow of the tent. Not half a dozen feet from him two of the Ree scouts crept out into the night. Hunched down near the ground, they stole across the Indian encampment, keeping in the shadows.

This was curious. Jones didn't know what to make of it at first. Then one of the Ree reached for something hidden in the waist cord of his breechclout. The only light in camp came from the star-filled sky, but it was enough to glint off the long, thin blade of a knife. Jones scowled. Whatever these two had in mind, it would almost certainly amount to no good. He debated alerting the camp, but held back until he could determine for himself what mischief they were up to.

When their backs were to him, Jones eased out of the shadows, careful to make no sound. His woodcraft skills were not equal to those of the Indian, born and raised in this wilderness, but these two seemed so intent on their mission that Jones found he could trail them at a distance with little trouble. They made their way through the Arikara section of the camp and moved stealthily in among the tents of the Sioux. Here they halted and sat motionless in the dark, waiting.

Jones drew up too and squatted on his haunches to present a smaller profile. His boyhood hunting trips with his father had taught him that a man who did not move was likely to be overlooked, especially when he had the night to conceal him. And so it was when one of the Ree chose to peer over his shoulder. With the light of the night sky upon the Indian's face, Jones recognized Bloody Knife, the Ree chief. From Jones's position, it seemed that the man was looking directly at him. He held his breath and dared not flinch. Finally the Indian's eyes shifted away from him and moved slowly around the sleeping camp.

Within the range of Jones's voice were over a thousand sleeping soldiers and civilians—and only he was aware of this treachery afoot. Should he cry out and awaken the camp? Not just yet. Not until he knew more about what the two Indians were up to.

The Ree crept forward again. This time they had set their sights on a particular tent. Jones followed along at a safe distance as the Indians drew up silently alongside the dark canvas and exchanged glances. Bloody Knife put his blade to the cloth and very slowly began to saw an opening in it.

Jones was still too far away to see what they had in mind. He had to move closer. His foot came down on something in the dark grass that gave forth a sharp crack. At the sound Jones froze, and the same instant the Indians looked up.

His position, fully exposed upon a gray patch of ground between two tents, was not a good one. Even assuming the unmoving pose of a statue could not hide him now.

Bloody Knife shot a glance at his companion and growled something low in his throat. Immediately the other man leaped to his feet and, drawing his knife, dove toward Jones. In the moment it took the Ree to cross the few dozen feet of open ground, Jones saw that Bloody Knife had resumed his sawing at the canvas.

He couldn't think about that now.

In a heartbeat the Arikara scout was upon him, his knife held low as if aiming for Jones's gut. At the last instant he feinted with it and snuck a rounding blow with his left fist at Jones's jaw.

Jones's eyes had been fixed upon the knife, and the blow caught him off guard. He staggered back a pace or two before regaining his balance. It was suddenly plain to him that this Ree had no intention of killing him, only delaying him long enough for Bloody Knife to accomplish whatever mischief it was he was up to.

The Ree dove for Jones's neck, but to his stunned surprise, Jones's fist stabbed out in a short thrust that smacked soundly upon the Indian's chin. It was followed by a second blow, then a third, so closely spaced that they seemed to have come all at once.

The jabs had stabbed out so automatically that Jones had hardly been aware of delivering them. He was only a year out of college, and therefore, it had only been a year since he had captained his school's boxing team. After the initial shock of the Arikara's attack, all the old reflexes came back to him. Jones hunched down into a crouching stance, elbows and fists protecting his vitals while his feet began their long-unrehearsed but never-forgotten dance steps.

Those first reciprocating blows had stunned the Indian, not so much by their violence as by the fact that they had come so unexpectedly. Before he had fully recovered, Jones darted in, weaving, and again delivered the famous three-blow volley that had won him the state championship back in '71. He bloodied his opponent's nose and sent him staggering; the knife went sailing somewhere out into the darkness.

Gatling Gun Jones is what he had been called back in his college days, mainly because of the rapidity of his fists and the renowned three-blow volley that he could deliver like no one else. Pugilism had been the only sport that Jones had ever excelled in, probably because of his height, his reach, and his natural agility. But there had been another reason as well . . . Fat Walter Gottlieb.

Walter Gottlieb was a pugnacious fifteen-year-old who saw the scrawny twelve-year-old Nathaniel Jones as easy fodder for his gluttonous fists. And Jones remembered tasting his own blood more than a dozen times that summer before his exasperated father had hauled him off to the Knuckle and Glove Saloon and put him in the capable hands of its owner, Simon Long, an old fisticuffer from before the civilizing days of the Marquis of Queensberry.

Simon Long was a soft-spoken man with a crooked smile and a battered, pockmarked face that had stopped its share of fists and clubs in its day. He took Jones under his wing that winter, teaching him the fine art of pugilism in a room behind the saloon every Wednesday and Friday afternoon after school. Throughout the cold months Jones kept warm by honing his newfound skills, and about that same time, puberty kicked in, and he grew six inches in height as well. The next summer Fat Walter Gottlieb, who had also grown a half dozen inches, found a tougher, sturdier Nathaniel Jones. After the first shove, Gottlieb never laid a glove—well, a fist—on Jones again.

Now, as he weaved and darted, piercing the chinks in his opponent's defenses with solid blows, Jones knew that this was an entirely different sort of contest. This savage was hard and nimble, he wasn't Fat Walter Gottlieb, and this was not a twenty-four-foot padded ring, nor were either of these two men concerned about what the Marquis of Queensberry considered fair fighting.

Jones's fists shot out like pistons, yet the Indian shrugged off blows that in days past had sent contenders to the canvas for the count. Even though he was reeling beneath Jones's precision pounding, he still had a trick or two left up his sleeve. Unexpectedly, he dropped to the ground and swung one outstretched leg in a circle. It caught Jones behind the knee, and as he went down, the Indian sprang to his feet and dove with clutching fingers aimed at Jones's throat.

Jones turned at the last moment, leaving the Ree clenching a fistful of grass. Jones leaped to his feet and tossed a quick glance back toward the tent where Bloody Knife had been cutting away. The chief was no longer there, but from inside the tent he could see a struggle of some sort in progress. Then the Ree was back on his feet moving warily, staying just out of reach of Jones's lightning fists.

Jones was only vaguely aware of the small audience that had emerged from the surrounding tents, standing back in the shadows, watching, giving the two men lots of room to end this battle. And he knew that end it he must, for already he felt his breath burning in his throat and his heart pounding. He'd been out of training too long to keep this pace up for very much longer.

With the cry of a savage beast, the Ree sprang. Jones had been waiting for this rush, but he'd not been prepared for the whooping yell that accompanied it. It startled him, and he nearly lost his concentration. Then his head cleared and with rapid precision he found each one of the Indian's breaches and plugged them with solid blows from his speedy left fist and damaging right hooks. The Ree's defenses went to pieces as he backpedaled, stumbling. Jones plowed in, driving him back with powerful punches that had defeated so many opponents in the past.

With one final blow, Gatling Gun Jones laid the Ree out flat. Then, nearly buckling but catching himself at the last moment, he stood there heaving in fiery breaths while all around him came the low, appreciative cheers of the Santee scouts who had witnessed the battle.

He remembered the tent and Bloody Knife, and turned, preparing to take up that cause if need be. But by this time two Santee Sioux had Bloody Knife by an arm and were hauling him out. As Jones watched, another man emerged from the tent. It was old One Stab, looking somewhat bewildered, as if only yet half awake.

For all the commotion, amazingly, the camp still slept on, except for the Santee scouts, among whose tents the struggle had taken place. Now someone ran off toward Custer's dark tent, and in a moment the lieutenant colonel, sleepy-eyed and dressed only in a long white nightshirt, came stepping gingerly across the trampled grass.

Two Santees hauled the fallen Ree off the grass as Custer came to a stop, massaging the tender ball of his pink left foot. Jones found himself being carried along by a crowd of Sioux who circled around Custer.

Custer looked at the Ree, who was only now coming groggily awake. Even in the darkness, it was apparent the Indian's face was a mess and his clothing darkly streaked where the free-flowing blood from his nose still spilled.

"Bear's Ears? . . . Bloody Knife? . . . Jones?"—this last accompanied by open amazement. "What is this all about, Mr. Jones?"

"I as yet have no idea what it is about, General. All I know is that these two were up to no good."

One Stab sidled up alongside Custer and said something. A nearby Sioux gave a passable translation. The Ree, it turned out, were trying to murder the old chief in his sleep. Custer frowned, then glared at Bloody Knife and said as if speaking to a disobedient son, "You ought to be ashamed of yourself."

Bloody Knife lifted his chin indignantly and looked away.

Custer glanced at Bear's Ears. "Who did this to you?"

The Ree refused to speak, or perhaps his wounds made it impossible. The Santee, however, were eager to answer the question for him.

"You, Mr. Jones?"

"It was I, General."

Custer looked at Bear's Ears again, as if not believing his eyes, then back at Jones with a new respect. "But how did you manage it?"

Again Jones shrugged his shoulders, and the only reply he could think of was, "Indiana State Collegiate Boxing Champion, 1871."

# EIGHT

The Ree were unrepentant over the attempt on One Stab's life, and there was no doubt in Jones's mind that before Custer was through with the chief, the old fellow was likely to encounter the blade of one of these vindictive Arikara scouts. Custer knew this too, and put an extra contingent of Santee and a couple of his own men to the job of ensuring One Stab's health—at least until the expedition had left the Black Hills.

The next day Custer took a company of men up the side of Harney's Peak. Jones and Donaldson accompanied the little group. The climb was exhausting, but as Donaldson later wrote of it, "The view was worth infinitely more than all that it had cost us."

The photographer, Illingworth, had hauled his equipment up the mountainside on the backs of two horses. He set up his darkroom, tripod, and camera, and after focusing the apparatus on some distant landscape by means of the ground back glass, he went about preparing and exposing several wet-prepared glass plates.

"It's a grand sight, is it not, Mr. Jones?" Donaldson said with a hearty laugh, sweeping an arm across the vista that opened below them.

"Yes, indeed." Jones drew in a deep breath and reveled in the pure perfume of the land. "Ah, drink in that clear air." From the top of Harney's Peak, they could see all the way to Bear Butte to the north and eastward to the plains beyond the Cheyenne River. To the west, the Black Hills rolled away in giant waves of granite peaks with limestone and white marble ledges and outcroppings glinting in the sunlight, crowned everywhere the eye looked with the tall pine tree. It was pristine. Unmarked by man. Beautiful!

"Invigorating!" Donaldson pronounced, expanding his massive chest and grinning through the forest of his long black beard.

"Here's some'tin' wots even more invigoratin', Prefesser," said a soldier, handing him a tin cup.

"What is it?"

"Champagne, sir? An' one for you too, Mr. Jones. Say, I heard wot you done to that blackguard Bear's Ears last night. Word of it is all over camp, an' One Stab is mighty grateful too, the way I hears it. 'Tis a pity I missed the show."

The soldiers in charge of the company's mess had broken out bottles of champagne and were passing drinks around. Everyone drank a toast to the man for whom the peak was named—Col. William Harney, who in 1856 had explored the region around the base of these Black Hills—and then another to "General Custer, Prince of the Prairies and scourge of the defiant savage!"

Custer smiled indulgently, lifted a cup to the men in return, and took a sip. Later, Jones learned that Custer's cup had contained water, not champagne.

As most of the expedition had been, this little side excursion was half a scientific investigation and half a "Sunday afternoon picnic." Lt. Col. Fred Grant, acting aide-de-camp to General Sherman, and the President's son, got falling-down drunk—again—and was soundly reprimanded by Custer—again. But all in all, the men had a glorious time and no one minded that they did not return to camp in Custer Park until after one o'clock the next morning.

Later that day they moved the tents a few miles down French Creek where there was fresh grass for the animals. Ross and McKay immediately began panning the new site, and within minutes the cry of "Gold!" resounded once more throughout the encampment. This time the men were pulling nuggets from the grass roots and digging them from the streambed. Custer seemed impressed with the finds and prepared another report.

Jones joined the gold-mad crowd, panning away most of the afternoon and ending up with what McKay estimated to be fifteen dollars' worth of the yellow medal. "Not bad pay for a day's work."

Carson Grove was still in a grumpy mood as he studied the vial that Jones showed him later that evening.

"So, you gonna be a mining man now?" he inquired cynically.

"I can't see as panning for a little gold portends a change in my career, Mr. Grove." Jones was confused by Grove's cantankerous disposition, and becoming a little annoyed at it.

Grove merely frowned as he curried his gray beard with his fingers, discovering in it the bits and pieces of dinner that had missed his mouth. "Gold has turned a man's head before."

"Just what is it that has been bothering you? What's wrong with us finding gold in these hills?"

"Already spoke my feelings on the matter, Nate."

Jones studied the old man narrowly. "You said you were worried about what might happen to the Sioux, and about the bloodshed that might come of it. But I hear something else in your voice as well."

Grove laughed. "Well, not only is you a writer, but you are a psy-chy-otist too. So, what is it you think you hear in my words?"

Jones thought a moment, then shook his head. "I'm not sure."

"Hah! Caught you out, didn't I?"

"If I had to put a word to it, I'd say what I'm hearing is envy."

"Envy?" For once Grove was speechless.

"Good evening, Mr. Grove." Jones went back to his tent where he found Donaldson humming a tune as he meticulously arranged pedals, leaves, and stems between sheets of stiff brown cardboard and stacked them atop each other in one of the half dozen plant presses he kept beneath his cot.

Jones unscrewed the cap to the inkwell and settled his writing table upon his knees.

"Another report for the folks back home?" Donaldson inquired.

"Custer says he's sending a rider off to Fort Laramie tomorrow or the next. I figure if I dash off another dispatch to your publisher it would help justify the vast salary he's paying you to be out here."

Donaldson gave a genuine laugh. "I didn't know you once had a career in boxing."

"Only a couple years of it while in college."

"Obviously a profitable course of study," Donaldson observed wryly as he went back to work compressing the plant press, aided by his knee and his more than ample bulk.

Custer held back his dispatch rider yet another day. Instead, this Sunday was lazily spent. Many of the men chose to pan for gold along with McKay and Ross, who had begun another hole and were pulling real nuggets from it. Colonel Hart was sent southeast along French Creek with two companies of the seventh to explore the creek's course. It was generally believed that the creek joined up with the south fork of the Cheyenne River somewhere to the east. Some of the men scrounged up a ball and ball bat and organized a game of baseball, which occupied them most of the afternoon.

Jones watched the two teams knocking the ball across a grassy vale for a while. Tiring of that, he retrieved his battered gold pan from a soldier who had asked to borrow it that morning and got to work swirling little yellow nuggets from the gravel bars along French Creek.

There was not a more delightful spot on earth than Custer Park that afternoon. It was warm out in the open, but only a few paces one way or the other, a bough was waiting to provide shade. Everyone was amiable. Champagne and whiskey kept many of the men pleasantly intoxicated while the brass band kept the wonderful valley filled with music. Over most everyone's protest, they managed to play "The Little German Band" three times that day. Someone commented that if he had it rightly ciphered, that particular tune had been played 572 times since they'd ridden away from Fort Abraham Lincoln. He may have exaggerated some, being half drunk and feeling feisty.

Nothing more had followed the incident between Bloody Knife and One Stab, and Jones had not seen Bear's Ears since the fight the night before. The defeated Ree was keeping to himself in the Indian quarters, on the Arikara side, while One Stab had suddenly found himself with more companionship than he reckoned comfortable. He complained that he was worried about his family and wanted to be on their trail soon, but Jones figured that was only an excuse. It was his hair that One Stab was really worried about: keeping it securely attached where it belonged rather than hanging from the lodgepole of one of the Ree.

As the day wore on and shadows began to lengthen across the valley floor, Jones put away his pan and went to look for Carson Grove, hoping the old man's mood had sweetened some. He hadn't realized how much he enjoyed Grove's company until he had been without it for a couple days. He found the meat hunter sitting alone in front of his tent, running a cleaning rod down the barrel of his Sharps rifle. It must have been out of boredom, for Grove hadn't fired the rifle since that hunting trip when he'd broken his leg.

"The leg still itch?"

Grove turned with a start. "Oh, it's you, the gold

miner." He pretended to be surprised at seeing Jones standing there, but Jones knew Grove had heard him approach.

"Can I get you anything?"

"Just because my leg's busted don't mean I'm helpless."

Jones winced. Grove was souring, not sweetening.

There was a blackened coffeepot sitting near the banked coals of Grove's fire. The coffee smelled good, but he didn't offer Jones any. It was plain he didn't want company.

"Custer is sending out a rider to Fort Laramie early tomorrow morning. I need to get my dispatches together and ready for him." Jones started to leave.

Grove said, "I hear you was a hero the other night."

Jones stopped and looked back. Grove prodded the coals of his fire with a stick as if suddenly distracted by them, or maybe he was simply uncertain about what he wanted to say next.

"I talked to One Stab today. He's mighty grateful you were there to stop Bloody Knife."

"I only did what anyone would have in the same situation."

"Maybe, but not everyone could have stopped a man like Bear's Ears. The Santee were mighty impressed. They've given you a name."

That was news to Jones. "I hadn't heard any of this."

Grove kept his attention on the coals. "Oh, you will."

"What sort of name?"

"They are calling you Ma-za-chat-kah."

"Ma-za-chat-kah?" Jones stumbled over the odd syllables. "What does it mean?"

Grove continued poking about in the coals. "I reckon a close translation might be, 'Iron Left Hand.' "

Jones laughed.

Grove looked up at him without a hint of a smile on his face. "I haven't heard anything for certain, mind you, Nate, but if I was you, I'd keep an eye out for Bear's Ears. An Indian defeated in combat can go one of two or three different ways. He'll either ignore you completely, which would be for the best, or he will seek revenge—not a healthy course for you. Or he might look upon you with a certain bit of honor, and accept you as an equal—which might be as bad as him looking to lift your scalp, depending on your point of view. I don't know Bear's Ears, so I don't know which way he'll lean. Just a word of warning.'' Grove went back to stirring his fire.

Recalling the stealth with which Bloody Knife and Bear's Ears had stolen through the sleeping camp in their attempt to murder One Stab, and the warning that Grove had given him, Jones did not sleep well that night. Donaldson's snoring didn't help either. Jones had slipped his revolver under his pillow, and kept a hand on it all night, but even that hard, reassuring lump beneath his head did not comfort him much. With the faint, gray light he dressed and went outside.

Custer was already up and about, assembling five companies of cavalry for an exploration of the south fork of the Cheyenne River. He had been conferring with Colonel Grant and Major Forsyth when Jones strolled over. The two officers went off in different directions and Custer looked at the correspondent and grinned. ''Well, if it isn't Mr. Jones.'' In the cool of the morning, his words were accompanied by a puff of white steam. ''I ought to have you show me some of your moves.''

Custer dropped into a crouch, weaved, and threw a couple of passable punches at the brightening sky. Laughing merrily, his blue eyes like twin sparks of light, he clasped Jones amiably by the shoulder and guided him toward the picket line, where soldiers were saddling their horses. ''You know, I was something of a fighter myself in my younger days.''

Jones liked this man. There were so many stories circulating about the famous Indian fighter that it was hard to ferret out truth from lie, fact from fiction. He knew that Custer curried the favor of the press and squelched those stories that he considered unflattering to either himself or his Seventh Cavalry. Just the same, Jones found the man friendly, easy to talk to, and possessed of a great zest for adventure and a keen sense of fair play. He knew that Custer was devoted to his wife, Libbie, constantly writing her long letters about his adventures. Although they had no children of their own, he assumed the role of schoolmaster for the children of the people who tended their big house at Fort Abraham Lincoln.

Custer was a man of temperate habits and impeccable character. He looked to the humorous side of life so often that one wondered if he ever took a matter seriously. Needless to say, the lieutenant colonel was also a brilliant tactician, even though his daring feats sometimes bordered on the reckless.

They walked over to Lonesome Charley Reynolds, who was examining the hoof of his cavalry mount. Upon his saddle was the canvas bag holding the letters and dispatches bound for Fort Laramie, and from there via telegraph wire for the various newspapers across the country. Charley wore a red shirt under a dark corduroy vest. A wide, black slouch hat sat upon his head, and .44 Colt's revolver upon his hip. Custer would escort him this day to the edge of the Black Hills. Tonight, upon a fresh mount and lightly provisioned, he would steal out of the hills and make a mad dash across hostile Sioux territory for distant Fort Laramie.

More important than all the personal letters and the correspondents' reports, Jones knew, were those few words Custer had hastily written officially describing the gold and silver finds. Considering the tough economic times the country was presently suffering through, those words could very well ignite a wildfire of excitement, and a gold rush that might equal California's in '49, or Colorado's in '59. Carson Grove's prediction just might come true, Jones mused as Custer and Reynolds shook hands and spoke for a moment about the journey.

Custer put his reports in Lonesome Charley's care. Charley packed them into the canvas bag along with all the personal letters he was to carry, and then Custer shouted to the men, "Boots and saddles in fifteen minutes!"

Excusing himself and bidding Jones farewell, he went off to attend the affairs of readying his troops and supply mules for the three-day trip.

Jones returned to the tent and fell on his cot, but with the new day brightening against its canvas, he felt a restlessness to be about something—anything but lying there. Sitting up, he glanced around the tent. Spying the gold pan in the corner, Jones knew what it was that was making him anxious.

Ten minutes later he was hunkered down on the bank of French Creek with two dozen other early risers. An hour later nearly fifty men lined the banks. Jones took his pan farther down the creek as more men joined the gold seekers. The growing population pushed Jones farther and farther downstream, but he was hardly aware of this as he worked the tiny nuggets from the coarse gravel and pulled yellow grains from the black sand at the bottom of his pan. As the hours sped past, he paid little attention to anything else around him. It was well after noon when all at once the sound of footsteps crunched up behind him and a long shadow fell across the swirling water.

Startled, he turned and found himself looking up into Bear's Ears battered, swollen face.

The Arikara's bruised cheeks, blackened eyes, and swollen, bent nose made his fierce face even more frightening. His long black hair tumbled down around his shoulders, and on his dark cheeks were two slashes of red war paint. He was naked except for his woven sandals and breechclout, and the knife that hung at his waist.

They stared at each other a long, silent moment. Then Bear's Ears said, "Ma-za-chat-kah."

Jones stared, dumbfounded.

"Ma-za-chat-kah," the Ree repeated.

Then Jones remembered. It was the name the Santee had given him. Bear's Ears was addressing him by his Indian name! Slowly Jones stood. He was taller than the Indian, but Bear's Ears was powerfully built, with wide, muscular shoulders and thighs of corded muscles. Jones imagined that the man could have trotted tirelessly at a comfortable pace all day long if he chose to.

The Indian spoke again, but Jones understood none of it. He thought fleetingly that having someone like Carson Grove nearby to translate would have been of great benefit to him right now. But Grove wasn't nearby. No one was nearby except the savage, Bear's Ears—and a second warrior who Jones suddenly noticed, standing back a few paces.

"You brought your second along, I see, and I have no one in my corner. I'm afraid you have me at a disadvantage."

Bear's Ears cocked his head in curiosity. If he *had* understood any of that, the meaning had completely passed him by. Then quite suddenly, Bear's Ears reached for him. Jones instantly stepped back, but the Indian managed to clasp Jones's right arm, and to his surprise he gave it a hearty shake in the same manner that Jones remembered seeing the Sioux war chief, Crazy Horse, grasping and shaking Carson Grove's arm in friendship.

Bear's Ears spoke again, and this time his friend stepped up. He was every bit as powerfully built but stood a full head taller than Bear's Ears, taller even than Jones himself. He wore an expressionless face and his dark eyes studied Jones intently as if he was somehow assessing him. Bear's Ears kept talking, occasionally jabbing a thumb at his friend. Jones managed to smile and kept nodding his head—partly out of courtesy and partly from sheer confusion.

Suddenly the two Indians grinned and looked at each other. Bear's Ears wheeled around, and without another word he and his companion marched stoically back toward the Indian quarter of the encampment.

Jones didn't quite know what to make of it, but with adrenaline pumping through his veins, he knew one thing: It would be fruitless to try and resume his new avocation. Looking down at the gold pan in his hand, he dumped the half-worked gravel back into the creek, and shaking his head in mild amazement, returned to camp.

# NINE

As he headed back to his tent, a couple of Santee scouts sharing a bottle of whiskey stopped him and jabbered amiably with him. They were feeling no pain as they slapped him on the back two or three times, spoke a few rapid-fire sentences, and called him "Ma-za-chat-kah" over and over.

Jones smiled and nodded his head, wishing the hell he knew what they were saying. Seeming finally satisfied, the two Indians went happily on their way, swaying like willows in the wind, singing a song that must have been what Sioux sang when they got drunk . . . except that it sounded suspiciously like a poor rendition of "The Jug of Punch," a ditty the Irish soldiers sometimes crooned after they had sipped a wee bit too much John Barleycorn.

Jones spied Buckskin Joe across the camp and made for the man.

"Well, how is the Champ today?"

Jones grinned. "Have you seen Mr. Grove around?"

"Sure have. Him and old One Stab are over yonder." Joe pointed toward the Indian quarter of the camp. "Palavering, most likely. I haven't figured out which one of 'em is the bigger liar."

"Thanks." Jones turned toward the Indian camp, and Joe said, "Keep your left up, boy. My money's riding on you."

That was an odd thing to say, Jones thought, but he gave it only passing notice. He found Carson Grove where Buckskin Joe said he would be. His leg was propped up in one folding canvas chair and his tail end comfortably ensconced in another. One Stab was similarly reposed in one of the army's canvas chairs, and the two of them seemed to be talking of old times.

Telling lies, more like it, Jones mused as he strolled up to them. Along the way he was stopped by three more Sioux, four soldiers, a bullwhacker, and one of the black-smiths, everyone congratulating him and wishing him good luck. He graciously accepted their kind words, somewhat confused as to what had brought it on so sud-denly. His run-in with Bear's Ears had taken place days ago. Could it be that only now was the whole camp learn-ing about it? He supposed that might be possible, consid-ering that the camp consisted of almost two thousand men by the time you added up all the extra civilians Custer had brought along just to support the expedition.

"Well, here's old '49er Nate." There was no vinegar in Grove's voice this time. One Stab grinned crookedly and beckoned him over with a scrawny, sun-darkened arm. They were both in high spirits. On the trampled grass between their chairs was a bottle of whiskey, and judging by the level of liquor in it, they were well on their way to rip-roaring headaches.

One Stab said something to Jones, then offered him the bottle.

"No thanks."

One Stab insisted.

"Better take a swig of it, Nate, otherwise you'll offend the chief. He's thanking you for what you done the other night."

"Well, in that case . . ." Jones took the bottle. He didn't mind whiskey on occasion, but the stuff that the sutler had brought along was sharp as turpentine and tasted like it had been aged in a pair of old cavalry boots. Fortunately, one sip was enough to satisfy One Stab, and the chief greedily snatched back the bottle and poured a goodly amount down his scrawny throat.

"I just saw Bear's Ears down by the creek," Jones offered.

"Is that a fact?"

"He didn't seem to hold any grudges."

"Like I told you, Indians are an odd lot. You got to watch 'em with both eyes until you win their trust. After you do, they'll treat you like one of the family."

Jones wasn't certain he was ready for that sort of intimacy with these wild men of the plains; then he thought of Morning Snow Woman, and suddenly he wasn't so sure. He wanted to ask One Stab about her, and about the man who had challenged him back at the Indian camp, but it was a subject he didn't care to explore through an interpreter, which was the only way he could communicate with these Sioux.

He put the girl out of his thoughts. It was foolish to pursue such a clearly impossible course anyway, he chided himself. A roar of cheering erupted from across the camp, over at the makeshift baseball diamond. The two teams gathered up the balls and bats, slapped one another on the back, and headed toward the sutler's wagon, where a large supply of whiskey and champagne was waiting.

"Wonder which team won?" Jones said, thinking aloud.

"I don't care much for baseball, but I am sure gonna be at the match tomorrow mornin'."

Jones looked back. "Match? What match?"

"Nate, sometimes you're thicker than January molasses."

"I haven't heard of any match."

"The boxing match, of course," Grove said, exasperated.

This was news to Jones. "I hadn't heard. Who are the contestants?"

Grove gave him a wondering look. "You're serious, ain't you?"

He shrugged his shoulders. "I don't think it so odd that I hadn't heard of this boxing match. After all, it's a big camp, and besides, I've been down at the creek all afternoon."

Grove just looked at him. He turned to One Stab and spoke some quick Sioux. The old chief's leathery face cracked in a drunken, gap-toothed grin and they both laughed.

"I don't see what's so humorous."

"Didn't you just say you talked to Bear's Ears?"

"To say we spoke is an exaggeration. He did all the talking, but frankly, I understood none of what he was saying. I smiled and nodded my head, of course, and tried to be polite to the fellow."

"He had a friend with him, didn't he?"

"Yes. A big fellow with a surly scowl."

"His name is Two Bulls, and he's the Ree's top-notch down-in-the-dirt, eye-gouging, tooth-and-nail brawler, and he's the Ree's champion for tomorrow's match."

Jones began to get an uncomfortable feeling about all this. "And who is the other contestant?" he asked cautiously.

Grove considered a moment. "You know, Nate, it might be a good idea if you learn a few Indian words if'n you intend to talk to 'em. Leastwise, enough to know when to nod your head and when not to."

It was too late to back out of it. Word of the contest had spread throughout camp like butter on a hot skillet. Hundreds of men had already placed bets on the outcome of the match, and Jones found himself the center of attention. A cadre of advisers, admirers, and self-proclaimed pugilistic experts suddenly developed around him.

Jones demanded to know who was promoting the fight, but no one seemed to have an answer to that. Seeing that his fate was sealed, and that the fight must go on, Jones spent the remainder of the afternoon and evening in training. Two Bulls was enjoying a similar burst of adulation over in the Indian camp, and a medicine dance was in progress to ensure the Great Spirit's helping hand in the matter.

Jones ate a good dinner, went to bed early, slept restlessly, and awoke at dawn. The camp cook gave him a cup of stout coffee and a hard biscuit. It was all he cared to eat; experience had taught him that he fought best on an empty stomach. As the morning sun climbed in the perfectly blue sky, Jones sprinted around the perimeter of the camp a couple times to limber his muscles, then took a few moments to examine the makeshift ring, which consisted merely of a square of freshly felled saplings laid out on the ground, stripped of their leaves and branches.

The fight was scheduled for ten o'clock. A baseball game that had also been slated for that time had been temporarily postponed. By nine-thirty men from around the camp began to swarm the ring site, shouldering in together; soldiers, Indians, bullwhackers, blacksmiths, cooks, wranglers, hunters, and journalists. Knappen and Curtis managed to secure ringside seats, right next to Carson Grove, who had hobbled in early enough to set up his canvas chair. Latecomers mounted nearby rocks or clambered atop wagons and into the lower branches of trees to secure a bird's-eye view.

A bullwhacker by the name of Cawood who claimed to be an ex–Indian fighter was trying to explain the way an Indian thinks when Kinsey and his partner, Sink, pushed their way into the center of the circle of advisers and well-wishers.

"You gonna whup that Injun, Deadeye," Kinsey said, sucking a fat cigar and looking very much like men Jones remembered seeing at the bar of the Knuckle and Glove Saloon when he'd been a kid under the tutelage of Simon Long.

Jones was rubbing liniment into his knuckles. "I'm going to try."

Kinsey let a grin slide across his face, but Jones had the feeling there was no humor behind it. "You better try mighty hard then, Deadeye."

Jones caught the veiled threat. "What's it to you if I win or lose?" He figured that like most of the camp, Kinsey had placed a bet on him. He didn't want to let anyone down, but Two Bulls was a formidable opponent, and by now the Indians had figured out his fighting style and were surely working a dodge against it.

Kinsey removed the cigar from his teeth. "Now, is that any way to address the man what got you this fight in the first place?"

"You?"

"Me."

Jones gave a short laugh. "Thanks a lot, Kinsey. I ought to let you take my place."

"No, that wouldn't be so good an idea. I'm not a fighter. But I heard from the Sioux that you got real talent. They've taken to you. Given you a name, even. Iron Left Hand. Ain't many white men so honored."

Jones ignored the sarcasm in Kinsey's voice.

"Besides," Kinsey went on, "There is a lot of money changing hands, and guess where the big dollars are landing?"

"Two Bulls?"

"Naw. Fact is, I had a hell of a time finding takers for all the money that come in since I put this fight together. Believe me, it's been a real job. I'm earning my twenty percent." Kinsey leaned closer and his voice lowered threateningly. "So I hope you know that you better earn yours. You do good out there this morning and I'll see that you get a generous cut. You do bad and . . ." He let his words trail off ominously.

Sink grinned, opened a long folding knife, and prominently displayed it as he cleaned his fingernails.

"I got faith in you, Deadeye. And I got a considerable amount of money there too. I hope you don't let me down." Kinsey stuck the cigar between his teeth. Someone said, "It's time. That big Injun is climbing into the ring."

Jones shook his head as if to dislodge the incident and put his thoughts on the contest ahead as his supporters followed him to the ring. A round of cheers rose from the crowd, and a chorus of low grumbling from the Ree and Sioux that Jones roughly translated as boos.

Jones stepped over the saplings into the ring, and it was the collegiate championship all over again, only this time it would be fought in the wilds of the Black Hills instead of a university gymnasium, and with bare knuckles instead of the gloves he had worn as he'd fought his way to state champion. Not a great difference, he told himself, looking at the scowling giant of an Indian in the opposite corner.

A man stepped into the ring brandishing a revolver. "We ain't got no bell here, so this here Colt will sound the rounds. I'll be the referee, and Bloody Knife will make sure I keep it fair. Me and Bloody Knife talked it over and come up with the rules. You might say they're a cross between the London Prize Ring rules and the Queensberry rules. To make it simple, we just call 'em the Black Hills rules."

There was laughter among the audience. The man in the ring continued. "We kept it simple. No hittin' or kickin' below the belt. No hair grabbin' or bitin'. No kickin' a man when he's down. This match will be bare-knuckle fisticuffs. Three-minute rounds. A downed man's got thirty seconds to either stand up or crawl to the center of the ring, to this mark." He dug a deep X in the dirt with the toe of his boot. "Each contestant is allowed one man to act as his second, and that feller can help him to his feet. You'll fight as many rounds as it takes. 'Nough said about that. Any questions?"

While he was speaking, a Ree was giving a running translation to Two Bulls. The big Indian seemed to understand the rules, and he shook his head. Jones didn't have any questions either.

"Good. You can each choose your seconds now."

Two Bulls nodded at Bear's Ears, who stepped into his corner.

Jones's view swept across the faces of the hundred or more men there. Who could he choose? He felt as if he was being swept along in a flood. This whole affair seemed to have been taken out of his control, rushing him headlong into something he had no way of backing out of. *A second?* Weren't these decisions supposed to be made before the match? *"The Black Hills rules"!* He would have laughed if he had the time. *Who would he choose?*

"I'm Jones's second," a voice said, and when Jones turned he saw Ro Kinsey standing there with a towel over his shoulder and a bucket of water with a ladle in his right hand. He frowned. Kinsey would not have been his choice if he'd had time to make one. He started for his corner.

Knappen stood up and said, "Just remember to keep your head down, your guard up, and them elbows tucked in close."

Jones paused near the younger correspondent and looked back at Two Bulls. "I guess the Black Hills rules don't cover things like weight divisions."

"Lo might have twenty or thirty pounds on you, but you got the training, and the brains"—Knappen tapped himself on the noggin—"and the men are counting on that. I've got ten dollars riding on you."

Jones glanced over at him and frowned. "Ten dollars! Why did you do that?"

"We all heard how you whipped that Bear's Ears the other night. The Sioux were mighty impressed by that."

Through the whirl of confusion, a thought suddenly occurred to Jones. "Who took your bet?"

"What do you mean?"

"I mean, if everyone is betting that I will beat that big fellow, who other than the Indians are betting against me? Who is covering all the bets?"

Knappen shrugged his shoulders. "I don't know. I just

gave my money to that fellow Kinsey. He said he'd handle it.''

"Kinsey?" Jones's eyes compressed slightly, then he speared Knappen with a sudden look and lowered his voice so that only his fellow journalist could hear him. "How did you do in that poker game the other night? Donaldson said he lost a bundle.''

Knappen frowned. "I lost every penny too.''

Jones remembered Carson Grove's warning. "I'll do my best to see that you don't lose that ten dollars.''

"You'll run all over him like the Northern Pacific Railroad!" Knappen exclaimed, slapping Jones on the back as the fighter made his way to his corner, where Ro Kinsey waited for him.

"You ever second at a fight before, Kinsey?"

"Nope. You ever fight under Black Hills rules before?''

"I reckon we're both green at this.''

"Reckon so, Deadeye.''

Jones glared at him. The man seemed to enjoy being obnoxious.

The revolver roared and Jones put Kinsey out of mind as he turned to face the big Arikara. He could only afford to fight one battle at a time.

Jones began his smooth, rhythmic dance. In spite of having been away from the ring for a year, he felt surprising light on his feet as he circled the big Indian, his fists wheeling slowly. Two Bulls was circling too, wary, his eyes focused, a tight smile carved into his broad, dark face. He seemed to care little about fistfighting. His fingers were open and slightly curved, like meat hooks looking for something to sink into.

Jones feinted right and immediately snuck in a left jab that smacked soundly into Two Bulls's chin. The Ree sprang for the flying fist, but Jones backpedaled out of his reach. Two Bulls ground his teeth and without warning leaped like a cat. Jones eluded him, and it became immediately apparent that they were fighting two entirely different matches. Two Bulls neither knew nor cared any-

thing about boxing. All he wanted was to get Jones in his
giant grasp and turn this match into a knock-down-drag-
out, and the Black Hills rules be damned!

They circled like sharks, taking the measure of one another, searching for the chinks in the other's armor.

Two Bulls suddenly dropped to the ground and swung
a leg. It was the same maneuver that Bear's Ears had used
on him, and Jones had been waiting for it. In an instant
he darted out of the way, but the Ree was back on his
feet as if he had springs strapped to his back. Without
breaking stride, he ducked his shaggy head and burrowed
it into Jones's gut.

The wind went out of Jones. They rolled across the
ground, Two Bulls groping for his eyes and throat and
getting hold of an ear instead. His weight was tremendous,
and Jones found it impossible to throw him off. Two Bulls
yanked his head back by the hair, exposing his throat, and
Jones decided right then and there that the Ree had *not*
understood the rules.

He freed his fists and slammed them both into Two
Bulls's temples. The Indian lurched away and Jones's foot
rammed into the man's chest, sending him flying back
into the arms of the crowd outside the ring.

A wave of cheers rolled up from the men and broke
upon Jones as he shook his head, clearing it.

Two Bulls came charging back, and just then the revolver roared, signaling the end of the round. But that
didn't stop the Indian, who launched himself at Jones. A
half dozen men swarmed in to tear the two men apart and
drag them back to their respective corners.

"I don't think," Jones panted, trying to catch his
breath, "that that Indian understands the rules."

Kinsey ladled up some water. "He's just an Injun. They
only know one way to fight—dirty. Here, drink this."

Jones took a sip, then shoved the ladle away. "Ugh.
Where did you get that? Downriver of a buffalo?"

Kinsey gave him a bewildered look, then put the ladle
to his lips. "What did that Injun do to you out there,

Deadeye, rattle your brains? There ain't nothin' wrong with this water.''

*Bang!*

Jones stepped back out into the ring, moving into his dance as Two Bulls slunk across the ground, hunched low, his hands weaving like rattlesnakes about to strike. Two Bulls sprang. Gatling Gun Jones's fists found an opening and fast as a sewing machine stitched a line of punches across the Indian's face, drawing blood from lip and nose. Two Bulls reeled back, stunned, and dragged a hand across his face, seemingly amazed to discover blood there.

The crowd was roaring. Jones was finally getting a handle on this contest. The thing he had to keep in mind was that it was deadly to let the huge Indian get ahold of him.

Easier said than done.

Two Bulls snarled and lumbered forward. He changed his tack then and aimed a toe for Jones's groin, connecting instead with a hip as Jones leaped aside just in time.

The boos from the crowd went over Two Bulls's head. He tried the move one more time. This time Jones caught the leg and shoved it skyward, and Two Bulls crashed to the ground, arms flung wide, surprise showing in his bulging eyes.

The men cheered.

Two Bulls gasped.

Bloody Knife bent over him and said something. Two Bulls grunted and batted away his friend's hand as he rolled heavily and worked his way back to his feet.

*Bang!*

Breathing hard, both men went back to their corners.

"You've got him on the run, Deadeye! Another couple rounds like that and it will be all over."

"You're dreaming, Kinsey. That Indian is harder than nails, and getting madder by the minute."

"Here, take a drink. You need the water."

There was no denying that, and Jones drank deeply, ignoring the buffalo-piss taste. Kinsey wiped the sweat from his face and eyes with the towel.

*Bang!*

They fought another round, and by time the revolver ended it, the Black Hills rules had been forgotten by everyone, including the referee. The contest had turned into a free-for-all. Jones felt the strain of the battle. He was slowing down. His year out of training was beginning to show, and he wondered again how he had allowed himself to be suckered into this match. Two Bulls had yet to seriously lay a hand on him, but Jones didn't know how much longer he could keep the big Indian at bay.

He took another long drink, drew in deep breaths, shook the fog from his brain, waiting for the . . .

*Bang!*

They circled. The Gatling-gun fists had slowed to mere repeating-rifle speed. His feet had taken on some extra weight too. Jones had to concentrate now. The moves that before had flowed naturally were now dependent on deliberate thought.

He shook his head.

Two Bulls darted past and a fist caught Jones on the cheek.

Jones danced back, opening the distance between them. The punch had not been particularly hard, a glancing blow was all, but as he stood there, his head began to spin. Two Bulls's image wavered, and for an instant Two Bulls became Four Bulls. Then the forms merged into one again. Drawing in a long, ragged breath, Jones shook his head to clear his brain and charged forward, landing a solid punch to the Indian's already crooked nose.

Fresh blood streamed down the Ree's face. Two Bulls slung it from his mouth. Enraged, he threw caution to the wind and tackled Jones at the knees. They went down together, rolling across the ground, Jones fending off the Indian's blows, unable to do anything but protect his face.

*Bang!*

But Two Bulls didn't break; instead, he continued his unrelenting attack. When the referee tried to separate the two men, Two Bulls swung a fist that buckled him over, then turned his assault back to Jones. Finally a half dozen men crowded into the ring and hauled the two men apart.

Staggering, Jones made it back to his corner.

Kinsey spilled a cup of water over Jones's head and vigorously wiped him with the towel.

"What happened to you out there? You're fighting like an amateur."

Jones glared up at him, pulling long, burning breaths into his heaving lungs. "I *am* an amateur! And I don't know what happened. I'm feeling . . . feeling not all together."

"Well, you better get together right quick or a lot of men are gonna lose a lot of money. Have another drink. You look horrible."

Jones took a long swallow, then said, "Maybe we ought to call it—"

"Hell, you can't do that. Get yourself together, Deadeye, and show that Injun what for. There is more than just money riding on this fight—there is white man's honor as well. Here, take a swig of this." Kinsey shoved a bottle into Jones's fists.

"I don't need this."

"The hell you don't."

Maybe he was right. At this point, Jones figured, a shot of whiskey couldn't hurt. He tipped back the bottle.

"There, that'll straighten you right around. Now get back in there and set that Injun on his butt!"

*Bang!*

Jones moved wearily into the ring, his fists wheeling. As Two Bulls circled around him, Jones knew something was wrong. He'd fought hundreds of opponents, and even on his worst days, he'd never experienced the odd sensation that was spinning through his brain now.

Two Bulls lunged forward, and Jones just managed to avoid his meat hooks. His once nimble dance had ceased and now he just turned in a circle, flatfooted, trying desperately to keep the big Indian in sight.

Two Bulls faded then; he just disappeared from Jones's sight. Jones blinked, amazed. A fist shot out from somewhere to his right. Jones spun with the punch. Another caught him low. He buckled. An uppercut wrenched his head back.

Jones tasted his own blood. He staggered in a spiral and a moment later slammed into the ground. The world did a couple more spins, he felt vaguely ill, and then the lights went out.

# TEN

The world was still rocking beneath him as daylight once again savaged his closed eyelids. He groaned and when he tried to open them, a million needles shot into his brain.

"I was gettin' worried about you, Nate," a familiar voice said.

Jones licked his lips, trying to work moisture into them. "Grove?"

"I'm here, Nate."

The sound of the old man's voice was reassuring. Jones opened his eyes again, slowly. Through the blinding glare Carson Grove's bearded face came into focus. Jones was lying on a cot, and the sky overhead had taken on a muted, tan tinge. Oddly, he was still reeling . . . and then he knew the truth: He was inside one of the supply wagons, or ambulances.

"Water." His tongue was as thick as a barber's strop, his mouth as dry as the bottom of an alum barrel. Grove fetched him a cup and lifted his head to drink it. Jones moaned and afterward shut his eyes and said, "Are we moving?"

"Yep. Custer come back last night and we got going this morning."

Jones's eyes sprang open. "How long?"

"Two days. You know, Nate, a man with a weak jaw ought not step into a ring like you done."

"Weak jaw? I've never had a weak jaw in my life!"

"Well, you sure went down like a bag of bullet lead when that Injun connected." Grove smacked a fist into his open palm. "*Whoomp,* just like that and you was down for the count . . . and then some."

Jones rolled his head. "I don't understand it."

"What's to understand? Two Bulls whupped your hide."

"No, I mean, there at the end, it was almost as if I wanted to go to sleep."

Grove laughed. "And that you did."

Jones didn't want to talk about it anymore. The effort was too great, and the more he thought about it the clearer he saw the faces of all those men who had believed in him, who had lost their money because of him! He'd let them down.

Jones asked for another drink of water, then shut his eyes and pretended to fall asleep again.

The expedition cut a wide swath through the peaceful Black Hills as Custer led the company of men, wagons, and cattle north on the final leg of the exploration, and then back to Fort Abraham Lincoln.

In the dead of night a few days before finally breaking free of the Black Hills, Custer secretly summoned Chief One Stab to his tent. He thanked the chief heartily for his help and loaded him down with gifts and provisions, then quietly let the man leave, giving One Stab a good head start so that come dawn, the Arikara would not be able to catch up with him. When Bloody Knife learned the next morning that the scrawny neck he had so desperately wanted to wrap his fingers around had managed to slip through his clutches, he fell into a deep depression, and climbing sullenly onto his horse loped to the tail of the expedition, where he rode the rest of the way brooding over his loss.

*August 14th, 1874. It has been some time since I last added to my journal. I still don't know what happened to me that morning when I stepped into the ring with Two Bulls, only that I was carried out unconscious and remained so for most of two days. All I can think is that I was ill at the time, and hadn't realized it. I am fortunate, therefore, to have not perished. Other men had died during the expedition from sickness, mostly dysentery. I have decided, however, that my boxing days are behind me, and never again will I be tempted to enter into another contest of fists. With the help of my friend Carson Grove, I have begun to understand the Sioux language. Never again will I permit ignorance to pull me into something I have no desire to do. We live and learn.*

*Today we left the Black Hills, and I will miss the cool, lush beauty of them. Custer has brought us to Bear Butte, where we will rest a few days while we prepare for the long, demanding push north to Bismarck and Fort A. Lincoln. The scientists are working on their notes and cataloging their discoveries. Custer's personal wagon, I am told, is packed with specimens of wildlife which he has collected and intends to send back East to zoos.*

*There is talk among some of the men to immediately return to these hills and begin prospecting for gold once the expedition disbands at Bismarck. These plans are being made on the quiet, for it is known that the government will not permit white men to enter the Sioux's land to look for the precious yellow metal. I have been asked to join a forthcoming expedition back to these hills. My inclination is to accept the invitation. The feeling among the men is that the government will work some treaty with the Sioux to take back the Black Hills, and those men who brave the dangers now, and make the first*

*claims, will become rich in a matter of only a few
months. Yes, the prospects are certainly inviting.*

On a hill overlooking Fort Abraham Lincoln, Custer
brought the mile-long column to a halt and glanced back
along the train of covered wagons and mounted cavalry.
A satisfied smile eased across his lips. It had been a good
expedition, well accomplished, and not one man lost to
the hostile Sioux. Another feather in Custer's cap, another
glowing page scribed in the future history books of this
grand country.

What more was there to life? Custer suspected he had
a long, profitable future ahead of him, and next year there
would be another expedition, perhaps even a return to the
Black Hills.

Feeling suddenly all-powerful, and calling to his head
musician, he ordered the brass band to strike up his favorite tune.

To the relief of everyone there, it was *not* "The Little
German Band," but "Garry Owen," Custer's personal
battle hymn. He rode at the head of his Seventh Cavalry
as they came triumphantly into the quadrangle of the fort.

Libbie was there to greet him, as were the wives of the
other officers. For Custer, the expedition was at an end.

But for other men, the adventure was only just beginning.

Jones found Carson Grove in a Bismarck saloon a few
days later. He was sitting alone in the corner, that long
Sharps rifle of his lying across the table. The heavy cast
on his leg had been replaced with a couple splints, and
although he still had to hobble about on a government
crutch, he was nearly mended.

"Pull up a chair, Nate," Grove said happily when
Jones stopped at his table. "Here, have a swig."

Jones took some of Grove's whiskey and passed the
bottle back.

"You never was much of a drinkin' man, Nate. I'd seen
that right off."

"You're hitting that stuff kind of hard, aren't you?"

"Well, tell you what. In a day or two I'm heading out of here. I reckon this will be the last celebrating I'll be doing for some time."

"Where are you going?"

"West."

"That leaves it wide open."

"Wide open is the way I prefer it, Nate. How 'bout you?"

Jones glanced around the saloon. It was largely filled with civilians, but here and there stood a few soldiers, including a couple cavalry officers Jones had become acquainted with while on expedition. He lowered his voice and said, "A few of us men have decided to go back to the hills and stake out claims. A fellow by the name of Kansas Knutsen is organizing a party this very minute. But we got to keep it quiet, because Custer has forbid any white man to return to the hills."

Through his inebriation Grove managed a small scowl. "You ought to listen to the gen'rl and think twice about that. Them Sioux ain't happy about white men in there. They left us alone this time because of Custer and a thousand of his soldier boys, but a bunch of white men alone . . . well, that's inviting a scalping if I ever heard it."

"The Sioux seemed to have accepted me. I don't think I will have trouble with them."

"Ha!" Grove roared, and when some of the heads in the saloon turned toward them he lowered his voice. "Them was friendly Sioux. They already come to terms with Unky Sam. But I guarantee that Sitting Bull and Crazy Horse won't be so cordial when they come a-visitin'."

"I've already decided, Mr. Grove. I don't have anything back East to return to. Donaldson has already departed, and it was he who enlisted me to help him write his reports. Besides, I've already told them I'd come along. I've bought my supplies, and a rifle, and we will be leaving in a few weeks."

"What kinda rifle?"

"Winchester, 1873 model. It's a good shooter."

Grove huffed. "Repeating rifles are only an excuse for bad marksmanship. What caliber?"

".44 Winchester Center Fire. That way I only have to carry one size bullet for my revolver and rifle."

"Hope you only have to shoot at Injuns then. You run up agin' Ol' Ephraim and you might as well throw rocks at him."

"I think that's an exaggeration, Mr. Grove."

"That's the voice of one who's been there, Mr. Jones," Grove came back caustically.

Jones grimaced and shook his head. "Here I thought your disposition had sweetened up." He stood. "Well, I just came to say good-bye. I know you'll be pulling out soon, and likely we'll never meet again. I wanted to tell you that I have appreciated your friendship, Mr. Grove. I wish you good luck." Jones started toward the door.

"Nate." Grove motioned him back to the table.

"Sit a spell longer. I got something I want to tell you."

"What is it?"

"I've been cranky, it's true, and I reckon I owe you an explanation before you leave. Remember when I told you that you reminded me of someone?"

"Yes. A man named Pierre Fontenelle."

"He was young, maybe your age. He'd just joined Bridger and me in Missouri a few weeks earlier. He was green, but he was a fast learner. He wanted to make his way in the mountains, and Bridger said he'd take him along.

"I made a mistake. I talked my partners into setting out some traps in the *Paha Sapa*. I said it would be all right 'cause at that time I had me a Sioux wife. . . ."

"One of three," Jones pointed out.

Grove grinned.

"Well, the short of it is, we come upon One Stab and he didn't care a whit who I was married to. He run us up and down those hills like one of Custer's hounds after a jackrabbit. I thought for certain my heart and lungs was gonna bust through my chest, but we made it out of there all right—except for Frenchie. And he would have made it too, except scrambling up out of a gulch he fell and come up holding the grandest gold nugget you'd ever seen—big as a walnut, and shaped like a horseshoe. Gold fever come down on him with a vengeance and Fontenelle forgot all about the Sioux hot on our tails. He stopped thinking straight, and all he wanted to do was to linger there and find some more gold. I finally got him moving again, but by that time it was too late. He took an arrow in the back and went down. We had to leave him there."

"That must have been a hard thing to do."

"It was either that or end up dead too. The point is, I'd seen what gold will do to a man. It scrambles his brains. It gets him kilt! When I seen you and them men digging out them nuggets from your pan, I was really seeing Frenchie Fontenelle clutching up that nugget and calling it his 'lucky horseshoe,' and then the next minute falling with a Sioux arrow in his back.

"You go back there now, Nate, and you're liable to end up like Frenchie."

"Maybe you're right, Mr. Grove, but I have made up my mind."

"Well, a man has the right to do what he thinks best." Grove stuck out a hand. "Until our trails cross again, God be with you, Nate."

"Thanks. And you take care too."

"I always do."

Jones paused at the door. The warning weighed heavily on him, but this was something he had to do. The Black Hills were calling to him.

It would be almost another year before he understood the reason why.

# ELEVEN

*October 23rd, 1874—Near Bear Butte, Dakota Territory*

Winter came early to the Dakota plains. A cold wind rippled the short, stiff brown grass and buffeted the small company of men making their way south along the trail left by Custer's returning expedition. There were twenty-eight in the party. Most rode horses, but some found places in the two freight wagons, hitched together and pulled by an eight-yoke of oxen, where all their supplies had been loaded. On the seat of the freighter, Nathaniel Jones turned up his collar to the wind and cracked the long whip above the ear of the off-side lead cow.

"Get your fanny back in line, Clementine!" Jones barked, expertly tugging one of the reins as if he'd been bullwhacking all his life instead of just these last eighteen days.

On the seat next to him, Shorty—he had given no other name than that, and none had been asked for—nodded his round head, open approval on his weathered, mustachioed face. Shorty was five feet tall, but sitting there next to Jones, he appeared normal size. It was from the waist down that nature had played her joke upon him, and from a distance, if you happened to spy Shorty with his feet planted squarely on the ground, you might mistakenly think he was standing in a hole up to his knees.

"She understood that, all right, but only 'cause Clementine is a sensitive lady. You try them sweet words on Esmeralda, you might as well be talking to the wind." Shorty's instructions had been accompanied by gray puffs of steam in the chill afternoon air.

"I'll keep that in mind, Shorty." Jones enjoyed bullwhacking, but the cussing that went along with the job was something he'd not yet gotten comfortable with. Just the same, every bullwhacker he had ever met had told him the same thing: Cussing is all that dumb animals like oxen understand. Cattle, he'd come to learn, were powerful creatures with a mind of their own, and they had only one pace when put to yoke—slow. But it was a steady slow. Cattle got you to wherever you wanted to go according to *their* schedule, not yours.

Kansas Knutsen, one of the men who had organized the party, rode up alongside the freighter. Knutsen was a tall, heavy-boned man, a Texas cowboy by trade who had been one of the wranglers along with Custer on his expedition into the Black Hills. He'd met Jones there while panning flecks of gold from French Creek, alongside the other greenhorns, and like Jones and a couple other men along on this illegal trip, he'd been bitten hard by the gold bug.

Knutsen had been riding ahead, scouting the trail which Custer had left behind. It was an easy thing to follow. The wagons, four abreast, had left deep furrows in the gumbo soil that would remain for twenty years or more, if Raynolds's old trail to the Yellowstone was any indication.

"If my memory serves right, that's Bear Butte in the distance." Knutsen said it straight out, but Jones sensed that he was asking for confirmation. They had all seen the butte as they were leaving the Black Hills, but that was approaching it from the south. Coming down from a different direction can make landmarks hard to read.

"That's Bear Butte, all right. I seen it once from this direction, only I was a little farther west," Jones said.

Knutsen pushed the wide Stetson farther back on his head. "I figured we was right on trail. Can't hardly miss tracks that Custer left behind. Another day and we'll be off these wide-open plains, and I'll breathe a little easier, Jones."

So far they had seen no Sioux, but Jones knew it wasn't the Sioux that concerned Knutsen. That night they camped at the base of Bear Butte on the same ground Custer had stopped and rested before making the hard push back to Fort Abraham Lincoln two months earlier. The fire rings were still in place and other than some dirt that had blown into them, they appeared as if they had been left behind only a couple days ago. There was even a stack of firewood which made stopping real convenient.

Jones strolled through the abandoned camp, which had taken up more than a hundred acres when Custer had stopped, noting here and there the prints of unshod ponies or the impression of a moccasined foot. The Sioux had come through and scouted the place since Custer's departure. Some of the tracks looked fresh. If Carson Grove had been here, Jones was certain, he'd have been able to read more into them than his own untrained eyes could.

The campfires were burning when Jones got back, and the smell of cooking food filled the cool evening air. There had been no lack of game along the trail, and tonight, like most nights, they'd feast on meat. Jones wandered over to the cook fire, where a young man named Jim Johnson was quartering potatoes into a black pot.

"Antelope stew, Mr. Jones," Johnson told him, chopping happily away at the potatoes.

Johnson had not been on Custer's expedition. Of the twenty-eight men along on this trip, only Jones, Knutsen, a smithy named Conner, and a bullwhacker called Hefty Ragland had been to the Black Hills with Custer. That made Jones one of the leaders of what was generally becoming to be known as the Knutsen-Jones party. It was his memory of the landmarks, and the notes he had recorded in his journal, that made him so important to the success of this trip back to the hills.

The rest of the men had swarmed Bismarck and Fort Lincoln once Lonesome Charley's dispatches reached Fort Laramie and the news of there being gold in the Black Hills was wired around the nation. Almost at once the military had its hands full trying to keep illegal prospecting parties, like theirs, out of the hills and off of Sioux land.

Jones poured a cup of coffee from a pot banked in a bed of coals.

"We got General Custer to thank for making this trip a real cakewalk," a man named Harley said. Dave Harley was a grocer who had lost his business in Chicago during the Panic of '73 and had come west at the news of gold. His wife and four children were still back East, living with his parents.

"How so?" Jones asked, relishing the strong coffee after a long day handling the team.

"Well, every place we've stopped so far, there's been a fire ring already put together and a stash of wood somewhere nearby." He laughed.

"He sure has marked the way plain enough," a man named Jacob Ackerman said, fishing a bit of ash from his coffee cup with a dirty finger. Ackerman was nearing forty, Jones judged, though the man never spoke of himself or his past. He was a quiet man, always frowning, and when he did speak, he measured out his words as if they were money. He wore a dark, neatly trimmed beard with a streak of gray through it that looked as if he'd drunk cream and dribbled some out the corner of his mouth.

Jones said, "And every place we've stopped has recently been visited by the Sioux. You can thank Custer for that as well."

"You said the Indians didn't bother you the whole trip," Harley reminded him.

"Custer had nearly the entire Seventh Cavalry with him. The Sioux don't have feathers for brains." Jones grinned, suddenly recalling where he'd gotten that phrase from.

"The Sioux ain't gonna bother to run us out," Knutsen said, coming into the circle of the firelight and reaching for the coffeepot. "Not when they got the United States Army doing it for them."

Jason Hormell had been quietly listening to this. Now he said, "It ain't fair! This country is in an economic whirlpool, and our government is keeping us from searching for the gold that might pull us free of it."

"Ain't that true," Harley said. "I lost my store and my family had to move in with my folks just to keep body and soul together." He looked earnestly at Jones. "You were there—tell me again what you saw. There *is* gold on French Creek, ain't there?"

"I panned it myself. Ross and McKay both said a fellow could make twenty to forty dollars a day in some places. There is gold there, or I wouldn't be going back," Jones said.

An uneasy grin moved across Harley's face. "I just needed to hear it again. I spent every last dime I had to make this trip, and I ain't gonna let President Grant or Phil Sheridan or George Armstrong Custer keep me from my God-given right to do for my family. My God, ain't these people ever heard of Manifest Destiny?"

"I wonder if Manifest Destiny includes running the Indians out of the country and breaking our treaties with them," Knutsen said easily.

Harley's voice rose. "It don't mean letting my family starve, either."

Jones said, "According to the Laramie Treaty of '68, this is all Sioux land, and we are breaking the law just being here."

"I know that," Harley said, getting his emotions under control. "But what the hell are they doing with it? They don't live on it. They hunt some and pass through, and that's all. They ain't got no reason to hold on to something they don't use."

"It's important to them," Jones said. "It's where their Great Spirit hunts. To the Sioux, it's sacred land—at least that's the way I understand it."

Harley grunted disgustedly. Jones was grateful when Johnson called them to dinner and the conversation turned to the next day's travel, and what they were going to do once they reached French Creek.

The next morning Knutsen came to Jones as the company was preparing to leave.

"I'm going to ride into the Black Hills and make sure Custer's track is still clear. That was some pretty hard ground we crossed coming out, not like the silty gumbo where a wagon track shows practically forever. I'd like you to ride with me. You have a good memory and that might be of help if I should lose the trail."

"I'll ride with you," Jones said. "I always did prefer the back of a good saddle horse to the hard seat of a heavy freight wagon."

Knutsen gathered his reins and shoved a boot into the stirrup, and was about to swing onto the saddle when Dave Harley rode up.

"Did I hear you saying you was heading into the hills today?" Harley nodded his head at the rising land to the southwest. From this position it was easy to see how the Black Hills got their name.

"Jones and I are going to scout ahead," Knutsen said. "We both remember the way we came out of them, and by putting our heads together we should have no trouble figuring the way back in."

"Mind if I ride along?"

Knutsen glanced at Jones. Jones didn't mind the extra company and nodded his head. "Sure, you can ride along, Harley. You have a rifle?"

"Got one in the wagon."

"You might want to take it with you."

Harley frowned. "Expecting trouble?"

"No," Knutsen said, swinging up onto his saddle, "but I like to be ready for it if it comes."

They rode away from the party of prospectors with the morning sun warm upon their backs, driving the October chill from their bones.

"Ain't that a sight," Knutsen said, reining to a halt to study the heavily forested hillsides rising before them, only ten miles away.

"Finally," Harley exclaimed. "How far is French Creek?"

"It's still a good two or three days' ride," Jones told him. "According to the maps that Ludlow was making of our progress, French Creek was down at the southern end."

"Wouldn't it be faster to just follow these hills south to the place, rather than push our way through them?"

"It might be," Knutsen said, scanning the rising land in the distance, "but the longer we remain out on these plains, the more chance we got of being seen by the army."

Harley grunted. "It's a sorry day when you're more worried about our own army than about Indians."

"Come on, let's get moving," Knutsen said.

"Hold up!" Jones said suddenly, and the urgency in his voice brought their heads around.

"What is it?" Knutsen asked, turning.

Jones pointed back the way they had come, at the lumbering ox team still visible in the distance. "What's that?"

"It's the freight wagon, that's all," Harley said with a note of impatience.

"No, past that—past that rise of land just after Bear Butte."

Their view shifted and fixed upon a cloud of dust rising into the air beyond the freight wagons, tinged yellow by the low morning sun. To the men down below, it would still be invisible behind the higher ground to the east.

"Indians!" Harley cried.

"We don't know that yet," Jones said, peering hard at the growing haze.

"If it is the Sioux," Knutsen said thoughtfully, "we're too far away to get to our men in time."

Jones said nothing, but his heart had climbed into his throat as the cloud expanded. Then suddenly the horsemen burst over the rise into view. At the head of the riders was a soldier carrying a guidon, and behind him galloped maybe forty cavalrymen.

Jones felt a wave of relief wash over him: It wasn't the Sioux. Then, just as swiftly, the relief turned to despair. They'd been discovered by the military, and surely they would be turned back now.

"Damn!" Knutsen exploded. "They've found us."

"Sonuvabitch!" Harley growled. "Maybe they found *them*, but they ain't found me. I ain't letting the army keep me from what I got a right to." Wheeling his mount around, Dave Harley put his heels to its flanks and drove the animal into a gallop.

Knutsen glanced at Jones. "What do you think?"

Down below the cavalry had caught up with the freighter and had encircled it.

"It's not as if we haven't been expecting it, Kansas," he said. "Those men will be taken to one of the forts and sent home, and our supplies will be confiscated." Jones looked over at the tall cowboy. "You and me, we got a choice to make. We can either ride down there and turn ourselves in, or follow ol' Harley there and make the best of it on our own."

"We ain't got no supplies now," Knutsen pointed out.

Jones considered this a moment. "We've got our guns, our blanket, and what's on our backs and in our saddlebags. I've a friend who predicts that these hills will be overrun by prospectors in no time. I think he's right, and if he is, it won't be long before we will be able to buy whatever we need . . . if we've got a claim or two staked out already. But if we go back, someone else will make it in ahead of us."

Knutsen sat there a moment in silence, watching the scene below. Soldiers and prospectors were discussing the matter, but the outcome was certain. Already the boys in blue were inspecting the cargo. The cowboy dug a plug of tobacco from his shirt pocket and filled his cheek.

"Reckon I didn't come all this way only to be turned back at the gate, Jones."

"Reckon I didn't either. No sense in crying over what we lost down there."

Jones and Knutsen turned their animals toward the Black Hills and kicked them into motion.

Winter settled in on the Black Hills; there was already a crust of ice on the flattened grass where Custer's troops and the civilian corps had camped in Custer Park that wonderful week last summer. Jones, Knutsen, and Harley found the place easily, and with no trouble from the Sioux either. That was both a blessing and a concern, for Jones knew the Indians had to be watching their *Paha Sapa* closely now that Custer had been through it and had sent back word of the gold discoveries.

For the first few weeks they were alone. They busied themselves hunting, laying in a supply of food and firewood, and constructing crude shelter, their only tools being their hands, their sheath knives, and their brains. They awoke several mornings with snow covering the pine bough roof of their shelter, but fortunately, game was plentiful and there was dead wood in abundance, so that they always had a fire blazing and meat available.

They were not once disturbed by the military, but sometimes they would awake to discover the footprints of Sioux warriors who had entered their camp during the night. Nothing was ever taken, including their horses. The Sioux were merely keeping an eye on the place, and now and again reminding them of it.

During their fourth week, three prospectors wandered into Custer Park from the southwest, leading a train of six pack mules. Jones had been gathering firewood when the party appeared suddenly through the swirling snowflakes that had been falling for two days.

He dropped the load of wood and hailed them.

They drew up as Jones strode out of a stand of fir trees. "Welcome to Custer Park," he called when he was a dozen feet from them.

They were bundled up like Eskimos against the cold: Buffalo coats, rabbit skin gloves, wolf fur hats, and woolen scarves. The fellow in the lead stopped and tugged the scarf off his mouth.

"So, this is it? Where Custer found gold?"

"It is. Where you from?"

He looked around the place as if he'd been given a glimpse of what lay beyond the Pearly Gates. "Stepped off the train at Cheyenne two weeks ago. I'm Willard Sanders, and that there is Kevin McClusky and Ralph Henderson. We're partners, and Omaha is our home. Find much gold yet?"

"I'm Nathaniel Jones. We've got a camp not far from here. Come on over. Can't offer you much, but there is hot meat and water, and shelter from the weather."

"We could sure use some hot coffee?"

Jones frowned. "You and me both. I'd surrender to the cavalry about now for a cup of coffee. We had plenty of supplies when we left Bismarck, but we lost them all when the army turned back our party. My friends and I were away at the time. We've just been waiting for someone to show up. Haven't even got any gold pans."

"Well we got coffee in our packs. You supply the hot water and you and your friends are welcome to some."

The newcomers were a gladdening sight to Knutsen and Harley, who so far had had to get along with only the meager supplies they'd had with them when they escaped the soldiers. The party from Omaha set up housekeeping next door, anxious for any news of their discoveries and happy to share their supplies, which included axes and extra gold pans. Their stock of clothes was on the scant side, but Jones and the others had already stitched together heavy deerskin jackets.

With the axes and tools the men from Omaha had brought with them, the six men built a large cabin. When the weather broke, they used the time to search out likely gravel bars and work the material down to black sand. There was gold to be found, but not, it was starting to seem, in the abundance that they had hoped or as the newspapers had described it—"gold nuggets dripping from the grass roots." Yet, around the fire pit when the day was through, Jones and the others talked about their future wealth as if the gold was in their pockets already.

So far as Jones knew, they were completely alone, except for their occasional night visitors, who made no noise, took nothing, and left only footprints in the snow. Sometimes Jones would climb a nearby rock and look out across the valley. It was a beautiful place in the winter, often veiled in fog, pine boughs trimmed in white-ice lace, and so quiet that he could hear the fat snowflakes falling softly all around him.

Weeks slipped by and the date became lost among the cold days that mounted up. They suspected that Christmas was due to arrive, but no one was certain exactly when. They had staked claims on French Creek and after a month's work had collected what amounted to only about a hundred dollars in tiny gold flakes. Their enthusiasm was wearing a bit thin.

The men from Omaha were friendly and industrious. Jones became close friends with Ralph Henderson, who, he learned, had written a book once. The two men talked of the literary world, and Henderson was surprised to learn that Jones had penned most of A. B. Donaldson's correspondence, which Henderson had read with relish, planning for the day he too would go to the Black Hills and strike gold.

Henderson was in his late thirties, a widower with two children who were now living with his sister. Although he had never gone to college, he read voraciously and had amazing recall. He had at least a passing understanding of most any subject, and oftentimes he could speak with great authority. Jones enjoyed their long talks on days when the weather kept them inside and near the fire.

Jones and Henderson were having one of their frequent discussions one afternoon, working a sluice box they had cobbled together out of hewed fir trees, when all at once a rifle shot echoed up the valley. Henderson gave Jones a quick glance, then both men grabbed up their rifles and hurried in the direction of the shot. It might be Indians, but then again, it could be that another group of prospectors had entered Custer Park.

Cutting through a stand of trees and up and over a spit of rocky land, they descended the other side and drew up. Below were six covered wagons moving slowly up the valley. A rider coming in from the south had a freshly killed buck in tow at the end of a rope. Jones made a quick count and came up with twenty-three men, and one woman.

"The territory is beginning to fill up," Henderson noted with a grin.

"Let's go down and welcome them."

The wagon train came to a halt and a man on horseback rode out. Jones raised a hand in greeting. In their buckskin coats and rabbit fur hats, the last thing he wanted was for this man to mistake them for Indians and decide to use them for target practice.

The horseman drew up. "White men?"

"I was when I left Omaha," Henderson said.

The men shook hands and traded introductions.

"My name is John Gordon, and we've been on the trail over two months. Left Sioux City on October sixth. I take it this is Custer Park?"

"It is," Jones said. "What date is it?"

Gordon thought a moment. "I believe it's December twenty-third."

"Christmas is two days off. We sort of lost track of the time."

"How long you fellows been here?"

"About two and a half months," Jones said. "Ralph here and his partners came in after us."

"Find any gold, Mr. Jones?"

"Some, but we've been busy getting ready for winter."

Gordon glanced at the gray sky. "Seems winter has already come. How about Indian trouble?"

"None so far, but they're around."

Gordon said, "Well, we'll need to build some kind of defense against them. We got a woman and a child along."

Henderson said, "This will be a hard winter for a woman."

Gordon nodded in agreement. "I know, but Annie is a tough little lady, and she's got a husband. She'll make out all right."

"We have a cabin a little way up the valley, and some claims already staked out, but there is still plenty of French Creek available to you and your people."

"We were counting on that. It's why we dodged the army and took our chances against the savages, hoping to be the first here."

"You're one of the first," Henderson said, grinning. "Welcome to Custer Park, Black Hills, Dakota Territory."

# TWELVE

The Gordon Party made camp about a mile south of Jones and the others, circling their wagons for protection against the Sioux and setting up their tents inside. A couple days later, John Gordon, Ephraim Witcher, Thomas Russell, David Tallent, and Charles Cordiero came visiting. It was Christmas Day, but all that Jones and the others had to offer their guests was coffee, beans, and venison. The men had brought along a bottle of rye whiskey, however, and were eager to share it for any news of gold and Indians.

"There is gold to be found, but it takes a lot of work. It don't come easy like the newspaper made you think," Kansas Knutsen said, relishing his first sip of whiskey since the cavalry had commandeered their freight wagon.

"Tell us about the Indians," Russell said.

Jones said, "They've left us alone so far, but they are around. You'll see their tracks soon enough."

Eph Witcher gave a shiver, which was probably unrelated to the chill wind whistling through the chinks in the log cabin, and said, "I told you we ought to have turned back. This venture is gonna get us all killed."

The others ignored him, and Jones got the feeling that

they had heard this complaint from Witcher more than once.

"Why do you think that is?" John Gordon asked.

"I suspect they're just waiting to see if the government is going to enforce the treaty it made with them."

Gordon frowned. "You mean they're waiting to see if we will be hauled outta here by the scruff?"

"I think that's it."

"And if we ain't?"

"Well, to hear Crazy Horse talk, he isn't about to let any white man stay in their *Paha Sapa,* even if it kills him and every one of his braves."

Gordon's view narrowed. "When did Crazy Horse say that?"

"A few months back. I heard him myself."

"You spoke to Crazy Horse?" There was a note of alarm in Gordon's voice.

Jones grinned. "Didn't I tell you—he and I are kin."

The men of the Gordon Party were momentarily struck dumb. Knutsen and the others chuckled. They'd already heard the story of Jones's sudden adoption by Carson Grove in order to preserve his hair. Now Jones told it again, and afterward everyone had a laugh, and another long drink, and the talk resumed.

Gordon said, "Well, I'm not going to let the savages drive me out, not after all we gone through to get here. We got guns, plenty of them, and ammunition too. Soon as we can, I say we build us a stockade. A big one. One that will keep the Indians out and make the army think twice about trying to run us off of this land."

There was general agreement that a fort would be a prudent thing to have.

The men immediately began felling trees. Hundreds of them toppled beneath the blows of the sharp axes and as the days passed, trenches were cut into the frozen ground, three feet deep, and a stockade of sixteen-foot trees was erected. Every eight feet along the wall they built portholes to shoot out of.

"Be them the damned Sioux or the damnable government, I intend to hold my ground!" Gordon affirmed in open defiance. And when they had finished the double gate, wide enough to drive a freight wagon through, and had built two corner towers to survey his domain from, John Gordon carved a sign and hung it over the gate.

FORT DEFIANCE

While excavating the foundation for one of the towers, they'd discovered their first gold. The find delayed construction for several days as every man had a turn at panning the soil and extracting a few small nuggets for his pocket. The work resumed with renewed excitement and in a week seven cabins began to take shape inside the walls of the stockade. They were crudely built, roofed with logs split in half, hollowed out, and overlapped to form long gutters through which melting snow ran in torrents, keeping the ground continually soaked that winter.

Meanwhile, the men up the valley worked their claims during the day and at night weighed their finds on a crude beam scale that Henderson had constructed from scraps of iron the Gordon Party had brought along.

"Not even half an ounce," Willard Sanders complained one evening in late January. "I hope this does not portend of things to come this new year. I'd make more money cutting ties for the railroad than what I'm turning up here—and it would be steady pay."

Kevin McClusky, who had worked on Grenville Dodge's Union Pacific Railroad with Sanders, shook his head. "You'd not be makin' more money, laddie, but at least you'd have a dry roof over your head and decent victuals on your table."

"There wouldn't be the worry about the Sioux or government either," Henderson added thoughtfully. He sighed. "I wonder how my kids are doing."

A bad case of homesickness had overtaken the friends from Omaha. "Your kids are just fine," Jones said, trying to encourage Henderson. "They're with your sister, after all.'' He didn't want to see his new friend leave, but he'd heard this line of talk before, on the expedition, from soldiers who suddenly turned up missing one morning. Custer labeled them cowards and deserters, but Jones knew it was just the weeks and months away from family and sweethearts, and the low pay, that made most men steal away at night.

The wind moaned softly through the cracks in the logs of their cabin and teased the flames of their fire.

After a moment, Harley said, ''I miss my family too.''

''How many kids you got?'' Henderson asked him.

''Four. Two girls and two boys. The oldest is twelve.''

Kansas Knutsen propped a boot on a log they used as a chair and worked a stick with his skinning knife, slicing long, thin curls into the fire. ''I got me a boy somewhere. He left home when he was fourteen and I ain't heard from him since. I'd hoped he'd come back for his ma's funeral.'' Knutsen sliced another curl of wood into the fire, and a full minute passed in silence before he said, ''I reckon Billy never got the word.''

Other than a mother and father back in Indiana, and a sister down in Kentucky, Jones didn't have anyone to miss—not a wife or children, as these men had. He felt fortunate not to be so burdened, but still something nagged at him, an uneasiness gnawed at his gut. It *would* be kind of nice to have someone to miss, he thought. To have someone who would be missing him right this minute. Without warning, the vault of his memory opened wide, and there he saw a face.

He had forgotten about Morning Snow Woman, but he obviously hadn't gotten over her. Now she filled his brain, and stalked his heart, and he felt suddenly foolish. Could he not forget the beautiful wild savage? How could she have so completely captivated him? And in such a short encounter! It had been only a few moments out of his life, and in that brief time the woman had entrenched herself in his heart.

The vision faded, leaving a heavy stone buried in the center of his chest. *She is probably already married to that young buck with the threatening name.*

That thought made him even more depressed.

"What's wrong with you?"

Jones glanced up and discovered they were all looking at him. "Me?"

"You're wearing a frown longer than the Rio Grande," Knutsen said.

"Nothing's wrong," he lied. "Listening to you five complaining would give anyone a long face."

Sanders laughed. "Yeah, reckon we *were* sort of crying in our whiskey."

"Speaking of that," Knutsen said, running a tongue over his dry lips, "I was down yonder visiting with our neighbors, and just happened to trade some dust for this." He reached back into his bedroll and brought out a bottle. "I was gonna save it for a celebration, but I was only fooling myself." He yanked the cork and grinned. Knutsen carefully measured equal amounts into six cups, then recorked the bottle and set it on the ground between them. "To your health, gentlemen," he said, raising his cup to them.

"To your health," they chorused, and took a drink.

Jones was getting to where he rather liked the bite of a good whiskey, and this fare was much better than what the sutler had brought along on Custer's expedition.

"That wiped away your frown, Mr. Jones," Knutsen declared.

"I do believe it did, Mr. Knutsen," Jones replied, pretending his spirits had lifted; but inside, the weight in his chest remained.

Still, he had to admit that the evening passed more pleasantly once Knutsen brought the bottle out.

A little while later, when the bottom of the bottle was in clear sight, Knutsen suddenly looked up and stared at the door of their cabin.

"You hear something?"

The men went silent, listening. They had heard it too.

"Horses," Jones whispered, grabbing his Winchester.

The men dove for their guns. Jones eased up alongside

the door and lifted the latch. Motioning them away from the firelight, Jones pushed the door open.

The night flooded in. When his eyes adjusted, Jones saw only the fat snowflakes gently drifting down from a gray sky. He stepped outside, Knutsen and Sanders right behind him. A few feet from the cabin, Jones knelt in the snow and placed his hand on the fresh hoofprint of an unshod pony. The hairs on his head stood straight up as he shot a glance around the grounds and saw more prints.

"Sioux!"

"They was here, all right," Knutsen said. "But they are gone now."

Dave Harley stuck his head out the door. "What did you find?"

"The Sioux have been here, but they rode off," Knutsen told him.

Jones stood, turning slowing toward the dark wall of trees across the little valley, indistinct through the falling snow. A spider crawled up his spine as he peered hard into the night. "I don't think they have left, Kansas," he said as a form slowly emerged from deeper shadows beyond the veil of snow, and then another, and another, until eight riders had appeared, halting just at the edge of their view.

Knutsen levered a shell into the Winchester's chamber and threw the rifle to his shoulder.

"No, wait," Jones barked, pushing the barrel away.

"Wait for what? To lose our hair?" Knutsen shot back.

"I don't think that's their intention."

Knutsen slowly lowered the rifle. The white men and Indians watched each other across a distance of maybe fifty yards. A minute passed, but it seemed like ten before one of the Indians rode forward.

He was wrapped in a blanket, with the barrel of a rifle protruding from it, but pointed away from them. Through the softly falling snow Jones noted the dark, searching eyes and the two feathers in the man's long black hair. He looked somehow familiar, yet Jones could not place the face. Someone he had met on the expedition, perhaps?

"Ma-za-chat-kah."

For an instant Jones did not understand. Then it struck him: This Indian was calling him by the name the Sioux had given him. Suddenly Jones remembered where he had met this man before.

Jones gulped, steeled himself, and stepped forward. "I am Iron Left Hand. Why does the great war chief Crazy Horse ask for me?" Without realizing it, he had fallen back on the limited Sioux that he'd learned on the expedition after his fight with Two Bulls. Some of it he'd picked up from the Sioux, but most had come from Carson Grove, who'd taken on the job of giving him enough understanding of the language to avoid any further misunderstandings.

Clumsy as Jones's words were, Crazy Horse understood them. "You are spoken of highly among my brothers, Iron Left Hand, son to Carson Grove." Jones wasn't certain, but he thought he detected a note of mocking. "Therefore I call you brother as well. I have come to give you this warning: You have built your lodge on Lakota land and you must leave. You have come to hunt for the yellow rock. This you cannot do. Your Father has signed a treaty with the Lakota."

"The President did make a treaty with the Sioux in 1868, but Crazy Horse did not sign it."

"I do not make treaties with the White Father, but my people did make the treaty, and I will see that it is honored. We have waited long, but the Father in Washington does not come and take his sons out of our land. We have no more patience. Lame Antelope is gathering a great many warriors. Soon he will be ready and will strike the fort you built. Many will die."

"You would permit this, Crazy Horse?"

The young war chief nodded his head gravely.

"There is a woman and a child in the fort."

"They will die. All will die. You will die too, Iron Left Hand, if you do not leave this place. I have given you this warning."

"When does Lame Antelope intend to attack?"

Crazy Horse shook his head. "The warriors come from many clans, but soon, Lame Antelope will be ready."

"I have spoken to the people in the fort. They will not leave. They have many guns."

"Then many will die."

"And you as well, Crazy Horse."

"Then it will be a good day to die." Crazy Horse reined his horse around and rode back to the waiting warriors. A moment later they had all faded into the night.

"Damn!" Knutsen hissed as if he had been holding his breath the whole time. "What was that all about, Jones? What did that Indian say?"

Jones stared hard into the night at the spot from which the Sioux had vanished.

"Well?"

With a frown pulling heavily at his face, Jones wheeled back to the cabin. "Come on inside, Kansas. I'll tell you and the others."

John Gordon rang a huge triangle to summon them in from their claims. When they had all gathered together inside the stockade, Jones told them about Crazy Horse's night visit. Afterward, a dozen questions were flung at him.

"When did he say the attack would come?" Dave Aken demanded.

"He didn't know. But he thought it could be soon."

"What can we do to protect ourselves. We're less than thirty men strong," Eph Witcher moaned.

Jones had no answer to that. "There is not much any of us can do against a big Sioux war party. Crazy Horse says his braves are prepared to die to keep the *Paha Sapa*. It's their line in the sand. They've only been waiting to see if the cavalry would move us out first."

"We ain't seen hide nor hair of a soldier since coming here," Tom Quiner declared. He sounded almost disappointed.

"It's the weather," Jones assured them. "This hard winter and deep snow has made it impossible for the army to search us out. Come spring, however, you can bet they will show up.''

''If the savages don't get to us first,'' Witcher lamented.

''We all knew the risks in coming here,'' Gordon said, trying to quell some of the unrest.

''But now we got a plain threat,'' Black Dan McDonald said.

''From none less than Crazy Horse hisself,'' Thomas Russell pointed out.

Charles Cordiero stepped forward and said, ''What I want to know is, why did Crazy Horse come to you, Jones? What kind of special arrangement have you got going with him? Are you figuring to have your Sioux friends run us out so you and your partners can take over our claims?''

Charles Cordiero was called ''the Moor'' by some in the party. He had a fierce temper, and his words pulled weight. He, Gordon, and Russell seemed in a constant struggle for control over the other men.

Someone at the back of the crowd said, ''Is that right, Jones? You cut a deal with the savages?''

It didn't take much to turn the prospectors' fears toward some object they could lay hands on. The Sioux being out of reach, Jones seemed as good a target as any.

David Tallent spoke up. ''You told us yourself that Crazy Horse thinks you're kin. . . .''

''If I cut a deal with the Sioux, would I be here now giving you warning?''

''You would be if you thought you could drive us out,'' Cordiero growled, pushing his way to the front of the crowd.

Russell stepped alongside Jones and threw up his arms. ''Men . . . men! Settle down now and let's think this thing through. Mr. Jones has come in friendship. He would not sell us out to the Sioux, and if he has some connection with Crazy Horse we ought to consider that a blessing, not a curse. At least now we've got some warning. This

Lame Antelope and his warriors might have caught us all napping otherwise.''

The prospectors saw the logic in that, and tempers cooled.

''That still leaves my question unanswered,'' Witcher shouted. ''What do we do to protect ourselves?''

Russell looked helplessly to Jones.

Jones said. ''My feeling is that like the cavalry, the Sioux will wait until the weather warms up some and this snow melts off. In the meantime, there is only one way an army of men will come against us, and that is by following the valleys. The hills are too rugged and too heavily wooded for a large war party to cross. Our cabin can serve as a lookout on one end of this valley, and you can keep watch on the other. You might want to station some men farther down as well.''

''That makes sense,'' a man named McLaren said.

Russell said, ''There's that cave west of here. I'd be willing to set up camp there.''

''I'll go with you, Thomas,'' Dave Aken offered.

Gordon said, ''That will give us eyes in three directions, and the fourth is nearly impassable. It's a good start.''

Jones was anxious to be back at his own place and away from here. He'd seen today that in spite of the appearance that all was well, these men were really a quarrelsome, fragmented group, barely hanging together. Gordon and Russell openly disliked each other, and Charles Cordiero was a shark waiting to see which of the two men was weaker so that he could attack and take over. They had discovered some gold; not so much as to make any one claim more valuable than any other, but enough to put them at each other's throats. Gold sometimes did that to men. Yet Jones felt these men's problems had begun long before the Gordon Party reached the Black Hills.

# THIRTEEN

When Jones got back to the cabin Sanders and McClusky were packing their mules.

"The little gold we worked out of these hills so far ain't worth losing our scalps over, Jones," Sanders said.

"The three of you leaving?"

"Henderson is staying, but Harley is coming with us."

"Harley?" That was unexpected. Of the four of them, Harley had boasted the loudest of staying regardless of what the army and the the Sioux did.

Jones tied his horse to the hitching rail and went inside, where Dave Harley was putting his few belongings into his saddlebags. "Heard you were pulling out."

Harley looked away, frowning as he placed a box of .44 shells atop the small poke of gold nuggets. "This ain't working out like I expected, Nathaniel. I figured we'd be pulling more gold outta that creek than we could carry, that I'd come back a rich man and buy the family a house somewhere, and maybe open up another store."

Jones sat on one of the rope beds. "There is money to be made. I'm sure if you stick it out you'll see."

Harley frowned at a sock he was packing and shoved a hand inside it. Two fingers came through the toe. He looked over, wiggled them at Jones, and grinned. "I'd only be kidding myself if I did. I've come to learn something about myself these last couple months."

"What's that?"

"I've learned that in spite of the hard times this country is going through, I'm happiest when I'm home with my wife and family. I miss the city where I grew up. This ain't something I *just* decided on, you understand, but after last night, I had to stop and think about what was important to me. Being rich would be nice, but the risk of freezing to death or dying from a Sioux arrow, and not ever seeing my family . . . well, it just isn't worth it."

Harley gave a short laugh.

"I should have realized it when we lost the wagon and our supplies. We really weren't prepared for what we wanted to do here, Nathaniel." He lifted the saddlebags and said, "Look, I'm going out with about all I came in with. The gold I found will just about pay for what I spent to come out here."

Jones clasped his hand. "You've got good reasons. Can't say as I blame you, Dave. Good luck."

"Thanks."

Outside, the men gathered their mules as Henderson and Knutsen strolled up from the creek to say their good-byes.

"Will you see that my kids get this?" Henderson asked, handing Sanders a sealed envelope.

"I'll see that they do, Ralph."

After the party had disappeared down the valley, Kansas Knutsen glanced at Jones. "How did Gordon and the others at Fort Defiance take the news?"

"They got their backs up. Some accused me of wanting to run them off of their claims, but I don't think anyone really believed that. They're going to stay right where they are."

Knutsen winced. "Wonder how many men have died from pigheadedness."

"You talking about them or us?"

"Both."

Henderson said nothing, but Jones got the feeling that he was rethinking his decision to stay.

The sky was graying, and a cold wind was suddenly in the air. Jones shivered, buttoned his coat, and stared down the valley. The six of them had grown close over the months, and it was hard to let them go. They were probably passing the fort by now. The thought made him suddenly angry. Why had he wasted his time on those newcomers anyway? Why, for that matter, was he staying? His claim was barely paying, and now that the Sioux were amassing to attack the fort, and their cabin as well. Was it worth it?

Jones remembered that when Custer's expedition had started north, the gold had become more abundant, though not so easy to take from the ground as it was down here on French Creek. Jones briefly considered striking out on his own and working his way north. At least if he was alone, the Sioux might not bother him. Then he thought of his friends. He couldn't abandon them now.

January ended without incident, and one morning in early February while cleaning out the cabin Jones discovered a tin mirror that had belonged to McClusky. It was stained and grimy from having been wedged in a chink between two logs for so long. Jones polished it on his sleeve and was stunned by what he saw. He blinked, then stepped outside into the sunlight and looked again. He hardly recognized the face that stared back at him. The usually trimmed mustache had grown into a shaggy beard, light brown and streaked here and there with reddish gold. His skin was ruddy, drawn tight across his cheeks like buckskin drying in the sun, and his eyes seemed harder than he remembered, with a wariness he could not recall ever seeing there before. He was looking into a stranger's face.

He had changed, and he could not remember when it had happened. He looked back at the shiny piece of tin and curried the beard with toughened fingers, then glanced at his hands. A callus had developed on his palms from the gold pan, and his fingertips were rough as a bastard file.

The eyes, the mouth, the skin were all his, yet somehow they reminded him of someone else.

*Carson Grove!*

He looked back at the mirror, amazed, and would have remained staring at it in mild wonderment had not the sound of hoofbeats interrupted him. A man was riding up the valley, and after a moment Jones recognized him.

Charles Cordiero came toward the cabin on a stout sorrel mare. He was buttoned tightly into a gray corduroy coat, with a black, flat-brimmed head on his hat and a scarf around his ears. A rifle stuck out from the saddle scabbard, and as the man reined to a halt, Jones noted the butt of a Remington revolver peaking through a slit in the coat.

Cordiero leaned forward in the saddle. "Where are your partners?"

Jones inclined his head toward French Creek. "Down there somewhere."

"Working their claims?"

"I suspect so. What can I do for you, Mr. Cordiero?"

"Gordon is calling a meeting. He wants you and your friends there."

"When?"

"Tonight."

"What about?"

"Be there and you'll find out." Cordiero reined the horse around and started back the way he had come.

"What was that all about?" Kansas Knutsen said from behind him.

Jones glanced over his shoulder as the cowboy stepped away from the corner of their cabin. "Thought you were down by the creek."

"I was. Come up to warm my hands by the fire. I do believe I've got a touch of arthritis settling in."

"Gordon is holding some kind of meeting."

"So I heard. That Cordiero fellow sure ain't one to talk your ear off."

"He doesn't like us."

Knutsen grinned. "Ain't that just a shame. Ought we take it personal?"

Jones gave a short laugh. "I wouldn't. The feeling I get is that he doesn't like everyone about equally."

They rode the short distance to Fort Defiance later that evening, after their work was done and dinner eaten. Jones noted that a great swath of trees had been cut down from the hill beyond the stockade. Several of the wagons that stood outside the stockade had been disassembled down to their axles and wheels for their wood, and now new flumes made their crooked way down the denuded sides of the valley, past fresh mounds of rock and dirt.

The large gate swung open for them and closed immediately after. Gordon came over, shook hands, and invited them into his cabin, where six or seven other men, including Charles Cordiero, were crowded together.

"We've been fortunate, gentlemen. The Indian scare has not come to pass, and it is time to make some decisions. Open your coats and warm yourselves at the fire. I got coffee here, and if that don't suit your tastes, something a wee bit stronger."

Jones took a cup of coffee and felt it warm his insides while Gordon's blazing hearth did similar service to his outsides.

"I'm glad you men could make it. We have been waiting."

"We got your message, but no more. What is this about?" Jones asked, eyeing Charles Cordiero.

"I've been thinking over our problem, Mr. Jones. It seems to me it's twofold. On the one hand, we have the Sioux, who are slinking about these hills and have threatened to take our scalps if we don't leave. On the other, we got the government, a scalp-taker in its own way, which intends to deprive us of our property if we don't leave. Spring ain't far off and come the warmer weather we are going to have to face one or the other of these foes, maybe both. I've been hoping more men would make their way into these hills, but so far it's been only our party and yours."

"You think more men would help?"

"I do. For one thing, it will give the savages pause if they find a hundred well-armed men here instead of just thirty, and for another, Americans just being here will give us more of a voice in Washington. We might even send a representative to demand the government grant us the right to stay."

"What about the Sioux rights granted to them by the Laramie Treaty?"

Gordon groaned. "Only words on paper, Mr. Jones. Let the government negotiate a new treaty. There is gold here, the substance of prosperity, and this country is in sore need of that right now!"

Henderson said, "Suppose all that you say is true. Just what is it you are proposing, Mr. Gordon?"

"Just this: If we built a town, our claims would be that much stronger."

"A town?" Knutsen said. "A town needs people."

"And so it shall have. The day after tomorrow I'm planning to return to Sioux City to recruit men, and maybe even some women. Eph Witcher is coming along with me, and between the two of us we will show them that there is gold in these Black Hills. I intend to bring people back with us."

Jones noticed the anticipation on Witcher's long face. Leaving was exactly what the man had wanted to do even before he'd arrived, according to what little Annie Tallent had once told him. Jones wouldn't have been at all surprised if Witcher hadn't planted the idea in Gordon's brain in the first place.

Gordon was saying, "We'll organize a whole new party. Once we show them our gold, and tell them that the Indians have been all posturing and no action, I know we can bring at least a hundred in by summer. In the meantime, those remaining here will lay out a town site. We've already got a name for it: Harney City."

"The Sioux aren't just making a show," Jones warned

him. "If you bring more people into these hills, more people will die."

Cordiero said from the back of the room, "How would you know that, Jones, unless you've been talking with Crazy Horse again." His voice held the sharp edge of accusation. Cordiero shoved off the wall he'd been leaning against and placed himself squarely before Jones. "What kind of agreement did you make with that savage? Have you betrayed our strength to him in exchange for your life?"

"Charles!" Gordon said sternly. "We don't need any dissension among us. We are fighting for our future here, and we've invited Mr. Jones and his partners to join us, to be part of that future."

Jones's and Cordiero's eyes locked until finally Cordiero swung away and went back to the corner, where shadows hid his expression. Jones looked back at Gordon. "Just what *are* you proposing?"

"A combining of forces, Mr. Jones. A joining of efforts. I'm inviting you to accompany Mr. Witcher and myself back to Sioux City. You were on the Custer Expedition, so that makes you one of the first white men ever to come to these hills. You'll be a celebrity. Between the three of us we'll visit every town within a hundred miles of Sioux City. We'll gather hundreds of people willing to risk the dangers for the reward of gold and the chance to start a new city right here in the heart of the Black Hills, in the Land of Gold. Then the Sioux will have to think twice about attacking us, and the government will have to listen to our voices. What do you say, Mr. Jones?"

Carson Grove's predictions were coming true, and Jones was being thrust into the middle of it . . . and he did not like that.

"Even if you do manage to round up all the people you say you can, the military isn't going to allow you to return. They'll stop you before you go fifty miles."

"We made it once with six wagons. The army didn't stop us then. We can do it again."

"You were lucky."

Cordiero spoke up. "Don't you see that he's trying to talk you out of it, Gordon? Why is that, Jones? Is it because you don't want any more white people to come here? Is it because you know that Gordon is right, that a town built on this site would keep the Sioux away and give us a lever to use against the government?"

"Mr. Cordiero," Gordon said, his patience strained. "Let the man speak his opinions. He must make up his own mind."

Jones glanced at his partners, but their faces revealed nothing of how they felt. "I have had no further communication with Crazy Horse, Mr. Gordon; I would have told you if I had. But Cordiero is correct when he accuses me of not wanting any more people here. I'm beginning to wish I had never come, but that wouldn't have changed anything."

"I don't follow you."

"The government is only doing its job when it tries to keep us out. These hills belong to the Sioux, and the Sioux intend to keep them. You bringing a hundred, or even two hundred people here will only make matters worse. You'll only get a lot of people killed. We are not talking about a few hundred Sioux—there are thousands of them. When Custer came through it was reported that there were five thousand warriors amassing."

"But we have rights too."

"You . . . me, we are all here illegally. Your town will be illegal, with no weight of law behind it, and it will only add fire to the pot of trouble that's already simmering. I have no doubt that one day the Sioux will be removed from their sacred *Paha Sapa,* just like a hundred years ago the Sioux removed the former inhabitants of this land. That's the way of things— the way it has always been, the way it will always be. Some people even call it progress. But until that time, we must abide by the law and the treaties. Let the government negotiate new treaties if it must; then the hills will be open to everyone. In the meantime, I've made my choice to be here—but I won't influence anyone else.''

Jones looked at his friends, but when he spoke, it was still to Gordon. "I can't talk for Henderson or Knutsen. They can do as they please."

"I was hoping you'd see it differently, Mr. Jones. But like you say, we all have to make our own choices, and to live with the results of those choices. I, for one, intend to follow through with the plan I've just laid out before you, and I think I have the support of every other man in this room."

Henderson and Knutsen said nothing. Jones still didn't know where they stood.

That night, as the other men slept, Jones extracted his journal from his saddlebags—where it had remained over all the long months since the cavalry had turned back his party—and mixing a fresh batch of ink, made a long-overdue entry.

*February 4th, 1875. I can almost hear Mr. Grove whispering in my ear, "I told you so." His predictions so far have been flawless, and if the remainder of them hold true, we are in for a time of bloodshed all through the Black Hills.*

*Most of the men in this lovely valley would like to erect a town. They would call it Harney City, and populate it with unsuspecting pilgrims from back East who would be showed Black Hills gold and told of the land's hidden riches.*

*I've been invited to become a part of this venture, which will certainly fatten my wallet more than working claims that have proven marginal at best. I should jump at the chance, but a part of me resists, and I don't know why. A town, if successful, would fulfill many of my dreams. Still, within me there gnaws an emptiness which I cannot identify. An uneasiness troubles me as well, which Mr. Henderson has identified as a longing to do justice by the Sioux.*

*That sounded horribly righteous, but I could not deny it, either. I am beginning to wish I had never come back here, and have considered abandoning my pursuits and returning to civilization. Who knows, I may yet do that.*

*But for now, I intend to stay on. I'm not sure why. Mr. Grove has correctly predicted so many things that I'm not surprised that he got his opinion of gold fever right as well. It does scramble a man's brains, and it is likely to get him killed as well.*

# FOURTEEN

Two days later, Gordon and Witcher left for Sioux City. A sense of foreboding settled over Fort Defiance as the two men rode away. The next morning a storm swept into the hills, which drove the men off their claims and herded them together around the big fire in the center of the compound that Annie Tallent made sure was always blazing. The tall, log walls of their stockade rebuffed the chill winds and reflected some of the heat from their fire back at them while the men waited, restless to get back to their diggings. Some stood around drinking coffee, or whiskey; others took to squabbling between themselves. The more industrious among them used the time to repair tools or mend clothes.

The snow and winds blew themselves out after a week, and on the fourteenth of February, Thomas McLaren and Charlie Blackwell decided they had had enough of prospecting life. They quit the party and left the Black Hills for Fort Laramie; then it was on to the rail line at Cheyenne, and a quick trip back home.

With the break in the weather, the prospectors laid out the town site of Harney City in preparation for Gordon's return and the people he intended to bring back with him.

They formed the Custer Mining Company and registered all their claims with it, which amounted to nearly all of Custer Park. Any pilgrims coming in with Gordon would find the land already claimed, which would turn a tidy profit for the men already there. The green prospectors would have to purchase claims from them!

Russell and Aken had abandoned the cave and moved back into the stockade. The fear of a Sioux attack dimmed and was consigned to the back room of their brains as more immediate concerns took over. Cordiero and Russell jostled for control of the party, with men lining up in each camp. Everyone saw the fight that was coming. Some could not so easily forget the Sioux always lurking nearby. For others, it was simple homesickness beginning to gnaw at them.

On the sixth of March, Red Dan McDonald, Newton Warren, J. J. Williams, and Henry Thomas pitched their belongings onto the back of the last donkey and trod the now well-worn path out of the Black Hills, leaving only eighteen men at the fort. When they made it to Fort Laramie several days later, the army managed to nab two of them. There had been five attempts that winter to locate the Gordon Party, but now, with their hands finally on a pair of *guides,* and with the break in the weather that they had been waiting for, the opportunity was ripe.

At once Captain John Mix readied his troops for a sixth, and perhaps final push into the Black Hills. News that Lame Antelope had over three thousand warriors camped near the Hills made Mix's task of finding and removing the elusive group of white men even move urgent now.

The temperature was mild and the ground damp from the winter's snowmelt. April held all the promises of spring that warm morning as a pleasant, pine-scented breeze came up the valley. Jones paused, leaned on the mattock that he'd been using to excavate a new pit, and took a moment to look around the claim he had worked all that winter. He took a fresh look at the land, and was suddenly stunned by what he saw.

Last fall they had come into a pristine valley, but now it was all changed. A giant gopher had invaded the Black Hills and had left huge mounds of overturned earth in its wake. The forests had been hacked back where their cabin stood, and through the use of ax and muscle, he and the others had managed to erect a complex spider's web of flumes, chutes, and sluice boxes. Panning for gold had taken them far from the banks of French Creek, and everywhere they went in search of the precious metal, water had to follow. Instead of the deep grass that Jones remembered from the Custer Expedition, vast fields of muddy and torn ground now stretched along the creek, whose waters had become clouded.

It was a wonderful display of man's industry, he thought just then. If only the work had resulted in the wonderful fortunes they had hoped for.

It hadn't.

The entire winter's take amounted to something around six hundred dollars per man. He looked around again. Acres of ground turned inside out, a back that ached, fingers that had grown stiff and sore, and for what? Six hundred dollars? True, it was more money than he could have earned back East writing newspaper articles . . . but then, it had been infinitely more work as well, and accompanied by the dangers of frostbite, wolves, bears, and the Sioux, who had, thankfully, caused them no harm—yet.

Jones looked toward the north, remembering McKay's excitement when he'd dug down to bedrock and discovered the underlying gold. It had been a richer find than what they had turned up here on French Creek, but the gold had been harder to get to as well.

Then again, it was surely no more work than what he'd already put in this winter, Jones decided.

Turning, he peered down the valley at the rising plume of smoke from Fort Defiance that stood above the trees. The men there had been hard at work clearing ground and making big plans for their new town site. If Gordon was successful, hundreds of men would be ripping apart the ground come summer. Jones had already registered his claim with the Custer Mining Company, and like the others, knew it would be an easy thing to sell once all the pilgrims began spilling into the hills.

"Maybe it's time to move on," he thought out loud.

If there were richer diggings north of here, he mused, now would be the time to go and find them. He could sell out here and use the capital to develop better ground. The weather had turned, and Jones was itching to be on the move.

It was hard leaving; he'd grown close to these men. But the time for him to move on had come. He packed only the necessities on one of the three remaining mules: a shovel, a pick, a gold pan, a frying pan, some coffee, baking soda, flour and beans, matches, a towel, a tin pail, and five boxes of .44 Winchester Center Fire ammunition for his revolver and rifle.

The men shook hands and Jones turned his horse away. At the top of a ridge he stopped and looked back. Knutsen and Henderson were still standing at the door of their little cabin, watching. Jones raised his arm in farewell and urged his horse into the forest.

For a long time, he stuck near the old tracks left by Custer's wagons a year before—time did not quickly erase the traces of man from this land. He rode ahead warily, on the lookout for sign of the Sioux. So far, the Indians had left the white intruders alone, but Jones knew that would not last.

He made camp an hour before sundown and heated coffee and over a small fire, roasted a rabbit he'd shot. Alone in this Black Hills wilderness, he was careful not to do anything to attract attention to himself. He'd seen grizzly bear in the distance that day, and had heard the howling of wolves nearby. A fire might keep them at bay, but too much of a fire would be an open invitation to any passing Sioux.

The next day he came upon seven prospectors camped at the head of a little valley. They were relieved to learn that Jones was not a scout for the cavalry, and starved for

news from the outside. Jones had none of that, but he did
tell them of Gordon's stockade. This group, led by a man
named Bill Smith, had been prospecting since February,
having snuck into the hills under the cover of a snow-
storm. They had found a little gold, but no big strikes—
no glory holes. It had been a lot of hard work for a small
poke of metal. But it was enough to drive men like Smith
and his partners on, in the constant hope that the next
shovelful of dirt would hold the answer to all their
dreams.

Smith said they'd had no contact with the Sioux, but
that the party had come well prepared with repeating rifles
and two cases of ammunition. They were interested in
what Jones had to tell them of Fort Defiance and Gordon's
plans for a town.

Jones spent the rest of the day with these men and the
next morning was on his way again. He traveled leisurely,
for he had no particular destination in mind; "north," like
Carson Grove's "west," left it wide open. He even considered riding to the end of the Black Hills and surveying
the plains the lay beyond, to see if he might spot the
reported encampment of Lame Antelope and the warriors
that Crazy Horse had warned him about. Along the way,
Jones spied the evidence of prospectors having invaded
the area. New excavation pits pockmarked the land and
abandoned campsites littered with tin cans seemed to have
sprouted everywhere.

Jones spent a second night beside a small campfire, the
silence of the Black Hills pressing down all around him,
the cold, clear sky a black bowl awash with stars. Occasionally a bright streak would shoot past, only to burn
itself out a moment later. He spread his bedroll on the
hard ground, not caring anymore that it wasn't a soft bed,
or even a taut army cot. The forest had become home to
him these past many months, her sounds familiar enough
that he could read any danger in them. Tonight, there was
none, and propping his head in the curve of his saddle,
he let the soft sounds loll him to sleep.

The next morning, Jones had no idea how far he had

come as he rode beneath a warm morning sun along the line of a forested ridge. He suspected that he was nearing the northern edge of the Black Hills, and if he could only find a peak high enough, he was certain, he would spy Bear Butte not too far to the east. He reined to a halt and studied the forest. To his left the land fell off toward a valley, and to the right it climbed. Perhaps up there he'd have a wider view.

He'd started his horse in that direction when all at once the distant boom of a rifle echoed up from the valley below. The trees blocked his view. Curious, he swung out of his saddle and taking the Winchester with him, started for the edge of the trees. As he drew nearer, a valley below opened up. It was a long, narrow rift in the land, with pine and fir trees rimming it, and at the bottom where a stream flowed, spring grass was greening up.

He studied it a moment, saw nothing, and was about to return to his horse when at the head of the valley two figures broke from the cover of the trees, running wildly.

They were too far off to see clearly, but Jones knew they were Indians. A man and a woman—he could make out that much as they fled recklessly into the valley, looking over their shoulders as they ran. Then the man stumbled and fell. The woman wheeled around and dragged him to his feet. At that same moment a grizzly bear burst into view.

The man and the woman stumbled on. She was fleet of foot, but the man was having trouble keeping up. To add to his problems, he was frantically trying to reload an old single-shot rifle as he ran: spilling powder down the barrel, thumbing a ball in place, and fumbling the ramrod in after it.

As Jones watched the bear gaining on them, he suddenly remembered his own rifle, and the next instant he leaped from his cover and waved it overhead at them.

"This way! This way!" he shouted in Sioux.

But the two fleeing people didn't hear him. The man had gotten his rifle reloaded and with the grizzly nearly upon them now, he turned to fire.

The beast pounced, knocking the rifle from his hands and smothering him beneath its great bulk. At the same time the woman spun around and fearlessly dove to his aid, grabbing the rifle out of the grass and firing.

The bear roared as the ball cut into its hide. Forgetting the man beneath its giant paws, it put its small eyes upon her.

She was young and swift, but even that couldn't keep her ahead of the bear for longer than a few more seconds. Jones had been charging up the valley himself, and now, as the bear closed in on the girl, he threw his rifle to his shoulder and fired a shot. The bullet went wide.

The sound of his shot was the first indication to the woman that someone else was nearby, and to the bear as well. Jones levered a fresh round, steadied his sights on the fierce bruin, and fired again.

Its anger raging, the giant beast broke stride. It shook its massive head and with its weak eyes searched for this new enemy. Jones fired a third shot, which seemed to have no effect on the bear except to alter its plunging charge. The girl had changed course as well, and suddenly both she and the grizzly were barreling down on him.

They drew nearer as Jones took careful aim.

Now that she was much closer, he saw that the girl was young and tall, her long black braids flying and a wide, terrified look upon her face. . . .

*Her face!*

The shock brought him to a halt as she flew past him.

*Morning Snow Woman!*

Stunned, he stood there with the rifle still against his shoulder, but his eyes traveling back, watching the girl as she fled. Then an earthshaking roar broke his trance. Jones took off in a run after her. A few dozen paces behind the girl, he turned and fired several shots over his shoulder as fast as he could lever a new round into the chamber. Running and firing, he was missing the bear as often as he hit him. And even when his bullets did meet their target, they seemed to make no difference at all. Blood was streaming down the bear's dark coat from a half dozen different places, but his energy had not in the least diminished.

Then the hammer of Jones's Winchester snapped down on an empty chamber. He flung the useless weapon back at the bear, which was now so near that Jones imagined its hot, foul breath on his neck. The rifle harmlessly smacked the bear across its nose and was instantly trampled beneath one of its huge clawed feet.

Jones caught up with Morning Snow Woman, but the nearest tree was still several hundred feet away, and the grizzly was less than a dozen. Stretching his strides to the limit, he grabbed her under an arm to hurry her along, but then, as luck would have it, a branch hidden in the new grass reached up and snagged his foot. Jones reeled forward, plowing headlong into the ground, taking Morning Snow Woman down with him.

Scrambling, Jones twisted around as the great shaggy creature reared on its hind legs above them. Its roar thundered like a driving locomotive; its huge paws and sharp, curved dagger claws rose in the air and momentarily blocked the sun.

Jones had never stared death in the eyes before, yet all he could think about was protecting Morning Snow Woman. He threw his body across hers—a futile gesture, he knew, but it was all that he had left with which to protect the girl as the great beast lunged.

What happened next was an impossibility, or so it appeared to Jones. Claws, fangs . . . all nine hundred pounds of raging death seemed to stop in midair and hang there a brief instant; and then, as if someone had yanked a rug out from under it, the griz flipped over onto its side and crashed to the earth. Jones grabbed Morning Snow Woman and heaved her aside as half a ton of quivering muscle and fur came to a rest.

A second later a distant boom echoed down into the valley from the ridge above. Jones looked up and spied the white puff of smoke among the boulders. Then he remembered the girl.

"Morning Snow Woman! Are you hurt?"

She sat up and stared at him, confused.

"It is I. Nathaniel Jones. Don't you remember me?"

Her black eyes widened, searchingly, then she reached up and touched his shaggy beard. "Nathaniel Jones?"

"Yes! I . . . ah, I guess I have changed a little since you last saw me."

"Hair grow on face," she said, then suddenly her eyes narrowed. "Grandfather!" She leaped to her feet and ran back toward the fallen man. Jones followed her, at the same time watching a figure in buckskins coming down the hillside. The man was still a good distance off, but Jones grinned anyway. There was only one rifle that spoke with that voice and punched with that fist, and Jones knew who had pulled the trigger.

"Carson Grove!" Jones greeted when the old mountain man was still half a hundred paces away.

Grove walked with a limp, peering hard at Jones as he came across the valley.

Jones laughed. He was getting used to people's not recognizing him. Six months wintering in this wilderness had hardened him and given him more girth about the shoulders, and the wild beard he wore had pretty much erased all vestiges of the civilized man he'd once prided himself as being.

Grove had a wary look upon his weathered face as Jones rushed forward. The old hunter drew up and waited, studying Jones hard, and the next instant he roared, "Well, if it ain't young Nate!"

They clasped hands, then stood back and took to peering at one another.

"What are you doing in the Black Hills?" Jones asked. "The last time we said good-bye, you said you were heading west."

"I did, and I am. These hills are a mite west of Bismarck, if I read my maps right."

"You have no idea how happy I am to see you."

Grove slanted an eye at the mound of fur and said, "I reckon I know. I was that happy once, when Jim Clyman's ball busted the spine of another griz a few years back. What did I tell you now, Nate? I seen you from up there popping away at Ol' Ephraim there with that pitiful pip-squeak of a rifle. You're just lucky I happened to be passing by and heard your shots. I warned you to get yourself a big-bore rifle. One with oomph!"

Jones frowned. "I would have stopped him if I had the time to aim properly."

Grove gave a short laugh, then nodded toward the woman up the valley, bending down now over the fallen man. "Who is that there?"

"You'll never believe this, but I too was drawn here by the sound of a shot, and came upon the scene just as you did. That's how I got drawn into this. But then guess what I discovered."

Grove stood patiently, waiting, leaning on the long, heavy barrel of his Sharps.

"That young lady is Morning Snow Woman! You remember her?"

"Sure do. That's the gal you ain't got no interest in at all, but jest the same every time you mention her name you gush like one of them Yellowstone spouts."

Jones paused and said thoughtfully, "Wonder what she is doing here, anyway."

"Who's the feller with her?"

"I don't know. She said it was her"—Jones looked up with a start—"grandfather!"

"One Stab," both men said together.

Jones retrieved his Winchester from the trampled grass as he and Grove hurried to One Stab's side.

"How is he?" Jones asked, kneeling beside the old man.

Morning Snow Woman glanced up, an uncertain look on her lovely face.

"He is alive," she said quickly in her native tongue.

Without thinking, Jones lapsed into the Sioux language as well. "We need to get him to shelter."

Grove was examining the claw wounds that had raked the old man's chest and laid the skin open. "There's lots of blood, but the wounds ain't deep. He'll need some stitching up, though. I got me a cabin nearby."

They cut saplings and rigged up a travois and attached it to Jones's horse; Grove's animal was already carrying a quartered elk. One Stab was conscious by the time they lifted him onto the horse. He was surprised and pleased to see the two men, but mostly, Jones figured, he was relieved to find his granddaughter unharmed. Grove found the old chief's rifle not far away, and when he paused to study the piece, a curious frown pulled at the corners of his mouth.

"What is it?" Jones asked.

"Nothing," Grove said brusquely, then, "Except, I ain't never met an Injun yet who knew how to take care of a rifle. At one time this here was a fine J. Henry Lancaster. Now look at it—a hunk of rust is all," he groused as he laid it upon the travois next to One Stab.

# FIFTEEN

Carson Grove led them up over two ridges and to the edge of a steep gulch. They stopped near a pile of brown rocks, and Jones peered over the edge. He was amazed by the amount of dead wood littering the forest floor beneath the towering Douglas firs.

"Looks like fire or flood came through here once."

"It was fire, and you should have seen this gulch thirty years ago. Couldn't hardly cross to the other side without getting your clothes black from the charred wood. Not that we was worrying much about that at the time, you understand," Grove said with a curious grin.

"You've been here before?"

Grove nodded his head. "Me and my partners come huffing up this side of the gulch with ol' One Stab there and his warriors hot on our tails. We was a lot younger men back then, you understand." Grove looked around, remembering that event of so many years before. "Yep, I was here, Nate. My, how the years have changed this place. There warn't one tree left down there over two feet tall, and now look at 'em. Most of the old wood has rotted and gone back into the ground. But there's still plenty around, as you can see. Right over there, that's where

Frenchie found his gold nugget. And over there a few feet, that's where he died because of it.''

He stared at the spot a moment, then drew in a breath. "I built me a little cabin down the way a piece. Come along.'' Following a game trail, they descended the side of the gulch to a rustic log cabin near a fast-flowing stream.

"This gulch ain't got no name on no map as far as I can tell. I just call it Dead Wood Gulch, and to make it convenient, I've been calling that Dead Wood Creek. It flows into another creek up ahead. I ain't bothered naming that one. Names are only good so long as there is someone here to use them, and this place is so far from the findings down along French Creek that I reckon them prospectors will never make it here. Leastwise, I hope not . . . not until I leave it.''

"It hasn't been all that profitable down south, Mr. Grove. I just came from Custer Park.''

They carried One Stab into the small cabin and laid him upon a blanket on the dirt floor. Grove had no bed, and only a log turned on its side for a chair and another with one side hewed flat for a table. His fireplace was merely a circle of rocks beneath a hole in a roof made of pine boughs. It didn't appear that Carson Grove intended to stay very long.

Grove got to work on One Stab, cleaning the wounds while Morning Snow Woman busied herself collecting medicinal plants and boiling a concoction in a black iron pot.

He found a needle and thread among his things and crudely stitched the flaps of skin together. Afterward, Morning Snow Woman applied her poultice. They made One Stab as comfortable as they could. The old chief asked for whiskey and Grove dusted off a bottle of rye that he said he'd been saving for a special occasion. Being alive was special enough for One Stab, and he guzzled it happily.

Morning Snow Woman left, and a few minutes later

returned carrying a load of wood that would have tested the strength of Jones himself.

"Let me take that," he said, hauling it near the fire.

"Grandfather must be kept warm."

"There is plenty of dead wood around for that," Grove said. "One thing I ain't had to do much of is cut firewood."

Morning Snow Woman tended to One Stab's wounds, gathered wood, collected herbs and roots, cleaned the cabin, cooked a stew with some of the elk meat Grove had brought along, carried the blankets down to the creek, washed them, then hung them to dry over some low branches.

Jones watched her going about the chores, amazed at her boundless energy. He helped her with some of them, but soon he tired and found himself sitting next to Carson Grove on a stump outside the cabin.

Grove was grinning to himself. When Jones inquired why, he merely said, "She reminds me of my first wife, Nate."

Jones leaned back against the rough wall of the cabin. When he wasn't watching the lovely Indian woman diligently taking over the chores, his view was wandering up and down the gulch.

Grove had his Sharps rifle on his knees, running a rod up the barrel. He carefully cleaned the black powder residue from around the breech and lock, and then oiled the steel parts.

"So, tell me, Mr. Grove, what *are* you doing here?" Jones finally asked. "I never expected to see you again, and certainly not here in the Black Hills."

The old man pretended not to hear him.

"Are you here hunting?" Jones asked.

"I do some of that," Grove allowed, wadding a rag and vigorously rubbing down the barrel.

"You doing it with a rifle, or with a gold pan?"

Grove glared at him.

"Don't deny it. I saw the pan behind the cabin."

"Well, what of it?"

"Who was it said that gold scrambles a man's brain? Who was it said that gold fever gets a man killed? Who was it said that the white man coming onto Sioux land was going to start a war or something?"

"You got a mighty annoying memory, Nate."

"Why *are* you here?"

"I got to spell it out for you, or do you jest like to see me squirm a bit? All right, I'm here for the gold. Same as you and fifty other men right now. There, I said it. Does it make you happy?"

"What changed your mind?"

"Who said my mind ever changed?"

"But back in the saloon in Bismarck—"

"Back there I already knew what I was intending to do. I said them things to you because I didn't want you coming here and getting hurt."

"I've taken care of myself all right so far."

Grove looked him up and down and grunted, giving a reluctant nod of his head. "You've toughened up, Nate. You'll make out all right if the Sioux leave you alone."

"I've had some visitors."

"Spill any blood?"

"No, but me and Crazy Horse had us a nice little talk."

"Crazy Horse! And he didn't try to lift your scalp?"

"No. In fact, he came to warn me about Lame Antelope."

"Hmm. I've heard that war chief was getting some of his boys together for something or another. Whatever it is, it won't amount to anything good." Grove looked at him, then grinned. "Crazy Horse come to you, did he?"

"He still believes we are kin."

"He does, does he? Well, I reckon I always could spin a good yarn."

"Tell me, Mr. Grove, have you found any?"

"Any what?"

"Why, gold, of course!"

Carson Grove looked around, and then, giving Jones a wink, he disappeared behind the cabin. When he returned he was carrying a leather pouch, working at the string that held it shut. "Stick out a hand, Nate."

He did, and Grove filled it with gold nuggets.

"You're staring, Nate," he said with a chuckle.

Jones looked up, speechless.

"I've got eleven other pouches as full as that one. This gulch is a gold mine, and nuggets are all over the place. Nearly every panful has one or two of 'em in it."

"How did you ever find this place?"

"Already told you—stumbled upon it more'n thirty years ago. Frenchie was the one who really found the gold."

"Have you filed a claim?"

"A claim? No, I reckon not. Ain't nobody else here so I jest work the whole creek. Figure I'll take what I want and leave. Maybe go on west to Calee-fornee and spend some time with Clyman. Maybe go hunt us a bear or two, for old times' sake." He laughed and held the bag open.

Jones dumped the nuggets into it and Grove carefully tied the mouth of it shut.

"You ought to file."

"Naw, ain't gonna do that."

"Why?"

"I file a claim and what do you think will happen? I'll tell you. Inside of a week this place will be swarming with gold hunters. Nope, I jest as soon keep it under my hat and work the creek until I'm ready to move on."

Jones looked at his friend. "But you still haven't told me *why*."

Grove studied the pouch, then hefted it as if judging the weight of the gold it contained and said, "Well, I already told you once, remember?"

"No."

"It was that day we went hunting antelope and I busted this leg. You asked me why I hunted for Custer if I was against all that he was doing. I told you why then, and my reasons for being here are the same. I ain't a rich man, Nate. Never have been, never planned to be—at least, not until now. A man sometimes has to do things he don't like, but he does them jest the same.''

Jones and Grove were friends, but Jones wasn't certain he could agree with the old mountain man's easy way of bending life's inconstancy to fit his needs. For now, he kept his misgivings to himself. And later that afternoon he took his gold pan down to Dead Wood Creek and fished out a half an ounce of nuggets in about two hours.

If nothing else, he had come upon a bonanza, and even if Grove wouldn't file, he certainly intended to.

Jones and Carson Grove slept out under the stars, giving the cabin over to Morning Snow Woman and her grandfather. At first the lovely Indian girl protested, insisting that she preferred a roof of stars to that of pine boughs, but in the end she agreed. Her grandfather, she reasoned, might need her during the night.

The next morning Jones was awakened early by a sound. He parted an eyelid and looked around. Nearby he heard Grove softly sawing . . . and then the snap of a twig. His hand went for the revolver and he quietly threw off the blanket.

The sun was not yet in the sky. To the east the sky had turned bright pink, but there were still deep shadows down in the bottom of Dead Wood Gulch. Jones moved quietly toward the creek from whence the sound had come. He drew up to listen, and a movement through the trees caught his eye. Crouching, he eased down the creek, keeping to the trees until the forest ended near the water. There he stopped abruptly at what he saw.

Morning Snow Woman was standing near the water, and as he watched her, she suddenly lifted the dress up over her shoulders and tossed it casually upon a boulder. Standing there, naked, she stretched toward the morning sky, arched her back as if working the kinks out of it, and stepped down into the cold, swirling water.

Jones stood dumbfounded, his view riveted upon the beautiful girl, already bloomed into the full beauty of womanhood, tall and as lithe as the branches of a young tree. Jones felt his body responding to her nakedness as she washed herself in the icy water as easily as a woman from more civilized realms might have bathed in a tub of warm water.

He knew he ought to leave, but his feet refused to budge. In a few minutes she finished her bath and, dripping, walked gracefully from the water. It was then that she spied him standing there.

To Jones's shock, she smiled at him, as if not the least concerned by her nakedness. Then she turned back to her dress and began brushing at it, fussing at a spot, before finally removing a bone comb from a pouch and tugging it determinedly through her long, wet hair.

Jones had to leave this very moment, or risk an encounter he was certain he was ready to initiate. Abruptly, he turned away and marched back to the cabin. Carson Grove was awake when he returned.

"What's wrong, Nate?"

"Wrong? What makes you think anything is wrong?"

"Well, your eyes are wider than the Great Canyon of the Colorado, and your face is nearly as red as its rocks."

Jones sat on his bedding. "Am I really all that transparent?"

"Something's got you worked up."

"I heard something this morning, Mr. Grove," he started, embarrassed by what he was about to tell the old man, but knowing just the same that it had to be said. There was so much about the Sioux that he just did not understand. "It was Morning Snow Woman, and she . . . she was taking a bath in the creek."

Grove shrugged his shoulders. "The Sioux are what you might call fastidious when it comes to washing up and such— you seen the way that gal fussed around my cabin. And why do you think she didn't want to sleep in it last night? I'll tell you why," he went on, not giving Jones a chance to reply. "It's because the place stinks!"

"But the thing is, when she discovered me there seemed not the least disturbed. In fact, she smiled at me and went about her grooming as if I were not there at all . . . and she naked as . . . as . . .''

"As baby mice?"

"Er, yes."

Grove laughed. "She got you flustered, I can see that. Was there anything wrong with her body?"

"Wrong? No! It was perfect—" His face was suddenly on fire.

"Well, then why should she be ashamed of it?"

"But—"

"You got to understand something about the Sioux, Nate. They don't fuss and fret over modesty like white women do."

"They don't?"

"Nope." Then Grove narrowed an eye, all at once dead serious. "But there's another thing you need to know, too. Although their womenfolk don't jump and screech when they are all naked and a feller sees 'em, the Sioux prize virtue more than most tribes. Not for virtue's sake, Nate— and don't get me wrong, a playful Sioux will give you a grand romp in the hay, if you happen to be the right man—but a virtuous Sioux maiden is a precious commodity, highly valued among the men of her tribe. And she usually keeps tight rein on that virtue right up to her wedding night, because it brings a higher purchase price from the prospective husband. More ponies, more beads, or whatever."

"Mr. Grove! I'd never consider—"

"Sure you would, Nate. Any man would with a woman as good-looking as that Sioux is. Oh, by the way, if you are intending to get intimate with her, they prefer to be called Lakota, not Sioux. Lakota is what they call themselves."

Jones was about to protest, but didn't. Grove was right: Properly enticed, he could easily succumb to Morning Snow Woman's charms. Jones cleared his throat and said levelly, "I will keep that in mind, Mr. Grove."

A few minutes later, Morning Snow Woman came back

to the cabin. Grove and Jones were inside, examining the claw wounds.

"He is warm," she said, wringing water from a cloth and placing it upon her grandfather's fevered brow.

"I ain't surprised," Grove said. "There is gonna be an infection."

She changed the poultice on his chest while One Stab watched, grinning. He glanced at Grove and said, "You do not sew very good, do you?"

Grove frowned. "I wasn't out to decorate your scrawny chest with any fancy stitchery, One Stab. Just wanted to get you back together before you fell all apart. Hell, you ought to thank me. The squaws in your village will think you're a right handsome fellow now with them new scars."

Although it hurt to do so, One Stab laughed. "The day I need your help to get a woman is the day the young men put me up in a tree."

"Well, if you keep on a-huntin' grizzly bear with that old rusty relic of a rifle, the day you go to rest in your sepulchre tree will not be far off."

One Stab waved that notion away and made a grunt. "I do not hunt the big bear anymore. That is the work of the younger men. This one, he come hunting me. What could I do, Carson Grove? My legs are no longer swift. I cannot climb trees anymore. All I can do is shoot back."

"Well, you're lucky young Nate showed up when he did."

One Stab nodded his head at Jones two or three times, and then his dark eyes darted back toward Grove. "Where is bear now? You did not leave him to wolves?"

"I skinned him out. Got the hide a-drying."

"I want skin."

"I don't know about that. It's gonna make one warm robe come winter. I kinda figured I'd keep it, since it was my bullet what put him down."

"I shot him first," One Stab protested.

Grove thought this over a moment. "I suppose you got a point there. What do you think your cut ought to be?"

"Cut? I want whole skin."

Grove shook his head.

"What good is half a skin?"

"Half? I was thinking maybe a quarter of it."

"Quarter! No. No good. I want whole skin, Carson Grove."

"You want it all, you'll have to pay for it. What have you got to trade?"

"Trade? I'm poor agency Indian. I have nothing anymore but what your government gives me!"

Jones followed most of the haggling, but did miss some of the words; there was much of the Sioux language he did not understand. Morning Snow Woman smiled at the bartering as she added herbs and roots to the boiling pot of medicine she had been preparing for her grandfather's wounds. When she went outside, Jones followed her.

"Where are you going?" he asked in his broken Sioux as she started into the forest.

"To gather more plants."

"For the poultice?"

"Yes."

"Can I help you?" he asked.

"I do not need help."

"Er, then, can I walk with you?"

She smiled as if embarrassed by his request, and said, "Yes."

They walked along a game trail, Morning Snow Woman stopping here and there to pluck a leaf or pry a root from the ground, then put it into a deerskin pouch. Jones was amazed that so early in the year, with sometimes only green shoots poking up through ground still moist from the melted winter's snow, she was able to find the herbs, worts, and roots that she needed. In a crevice she discovered a rat's nest and excitedly collected the droppings, wrapping them in a piece of doeskin and placing them into her bag.

"Does that go into your medicine?" he asked, shocked.

"It is good for wounds when boiled with other plants."

Between his broken Sioux and her broken English, they

managed to converse quite well. There was so much of her world he did not understand. Just walking with her, watching her collect the ingredients of her medicine, had opened his eyes to a science which he was only vaguely aware of, although how much of it worked and how much was superstition, he didn't know.

He was strangely at ease with this daughter of the wilderness. Her laugh was delightful, her smile hypnotic, and when she looked at him with those wide, dark eyes, he imagined he saw genuine affection there. Could it be that she found him as interesting as he found her? He could hardly hope that was so . . . yet he did.

"I thought I would never see you again after that afternoon last year. You cannot imagine my surprise when I recognized you."

"It is good you were near, and Carson Grove."

They had met for only the briefest time one summer afternoon back when Custer had come through the Black Hills, yet that single encounter had left an indelible mark upon him. He wondered if it had affected her in a similar way. He had tried to put Morning Snow Woman out of his thoughts, but had failed. They were from two different worlds that had accidentally come together once and then separated, he could accept that. But now it had happened again! It was said chance was blind, and yet . . .

A question had been nagging him, and now, he felt, the time was right to ask it. "Where are your people, your village, Morning Snow Woman? What were you and One Stab doing here alone?"

She pointed to the north and said, "My people are camped near the Belle Fourche. There are many who have come together for the winter."

"I thought you were living at the Red Cloud Agency."

Her lips compressed into a tight line that was not quite a frown, but very near. "No food at the agency. Government promise cattle and blankets. We got little of either. We had to go away and hunt or become sick."

"Did everyone leave the agency?"

"Not everyone. Most of the old people and the children

stay, but many of the young braves leave. Some of the older people too, like Grandfather. One Stab says he too old to live off of the white man's gifts. He has lived free for too many winters."

"What are all the young men doing? Hunting?"

She glanced down. "They prepare for war."

"I have heard that Chief Lame Antelope was gathering warriors together to fight the white man."

Her view returned to his face. "It is so, because you have come into the hunting grounds of the Great Spirit."

He winced at the open rebuke. They walked along the path in silence for a few moments.

"Is One That Kills in a Hard Place with Lame Antelope?" he asked, working his way toward the heart of the question that weighed on him.

"No. He says he will fight with Crazy Horse."

Jones didn't know how to say next he knew he must, except straight out. "Does One That Kills in a Hard Place still wish to marry you?"

She looked at him, searchingly. "He has sent ten ponies to the lodge of my grandfather. One Stab says it will be a good joining. His clan is strong, our clan is strong."

"One Stab thinks it will be a good joining? What do you think? What do your mother and father think?"

"My parents are dead."

"Oh. I'm sorry to hear that." Jones frowned as he tried to remember something he'd been told about Sioux courtship. Then he had it. "Has One Stab accepted the gifts?"

She averted her eyes. "He has not returned the ponies."

That was as good as an acceptance, and therefore a promise to give his granddaughter to this warrior. Jones's spirits plunged.

"How do you feel about it?" he asked, keeping his voice level.

"I will do as Grandfather wishes."

Jones hesitated. "But, do you love One That Kills in a Hard Place?"

Morning Snow Woman still did not look him in the

face. ''The joining will be good for our clans,'' she repeated. ''That is important.''

''But what about you? Will it be good for you? Isn't that important?''

She did not answer him.

''Well?'' he persisted.

She peered suddenly at the deerskin bag in her hand. ''I have gathered enough here,'' she said, and without another word Morning Snow Woman turned away and departed, leaving Jones standing there, watching her disappear around a bend in the trail that they had been following.

# SIXTEEN

"You're a strong old coot, One Stab, but those wounds are festering."

"Granddaughter make good medicine," he said, probing the burning flesh with the tip of his finger.

"I'd say you need a doctor," Jones said.

One Stab shot him a narrow glance. "White man's doctor? No good!"

Morning Snow Woman put a hand on his forehead to judge the fever. "My medicine is weak, Grandfather. The earth is only now awakening from its winter sleep. I cannot find the plants I need. They are only waking as well."

Grove said, "Jones is right—you need the care of a doctor. You might pull through it on your own, but I guarantee it will get a lot worse before its gets better."

"No white man's doctor."

"I'm not suggesting it, One Stab. You have a medicine man at your camp on the Belle Fourche, don't you?"

"Eagle Two Claws," Morning Snow Woman said. "He has the medicine to drive the sickness from Grandfather's body and to knit the skin together again."

"We ought to take One Stab to him," Jones said.

"How far is the camp?" Grove asked.

"One day's march," Morning Snow Woman said, "but with a travois, two days."

"You get your grandfather ready to travel." Grove glanced at Jones. "Let's get that travois hitched up, Nate."

Outside, they rescued the rickety conveyance from alongside the cabin. "Can Indian medicine really do anything for him?" Jones asked as they reinforced the travois, preparing it for the long journey to the Sioux winter camp.

"It works about as good as anything the white man can do—maybe better sometimes. But then, a lot of it depends on you. I've seen men die of a scratch, but I've also seen a man live with a leg blasted off when a keg of powder blew up once in a trader's camp."

"I am suddenly realizing how much I don't know about the Sioux."

Grove grinned. "The older I get and the smarter I think I get, the more I realize jest how dumb I really am. There is a wide world around us, Nate, and what I know about it is only a spit in the ocean."

Jones busied himself with the ropes that held the travois together. "Mr. Grove, what do you know about engagements?"

"Engagements? Get to high ground and good cover, and hope your powder don't run out."

Jones glanced up. "That's not the kind of engagement I was referring to." He saw that Grove was grinning.

"I know'd what you was talking about. Is that gal betrothed?"

"I'm . . . I'm not certain. But it sounds like she might be, and I don't think she's happy about it. One That Kills in a Hard Place has sent ten ponies to One Stab."

"And he accepted them?"

"She said he hasn't yet returned them."

"Well, then it sounds to me like he has agreed to the marriage—and how do you feel about that, Nate?" Grove asked, slanting a suspicious eye at him.

"Feel? Why should I feel one way or the other about it?"

Grove threw back his head and laughed. "You lie as convincingly as a politician the morning before Election Day, Nate. I'd seen right off that you was star-struck the moment you put eyes on the Injun girl. It was so plain that even her boyfriend saw it. That's why he wanted to lift your scalp, and he would have if Custer and One Stab hadn't stepped in."

Jones dropped the rope and sat on a rotting tree trunk. "You're right, Mr. Grove. I know it's crazy, but there is something about Morning Snow Woman that I've never felt with any other woman. I believed I had forgotten her, but she was never very far from my thoughts. I kept telling myself it was impossible, that we were from two different worlds. Then the other day, when I saw her again, all of that didn't make any difference. I was elated! How do I feel about her engagement, Mr. Grove? I feel like someone's got a tourniquet around my chest and twisting it tight."

"You know what that means, don't you?"

Jones looked up.

"You're in love, Nate."

He winced. "It means I'm going to have to try to get over her all over again. And this time will be harder."

"What! You gonna give up that easy?"

"I'm a fish out of water. I don't know the customs, hardly know the language."

"I ain't never know'd something so simple as that getting in the way of two people who want to be together."

"You think she feels the way I do?"

"I know something about Indian women, Nate. They ain't all that different from white women once you scratch the surface. She's as smitten with you as you are with her." Grove nodded his head at the Sharps rifle leaning against the cabin wall. "I'd bet ol' Big 50 on it."

This perked Jones up some. "What should I do about it?"

"It's two days to the winter camp. I'm sure an enterprising young fellow like yourself will think of something between then and now."

Before they pulled out Jones made a sign and posted it near the cabin:

THE GROUND ALONG THIS CREEK,
DEAD WOOD CREEK, ONE HUNDRED FEET
ABOVE AND ONE HUNDRED FEET BELOW
THIS CABIN IN DEAD WOOD GULCH,
CLAIMED BY CARSON GROVE AND
NATHANIEL JONES.
APRIL 17, 1875

Jones paused on the rim of Dead Wood Gulch and looked back at the little cabin, almost lost from view among the trees at the bottom.

"Now what's troubling you?" Grove asked when Jones lingered there as if trying to make up his mind about something.

"I don't like pulling out like this, Mr. Grove. You have a real bonanza claim down there, and you haven't filed on it. I don't like leaving it unprotected."

"You fret too much. Ain't gonna be anybody finding this place in years. They're all too busy down south in Custer Park. Everything will be here jest like we're leaving it. You wait."

Jones's mouth cut a stern line across his face. He wasn't so sure. He'd seen the signs of men all through these hills. He wanted more time to stake out a claim of his own. But everything was happening too fast. Two days ago he was wandering carefree through the Black Hills, nothing on his mind but finding a strike. Today he was hauling One Stab back home on a travois, and Morning Snow Woman had stepped into his life, turning it upside down. In that stretch of time he had sipped the sweet wine of jubilation and drunk the bitter dregs of despair. . . .

He only hoped that Grove was correct once again as he led his horse from the edge and joined the others already on their way.

The morning wore away toward noon as they traveled on, the travois cutting twin scratches in the hard ground

behind Carson Grove's mule. Morning Snow Woman
stayed near One Stab, and Jones stuck near her. It was
pleasant traveling beside the Indian girl, and Jones's
Sioux was improving with every passing hour. He'd point
out a feature or object, and she'd supply the word, sometimes finding his pronunciation humorous, other times
giving a playful scowl and warning that such an error in
inflection or intonation would have resulted in an insult
to the chief, his wife, and every dead Lakota spirit that
had ever crossed over into the hereafter.

Jones found her humor delightful, and the better he got
to know her, the more her betrothal to another man stung
like a knife twisted in his chest. At noon they stopped to
rest and made a fire to cook a couple squirrels that Jones
had brought down with his Winchester.

"Them varmints are just about the right size for that
rifle of yours, Nate," Grove said, hiding a grin in his
tangled gray beard. He wasn't about to let Jones forget
that it took his Big 50 to bring down that grizzly, or that
he had told him so back in Bismarck.

Morning Snow Woman gathered a handful of roots and
washed them in a swift, cold creek. Jones thought them a
bit too tangy. One tasted a little like a carrot, though it was
decidedly the wrong color. One Stab had no appetite. A fever roared through his scarecrow frame and all he wanted
was water to drink and a damp cloth for his burning brow.

Grove looked concerned. So did Morning Snow
Woman.

"We best be pushing on," Jones said. The sooner they
got One Stab to his people, and to the medicine that he
believed would heal him, the better off everyone would
be. But a part of him resisted, for as soon as they reached
the Indian camp, Morning Snow Woman, being promised
to another man, would be compelled to distance herself
from him.

They camped that evening near the northern edge of
the Black Hills. After eating dinner, gathering a supply of
firewood, and seeing that One Stab was as comfortable as
they could make him, Grove, Jones, and Morning Snow

Woman settled down. Grove sat with his back against a tree and worked on a ripped seam in his buckskin shirt. Morning Snow Woman kept herself busy around the campsite, and Jones wondered if she ever stopped to rest. She had boundless energy and seemed not to resent the work in any way.

So much had happened that he wanted to write it all down while he still had light and before the details fled his memory. He retrieved his journal and writing implements from his saddlebags, and after finding a comfortable nook against a smooth boulder was about to begin when Morning Snow Woman was suddenly standing before him.

"Come with me, Nathaniel."

Jones set down journal, quill, and ink and was instantly at her side. "Where are we going?" he asked, not that it made any difference. Being with Morning Snow Woman was all that he cared about.

"I wish to climb to that ridge and gaze out over the land of my people. I did not want to go by myself, for my heart is heavy, and I do not want to be alone when I am sad, Nathaniel."

They climbed a trail beneath the tall fir and pine. The ground leveled out, the trees parted, and beyond them the land fell away in waves of rolling hills, each less treed than the previous, until the vegetation gave way to grass prairie. In the distance Jones could make out the ribbon of cottonwoods that marked the passage of the Belle Fourche River. Morning Snow Woman stood gazing out, the evening breeze teasing her raven hair where it had come loose from the long braids.

"Why are you sad? Is it because of One Stab?"

"I am worried the fire in his body will drive out his spirit, but that is not the reason my heart is heavy."

"Then, what is the reason?"

As she stood there peering out into the distance, Jones again was riveted by the spark of alertness in her dark eyes, by her clear, olive skin, by the fine, sharp line of her cheekbone as the setting sun glanced off her face. Yet, he saw the deep-seated worry in that lovely face as well, and he wanted to help her however he could.

Still peering out across the carpet of prairie grass that spread away from the foot of the Black Hills, she said, "There are two things which trouble my spirit . . . but I may speak of only one of them, Nathaniel."

"What is it?"

She swept an arm past the vista that stretched before them. "All of this, it belongs to my people. But now the white man has come, and he will take it from us. Like the buffalo has been taken."

"What makes you think that, Morning Snow Woman? The land is yours, and there is still the buffalo."

"One Stab tells of the old days when buffalo moved like clouds across the prairies. Now they are few. The shining rails and the white meat hunters have pushed the great herds to where the frost comes from"—she pointed toward the north—"into the lands of our enemies."

Jones could not deny that the great herds had moved, or that the coming of the railroad had been a cause of that. He said, "But the land is still yours by a treaty. It will not be taken from you."

She looked at him and smiled patiently, almost forgivingly, in response to his naive statement. "Nathaniel, you do not even know your own people."

That stopped him cold. Fortunately, he didn't have to think of a reply, for Morning Snow Woman went on quickly, "You are here and Carson Grove is here. Already the sacred hills of *Wakan Tanka* are filled with white men looking for the yellow rock." Distractedly her hand went to her breast and clutched a small beaded pouch that dropped on a thong from around her neck; then she released it. "It has much value to the white man, but to the Indian its value is different. To collect it into great piles is foolishness. To the Lakota the land and all she brings forth, that is what is valuable. Because of the yellow rock, we will again be pushed from our lodges and put on reservations. This winter we saw how the white man provides for the Indian. That is why so many of us had to leave.''

"I am sorry if this is so. Carson Grove said it might happen.''

"Carson Grove has lived many winters. He is wise in the way of the white man and the People.''

"I should never have come back.'' Jones hesitated. ''But if I had not come back, I would not have found you again.''

She looked into his face searchingly, then quickly glanced away.

He stepped closer to her. She had resumed staring out at the darkening plains below. Tall and slender, with the evening breeze ruffling her hair and the hem of her dress, she might have been a statue. Although they were quite near now, she made no effort to open the distance. This closeness seemed so right to Jones that he wanted to reach out and draw her to him, but he resisted.

"Tell me, Morning Snow Woman . . . what is the other thing that has made your heart heavy?''

Like the statue he imagined, she did not move, did not speak at once. When she did all she said was, ''I cannot speak of it.''

He knew when not to press, and instead he just stood at her side, reveling in her nearness and struggling with the thing that had made *his* heart heavy as well.

As darkness settled over the land Morning Snow Woman turned away from the ridge. ''I must see how Grandfather is.''

They started down the hillside and Jones said, ''There is something I've been wondering about.''

"Yes, Nathaniel?''

"Why were you here in the Black Hills with One Stab?''

She looked at him, vaguely confused. ''He is my grandfather.''

"Yes, I know that. What I mean is, what brought you and your grandfather here in the first place? Your people are camped almost two days' march from here. There must have been some important reason why you two would make this journey alone.''

''We came to bury my father.''

This stunned him. ''Oh, I'm so sorry. I did not know you were grieving. This is the other reason for your heavy heart?''

''No. I am not grieving anymore. My father died three winters ago.''

Jones stared at her. ''And you only now got around to burying him?''

She smiled at his lack of understanding. ''He was placed in his burial tree when he went to be with the spirits of our ancestors. Every year when we returned to the *Paha Sapa*, Grandfather and I would visit the tree and tend to my father's needs. He had been Grandfather's only son, and now there is no one else left. This winter, when the white men came into the Sacred Hills, Grandfather and I returned to bury my father in the ground, for we feared the white men would discover his sepulchre tree and desecrate his body. Because there is no one left but Grandfather and me, and the burying is a family responsibility, we went together to do what we had to. Afterward, Grandfather gave me this.'' She touched the small pouch that hung from her neck. ''We were on our way back to the camp on the Belle Fourche when the bear attacked us.''

''What is in it?''

''It is a talisman from the Great Spirit. We call it a *Tukan*.''

Jones was confused. ''You call it a 'Grandfather'?''

''It is the same word, but it is also a name we call the Great Spirit. It was given to my father when he took my mother as his wife. Now, it has passed to me.''

''May I see it?''

She considered this a moment, then shook her head. ''No, not now. Perhaps someday I will show it to you.''

*Someday*? This was a statement that held promise if he'd ever heard one, and he let it go at that.

# SEVENTEEN

"Looky there, they've sent out a welcoming party," Carson Grove said from atop Nathaniel Jones's horse. Jones and Morning Snow Woman had traveled on foot, but Grove's leg was not as strong as it had been before he broke it. He'd divided his time between the saddle and the moccasins, favoring the saddle toward the end of their journey.

They had arrived at the Sioux encampment before noon the next day. They were spotted while still a mile away, and riders were sent out to meet them and inquire of their business. Immediately they recognized One Stab and Morning Snow Woman, and getting a quick account of what had happened, the riders returned to inform the rest of the tribe.

The tipis of this Sioux winter camp numbered about seventy-five, circled in groups according to clans, their door-flaps all facing east. Eagle Two Claws, the medicine man, was waiting to receive One Stab in his lodge when they came into camp. Grove and Jones were told to remain outside.

Grove wandered through the camp and in no time came up with a handful of old acquaintances—some past enemies, some past friends, and even a distant relative here and there. It didn't take Grove long to learn that something was up. There had been long meetings in the council tipi, in the center of the camp circle, between the chief warriors; Crazy Horse, American Horse, Man That Owns a Sword, and Young-Man-Afraid-of-His-Horses.

"Big powwow going on, Nate," Grove said, taking Jones aside. "The shirt wearers are making war plans."

"Shirt wearers?"

"Their four biggest war chiefs, sort of the tribe's headmen—the board of governors, you might say."

"We picked a fine time to show up," Jones said, feeling the pressing weight of the eyes of the young warriors upon them as he and Grove strolled through the camp.

"Don't fret now. We're safer here where they can keep an eye on us than we'd be alone up in them Black Hills."

Jones and Grove dropped in on One Stab. Eagle Two Claws was a young man, almost too young to be a medicine man, Jones thought. But then, maybe it was not all that unusual. Certainly in his own culture, young men were coming out of medical school as doctors all the time.

Eagle Two Claws allowed the two white men inside his lodge this time. The old chief was laying upon a pallet of buffalo robes, looking bored. The interior was dark, illuminated only by a faint glow of daylight coming through the skin wall of the lodge and from the smoke hole above, which had been closed down so that just a thin slice of blue sky was visible through it. The old man had been frowning, but now he brightened, obviously eager for company to break the tedium of the sickbed.

"Got you all lathered up, I see," Grove said. "How you feeling?"

"I hurt. It will pass." One Stab's scrawny chest had been smeared with some dark green concoction, with clumps of something that looked like black moss stuck to it.

Grove and Jones sat cross-legged on the floor mats, and Jones wondered how anyone could ever recover in this place. The air was heavy with wood smoke and as humid as a steaming jungle. Nearby was a pile of hot rocks and a clay pitcher, and as they spoke Eagle Two Claws poured water onto the rocks, raising a hissing cloud of steam in the close quarters.

Grove said, "You know what's going on here, One Stab?"

"I know. Talk of war with the white man."

"This would not be good. There are many soldiers nearby. Custer is at Fort Abraham Lincoln with his Seventh Cavalry, and as you know, there are many troops down at Camp Robinson and Fort Laramie."

One Stab shrugged his shoulders indifferently. "I too old to paint my face and ride into battle, Grove. But when I was young, I fought the white man. I fought you." He gave a gap-toothed grin. "Now young bucks fight the white man."

Grove frowned and shot Jones a worried glance. "Many will die on both sides. Is there anything you can do?"

One Stab's aged head shook from side to side upon the pallet. "They do not listen to old men when their blood is hot. It is war chiefs they take counsel of. Crazy Horse, Lame Antelope, American Horse—it is their words that the warriors hear."

Morning Snow Woman entered the medicine lodge and knelt beside her grandfather. "It is good that we are among the lodges of our people again, Grandfather. The medicine is strong and you will soon be well."

"I want to go to my own lodge."

"Soon, Grandfather."

"Me and Jones can carry him if you want."

One Stab shot Grove a warning glance. "No carry! I will walk when it is time." He looked at Morning Snow Woman and pointed to a bowl nearby. Grove helped him up as the girl put the water to his lips.

When they left, the sun had lowered toward the far-off upthrust of a blunt rock that the Sioux called *Mateo Tipi,* or Grizzly Bear's Lodge. Jones knew it by another name, Devil's Tower. Outside of the camp was a huge corral containing maybe three hundred horses and at least a dozen young men keeping watch. Off in another direction, men were busy piling dried branches in a clearing in preparation for a great bonfire.

"There will be a gathering tonight, and the braves will counsel with the shirt wearers," Morning Snow Woman said, watching the pile of brush mounting.

"Will there be a war?" Jones asked.

She looked at him with sadness in her wide brown eyes. "It will be so, for the shirt wearers have said it must, and Lame Antelope has had a vision."

"What was the vision?" Grove asked.

"It was a vision of blue soldiers raining from the sky, and of a river running red with blood."

"Which river?"

Morning Snow Woman shook her head. "The Vision Giver did not show him."

Grove looked suddenly worried.

"You don't believe in these visions, do you, Mr. Grove?" Jones asked.

"There is more to this world than what your two eyes show you, Nate. I've lived among the Sioux long enough to not cast aside the vision of a warrior as mere falderal."

Jones screwed his lips tight and said no more, for he knew that he was outnumbered.

Grove said, "We'll listen to what the shirt wearers have to say."

"Will they permit us to sit in on their war plans?"

"Well, we'll jest have to see about that, now won't we?"

Morning Snow Woman started toward the tipis of her clan circle. Jones and Grove exchanged glances, then Jones hurried to her side and said, "May I walk with you?"

Since they'd arrived at the Sioux camp she had become aloof toward him, and now he thought she seemed a little nervous. She hesitated, then said, "You should not accompany me. We must not be alone together."

"Alone? I'd hardly call the middle of this camp being alone."

Morning Snow Woman's wide brown eyes suddenly glistened. She blinked, and Jones saw moisture gathering. "Nathaniel Jones. I am betrothed to another. You must leave me now."

Jones was stunned. There was something devastatingly permanent in the sound of those words. This was the first time her betrothal had been spoken of with such finality. Up until now he'd at least clutched at the hope that the pending nuptials were still in a stage of negotiation, and that the outcome was yet uncertain. He stammered, then found his voice and said, "Is that what you really want?"

"It . . . it is what must be."

That wasn't good enough for him. "And I ask you again, is it what *you* want?"

"You put yourself in great danger."

"From One That Kills in a Hard Place?"

Her face tightened at the mention of his name. Casting her eyes down, she nodded her head.

Suddenly Jones was aware that three young men had assembled near one of the tipis and were watching them. Morning Snow Woman saw them too.

"They are of his clan," she warned. "You must stay away from me. This is not a safe place to be now. You and Carson Grove should leave before the sun goes down, and circle your sleeping blankets with brittle twigs tonight." Morning Snow Woman turned quickly and hurried to the tipis.

"She says I am to leave her alone. She says we are in danger. She says we ought to leave tonight. Frankly, Mr. Grove, I don't know which way to turn."

"You want to leave?"

"No!"

They walked on together near the common corral. Sioux guards watched suspiciously but made no move to confront them. The sun was setting, the clouds to the west showing their blood red underbellies. Across the camp a roaring bonfire licked skyward where warriors had begun to assemble.

From out of the darkening land to the east six Sioux horsemen galloped into camp, reining to a halt at the corrals. They were leading two horses loaded down with fresh meat. Eyeing the two white men with open distrust and curiosity, they turned their mounts loose in the corral and spent a few minutes rubbing them down with handfuls of sage.

"A hunting party. That one is asking what the hell we are doing here," Grove said, inclining his head at one of the young bucks as he spoke to a corral guard.

Jones gave the warriors only passing notice. He said, "You know these people, Mr. Grove. When a woman is betrothed, what does that mean?"

Grove dismissed the six newcomers and they resumed tracing a path around the perimeter of the winter camp. "It means the gal's parents, or in this case, her grandfather, has accepted the gifts of the buck interested in marrying her as proper payment."

"And she has no say in the matter?"

"Not much. But usually the interested buck is someone she's interested in too, or he would have been discouraged long before it got to the bargaining stage."

"Can she . . . change her mind?" That sounded like a bold presumption, and Jones tempered it quickly with, "I mean if, say, something were to come up?"

Grove narrowed a bushy eyebrow at him. "You mean if another young buck were to, say, come along?"

"Yes, exactly."

Grove puckered his lips and thought a moment. "I reckon if the young fellow was acceptable to the parents—"

"Or grandparent."

"Or grandparent. And I suppose if he came along with a better offer than the first fellow—"

"Say, twelve ponies?"

"Maybe."

Jones was feeling encouraged. "Then someone could

flip the tables on ol' One That Kills in a Hard Place after all!''

Grove stopped and looked at him. ''That is true, Nate— if One That Kills in a Hard Place doesn't cut this interloper wide open and gut him like a buffalo calf when he meets his challenge.''

Jones swallowed hard. ''His challenge?''

''Well, it is his right.''

This was not encouraging news. They started forward again, rounding toward the huge fire. Jones had retreated into his thoughts, studying the problem from a different direction, when he felt the sudden pressure of Carson Grove's grip on his arm. He glanced up. Four figures had stepped in their path and blocked their way. With their backs to the bright flames, Jones could not make out the Indians' faces, but their demeanor was unmistakable. They intended for Grove and Jones to go no farther.

''What can I do for you gentlemen?'' Grove said, his Sioux easygoing, but carrying a thinly veiled edge that even Jones was able to discern. It did not escape the four men either.

A powerfully built warrior stepped forward. Jones recognized him as one of the hunters who had turned their horses into the corral a few minutes earlier. The firelight glanced off his face, revealing his features more clearly. There was something familiar in that stern face. Jones tried to place him. . . .

''I speak to the one called Iron Left Hand.''

That voice! The same voice that had barked at Morning Snow Woman that day Jones had asked her to show him around the camp. And now the fierce features of his face came back to him as well.

*One That Kills in a Hard Place.*

Jones swallowed down a lump that had formed in his throat and said in his very best Sioux, ''I am Iron Left Hand. What does One That Kills in a Hard Place wish to say to me?''

The warrior was surprised at the sound of his own name. He studied Jones's face in the light of the bonfire, also recalling the past, and suddenly he too remembered.

"You!"

Jones steeled himself. "What do you wish to say?"

One That Kills in a Hard Place glared at him, a new, more deadly resolve hardening his face. "Once before you have crossed my path, Iron Left Hand. I warned you then to keep away from Morning Snow Woman. If not for One Stab and the Long-Haired Chief, I would already have spilled your entrails and fed them to the dogs, white spit."

Jones bristled. "You would have tried, red dog dung! But you would have ended up eating dirt."

"Ha! I have heard how well you fought Two Bulls. You fainted before his attack. It was *you* who ate the dirt! You are not man enough to fight me; therefore, you are not man enough for Morning Snow Woman. But since warning did not keep you from sniffing around the hem of her dress, I will fix the problem permanently." With the swiftness of a cougar, One That Kills in a Hard Place jerked his scalping knife from his clout. "I'll cut off your bull-bag and give it to Morning Snow Woman as a wedding gift, a pouch for her trinkets!"

Until now it had been merely an exchange of insults, but suddenly the matter had turned deadly serious. Jones could hardly believe what he was hearing, but instinctively he knew that it was not an empty threat.

One That Kills in a Hard Place crouched, judging his attack, preparing to spring.

Jones backed up a step, his eyes riveted on the red and yellow flames of the bonfire dancing along the long blade in the Indian's fist. Carson Grove's voice came from somewhere beyond his left shoulder, but it sounded as if it was far off—as if it was worlds away. "Now don't you think you got Nate at a disadvantage here? He ain't even armed."

"It is not my concern that this white skunk comes into my camp unarmed. It only proves he has wood grubs for brain."

"In other words, it makes no difference to you if a fight is fair or not?"

Jones could hardly believe his ears.

One That Kills in a Hard Place was getting irritated by Grove. "It matters little to me whether this buffalo shit is armed or naked as the day his cur mother spilled his afterbirth."

"Well, I reckon I'm glad you see it that way, buck," Grove said in an easy voice.

The Sioux warrior hovered a moment longer like a compressed spring. Jones's heart was in his throat, and as he took another step backward he felt something cold and hard suddenly being thrust into his hand. Instantly he recognized it by its shape and weight, and the next moment he swung his Big 50 around and leveled the half-inch bore at One That Kills in a Hard Place's chest.

In his easy voice, Grove said, "Since fair play makes no difference to you, buck, I figured I'd jest even up the odds a mite."

A wave of relief flooded through Jones. One That Kills in a Hard Place went rigid and suddenly lost his zeal.

Grove's unruffled voice droned on casually, talking to Jones, but in the Sioux language. "Now mind them triggers, Nate—it only takes a cat's whisker to set 'em off. And when you do blow a hole through that buck's chest, that bullet will likely make its way through three or four of them bucks before stopping, so be aware of what's behind him. Don't want to kill no dogs or horses unnecessarily."

The three warriors backing up One That Kills in a Hard Place instantly spread apart, out of the line of fire. Grove chuckled.

Jones thumbed back the heavy hammer of the Sharps. "Throw that knife aside, One That Kills in a Hard Place, and I'll get rid of this rifle." He did not particularly want to have it out hand to hand with this warrior, but it would end any respect he had earned with these people if he hid behind Grove's rifle now. And oddly, that was important to him. He had gained a measure of honor facing Two

Bulls, even though he had lost that fight. He had *earned* his Indian name, Iron Left Hand, and had no desire to sully it. He waited for the Indian's reply.

Apparently One That Kills in a Hard Place had heard how Jones had come about his name, and he had no desire to challenge him in a hand-to-hand match—at least not yet anyway.

"Soon we will meet again, white woman dung—"

Jones steadied his sights upon the brave's breast. "I'm sorry, I didn't catch that. What was it you just said? Perhaps you will repeat it?"

One That Kills in a Hard Place sucked a breath through clenched teeth, his eyes fixed upon the bore of the buffalo gun, and slowly said, "We will meet again, Iron Left Hand," a coiled-rattlesnake tension in his voice, its venom in his words, "and when we do you will feel the bite of my knife in your heart, and the dogs will lick your entrails from the dirt."

"I'm ready whenever you are," Jones replied. Their eyes locked in mortal combat a few seconds longer before One That Kills in a Hard Place broke it off. Then, turning angrily, he disappeared into the night with his three partners.

Grove glanced at his friend. "That was close, Nate."

Jones let go of a long breath. "I'm only glad he backed down, or . . ."

"Or what?"

He shook his head. "I don't know."

"You'd have blown his fool head off, that's what."

Jones handed the rifle back to Grove. "I suppose you're right."

"You know I am. Can't go making threats you ain't prepared to go through with—especially to a hotheaded, moonstruck Sioux buck that thinks you're after his gal."

Jones looked over, suddenly startled. "But I am!" he said, and all at once the realization swept over him like a stampeding buffalo herd. His voice carried more surprise than conviction. "That's exactly what I am."

"Am what, Nate? Talk sense."

But Jones was too stunned by the revelation he had just come upon.

"Nate?"

Slowly his voice returned. "That's exactly what I'm doing, Mr. Grove. I *am* trying to take his girl from him!"

In the leaping light of the bonfire a grin appeared behind the wild gray beard. "I know'd it. Know'd it right from the very start!"

Jones shook his head in amazement. "It's true. Everyone knew it from the beginning, everyone but me and Morning Snow Woman!"

"No, Nate, it was only you. She know'd it too."

# EIGHTEEN

Jones saw no more of One That Kills in a Hard Place that night. He and Grove were permitted to attend the council fire, and they stood at the outer edges of its light as one by one the shirt wearers spoke of the white man's invasion of their lands, and especially of the sacred Black Hills. There was poison in their words, and anger among the listening warriors, but finally Crazy Horse stood to speak and the crowd quieted down.

Crazy Horse had not erected his lodge in this winter camp circle, but had ridden up with his friend American Horse from the Dark Forest of Nebraska, where their winter lodges sat along Beaver Creek—*Capa Wakpala*—near Camp Sheridan. The closeness of the white soldiers, however, was a bitter taste in both men's mouths, and neither one spent as much time near their homes and families as they would have liked.

"For seven winters we have tried to live peacefully with the white man," he began, speaking in a low voice. "The Father in Washington made a treaty, and the Lakota People have honored it. We have taken their gifts, their food and blankets, and have put aside the old ways, but the white promises are like a feather in the wind. This winter there was no food. You have left the agency to hunt and return to the old ways, which were good. Now, the Hills That Are Black have filled with white men looking for the yellow rock. The sacred hills of the Great Spirit have become unclean, like a water hole with too many buffalo. The soldiers tell us they will take their men away, but still they remain. Only when they see the Lakota making war plans do they come and tell their young men to go away from the sacred land. And even then they sneak back in.''

Grove leaned close to Jones and said, "I heard from one of the elders, Bad Foot Running, that the army come and dragged all them squatters you was tellin' me about outta that fort and down to Fort Laramie.''

"The Gordon Party?'' This was the first Jones had heard about it.

Grove nodded his head. "I reckon you left jest in time, 'cause they come and hauled everyone out, including the woman. Bad Foot says they plopped her on the back of an army mule and rode her away from there. Afterward, a party of Sioux went and looked the place over, and come away with some fancy-colored cloth that the squatters left behind. Red, and blue, and white. Made some of their women mighty happy, and they made their bucks happy as well.'' Grove grinned and winked at him. "If you catch my meaning.''

"I do,'' Jones said, recalling Annie Tallent's red, white, and blue tent, which had gone up in flames that first week after the Gordon Party's arrival on French Creek, and how carefully she had trimmed away the burnt pieces, putting the good cloth aside for patches. "Then Lame Antelope never did attack?''

"Never had a chance. But if the army had delayed a week or two, he would have. I heard he had over three thousand warriors ready to ride.''

Jones returned his attention to the young warrior standing near the council fire. He was having some difficulty following Crazy Horse's speech. The war chief had grown more animated and his words were coming quicker.

"The white man only listens to words of war. Although we still have many young men, and many guns and horses, our people do not grow stronger, but weaker. Already many have gone the white man's way. They take his gifts and forget the old ways. One day soon, there will be no more young men who wish to keep the customs of our fathers. One day soon, all Lakota will accept the gifts and lay down their freedom. Then we will become like the dust in a dry wallow, and the wind will scatter us, and we will be a people no more!"

He paused, and the crowd gave him the approval he sought. When they'd quieted down, Crazy Horse said, "We cannot wait even one more winter. We must fight the white man here and now!"

Man That Owns a Sword stood and said, "Already the white soldiers are many. They have many guns and many horses. The Father in Washington has great corrals with many more horses. His war lodge is mighty and there is no end to the guns it keeps. How can we who are a great people, but few, fight an enemy such as this?"

"One Lakota warrior is as ten white soldiers," Crazy Horse exclaimed.

"That will not matter, for in the Place Where the Light Comes From are many young white men, and they are like the buffalo once were. As many as the bones of the buffalo are on the grass today. Many more soldiers will come. We will not be blown about like dry wallow dust as you say—our bones will be *buried* under this dust, and the grass will cover them over, and we will truly be a people no more."

Crazy Horse raised a clenched fist into the night sky, his long black hair flying loose in the hot wind of the fire. "Old women can sit around the council fires and lament the passing of our ways. As for me, I will fight to keep them, and to remain free. And if I die, then it will be a good day to die!"

The council meeting devolved into whooping and singing, some warriors smearing colored clay on their faces and bodies and leaping into an impromptu war dance.

Grove and Jones knew it was time to leave these Indians to their partying, for it could become dangerous to stay. They moved a little way outside the winter camp circle, spread out their bedrolls, and settled down without a fire.

Jones peered up at the stars, visible now that they were away from the big bonfire. He found Morning Snow Woman's face invading his thoughts and keeping sleep far away. He knew the time had come to make a decision, a decision he wasn't certain he was ready to make, but one that could wait no longer. There was still so much about the Sioux he did not understand, so many customs that were as foreign to him as Christmas and Easter would be to them.

"Mr. Grove?"

Carson Grove snorted and turned in his warm blankets. "Yeah?" he said sleepily.

"Did I wake you?"

"You did."

"Sorry."

"Well?" he grunted impatiently.

"I wanted to ask a question, but it can wait until morning."

"You got me awake now. Ask it so I can go back to sleep."

"You said it was One That Kills in a Hard Place's right to challenge me in battle. Is that some sort of Sioux ritual?"

"Ritual? Hell no. It's what any man who wants a woman would do, be he Sioux, European, Mexican, or . . . or . . . or a grass-skirted Polynesian."

Jones lay there listening to the low drumming and the hoots and yelps coming from the bonfire, which had shrunk to a heap of embers and a few struggling flames.

"Mr. Grove?"

Carson Grove rolled and glared at him. "I ain't gone nowhere—except to sleep."

"You ever get something stuck inside you that you can't shake? Even a year later?"

"Why don't you jest come out and say it, Nate?"

"I think I'm in love with her."

"You only *think* you are? That's something you better know for a-certain, not jest *think* you do."

Jones glanced over, his eyes narrowing in sudden resolve. "No, I don't think. I know it!"

In the darkness Jones could not discern the expression on the old man's face. Finally Grove said, "What do you intend to do about it, Nate?"

Jones peered back at the blue-black star-spangled bowl overhead. "I'm not sure yet," he admitted, "but I'll think of something."

Grove grunted and turned over, settling once again in his blankets. "You still have your revolver with you?"

"Yes. It's in my saddlebags."

"If I was you, Nate, I'd take to wearing it from here on out."

That had been an ominous warning to leave him with. Jones pondered it a while, and slowly his thoughts revolved around to One That Kills in a Hard Place. He could expect only no good, Jones decided, and Grove was most likely right—as usual. After tonight's confrontation and threat, it would be foolish to go around unarmed.

He became aware of the silence all around him, and when he glanced over, the Indians' fire had gone out completely, leaving only a smoldering pile sending thin tendrils of gray smoke into the dark sky. How late was it? The moon had arced considerably since he had last observed it. The council grounds were abandoned; the dancers and drummers had all gone off to their tipis and the camp circle below was mostly deserted, except for an occasional dark sentry moving about. A dog trotted through the faint shadows cast by a tipi in the moonlight, and at the brush corral a couple of men stood together, talking.

Perhaps he had dozed, but now he was wide awake—and he had come to a decision as well. Throwing off his blankets, Jones moved stealthily down into the camp circle, keeping the few camp police in sight as he slipped in

among the shadows of the tipis. He worked his way
around to the one belonging to One Stab and Morning
Snow Woman.

One Stab was still in the lodge of Eagle Two Claws,
and as far as he knew, Morning Snow Woman was alone.
Drawing up a few yards away, Jones felt around on the
ground for a pebble and cast it at the buffalo hide tipi. It
struck with a low thump and rolled bumping down the
sloping side. He waited a few moments, then cast a second
stone. In the quiet of the night, the sound of the pebble
striking the tipi seemed alarmingly loud. He glanced
quickly around, expecting at any moment to have the
camp police down on him.

But no one came.

He cast a third pebble, this one harder, and as it bumped
its way back down he thought he saw movement at the
base of the tipi. Then an edge of it lifted and Morning
Snow Woman's face peered out, wide-eyed and curious.
Her olive skin was bathed in the moonlight; it was the
loveliest face he had ever seen. She looked at him with
open surprise.

"I must talk to you," he said softly, but with an edge
of urgency.

"It is time for sleeping, not talking."

"Yes, I know, but I could not sleep. I need to talk to
you tonight."

Morning Snow Woman frowned; then, giving him a
nod, her head pulled back inside the tipi. He heard movement within, and two minutes later she came around the
side of the tipi and hunched down in the shadows with
him. She wore her beaded dress and moccasins, but her
long hair, freed from the braids, now hung loose and
nearly to her waist. With her hair unfettered and wild and
a spark of intrigue in her dark eyes, Jones was struck once
again by her beauty, and by something else—an animal
vitality that up until now she had kept hidden from him.

"You will get in trouble with the tribal police if you
are discovered. I should not be out here with you. Come,
let us go to the cottonwood grove nearby where we will

not be discovered.'' And taking his hand, she led him away through the night. They stopped among the thicket down by the swirling waters of the Belle Fourche.

She looked expectantly into his eyes and waited.

Jones's mouth went dry, and for a brief moment all that he had rehearsed in his brain fled from him. He was suddenly painfully aware of his deficiency in the Sioux language; for that matter, what he wanted to tell her would have been difficult for him even in English. He could only hope she would understand, and overlook the simpleness of his words and the awkward grammar that at this point was all he could muster.

''Morning Snow Woman, do you remember the first time we met?''

''Yes. You came with the Long-Haired Chief, Custer. You talked peace with my grandfather and then smoked a pipe. Afterward, you came to my second mother and her daughter—my sister—and me preparing food, and asked about it.''

''Yes, but that was not the first time. The first time was when you brought us water in Slow Bull's lodge.''

''I remember. You smiled at me.''

''And you at me.''

A half-embarrassed smiled crossed her pretty face now.

''I must tell you the truth. I didn't find you at your cooking fire by accident. I was looking for you.''

Her smile widened. ''And I will tell you a truth, Nathaniel. I knew that. It is why my second mother hid her smile as we walked away.''

''You did?'' But why should he be surprised? he asked himself. After all, hadn't Carson Grove already proclaimed it so? The old man's understanding of all that went on around him was uncanny! Jones swallowed hard and went on, ''I thought you were very pretty, and I wanted to get to know you better. But One That Kills in a Hard Place came and caused Custer and One Stab to separate us.''

At the mention of the warrior's name, Morning Snow Woman's smile faded and her lips compressed into a tight line. Jones felt her sadness, even though she did not speak of it. She didn't have to; it was written in her face. "Afterward, when I left, I hoped to see you again," he said.

"We moved our camp. The Arikara are ancient enemies, and One Stab feared they would return at night and attack us."

"I was very sad when I learned that your people had left."

She averted her eyes and said, "I had wished to see you again too, Nathaniel."

Jones's heart leaped within his breast. "I thought of you many times afterward."

She looked up and the smile returned. If he hadn't been one hundred percent certain before, he was now. He knew he had to say what was in his heart at once, for the time was right, and if he let this moment pass, he'd regret it all the rest of his life. There were two or three words in the Sioux language that meant love, but he had no idea which was the correct one to use in this case. Trusting that she would understand regardless, he picked *tehila*.

"Morning Snow Woman, I have come to love you in the short time we have had together. I ask you, will you marry me?" It sounded horribly stilted to his ear, yet it was the only way he could express what he felt through a language that he spoke so poorly.

But she understood perfectly. At once her face beamed, then just as quickly the spark left her eyes and they turned dull and lifeless. "I cannot."

Although a part of him had suspected that might be her answer, her words slugged him in the gut and took his breath away. "Why?"

She did not answer.

"Because of One That Kills in a Hard Place?"

She looked away.

"You don't love him. I see it in your face whenever his name is brought up. What is it then? Is it because I am white and you are Lakota?"

"No!" she said at once, as if even the suggestion of that was an affront.

"I don't understand," he said, gently this time.

"Grandfather has accepted his gifts. It will be a good joining of our clans."

Jones heard the struggle in her voice, and although the Sioux seldom showed emotion, he knew that Morning Snow Woman was fighting to keep hers under wraps. She stood up suddenly from the tree trunk on which they had been sitting and turned away from him.

He took her arm and turned her toward him. "Is there nothing I can do to change this?"

She flung her arms around his waist and pressed her face to his chest. For a long moment she held him as if she would never let go; then just as swiftly she released him and hurried away.

Jones stood there stunned, angry, hurt, and, most of all confused. Looking down, he touched the moist stain on his shirt where her eyes had pressed; then, as a man already dead, a man who had had his life crushed from him by that parting hug, he trudged away from the river and back to his bedroll up the hill.

For another hour he lay there trying to sort through his tortured emotions, expecting any moment to see the eastern sky pinked with the coming of dawn. But somewhere along the way he fell asleep, exhausted, and he would have remained asleep long into the morning had not something urgently tugged at his arm.

A faint light was in the sky, though not yet enough to show color. Jones came groggily awake, and then he looked over. Morning Snow Woman was there, her face intense, her voice low and urgent.

"Nathaniel, wake up."

"I'm awake," he said, and at the same time heard Carson Grove stirring in his blankets. It took a moment for the fog to clear his brain, then instantly he was alert. "What is it? What's wrong?" He was looking around for some immediate danger.

"I will go with you," she said, "but we must leave now, before the camp is awake and One That Kills in a Hard Place stops you."

Jones sat up, any lingering brain fog evaporating in the light of her words. "You would do this?"

"Yes."

"But it means leaving your people." Jones had learned enough about the Sioux to know that tribal and family links were extremely important to them. They derived much of their strength and sense of social importance from the family group of tipis, the *tiyospaye*.

"It is the only way," she said, not quite keeping the sadness from her voice.

A woman of virtue was of great worth to the Sioux, Jones knew, and one expression of that worth was the price a young man would be willing to pay for her. One That Kills in a Hard Place had offered ten ponies. It was surely an honor to her, to her family, and to the extended family of her clan. Now she was willing to throw all that away for him. To elope, he realized, would bring her down to nearly the level of a prostitute.

Carson Grove had levered himself up on one elbow and was scrubbing the sleep from his eyes.

Morning Snow Woman had braided her hair into two long coils that fell over her shoulders and had wrapped them in leather thongs, with a snowy white down feather from an eagle and a polished bone disk for ornaments. She carried a stuffed, parfleche bag over her shoulder like a handbag. It would have contained all her most precious belongings, Jones was certain of it. The light was still only a hint in the east, the perfect time to sneak away with her. It was what he had hoped for, a dream that only a few hours earlier had seemed all but shattered. Jones wanted Morning Snow Woman more than anything—but to secrete her out of her village and elope with her . . .

"No!" he said, standing and taking both her hands into his. There was confusion on her pretty face.

"Is it not what you want?"

"It is exactly what I want, only not like this. I want you, but I will have you according to the customs of the Lakota. I will not sneak you away from your people and steal your honor so that you can never return without seeing their scorn and listening to their ridicule. I will offer One Stab the proper price for a woman such as you. And if I have to, I will fight One That Kills in a Hard Place in battle, and settle the matter once and for all!''

She put her arms about him and hugged him, but this time did not pull away. When she finally stepped back, Jones said, ''Return to your lodge, my love. I will speak to One Stab this morning.''

As she walked away, Grove said from behind him, ''You done the right thing, Nate—the honorable thing. I jest hope to God it don't get you kilt.''

# NINETEEN

One Stab returned to his own lodge the next day, cranky and short-tempered. In his old age, he did not accept pain with the same stolid resolve of his youth. He had many winters under his belt, and figured that he had earned the right to grumble.

He was sitting upon a willow mat covered with a new, indigo, United States Indian Department three-point woolen blanket, scowling. Jones, who had been granted an appointment with the old chief, sat across from him, nervously running a finger around the neck of his shirt, perspiring more than normally. One Stab's narrowed eyes bore into him; then with a groan the chief reached for his pipe and pouch and methodically packed its pipestone bowl with tobacco. He fished a burning twig from the small fire that separated him from Jones and when he had the pipe burning just right he said, "What you have requested, Iron Left Hand, is not so easy to give."

"I love your granddaughter, and she loves me. She does not love One That Kills in a Hard Place. That has to account for something."

One Stab waved a hand in the air as if this was but a trivial matter. The air inside the lodge was stuffy and growing warmer by the minute with the sun beating upon it. "There is a matter of honor, and of unity. That is more important than love, a thing the white man places great value on. But how can a girl of seventeen winters know of love—or even a young buck such as yourself? The man and the woman, they often join because of these feelings, but then five winters pass and the brave returns to his lodge from a hunt to find his moccasins, war lance, and parfleche outside, and the door-flap closed."

"There!" Jones exclaimed, pouncing on that remark. "If it is so easy for a wife to divorce her husband, how hard could it be for her to oust a fiancé?"

One Stab considered this as if it had never occurred to him, though Jones knew it must have. In that moment of silence, Jones glanced at the figure sitting at the back of the tent. It was a man Jones had never seen before, tall, well muscled, of indeterminate age, although he guessed the fellow to be about forty. He had been there when Jones arrived, and throughout the meeting had remained absolutely quiet, hardly stirring upon his mat. Who was he? And why did he stare so? Jones wondered. His dark eyes never wavered, and the line of his mouth was as immovable as the frown of a cigar store Indian.

"This is a hard thing that you ask, Iron Left Hand."

"Oftentimes the most worthy goals are the most difficult," Jones said, waxing philosophical, and noting the stranger's eyebrows lift slightly as he did so.

One Stab said, "Your words speak truth, but of what profit are they to me? Words do not kill enemies or bring meat to the lodge. The joining of the Wild Horse Clan with ours is good for both. They have many strong warriors and we have many warriors and hunters. The joining will make us both stronger."

"Is that all your granddaughter means to you? A bridge to tie two families together?" It suddenly occurred to Jones that he was holding a couple of high-powered cards. But how much weight, he wondered, would they pull with the stubborn old chief? "Chief One Stab, I have done you and your granddaughter service, and now I wish to lay these before you so that you may determine the value of my claim to her hand in marriage. May I speak them now?''

One Stab appeared as if he had been hoping Jones would not think of bringing this matter up. He could do nothing less than stoically nod his head in acquiescence. ''Speak what you must.''

''I would not mention this, but I am a desperate man now that you would seem to deny my request and withhold the hand of your granddaughter from me. I have been a strong ally to One Stab. If you recall, I prevented the Arikara chief, Bloody Knife, from murdering you in your sleep. And later, I drew away the great bear from Morning Snow Woman and prevented the deaths of both of you.''

''Carson Grove killed the bear,'' One Stab pointed out.

''This is true, but he would not have come had he not heard the rapid fire of my rifle.''

With a frown, the old chief agreed. He sat there, his face drawn tight in concentration. Then suddenly he turned his head and spoke to the man at the back of the tent. ''What say you on this matter, Cousin?''

''There is truth in his eyes and in his words, Father,'' the man answered, addressing One Stab with the respect that a younger man gives to an old chief.

One Stab turned back, shaking his head in quiet resignation. ''What you request is a hard thing. It will cause much trouble between our clans.'' He considered a moment, then said, ''One That Kills in a Hard Place has sent ten ponies to my lodge. It is a big price for the woman you seek to have.''

''I will give One Stab *twelve* ponies,'' Jones blurted, not considering the problem that he owned only one horse.

A small gleam came to One Stab's eyes and he rocked back on the blanket and hitched his lips slightly to the left in a moment of contemplation. ''The Wild Horse Clan is very strong,'' he noted as if the thought was only a passing one.

But Jones understood. "I will give One Stab a Winchester rifle."

This perked him up. He glanced at the man behind him, then raised his hand, showing two fingers.

"All right, I will give One Stab *two* Winchester rifles."

"And cartridges?"

"Ten boxes."

One Stab smiled briefly, then put the frown back in place and casually fingered the blanket on which he sat. "Government blankets are thin. Cold when the wind comes from the north and brings the frost."

Jones was catching the drift of this game now. "I hear that the Hudson's Bay Company makes good, warm blankets. For your permission to marry Morning Snow Woman, I will give you one,"—he paused and glanced at the mysterious stranger—"er, two Hudson's Bay blankets."

This seemed to make the two Indians happy.

Jones drew in a sigh of relief and said, "Well, what is your word on the matter, One Stab?"

But the old chief wasn't ready to let him off the hook so easily. "I would drink with you, Iron Left Hand, but I have no strong water. The Red Cloud Agency has no good strong water, and tells the Indian he cannot buy any." He heaved his scrawny shoulders helplessly.

Jones grinned and said, "I might be able to get my hands on some good whiskey. Maybe even five bottles."

"Twenty."

"Seven."

"Fifteen."

"Ten, and that's my last offer." Jones would have gladly gone the twenty bottles of whiskey that One Stab asked for, but so far he had given in on every one of the old man's requests. To retain honor in the eyes of Morning Snow Woman's family, he had to resist at some point.

The stranger smiled thinly, and Jones saw approval in his face. He had passed a test of sorts, he was certain, and now it only remained to be seen if One Stab would go against custom and allow him to marry his granddaughter.

One Stab resumed puffing on his pipe, then passed it to Jones, who drew the smoke into his lungs and blew it out again. Taking it from him, One Stab passed it to the stranger, and he smoked too. Returning the pipe to the blanket before the small fire, One Stab introduced the man to Jones. "This is Elk Who Falls Running. He is Morning Snow Woman's second father. You have offered to pay a high price and have brought honor to our clan. We both agree to the price. You may marry Morning Snow Woman."

Jones was elated, but he maintained his composure and said with utmost aplomb, "Thank you."

One Stab turned to Elk Who Falls Running and said with obvious concern, "Take One That Kills in a Hard Place's ponies from the common corral and return them to his lodge circle."

Elk Who Falls Running nodded his head, wearing a tight expression that Jones read to be worry on his part as well. As the man stepped out of the lodge, One Stab picked up his pipe and looked at it, then fixed his stare on Jones. "Watch carefully, Iron Left Hand, and pray that the Great Spirit will be with you and that evil does not fall upon you."

"You speak of One That Kills in a Hard Place."

"He sometimes lets his anger rule his head. He is a very good ally, but a very deadly enemy." One Stab began cleaning his pipe, a signal to Jones that the meeting was over.

Jones stood. "Good-bye, One Stab."

"You will bring the gifts when?" His eyes lifted with the question.

"I must leave for a short while to gather all of them. You have requested much, and it will take me a little time to travel to the white man's villages and retrieve them. I will return in two moons."

"In two moons we will have moved the camp circle back to the Red Cloud Agency."

"Then that is where I will bring the price agreed upon."

One Stab nodded his head, accepting that, and resumed cleaning his pipe.

"Whoo-wee, she was an expensive little gal."

"And worth every penny of it, Mr. Grove!"

"Maybe, but she'll be impossible to live with now. Only a woman of high virtue comes at that price you paid for her. She'll never get her nose down outta the clouds. And how you figuring to pay for all them things, anyway?"

Jones patted the pouch on his belt. "I've got the gold from the six months of work I put in on my claim. It will buy what I need."

"And little else."

"There's plenty more where this came from," Jones said.

Grove snorted. "Maybe so, but hunkering down in that cold water is a helluva way to make a living. I know something of that. I done my share of it while following the beaver trail. What panning I done back there in Dead Wood Gulch last winter reminded me I was getting too old for that line of work."

"You intend to go back to your claim, don't you?"

"Been pondering it over some, Nate. Reckon I might jest settle in here for a while. I've already pulled more gold outta that creek than I've seen in twenty years, and these Oglala are right friendly folks. Besides, there is this widow woman I got to talking to the other day . . ."

Jones grinned. "The future Mrs. Grove number four?"

The old mountain man's whiskers parted in a wide smile, the crow's-feet at the corners of his eyes crinkling deeper. "You never know what might develop."

Jones laughed. "Who knows—might just be a double wedding."

"Don't go marryin' me off jest yet, Nate. This sort of thing needs to be pondered on for a while."

"Well, while you're pondering it, I need to find Morning Snow Woman and tell her the good news. I didn't see her. I thought she'd be waiting outside the old man's tipi.''

"Nope, a Sioux wouldn't do that. A Sioux is taught early on to guard her emotions and not make a show in public. I seen her go off a little while ago with a couple gals to collect wood. But I suspect she already knows. News of that sort don't stay kept under their caps, not in an Injun village.''

Jones strode off in the direction Grove said he'd seen her go. He found Morning Snow Woman a few hundred yards beyond the camp circle, in the grove of cottonwoods where they had talked the night before. She was with three other girls, and at least a dozen dogs, each hitched to a travois piled with more wood than it seemed possible an animal their size could carry. When he walked up, the trio suddenly found something to occupy them some distance down the Belle Fourche, leaving Jones and Morning Snow Woman alone.

"It's all settled,'' he said, hardly able to contain his elation.

"Grandfather accepted your gifts?''

"He did. He drives a hard bargain, but I willingly paid it.'' He took her into his arms and they held each other for a brief instant, then she released herself from him and stepped back, casting a shy glance at the three girls down the way. They were pretending not to notice, but Jones saw that one or another of them was always stealing a peek their way.

He said, "I must leave for the villages of the white man to collect the gifts I promised One Stab, but I will be back in two months, and then we will be married.''

"I will make a wedding dress, and a shirt for my husband to wear.''

Jones wanted to hold her and kiss her, but outward displays were frowned upon among the Sioux—and besides, he wasn't certain Morning Snow Woman knew the white man's practice of kissing. It was something he looked forward to teaching her. For now he'd have to get by on the radiance in her face, the wide expression of joy

in her dark eyes. Later there would be plenty of time—
their whole lives—to teach each other the customs of their
different ways.

"When will you leave, Nathaniel?" she asked.

"Call me Nathan from now on."

She nodded.

"And may I call you Snow? Morning Snow Woman is
rather a mouthful."

She shook her head briefly but firmly. "It comes from
the season of my birth, when the winds blow hard from
the land where the frost comes. Instead, you may call me
Mountain Rose, for it blooms in the new season—the season when I found my husband."

"Mountain Rose. I like that very much."

The girls had started back, slowly, so as to give the
newly engaged couple warning that they would soon have
company.

Jones said, "I will leave as soon as I can, Mountain
Rose. The sooner I'm off, the sooner I will return." When
the other girls arrived, Morning Snow Woman introduced
them to her soon-to-be-husband and told them of her new
name, and the meaning behind it. They were pleased and
happy for her, and they were quite eager to talk with the
prospective husband, and giggled when he turned an im-
properly pronounced word or used a stilted expression.

"I must go and make preparations to leave now. I will
see you in the camp circle later." Jones left, and as the
trees closed in around him, a tingle crept up his spine and
lifted the hairs off the nape of his neck. He slowed his
pace, listening intently now. He heard nothing out of the
ordinary, but just the same, alarm bells were clanging
away inside his head. He stopped, his back rigid, and then
all at once his hand swept for the revolver at his side.
Drawing it and spinning, he faced One That Kills in a
Hard Place and four other bucks.

They'd been creeping up behind him. They drew up
with a start and stared at the revolver in Jones's fists.

It wasn't as if he hadn't been expecting it. He had been

confronted by this Sioux warrior so many times already that now he wasn't even startled. One That Kills in a Hard Place had hate in his scowl, murder in his eyes, and a thick-bladed butcher knife in his right hand. The men with him carried bows with arrows already nocked. One even held an old caplock rifle similar to the ancient piece One Stab carried.

"Well, well," Jones said easily, "Grove was right. News does travel quickly through a camp circle."

"Hair-face dog! You have crossed my trace one too many times. Now you have stolen the woman I had bought to be my wife! For this you will die."

"I want no quarrel with you, One That Kills in a Hard Place, but if you do not back down now, *you* will surely die."

"I will die then, if I must, but not before my blade finds rest in your bowels." His friends drew back their arrows.

Jones was in a tight spot. At this range he'd get at least three of them, and perhaps all five, one with each of the cartridges he carried in his Colt. Just the same, he'd die in the fight; that was almost assured. If he could, he was going to talk his way out of this. If he couldn't, Morning Snow Woman would be widowed before she had even married.

"I did not know that a Lakota warrior needed four braves to help him kill one white man. I always thought the Lakota were mighty warriors, not girls."

One That Kills in a Hard Place's face darkened. "You have the gun, white spittle! Throw it aside and my bucks will not interfere."

"Last night it mattered not to you that I was unarmed. If I throw away my revolver I will once again be unarmed. Will you drop your weapon as well?"

"I have heard how you were given your name. I also know that Two Bulls drove you to the dust with his fists. I am mightier than that Ree shirt wearer. When I drive your face into the dust, I will put your neck beneath my moccasin and snap it like a dry twig for the fire pit."

Beyond them the girls had come up the trail, herding their pack of dogs, their arms wrapped around bundles of firewood. They stopped, startled, and stood there watching.

"Will you do this for the women to see?" Jones indicated the new arrivals with a nod of his head.

The braves glanced over, then back at him, not daring to let him out of their sight. One That Kills in a Hard Place said, "It will honor my clan to kill the hair-face that has brought them dishonor!" He spat the last word out as if it were a worm in his mouth.

"If killing me in front of Morning Snow Woman will bring honor to your clan, how much *more* honor would it bring you if you killed me in front of *all* the people of the village?"

"What is it you are saying?"

"I challenge you to a fight with empty hands, in front of all the people of your camp circle—if you're man enough to accept it."

"I accept, hair-face thief, but not with empty hands like children fight—with this!" He thrust his keen blade into the air.

"As you wish," Jones said boldly.

A smile settled firmly over One that Kills in a Hard Place's face. "Before the sun leaves the sky this day, you will die."

"That remains to be seen." Jones dared not let his nervousness show now. As a final act of bravado, he holstered his revolver, turned his back on them, and walked away, his spine stiff as a board, betting that One That Kills in a Hard Place's pride, and the eyes of the women upon him, would keep the Sioux faithful to his words.

"You jest can't seem to keep outta each other's way. You gonna make a career outta fightin' the entire Injun nation single-handed, bare-fisted?"

"It's not like I had much of a choice." Jones and Grove were making their way toward the circle of men and women outside the camp. In spite of his promise never to step into a ring again, here he was on his way to the most important—and deadly—fight of his life. "It was either talking him into this fight or shooting it out with the five of them."

"I would have taken my chance with Sam Colt's equalizer. You agreeing to go hand to hand with that buck, armed with butcher knives, is jest plain suicide! Injuns have been taught all their lives in this sort of fighting. Little boys practice it with play knives made out of reeds. Besides, you haven't fought in almost a year, Nate. You're outta shape, and if you don't mind me saying so, you've put on a few pounds."

"Thanks for the encouraging words."

"Sorry, Nate. Didn't mean it like that. It's jest I'm worried. This ain't like nothing you ever done before. There ain't no timed rounds, and no referee will pull you two apart. The only rules in that ring is that one of you is gonna live and the other is gonna die."

Jones managed a grin. "I know, Mr. Grove. And don't think I'm not having a case of the jitters."

"No shame in that."

Jones glanced at the bottle of whiskey Grove had tucked under his arm. "What's that for?"

"Why, it's for the celebration after you stomp that buck's face into the dirt . . . I hope."

The crowd parted for them as they approached the large circle scratched into the dust. Grove said, "I see someone I need to talk to, Nate. I'll be along to your corner directly," and he veered off.

Carson Grove hadn't seen anyone he needed to talk to. Instead he made his way through the crowd toward the knot of men standing around One That Kills in a Hard Place.

"You ready to take him on, buck?" Grove asked. He was suddenly the target of two dozen hard stares.

One That Kills in a Hard Place glared at him. "What are you doing here, hair-face? Spying for the white woman-stealer?"

"Hell, no. Why, it's jest plain the other way around. I come to wish you good luck."

"What is this you speak?"

Grove tipped the bottle up, then wiped his lips and said, "I'm plumb tired of putting up with that whelp, listening to him bad-mouthing the Lakota people. Why, he told me he thinks you are lower than buffalo shit down a prairie dog hole. He claims he's gonna tie you up by your braids and cut off your balls like them Texicans do to their bulls. Why, he said the most awful things about your mother, and he claims your grandfather got to know a sheep in an intimate way, if you know what I'm saying." Grove took another swig.

"You are his friend. Why you speak this?"

"Friend? Well, I admit I *once* was his friend. But that's all over with. I got a special feeling for the Lakota, right here, in my heart." Grove tapped his breast soberly. "I married the prettiest Lakota flowers that ever sprung from God's earth, and when a fellow shows he has no respect for the people I have grown to love, well, then it's time for me and him to part company. That's why I come over. To tell you I hope you slice him open like buffalo meat and hang his scalp from your lodgepole." Grove lifted the bottle again, then paused and glanced at One That Kills in a Hard Place. "Care for a nip to get you in a fightin' mood?"

"I already in fighting mood. Don't need your firewater for that," the warrior growled in his anger. But he snatched the bottle away just the same and guzzled it like water.

"Here now, go easy on that stuff. You don't want it slowing you down none." Grove took back the bottle and put it to his lips.

"Buffalo shit down a prairie dog hole ... ha! That white dog vomit will wish he had choked on his own afterbirth!"

"That's what I say," Grove passed the bottle back. It was intercepted by one of the braves and made its way around, finally ending up in the fist of One That Kills in a Hard Place, who drank deeply.

"Well, the fight is about to start. I better find me a good place to watch from," Grove said. He reached for the bottle, but One That Kills in a Hard Place and his friends were passing it around again. Grove frowned. "Go easy on that, buck."

The warrior only laughed, plucked the bottle from his group of admirers, and took another long drink. "Strong water is a woman! One That Kills in a Hard Place knows how to handle women."

Grove shrugged his shoulders. "Whatever you say, buck." As he walked away he added under his breath, "Although this *particular* woman has a kick like a mule."

# TWENTY

"Nathan!"

"Morning Snow Woman!" Jones was surprised to discover her suddenly standing there.

"It's Mountain Rose now," she said gently, with dark worry in her lovely wide eyes. Jones was surrounded by the men of the Eagle Claw Clan, of which she was a member. It was not so much that they were behind him as that they were honor-bound to support the future mate of one of their own. Likewise, on the other side of the dirt circle, One That Kills in a Hard place was engulfed in a crowd of his own Wild Horse Clan members. Although Jones had no way of knowing for sure, he figured the Wild Horses must outnumber the Eagle Claws five to one.

There was a whoop from the other side, and an empty whiskey bottle went careening out over the crowd.

Mountain Rose took his arm, her nails biting into his skin. "You must be careful, Nathan. I do not want to sing the mourning song for you." Those wide dark eyes traveled searchingly across his face. "You do not have to do this."

His heart was pounding, his forehead beaded with

sweat. "How can I back out now, Mountain Rose, and still have honor among your people, and more important, with you?"

Her words seemed to catch in her throat when she said, "You can give me to One That Kills in a Hard Place. It is what he wants. You would lose honor, but you would keep your life."

Jones was stunned. When he was able to speak he said softly, "And what about *your* honor?"

She averted her eyes and peered at the dirt beneath her moccasins. "I would be honored. I'd be the wife of a strong brave who fought for me, and paid many ponies for me."

"No, I will not give you to him. I will fight him and then I will marry you, just like I said!"

She looked up, a hint of a smile breaking through the gloom. "I have prayed to the Great Spirit for you, Nathan. I painted a rock in a secret place and have left an offering."

"I'll need all the help I can get."

"You'll do jest fine, Nate." Grove came out of the crowd and looked him up and down. "You jest weave and bob like you was trained to do, and keep away from his lunges. You know how to protect yourself; I seen you do it."

"You saw me beaten," he reminded Grove.

"You can't afford to lose this one. This fight is for keeps."

Mountain Rose removed the beaded pouch from around her neck and placed it over his head. "It will protect you."

"You've never told me what was in it."

"It is a *Tukan*."

"That means it's good medicine," Grove put in.

Jones had to leave it go at that, for the fight was about to begin.

"Lemme see your knife."

Jones handed it over.

"Here, use this," Grove said, pulling his big butcher

knife from its sheath. "It's sharper than a parson's tongue, and it's got a mite more reach than yours."

"Thanks."

One That Kills in a Hard Place stepped into the ring.

"Remember what I said, Nate: Play him out for a while. Keep back out of his reach; let him tire some. Never forget to keep your eyes on him. Friends ain't so easy to come by that I can afford to lose one."

On an impulse, Jones suddenly drew Mountain Rose to him and kissed her hard upon the mouth. She was startled. It was apparent that she had had no experience with kissing, but when he released her he felt she'd rather enjoyed it. He certainly had!

He stepped into the ring.

The two men circled at first, keeping apart, sizing each other up. It was much like every boxing match Jones had ever fought, but the glint off their blades from the lowering sun was a grim reminder that the Marquis of Queensberry would carry no weight in this contest. Then, with the suddenness of a rattlesnake, One That Kills in a Hard Place struck out. Jones sprang backward, just barely avoiding the bite of the Sioux's blade.

The Indian was quick on his feet; he recoiled and instantly launched a second attack, to Jones's left side. Jones backpedaled, half a step ahead of the darting knife, which had caught a piece of his shirt and laid it open.

The crowd cheered, and activity at the nearby betting stick picked up.

The warrior kept up his attack while Jones weaved and darted, staying always just out of reach of that deadly blade. At one point he backed himself into the arms of the onlookers and they shoved him into the ring. One that Kills in a Hard Place dove to drive home his attack. Jones saw an opening and shot a left jab into his chin, and followed immediately with an upward thrust, but his blade only scratched his adversary's exposed belly. The trickle of blood brought another round of cheers, this time from the Eagle Claw Clan side of the circle.

One That Kills in a Hard Place looked down at the scratch, his glaring eyes hardening as he lunged forward. This time the sharp knife caught Jones in the side, its blade glancing off a rib.

A bolt of fire raged through him as he leaped backward and stared at the red dripping from the blade in One That Kills in a Hard Place's fist. Jones pressed a hand to the wound in his side as slowly his shirt grew a crimson stain.

For some unexplainable reason the warrior didn't immediately follow up, which would have ended the fight then and there. Jones was momentarily stunned. His brain cleared at about the same time the Indian pressed his next attack—this time a little clumsily. Even wounded, Jones easily sidestepped it and roundhoused with his right, the clenched knife adding bulk to his fist. It caught the Sioux in the temple and staggered him.

He recovered almost at once, but stood there a moment as if confused, the great muscles of his chest heaving in the air, the fierce glare of his dark eyes seemingly unfocused now. Jones ignored the fire in his side and lunged low, delivering his renowned Gatling-gun attack. One That Kills in a Hard Place crumpled under the blows, the knife slipped from his fingers, and his knees collapsed. In a heartbeat Jones was atop him, yanking his head back by the braids, exposing his neck to the edge of his knife. He pressed it there, hard, and a line of blood appeared.

One That Kills in a Hard Place was no longer fighting. It was incredible that he had gone down so quickly. Jones could have killed him right then and no one would have stopped him. It was his right, and they all knew it. But at that moment Jones couldn't bring himself to do it, although he was certain that had the tables been turned the warrior would have cheerfully slit his throat.

Instead, he shouted to the crowd, "I, Iron Left Hand, will spare his life! From this day to the end of days, I declare my victory over One That Kills in a Hard Place!" Jones cut the warrior's twin braids and stood, his foot upon the fallen brave's back, holding the hair high, and giving a whoop of victory that surprised even himself.

He staggered. The flow of blood had reddened his trouser leg and showed no signs of stopping. He blinked sweat from his eyes and thought it curious that four or five Indians over on the Wild Horse Clan side of the ring had chosen this moment to lay down and take a nap. He looked again, startled, certain his vision was clouded by the pain that raged up his side into his neck and head.

Jones fought to maintain his balance and walked with dignity out of the ring. Grove caught him as he began to topple. The next thing Jones knew he was being borne away upon the shoulders of four Sioux warriors.

"I'm getting pretty handy at my stitching," Grove quipped as he poked a needle and thread into Jones's flesh and pulled it through. "Did that hurt?"

Jones grimaced and bit down on the rawhide strap Mountain Rose had put between his teeth. "Your bedside manners leave something to be desired," he mumbled around the leather.

Grove went on happily, "I've learned it works better if you tie off each stitch separately. That way it don't pull out later."

"I don't need a detailed account of it, Mr. Grove. Just get it over with." The sun had left the sky and the tipi was darkening as the last of its afterglow faded to black. A fire burned in the central pit, its wavering light dancing off the faces of Grove and Mountain Rose. Jones looked around. It was One Stab and Mountain Rose's tipi, but One Stab was not there.

"There, that should do it. The bleeding is about stopped, and it don't look like the knife cut into anything vital. I'd say you was lucky, Nate."

Mountain Rose had made a poultice from herbs and mosses and some river clay that the women from around the camp circle had donated. It was hot, almost unbearably so, when she laid it upon his red and swollen flesh, but after a few minutes the concoction seemed to draw the pain from his side and he was suddenly sleepy.

He still wore the pouch around his neck that she had

given him, and when he tried to return it she stopped him. "No, you will wear it now. It will help you get well, my husband."

He wasn't up to insisting and instead laid his head back on the pillow. Then, all at once his eyes sprang open and he looked at her. "What did you say?"

His sudden earnestness brought a puzzled look to her face. "I said it will help you get well."

"I mean, after that. What did you call me?"

She cocked her head to one side, uncertain of what he was asking. Grove grinned and said, "She called you her *husband.*"

Jones's eyes shifted from Grove to Mountain Rose, then back again. "But we aren't married yet . . . are we?"

Grove glanced around the tipi. "There's your saddle, your bedroll, your saddlebags, your rifle, and your revolver. You own anything else?"

"Er, not that I have with me."

"One Stab formally accepted your price for the girl and she moved your gear into her tipi. I'd say you was a married man, Nate. Congratulations!"

He was speechless as Mountain Rose's pretty face smiled back at him. "Where is One Stab?" he asked suddenly.

"My grandfather is staying with a cousin until we leave," she said.

Could it have happened so quickly? He had to admit, he was still woefully ignorant in the ways of her people. "But isn't there some sort of ceremony?"

Grove shrugged his shoulders and said, "Oh, I reckon there will be some feasting after you deliver on the goods, and if you wanted to, you could probably spend a night with one of her uncles' wives. . . ."

"No! I don't want that."

Grove grinned. "Is that a blush I see takin' shape?"

"No, it is not," he came back sharply.

"How much more of a ceremony do you need?"

"I don't know. I thought maybe we'd stand before a medicine man, or a chief, or something."

"That's the white man's way of doing it, Nate. If a Sioux woman can divorce her husband by merely tossing all his belongings out of her tipi into the common area, why can't she marry herself a husband by simply gathering his things *into* her tipi?"

He lay there, his head whirling, a multitude of confusing thoughts racing through it. "But I haven't even paid One Stab yet," he said finally.

"They know a trustworthy man when they see one, Nate. Your credit is good with them."

"We should let him rest now," Mountain Rose said.

Grove stood. "Night, Nate. I'll stop by in the morning."

"Good night, Mr. Grove," he said, distractedly.

Mountain Rose said, "I will come back later. Now you sleep."

She and the old mountain man left him there trying to sort out all the events that had raced by in less than one week. A week that had taken him from the Black Hills, a carefree wanderer in search of gold, to a Sioux camp circle, and a married man. It hardly seemed possible! Thinking about it jumbled his brain and made him weary, and he slipped into a deep sleep that might have lasted until morning had not something from the darkness awakened him. . . .

A year ago he would have slept blissfully on, completely unaware that someone was creeping up on his tipi, and he would not have awakened until an instant before his throat had been slashed. But a year of living in the wilderness had changed Jones. It had hardened his muscles, toughened his skin, numbed him to the rigors of cold, wet, and heat, and most of all, sharpened his hearing, so that now even the faintest sound out of the ordinary penetrated down into his subconscious, which never rested.

His eyes snapped open, but his body remained motionless, instinctively knowing that to move would be to give away his position. Shifting his view, he saw the moonlight coming faintly through the skins of the tipi—not enough to actually see by, but enough to accent the utter depth of the shadows surrounding him. He glanced to his right; Mountain Rose's sleeping pallet was empty. Slowly his view slid across the tipi. Piles of skins and his saddle and equipment were but indistinguishable lumps in the dark. His eyes stopped at the round opening. The door was folded shut. He heard a faint scraping and glanced toward the holster belt near his head. His revolver was gone.

Another sound turned his eyes back toward the door. Suddenly it was thrown back, spilling moonlight inside the tipi, and with it One That Kills in a Hard Place. The warrior paused, and in that moment Jones saw the ragged end of his hair where he had cut the braids, hanging loose close to his shoulders. And he saw something else too—the faint glint of moonlight off the long, deadly blade in the warrior's hand. One That Kills in a Hard Place advanced a step, and when he spoke, it was in a harsh whisper.

"Woman-stealer, wake up now so that you may know who it is that sends you on to the land of ghosts."

"I'm awake, buck. Is this the way a Lakota kills?"

"You have crossed me too many times. And now this!" His hand grabbed a fistful of his shorn hair. "But tonight you will be with the ghosts of your ancestors, and I will have your woman!"

Jones searched quickly for something to defend himself with. There was nothing but the pillow beneath his head— one side smooth for sleeping, the other decorated in bright quill and beadwork for day use. He had to keep One That Kills in a Hard Place talking.

"How can you stand in the council circle having killed a wounded man in his own lodge?"

"There are many here who will not be unhappy to have the white vomit removed from their sight." In an instant the Sioux leaped upon him, and clutching Jones's hair to throw back his head and expose the smooth skin of his throat, One That Kills in a Hard Place raised the knife high . . .

The four distinctive metallic clicks froze him in his

place even as the knife had started its downward arc. They were both suddenly aware that there was a third person in the tipi with them. Mountain Rose walked cautiously out of the shadows with Jones's revolver in both hands, its barrel pointed at the warrior's head. She slowly circled from behind them and stopped on her side of the lodge.

"What I have heard tonight tells me that you are a coward, One That Kills in a Hard Place. It was the workings of the Great Spirit that saved me from being joined to a man who brings no honor to himself or his clan."

"You would not shoot," he said cautiously.

"Back away from him or it will be you who will join his ancestors' ghosts tonight. They will laugh at your coming because a woman sent you to them," she said with deadly determination in her voice.

Slowly, One That Kills in a Hard Place lowered the knife and stood.

"You leave my lodge now, and never return. You will not be given another warning, One That Fears Women!" It was an insult greater even than Jones's cutting off of his braids. He stiffened beneath the sting of her words, and wheeling around, plunged out the door.

Jones looked up at her. "How did you know?"

She was still pointing the revolver at the open door. Slowly, she lowered its hammer, then the weapon, and finally she looked at him. "There was much talk among the Wild Horse Clan. I have many cousins there, brave warriors who told me in secret what One That Kills in a Hard Place was planning."

The pain flared in Jones's side. It had begun to bleed again. He lowered his head to the pillow. "It's nice to have family spread around."

She dropped to her knees and placed a hand on his forehead. "There is fire in you, Nathan. I will bring water to cool it." She started to leave, but he caught her hand.

"I appreciate your keeping watch over me."

"You are my husband. It is what I wish to do."

"I love you, Mountain Rose."

She smiled, then said hesitantly, "Yesterday you did the white man's custom. . . . the touching of lips. Show me again how it is done."

In spite of the wound in his side, he took her into his arms, and she came eagerly. After a few moments he was hardly aware of the pain . . . or of anything else.

# TWENTY-ONE

After a week among his wife's people, Jones felt fit enough to be on his way. He'd not seen One That Kills in a Hard Place since his night encounter with the man. Once the tribe had learned of his treachery he was shunned, and there was talk by the village police of a yearlong exile as a punishment. Instead, the warrior left with Crazy Horse a day later, vowing to take out his revenge on all white men. Many of the older men who heard this shook their heads in regret, and the keening of the women singing a death chant could be heard from many different quarters of the camp circle. A war cloud was swiftly overtaking the people of this land.

Jones hadn't seen his friend for a couple days. When he finally tracked down Carson Grove, the grizzled mountain man was in high spirits, sitting back against a tree, smoking a pipe and watching the Belle Fourche running past.

"I hear you're about to pull outta here, Nate. How you feeling? Say, you're looking fancy."

Jones grinned down at himself, and would have thumbed the lapels of his new shirt if it had had lapels.

"Rose made it for me," he said proudly, rolling the soft deerskin between his fingers.

"Rose, is it now? I figured you'd get around to shortenin' her name to something more familiar."

"She doesn't mind. She said the rose is a beautiful flower."

Grove laughed. "You got yourself a good woman there. Like I told you, can't do much better than a Injun wife." They started to walk back to the camp circle. "You take care of her, and she'll see to your every need. When are you pulling out?"

"Rose is packing up now. One of her cousins gave her a small hunting lodge that we'll live in until I can build us something more permanent."

"Where you heading?"

"I'm not certain." He gave a short laugh. "I've got a long shopping list to fill. I've been thinking of going south, to the railhead at Sidney. It's probably the nearest place to find the ponies I have to buy—other than Camp Robinson or Fort Laramie. But I sort of wanted to steer clear of the army outposts."

"Just make sure you get Injun ponies, not none of them Eastern crossbreeds. One Stab will be mighty particular."

"I'll keep it in mind." They strolled on in silence a few moments longer before Jones said, "What do you intend to do?"

The mountain man grinned and said, "Remember that widow I mentioned a while back? Well, she went and moved my forty-year gather into her tipi, so I reckon I'm gonna stay around a little longer, maybe through the summer. I don't know after that."

"Mrs. Grove number four! Congratulations. A man of your age . . . I am surprised." Jones paused to consider, then said, "I guess I'm really not surprised after all."

Grove pushed out his lower lip. "A man my age needs a woman to take care of him."

"What about your claim in Dead Wood Gulch?"

"It's yours, if you want it."

"Just like that? It may be worth thousands of dollars."

Grove shrugged. ''If it makes you feel better, put a sack or two of gold away for me, in case I ever need 'em in my *old age*.''

They came into the camp circle. Rose and three friends had packed a travois and hitched it to a dog. It was stacked with bundles tied down with rawhide thongs. Talk of gold reminded Jones of the beaded pouch. ''There is something I want to show you before I leave,'' he said to Grove.

Jones stepped alongside a tipi, out of view, and took the pouch from around his neck that Mountain Rose had given him as good luck just before the fight. He dumped something into his hand, then closed a fist around it.

''What you got there?''

''You once told me about the time that you, Bridger, Waller, and a man named Fontenelle were attacked by Sioux in the Black Hills.''

''Them days are long past. We buried that hatchet years ago.''

''You told me of the gold nugget Fontenelle found.''

Grove gave a short, derisive laugh. ''He called it his lucky horseshoe. Lucky, hell! It got him kilt! There warn't no luck in it at all.''

''Do you remember what it looked like? You described it for me once.''

''Remember it? I'll say I do. How could I ever forget? The nugget was about the size of my thumb-knuckle to the fingertip, and shaped like a horseshoe all right, with a piece of quartz or something set right in the middle like it was put there on purpose. But it warn't no lucky horseshoe.''

Jones opened his fist, and Grove's eyes went wide. ''That's it! That's Fontenelle's nugget!'' He stared at the twisted piece of gold for a long moment, then up at Jones. ''Old One Stab must have taken it from him and kept it all these years.''

''Rose told me that he gave it to his wife, but that she died shortly after and he kept it hidden until his son, Rose's father, came of age and took a wife. It passed to him until he was killed. Since Rose had no brothers or sisters, it went to her, and now she has given it to me.''

A look of fear came into Grove's eyes, something that Jones had never seen in the old man's face. Indeed, he had often wondered if Grove knew the meaning of fear, but here it was, clear as words written down on a page. ''Get rid of it, Nate! Get rid of that thing before it kills you too!''

''What do you mean? You don't believe there is some kind of evil tied up with this, do you? It's merely a chunk of mineral, nothing more than that.''

''Fontenelle had it in his hand and he died. One Stab's wife got hold of it and she died. Rose's father come to possess it next, and he's dead too.''

''Coincidence, that's all.''

''When you get that much coincidence running together, a smart man stops and reconsiders. No, throw it away before you or Rose are next!''

''Mr. Grove, if it was going to get me killed, what more perfect opportunity to work its evil than when I fought One That Kills in a Hard Place? If anything, it proves it is exactly what Rose claims.''

Grove eyed him oddly, then inhaled long, decisive breath and said, ''I wasn't gonna mention it, but seeing as how you brought it up, I reckon I better. That way at least you won't go around with any notions that could get you kilt.''

''What are you driving at?''

''Your little tussle with One That Kills in a Hard Place. That yellow rock had nothing to do with you besting the fellow like you done.'' As he spoke his hand went into the pouch at his side. ''This did.'' He slapped a glass vial into Jones's hand.

Jones turned it over and read the paper label pasted on it. ''Chloral hydrate?'' His face registered shock. ''You gave this to him?''

''I mixed it with the little bit of whiskey I had left, then pretended to drink from the bottle. One That Kills in a Hard Place wanted to make out like a big chief and show me he could hold his liquor, so I let him have it. Unfortunately, the half dozen bucks with him wanted to wet their whistle too. I was worried that he didn't get enough of it.''

"That's why you told me to stall."

"It needed time to work. But then, you ought to know all about that.''

"What do you mean?

"It will work when mixed in water, but it goes a whole lot faster with whiskey.''

Jones gave him a blank look.

Grove grimaced. "Know where I got that bottle from?'' He shook his head.

"Your fight with Two Bulls—the look in your eyes before you went down was sort of glazed and unfocused.''

"Yes, I remember. I was sick.''

"I thought so too—at first. But when it took you almost two days to wake up I knew there was more to it than that, so I paid Mr. Ro Kinsey a little visit. Tapped him aside the head with Big 50 one night while he was asleep and went through the things in his wagon. That's when I found that bottle. It looked like he had used about half of it on you. I used the rest on One That Kills in a Hard Place. If it wasn't that his friends helped him drink it, he might have never woke up. As it turned out, he and the others just got enough to put them to sleep for a few minutes. But that was all we needed.''

Jones stared at the empty bottle, hardly believing what Grove was telling him. "Then I was drugged!''

"It turned out Kinsey made a bundle off of that fight— and nearly kilt you in the doing.''

"All those men who lost money were cheated! And here I felt I'd let them down.''

"Cheating is the way Kinsey does business.''

Jones's fists clenched in anger. "And you did the same to One That Kills in a Hard Place.''

"I did, and I ain't ashamed of it neither. What was at stake there was more important than money.''

"I might have killed him.''

"You didn't, and you wouldn't have. I knew that."

Jones put the nugget away. "You're probably right," he said, but inside he felt vaguely cheated knowing that his victory was not of his own doing. Just the same, he felt some relief that his losing to Two Bulls had not been of his doing either.

Rose had finished packing their household goods; the women of the camp had given her gifts of those items she lacked for proper housekeeping. With the travois piled so high Jones feared the dog it was hitched to would collapse beneath its weight not a mile down the road, the new couple set off for Sidney, Nebraska.

Jones was in no hurry. Traveling slowly south with Rose was a delight, and there was so much they had to learn about each other. She brought camp life to a level of true comfort. At each stop she'd busily erect their tipi, cover the ground in buffalo robes, lay out their sleeping pallets, build the fire, cook the dinner, and clean up afterward. All that was required of him, he quickly learned, was to hunt and protect the lodge. This last was most important, she had warned him, for a single tipi out on the plains was always in danger of attack from hostile bands of renegades.

In no time he became accustomed to this lifestyle and fell easily into its pattern. In the course of things, his grasp of the Sioux language increased dramatically, while her English improved beyond anything she could have hoped for at the agency school. Life was perfect during those three weeks of travel, but the day they spied the bustling rail town of Sidney in the distance, Jones noted a change come over Rose.

"What's troubling you, Rose?" he asked as she fussed with the harness of the dog travois. To his amazement, the sturdy canine had not suffered in the least hauling his heavy burden these two hundred miles. Rose was taking longer than usual with the harness, and it was obvious she was stalling.

"My husband knows me so well already?"

"It's plain something is worrying you, my dear."

She looked at the sprawling rail town, still several miles in the distance. "That place frightens me."

"What frightens you about it?"

"There will be many people there. I know what the whites think of the Indian."

"They'll think you're wonderful. Just like I do."

She made a failed attempt at a smile, then frowned down at the new doeskin dress that she had made before leaving the Sioux camp circle. It was already showing signs of wear, although its bead- and quillwork was still bright and fresh. The frown deepened as her view traveled to the worn fancywork on her moccasins.

He knew what was really troubling her. "No matter what they think, Rose, you will be the prettiest woman in Sidney. If they don't treat you with the respect you deserve, they will have me to answer to." He took her into his arms and felt her grip his waist tightly. For a long moment they held each other, then she said, "I worry not only for myself, but for you, Nathan."

He laughed. "Don't worry about me, my dear. They don't call me Iron Left Hand for nothing." He took her hand in one of his, led his horse with the other, and with the dog trotting alongside, they marched down into the sprawling railroad town.

The wide streets of Sidney, Nebraska, were a tumult of activity, booming with commerce and jammed with dozens of freight wagons. A train sat on the Union Pacific right-of-way, its long black engine wheezing and pumping gray smoke into the clear Nebraska sky. The air was blue with the cussing and shouting of the bullwhackers. The streets stank of manure and rang from the clatter of chains, harnesses, braces, and rattling cargo and the rumble of huge iron-rimmed wheels. It was an assault upon their senses, coming out of the wild, empty Nebraska sandhills as they just had.

Rose's fingernails bit into his arm as they kept to the side of the road to avoid the passing freight wagons. Her eyes darted continually, seemingly unable to take it all in. She was strung tight as a fiddle string.

"Welcome to the white man's world, darling." He'd spent a good amount of time in her quiet realm, and even being city-bred, the shock of this was a bit of a strain on his hearing and smell, which the wilderness had honed to a keen edge. He understood something of what he knew she must be feeling.

They tied the horse to a hitching post on a side street off the main thoroughfare, and Rose ordered the dog to stay. The boardwalk was a somewhat safer route to take, but still Rose hugged close to Jones. Some folks coming and going gave the two of them curious looks, others smiled, and still others went on their way without noticing them. But mostly people just swung wide around them and closed ranks behind. Jones thought that curious, and paid it little attention at first. At nearly every storefront, Rose drew up and looked wonderingly at all the goods displayed behind the windows.

"Be careful—your eyes might pop out of your head."

"What are all these?"

"It is all that makes the white world go round. Things your people have not come to rely too heavily upon . . . yet."

"So many things! Who has the skill to make such things?"

"They are made in factories," he said and since he knew of no equivalent in the Sioux language, he went into a lengthy description of what factories were and what they did.

"These things—how does the white man acquire them?"

"He buys them with money—with gold." Jones touched the heavy pouches at his side. "Come, I will show you how it is done." He guided her through a doorway and up to the teller's window of the bank they'd been passing. Half an hour later, he'd exchanged his gold nuggets for gold coins and they were back out on the street.

"Now, let's do some shopping."

"Shopping?"

"Er, trading. What do you need?"

"I need nothing."

"Okay, then what would you like?"

This was obviously not something she had thought much about. "I don't know."

Jones was looking for a mercantile store where he might find the Winchester rifles he'd promised One Stab, plus a couple of good, heavy woolen blankets. He didn't know if he could find any of the Hudson's Bay Company's products in Sidney, but he was certain that heavy, quality blankets could be had. He spied a likely place down the street and picked up his pace, only to discover a moment later that he was alone.

"Rose?" Jones turned around, searching, and located his young wife a few stores down, her nose nearly touching the window glass. "What is it?" he asked, returning to her side.

"I have found what I would like," she said, pointing at the mannequin standing in the display window.

At the sound of the bell above the door, a man bent behind the counter, straightened, bumped his head, cussed mildly, and rubbed the injured spot. When he saw Rose and Jones, his view lingered a moment in surprise. Then he recovered and smiled amiably.

"What can I do for you folks?"

Jones stepped up to the counter. "My wife is interested in that dress in the window."

He was heavyset, with a fleshy face, friendly gray eyes, a receding hairline, and huge side whiskers worn after the fashion of General Burnside. "That's a lovely choice," he said, coming out from behind the counter. He smiled at Rose and went on, "I have several hanging up over here." They followed him to the back of the store, where a part of one wall was given over to ready-made dresses. "You might even find something you like better over here. And of course, you may try them on and see how you like them. Here is a mirror."

Rose turned and stopped, awestruck, her reflection looking back at her with wide-eyed amazement.

"Have you never seen a mirror?" Jones asked.

She remained staring a long moment. "Only a very small glass that looks back. I have never seen myself all at once."

The storekeeper chuckled. "Now you can see just how pretty you look. What size would you wear?"

"Size?"

"This is the first time my wife has been to a big town, or in such a large store."

"Hmm," the merchant purred, thinking. "Then I don't suppose you know much about this type of clothing? How to fasten the buttons up the back, perhaps nothing about the hoops, or whalebone corsets?"

Rose shook her head, overwhelmed, confusion blanketing her face. The proprietor smiled. "I think you will need help."

"My husband will help me."

"No, no, no, I think you need help of a different sort." Raising a single digit on his left hand, he said, "You wait right here," and with that he hurried through a back door. Jones heard his feet pounding up a flight of steps to the second floor of the building.

"Maybe I will not trade for the new dress after all, Nathan," she said, disappointment in her voice.

"Let's see what he has up his sleeve first." As he spoke, he happened to glance at the long looking glass, and was shocked to see a stranger staring back at him— a tall stranger dressed in a beaded buckskin shirt with long fringe dangling from the sleeves. This man was wide of chest and dark of skin, with a fierce beard encircling his face and a mane that might have been right at home upon the head of a lion. His canvas pants were worn thin and patched in half a dozen places. His boots, having worn out months ago, had recently been discarded and replaced with a pair of moccasins. With the battered black Stetson on his head, the rifle in one hand, his revolver at his side, and a heavy butcher knife thrust at an angle under his

holster belt, Jones suddenly understood why the more civilized folks of Sidney had given him and Rose a wide
berth.

Footsteps descended the stairs, and a moment later
there appeared a slight woman with a pretty face and hair
tied in a tight bun atop her head.

"This is my wife, Samantha. Dear, this is the young
lady who needs our help."

Samantha took Rose under her wing, whisking her into
a back room for a quick measuring session, telling her
she'd help her try on the dresses and assemble all the
"necessaries." Rose cast a helpless look back at Jones as
she was swept away. He nodded his head, telling her it
was all right. That seemed to reassure her some, and as
the door closed he called, "I'm going out for a little
while, dear. I will be back soon."

"She'll be just fine," the storekeeper assured him.

"I'm sure she will. Now, where might I find a barber
in town?"

# TWENTY-TWO

It is hard to believe that a simple thing like a shave and a haircut can change a man's life, but looking back on it in later years, Jones would see the progression.

He stepped out of the barber's shop feeling civilized again, and when he showed up at the store to collect his wife, he felt doubly civilized, for the woman waiting for him there, except in face and smile, was a different woman from the one he'd left in buckskins and moccasins.

"Rose!"

She smiled hugely at him and did a very feminine thing: She turned a graceful circle to let him see all sides of her, as if she were a debutante dressed up for her coming-out ball.

"You look beautiful!"

"The clothes of the white woman fit very tightly," she said, "and the shoes are like a strong hand holding my feet."

Jones laughed. "I reckon it's something that takes some getting used to."

Samantha said, "You have a lovely wife."

"Yes, I know." Jones bought a pair of trousers for

himself, a new hat, and a pair of sturdy boots, and paid for it all with a gold coin. Back out on the sidewalk, he took Rose by the arm and said, "Did you enjoy your first shopping trip?"

She was staring at his face. She touched his bare chin, laughed lightly, and said, "All of this from the yellow rock? Now I begin to understand." She touched his cheek. "I like you better this way, Nathan. You look like the man I first met at the hunting camp circle last summer."

"In that case, I will buy a razor at our next stop."

"You will trade for more today?"

"I still need rifles, ammunition, blankets, and twelve ponies. You, my dear, were a very expensive wife." That pleased her.

They made their way down the sidewalk, she a little unsteady in the new shoes, clutching the brown paper package that contained her old clothes and some new items she had acquired. Jones entered a hardware store and bought the rifles and cartridges. Their arms were getting pretty full by this time, so his next stop was a hotel, where they took a room for the night, deposited their goods, and went back out. He was getting hungry. At a cafe he guided Rose through another doorway into yet another new experience, and then spent some time explaining the purpose of a menu while they sipped their coffee. Rose, it turned out, had been exposed to coffee years ago and relished it whenever she could come by it.

There were so many new things to learn, and Rose was eager for them all. Jones enjoyed teaching her as well. They browsed the town of Sidney, becoming skillful at dodging the huge, rumbling freight wagons. He made a point of explaining every small detail of this white man's world. He found a store that sold heavy woolen blankets made in England, and bought two for One Stab and one for them. They collected their horse and the dog and made their way toward a livery where Jones hoped to get a line on a dozen ponies. He mentally counted the remaining money. Although they still had plenty left, buying the livestock that he had promised One Stab would leave them practically broke.

"Ponies? Ain't got no ponies, mister," the stableman said, eyeing Rose as if not quite sure what to make of this Indian dressed like a white woman. "Got a nice string of draft horses, though. Good, stout animals, they are. Can pull a wagon all the way to Custer Park and back. You want to know where the money's gonna be, I'll tell you, son: It's in freighting. The government just sent a professor by the name of Jenney to Custer Park to see if there really is gold in them hills. Already the soldiers can't keep prospectors out of the place. If he comes back and says there is gold there, why, this whole nation is going to be on the move, and you know what'll get them and their supplies there? It will be the driver, that's who. Now, don't go wasting your money on ponies. Buy yourself a string of real horses, and a wagon for them to pull."

Jones didn't tell him that he'd already been to Custer Park, and that there was indeed gold there. And he kept particularly quiet on the even grander strike that Carson Grove had made farther north in a narrow gulch he called Dead Wood. Acting innocent, he inquired further into what had been going on in the Black Hills.

"There are five hundred men up there right now, and already a freight bridge is in the works for crossing the North Platte. It won't be long before Sidney will be the main supply line to the Black Hills. We got the Union Pacific. We got the most direct route. We got us freighters coming in, a dozen a day. Once we fix the problem with them damned Sioux, why, there won't be any stopping the money to be made."

Jones felt Rose stiffen at his side. He said, "I thought the Lakota have been remarkably patient through this invasion of their land. Has something happened?"

"Where have you been, son?"

"Traveling."

"Then you don't know that a band of them savages attacked a freight team only three days out of here. Killed everyone aboard and burned the wagons to the ground."

"No, I hadn't heard." Jones glanced at Rose, then back at the liveryman. "Do they know who did it?"

"It was Indians! What difference does it make which ones? They're all the same—lying, thieving redskins!"

"But does the army know who?" he insisted.

The man must have seen the change come over Jones, for he casually backed up a step and said, "It was that chief, Crazy Horse, and a band of his bloodthirsty savages, that's who."

They left the horse and travois at the livery. Jones took Rose's hand and continued their search for Indian ponies, the dog trotting alongside, growling at anyone who passed too near to them. After he'd put some distance between themselves and the livery, he said, "Don't pay any attention to what he said, darling."

"I didn't," she replied. But it was an obvious lie.

Jones inquired at three other places, and got the same answer. There were horses for sale, all right—big, heavy draft horses or tall, Eastern-bred saddle horses; nothing that One Stab would approve of. It was at a livery a half mile out of town that Jones got his first good lead.

"There is a trading post up north where you can find what you're looking for, mister. It's on Bordeaux Creek and was built back a long time ago by the American Fur Company. Right now it's run by a fellow named Boucher, and he does lots of trading with the Sioux." The man glanced around the empty barn and lowered his voice. "In fact, he does more than he should. I hear that the Sioux get nearly all their ammunition from him, and if the troubles we been having keeps up, I wouldn't be surprised to hear that the cavalry don't run him out of there."

On the way back to the hotel, Rose said, "I do not like this talk I hear of the Lakota and the white man going to war. The warriors in our camp circle spoke of war, and even Crazy Horse, who had vowed never to speak out in the council circle, openly spoke of it. Will it come to that, Nathan?"

He did not have an answer. All he could do was shake his head and tell her that he hoped not.

"What will become of *us* if our people turn to war?"

"Whatever happens between our people, *we* will come through it together."

She smiled bravely, and they made their way through the crowded streets toward their hotel. They had just stepped up out of the street onto the sidewalk when a voice called out to Jones.

"Is that you, Deadeye?"

Jones's shoulders tightened. He knew that voice, and he knew too that Ro Kinsey was about the last person he wanted to see again. Slowly, Jones turned.

Ro Kinsey was seated upon the high-seat of a heavy freight wagon, clutching a rat's nest of reins in his fists, his left foot shoving forward on the brake lever.

"Well, it is you, Jones. I'd hardly recognize you in them Indian clothes." He laughed. Then he saw Rose and said, "Picked yourself up a squaw, did you. Look at you, Jones; I always knew hanging around with that flea-bitten mountain man was going to rub off."

Now Jones wished he had never gone to the barber and that his hair and beard had not been shorn. Kinsey might have driven right past him then, never realizing he was there. Instinctively his fists bunched at his side. Here was the man who had drugged him, made him lose the fight with Two Bulls, and cheated dozens of men out of their money.

"What are you doing in Sidney?" Kinsey asked.

"Just trying to stay out of the way of the riffraff. And you, Kinsey?"

"There's plenty of that here. Me? I'm driving a wagon for a living. The U.P. brings in the freight and I haul it out where it belongs. It's something to do during the day. At night I work my real job."

"What might that be?"

"Taking the suckers' money at the card tables. And believe me, Deadeye, this town is full of them! See ya around." Kinsey toed off the brake, cracked his whip above the horses' heads, and rolled on away.

"Who is that?" Rose asked.

"The proverbial thorn in the side."

She blinked, a blank expression on her pretty face. He grinned. "Someone I know from the Custer Expedition. Someone I hoped I would never meet again."

Sleeping proved a new adventure. The bed was too soft for both of them. Jones had been away from a real mattress so long that this one hurt his back. And Rose had never known such a thing. The mattress amused her at first, but when it was time to go to sleep, she adamantly refused to occupy it with him. She said that women sleep on the women's side of the lodge and men on the men's side. She took their new blanket to the right wall of the room and curled up on the floor near her dog, absolutely content. This arrangement would have to change, of course, but for tonight Jones was willing to let her have it her way.

He lay there in the dark listening to the racket coming from the street below the open window, thinking about what the liveryman had said. There was big money to be made in the freighting business, especially if the Black Hills really did blow wide open as most people were predicting. A man with a team of oxen or horses and his own wagon could make a good living.

He thought of the gold in the creek that flowed past Carson Grove's little cabin in Deadwood Gulch. There was plenty of money to be made there too, but he knew that more men went broke hunting out gold than became rich. And that once one site played out, it was pull up the stakes and move on to another. He was a married man now, and he wanted something more permanent in his life. He considered returning to newspaper work, but he hadn't written in his journal for months. Compared with his life of the last year, sitting at a desk in some stuffy newspaper office paled. He liked the active life, liked to be on the move, and . . . well, perhaps Kinsey had been correct in saying that a bit of Carson Grove had rubbed off on him.

He glanced at his sleeping wife, a full-blooded Lakota woman. How could he deny that Grove had not influenced his life at least a little?

The noise of Sidney was something he was not used to, having spent so much time on the quiet prairies or in the tall-pine cathedral of the Black Hills. The dog was fidgeting too, although Rose seemed to have had no trouble falling asleep. His thoughts turned to the more practical matter of money. If he was going to go into business—any business—it would require capital. After this shopping trip, capital was something he would be clean out of. His brain turned the problem over, restlessness keeping him awake.

After a while he dressed and went outside. Sidney was a town that didn't go to bed early; its streets were still busy, its saloons spilling their lights across the wheel-rutted tracks of the main street while piano and fiddle music invited passerbys one and all to enter the swinging doors. The only thing missing now was all the wagon traffic.

Jones found himself in one of the many Sidney saloons, bumping shoulder to shoulder with freight men, railroad men, shopkeepers, and anyone else who thought the night was for playing and not sleeping. There were drunks hunting up drinks, ladies of questionable virtue hunting up drunks, and cardsharpers, like hungry sharks, hunting up anyone who swam too near to their table.

Jones bought a beer and turned to study the busy barroom. He heard a familiar voice suddenly ring out above the crowd, and when he looked Ro Kinsey was raking a pile of coins over to his side of a table. Jones drifted across the room and took a place against the wall, near enough to watch the cards go around to three other players, but still out of sight.

One of the players looked familiar, and then Jones recognized him: Bradley Sink, Ro's partner from the expedition. So, they were still hanging around together, and still cheating folks out of their money—Jones saw the subtle eye signals that passed between the two men. He sipped his beer, watching the players ante up their money and the cards go around the table.

Ro dealt cards like warm butter spreads over toast. He was smooth as oil on glass, and by the end of the hand the pile of coins in front of him had grown handsomely. Carson Grove had warned Jones that Kinsey cheated, but Jones could not detect the method. Still, there was that continual eye-talk between Kinsey and Sink. Somehow, the other players were being fleeced; Jones was certain of it.

They went another round, and by the end of it, one of the other players was getting mad. Kinsey just grinned at him in his easy manner and assured him that the cards were bound to change any moment, and sure enough, they did the very next hand, and the fellow cooled down some.

Jones finished his beer and decided to move off. He had no desire to renew old acquaintances, especially with a man who'd nearly killed him with a dose of chloral hydrate. Ro Kinsey was someone he preferred to stay clear of.

Jones had made his way to the batwing doors when he stopped and turned back. No! Kinsey had nearly killed him, and had cheated a lot of his friends. Now, somehow, he was cheating these men too. However Kinsey was doing it, it required the help of his friend, Sink.

He made his way back to the bar and caught the attention of a skinny, bewhiskered fellow in a dingy white apron. "Another beer?" the bartender asked.

"No thanks. That was just to wet my whistle. I want a New York Roundhouse."

The gent eyed him narrowly. "A what?"

"It's what all the railroad men are drinking nowadays."

"Yeah? Where are they drinking it? New York?"

Jones smiled patiently and said, "Well, I can see how it might take some time to make it way out here in the backwaters of this nation."

"Backwaters? Fellow, I don't know what *you've* been drinking, but Sidney is the major supply hub of the whole middle of this here frontier!"

Jones leaned forward and lowered his voice. "Then I can see how it might be embarrassing not to know how to make a New York Roundhouse. Lucky for you I happened to stop in, before some big official of the U.P. come up and ask for one. It's what they're all drinking now, you know."

"No, I hadn't heard." The bartender looked suddenly worried. "You don't think they'd do something funny, like put my saloon off limits or something, do ya?"

Jones shrugged his shoulders. "I've known a few railroad tycoons in my days, and they're a queer lot. With all that money they sit on, not answering to anyone but themselves, they're likely to do just about anything."

"Er, say, you wouldn't know how to make one of them New York Roundhouses, would you?"

"I've seen it done. Had one in Omaha just last week."

"Could you show me?"

Jones nodded his head. "I'd be happy to help you out. Do you mind?" He pointed behind the bar.

"No, no. Come right around."

Jones stepped behind the bar and eyed the stock along the back shelf, pretending to be searching for the right bottles. But the bottle he was really looking for, he knew, would be hidden elsewhere. The bar was not well stocked; apparently you could order anything you pleased so long as it was whiskey, rum, or beer. Jones fought down a brief moment of panic, knowing that the fellow in the white apron was expecting him to concoct a new drink—one that was at least palatable, if not downright flavorsome!

"Let's see . . . some of this . . ." He picked up a bottle of rum and another of whiskey, and scanning the shelf, he spied a dusty bottle of brandy that apparently was not in high demand among the saloon's patrons. He grabbed it too. "Aha! Perfect." As he played out the charade, his view darted to the shelves under the long bar, which mostly held glasses, mugs, and barrels. A sawed-off shotgun lay at hand, just out of sight, but that wasn't what he needed. He was beginning to wonder if the bartender had any! He had to! It was common for bars to keep some of the stuff on hand to deal with the rowdy customers who plagued saloons. Then Jones saw the drawer. It was closed, but he was certain he'd find it in there. If only he could get to it without the barkeep noticing.

"I think I have everything," he said, carrying the bottles to a spot at the end of the bar. "Yes, rum, whiskey, and brandy. Of course, we have the beer, so that's all right."

The aproned man scowled. "You going to mix all them things together?"

"Oh, yes, but in a very precise ratio."

The scowl turned to curiosity.

"Now, I'll need a jigger."

"What for?"

"Why, to measure out the amounts, of course."

"I generally do it by eye."

"That might be all right for your common drinks, but you don't want to be making a New York Roundhouse that way. No sir."

"I got one over here." He fished around under the counter and came up with a dingy measuring cup that he wiped on his dingy apron.

"Hmm." Jones eyed the saloon's stock and frowned.

"What's the matter?"

"I need two more ingredients, but I don't see as you have them."

"What?"

"Well, back East they use a spot of grain alcohol and a splash of pineapple juice. I don't suppose . . . ?"

"Ain't got no pineapple juice, that's for certain." He thought, screwing his lips together. "Ain't got no grain alcohol neither, but got something almost as good. Got me some good Kentucky Lightning. Corn 'shine that I keep for myself in the back room."

"That will do."

The bartender hurriedly filled a mug of beer for a gent

at the bar, then slid out from behind the counter and disappeared through a rear door.

Instantly, Jones yanked open the drawer. There was a revolver, some papers, and a couple of stubby pencils. But he didn't see what he was looking for! Then, reaching to the back of the drawer, his fingers wrapped about a small bottle. He glanced at the label, shoved it into his pocket, and slammed the drawer a moment before the man returned.

The bartender set a small glass of clear fluid among the bottles. Jones took a whiff and recoiled. "Oh, that will do just fine." He began mixing, leaning heavily toward the moonshine since that apparently was a favorite of the bartender's. He made a point of explaining the amounts to the bartender, who carefully noted them down with one of the stubby pencils.

"Now," he said, holding the drink toward the lamplight and watching the yellow flame dance inside the mixture. "This is very important. You must precisely mix it with an equal amount of beer." By this time Jones had attracted a small gathering of curious men. He dumped the contents of the glass into an empty mug, then filled the glass with beer to exactly the same level and poured it in too, mixing it well with a spoon. "There you have it, sir, a New York Roundhouse—minus the pineapple juice, of course. And that is a pity, for the juice removes any lingering bite. Here you go—you may sample it."

The bartender took a tentative sip and smacked his lips, his eyes taking on the narrow look of a man whose concentration was firmly fixed. The onlookers held their breath. He frowned, then sipped again. His lips seemed to pucker involuntarily. He took another pull at it, this one long and deep. Then, slamming the mug upon the bar, he gave a long whistle and said, "She sure has a kick to her, boys! I like it!"

Orders for the new drink poured in, and the bartender went to work filling them. Jones said, "Only happy to be of service. Say, I see a couple friends. I'll just take a whiskey over to them and say howdy."

"It's on the house," the bartender told him, his hands flying to mix the various ingredients.

"I'll just help myself. I see you're busy there." Pouring out three whiskeys, Jones made his way out from behind the bar, breathing a huge sigh of relief. He paused to secretly pour a few drops of chloral hydrate into one of the glasses, then slipped the little bottle back under the bar and carried the drinks over to Ro Kinsey's table.

Sink glanced up, then Kinsey, giving Jones a smoldering stare as he set the whiskeys on the table. "If it ain't old Deadeye."

"Saw you two fellows here and thought I'd come on over and see how you were doing." Jones grinned.

"We're in the middle of a game," Kinsey replied, not trying to disguise his irritation at the interruption.

"So I see. You winning?"

"Some." Kinsey glanced at the whiskey glasses. "What's that for?"

"Bought you fellows a drink. For old times' sake." He pushed the glasses in front of each man, mindful of the one containing the chloral hydrate. "Don't hardly meet anyone anymore who was with Custer last year. Everyone's gone their own way."

Kinsey glanced at the whiskey. "That's decent of you, Deadeye, except I don't drink while I'm playing."

Jones shrugged his shoulders. "Well, save it for later," he said, taking a sip of his whiskey.

But Sink snatched up his glass without hesitation and tossed it back, downing nearly half of it in one swallow. He apparently had no qualms about mixing cards and whiskey. He smacked his lips in appreciation, but that was all. Not a word of thanks, not that Jones had expected any from either of them.

"You have room for another player?"

"Sure," one of the other men said.

"No," Kinsey barked, cutting him off. "I like it just the way it is, Deadeye. Now why don't you go off and find yourself another game. I'll stop by and visit later."

*Sure you will,* Jones thought. *You're sweet as molasses*

*when you want something, like keeping me from beating Two Bulls, but otherwise, it's "Don't bother me."* Jones just smiled. "Sure, Ro, I understand. I'll just wander around a bit. Maybe I'll stop back later."

"You do that, Deadeye."

There was the soft rustle of cards falling to the floor, and the next moment Bradley Sink slumped in his chair and followed them.

Kinsey jumped to his feet. "What the hell!"

Jones peered into Sink's blank face. "He's fallen asleep. Can you imagine that. He didn't look tired. My, my."

Kinsey came around the table, grabbed Sink up by the lapels of his vest, and shook him. Sink only mumbled something and grinned in his sleep. Kinsey let go and Sink sank back to the floor, out cold. For a moment all eyes in the saloon were on them.

Jones grinned and announced, "It's the lateness of the hour, boys. This poor fellow is just tuckered out." He and Kinsey dragged the slumbering man into a corner to join two other sleeping drunks.

"It's a shame about poor Mr. Sink," Jones said, shaking his head. "His falling asleep has ruined your game. . . . Ah, but perhaps not! I'll just take his place until he wakes up."

"No, I don't think so, Deadeye," Kinsey began, but he was promptly overruled by the other two players, who had already lost their week's wages to him and were chomping at the bit to win some of it back. Seeing no way out of it, Kinsey gave Jones a withering glare and sat back down. They called a misdeal and the cards went around again.

Jones removed the beaded pouch from under his shirt and said, "I'm going to try out this new good-luck charm."

Kinsey's luck took a dive. The next hour saw a substantial redistribution of wealth, with Kinsey making most of the payments and the others reaping the benefits. Kinsey growled, chewed the soggy end of a cigar, and even took to drinking while he played. In the end, he told them that he was broke and that he had to quit. This was all right with the others, who happily gathered in their winnings and trotted off to the bar.

Jones collected the money he had won and stuffed it into a pocket.

"I wish to hell I'd never run into you today, Deadeye. You ain't never been anything but bad luck to me."

"Is that the way you see it? Seems to me I heard somewhere that you made a bundle off of me losing to Two Bulls. Remember that fight? You were my second. You were there to make sure I won it."

Kinsey's eyes narrowed, hardening ever so slightly. "What are you saying, Deadeye?"

Jones's innocent grin widened out into a smile. "Nothing, only it's curious you should make more money by me losing than if I'd won." Jones put his hat on his head and started away, then turned back. "Say, I'm real sorry about your friend there. You know, the way he went down like he did, it almost looks like he was doctored up. I've seen it happen once or twice, you know. Chloral hydrate is what some use. It sure knocks a man off his feet." Jones shook his head in mild wonderment. "Wonder who would do such an underhanded thing like that. Well, good evening."

"Deadeye!"

Jones turned back from the batwing doors. Kinsey was in the grip of a quivering rage, and his expression had turned murderous. "I never forget a man who goes crosswise with me. I get even. I always get even, and it don't matter how long it takes."

"I'm sure you do, Ro," Jones replied easily, and stepped out into the night.

# TWENTY-THREE

The trading post on Bordeaux Creek was a long log building set partway into a hillside. There was a smaller log storehouse nearby, also sunk halfway into the slope of a hill, an old buffalo robe press out back that appeared in need of repair, and a small vegetable patch. Goats and chickens wandered about freely, and a milk cow and a few head of beef stood inside a crude rail corral. Jones was able to buy the ponies he was looking for there, just as he had been told he might. The proprietor, however, said he did not have all twelve ponies on hand and would have to locate some of them among the people he traded with. Told him it would take nearly a week, Jones and Rose set up their small tipi nearby to wait.

The post did business mainly with the Sioux, and Rose felt right at home. Daily, people from many different clans came to trade deer, badger, and coyote skins for knives, cotton prints, chief's coats, clay pipes, tobacco, and a hundred other things. (They hardly ever brought in a buffalo robe anymore. Years earlier, when the post had been run by the American Fur Company, buffalo robes were the mainstay of the business.) Through these folks Rose got caught up on the news of the tribe; One Stab, she learned, had returned from the winter camp on the Belle Fourche and was already back at the Red Cloud Agency.

When the ponies were finally all collected, Jones drove them west along beautiful pine ridges to the White River, then south to the agency. Soldiers from nearby Camp Robinson stopped him to ask his business when he and Rose drew near. He told them, and reluctantly the young captain in command let him go on his way. Apparently the agency frowned on Indians' maintaining large horse herds. Probably, Jones decided, because the horses had to be fed, and the government was now footing the bill.

Jones turned the animals, rifles, ammunition, and blankets over to One Stab, and in doing so fulfilled his end of the bargain. Rose was now unquestionably *his* wife, and One Stab threw a feast in their honor.

Afterward, as Jones and Rose lay in each other's arms in their dark tipi, Jones was thinking about the talk he had heard earlier when suddenly Rose said, "Your brow is like the trace of a travois in soft ground, and your breathing like that of a man running a race."

He hadn't realized his thoughts were so apparent, but then, he should not have been surprised. His wife, he was learning, was most perceptive. "It is the war talk I hear the warriors making. Already there have been battles fought and men have died, both Indian and white. I am concerned over this, and I am worried about your safety, Rose. And I am also trying to determine my next step."

"Next step?"

"We can't stay here with your people the rest of our lives. I have to find a way to support us."

"You can hunt and I can prepare the skins. What else is there that we need?"

He looked over in the dark at her. "You know there is more than that. You saw how it is in the white world. We need money to make our way in it, and I'm afraid I would not be very content living the life of a trapper."

She lay silent for a few moments, then asked softly, "Is it the yellow rocks that you wish to seek, to take to the white bank and trade for the coins that buy the things the Lakota trade skins for?''

''I've thought about it, Rose, but that's not what I want either. Prospecting is not a dependable business. It is good for some quick money, but it never lasts. Now that I am a married man, I need to think more toward the future, and find something I can rely on to make a living at.''

''Then what is it you seek?''

He lay there, considering. There were many ways he could go, but one kept coming back to him. ''I've been thinking about buying a wagon and a team of oxen and going into the freighting business. There's lots of money to be made in it, what with all the folks moving west and the railroad lines so widely placed. It would be dependable, steady income, and I think I'd enjoy the work . . . at least for a while. After I get a good start maybe I'd buy a couple more wagons, hire on employees, and concentrate on the business end of it. That would be years down the road, of course. In the beginning it would be plenty of hard work, but I'm still young.''

''All this you say, I do not understand. Business? Employees?''

''I know, darling. It must sound awfully strange to you, but it is the way of the white man.''

''Then, my husband, it is the way you must go. And I will go with you.''

He pulled her closer and kissed her. She responded, having already learned to relish the pleasure derived from this custom. They made love again, and afterward, as they cuddled and he tottered on the verge of sleep, she leaned closer to his ear and whispered in it.

For a long, drowsy moment Jones just lay there, impending slumber deadening his reaction. Then all at once he put her words together and sat straight up.

''What did you say?''

She smiled contentedly and said, ''I am carrying your child, Nathan.''

He was stunned; joy, surprise, and apprehension all jostling together in his brain. He swept her into his arms, kissed her hard, and told her he loved her.

"A baby!"

"Are you pleased?"

"Yes, very. But are you certain?"

She nodded her head.

He hugged her again, and all of a sudden the idea of setting a course for their future became even more imperative. He was wide awake now, and stayed that way for the next several hours, forming his plans while Rose— no longer seeking the women's side of the tipi, as was the Lakota way—slept peacefully beside him.

Jones spent the next couple months camped near the Red Cloud Agency so that his wife could be with her people as the baby inside her grew and began to swell her belly. He discussed his plans with Carson Grove, who had moved his lodge and his new wife some miles away and had returned to the occupation that he knew best—trapping. Grove thought the freighting business had merit, but pointed out that there was the problem of finances. Jones had spent everything to pay off One Stab.

"I still have some gold put away," Grove offered one evening as they sat around the campfire in front of his lodge, smoking their pipes.

"I appreciate that, Mr. Grove, but I'd rather earn the money myself."

"I can understand that. A man's got to make his own way in the world. You got any plans on how you're gonna do it?"

"Yep. I know Rose might not approve, but I thought I'd go back to Dead Wood Gulch."

Grove nodded his head. "Sure enough there's still plenty of yellow in that crick. But it will take you several months to get up enough money for a stake in that freightin' business."

"I got time. The baby's still five or six months off. I figured I'd leave Rose here with her people while I returned to that cabin you built. I ought to be back by Christmas if the snow isn't too bad this year."

Grove nodded his head, thoughtfully pulling at his pipe. "When you gonna tell Rose?"

"I've been sort of putting it off, but I'll mention it tonight. Give her a day or two to think it over. I know she will agree, although she still has some pretty strong feelings about white men going into the *Paha Sapa*."

Grove didn't reply at once. When he did, there was a note of resignation in his husky voice. "They'll all have to get over that, I'm afraid. Ain't no way to keep white men out of a paying goldfield once they find one, and that's what them Black Hills is turning out to be."

Later that night Jones put the proposal to Rose. She listened to him without interrupting. When he had stated his case, she resumed her beadwork on the cradleboard she was making. "It is a sacred place, Nathan—the hunting grounds of the Great Spirit, and the resting place of my father."

"I know what the place means to your people, Rose, but the fact is, the Black Hills are already overrun with prospectors. This may be my last chance to work that stretch of creek before Dead Wood Gulch is discovered." He took her by the shoulders and turned her toward him. Slowly her face lifted until he was looking into large, dark, lovely eyes. "We must face the truth. The *Paha Sapa* will never be the same as it once was. The army can't keep the prospectors out. The Lakota will make war with them, but eventually they must lose. One day soon, the government will make a new treaty with the Lakota, and the Black Hills will be lost forever. It is not the way I want to see it happen, especially not now, now that I have become so close to your people . . . and you, my dear."

"What you say is true. The old ways are vanishing, just as the time of the buffalo has gone. I do not understand the ways of the white, even as you do not understand the ways of the Lakota, but I know it is important, this thing you must do." She gently touched his cheek. "Be careful, and come back quickly. A father ought to be near when his child is born."

"I will return as soon as I can. By Christmas; no later."

"Christmas?"

He smiled. "A white man's feast during the season of the winter count. It tells of the time when the Son of God came into our world."

"Then I will look forward to Christmas of the winter count, and your return, Nathan."

There was the nip of fall in the air as Jones stood by the brown rocks that seemed to hang from the very edge of the gulch. Carson Grove had appropriately named the place. Dead Wood Gulch was littered with the fallen trees of some bygone calamity. The destruction was clearly evident from this vantage point, from which he could see far up and down the gulch in both directions and into the branching ravine that ran back to his left. This ravine was by far the easiest route down into the gulch, and the one he and the others had taken that spring day when they had carried One Stab to Grove's cabin. Like so many other things in his life of late, that event, only a scant five months past, seemed like it had happened aeons ago.

The cabin appeared undisturbed when he arrived. Once again, a Grove prediction proved correct: No one had yet found the secluded place. Jones's crude sign that proclaimed his and Grove's ownership of the claim had fallen over. He set it right again and spent the rest of the day clearly marking the boundary of his claim. Next, he cut pine boughs to repair the roof, and for the following several mornings he worked on readying the cabin for the winter, while the afternoon hours were devoted to prospecting: working shovelfuls of dirt and gravel down to fine black sand and the precious yellow nuggets contained amongst it. He dug a pit down to bedrock, which was only a few feet beneath the surface, and here he found a layer of gravel rich in golden flecks.

Jones enjoyed the aloneness of this place where he could work undisturbed, yet he missed Rose, and wished she could have come along with him. His solitude was broken on the fourth day when a party of four prospectors making their way north from Custer Park arrived in the gulch. It seemed he had beat the first party into Deadwood Gulch by a matter of days!

Their names were Patterson, Blanchard, Verpont, and Albien. Jones was eager for any news on the activity down on French Creek. He heard again how the cavalry had removed everyone from Fort Defiance but how almost at once the miners had slipped back in.

"It's like trying to dam a river with a sieve," Blanchard told Jones. "The military can keep some of the gold hunters back, but others are constantly slipping past them."

"Small camps are springing up all through the hills," Patterson went on to explain, "some nearly qualifying as towns."

There was also the frightening news of Sioux attacks on small parties of prospectors. "There is real trouble brewing," Blanchard said, shaking his head. "It seems a rifle and revolver are more important than a pick and shovel these days."

Jones told them of his discovery, and that he called the place Dead Wood Gulch, and the creek from where it branched off by the same name. He hadn't had time to explore much past his own diggings, so he couldn't tell them what lay beyond, where the gulch branched.

The men spread out along the banks of the two creeks, turning over the ground, panning out the dirt, looking for claims of their own. Hardly had two days passed when another group of men came down the creek that joined with Dead Wood Creek. They had come into the Hills a few weeks before by way of Spruce Gulch and had been working their way down a valley they named Whitewood. The creek they were following was named after the valley. The leader of the party, Frank Bryant, showed Jones an old map that had been drawn by three employees of the American Fur Company way back in the 1830s. Jones noted their names: Tom LaBarge, Lephier Narcouter, and Charley DeGray. When he got back he would ask Grove if they had been friends of his.

There was lots of room in the gulch, and the men all took off in different directions, digging holes, felling trees, staking claims, and building cabins.

By the end of October, Jones had panned several thousand dollars from the rich ground. He noted wryly, as he sat in front of his cabin one evening filling a leather pouch with nuggets and flakes that the gulch was all of a sudden a very busy place. Almost a dozen cabins lined the banks of the two creeks, with wood smoke from their fires scenting the valley floor and rising to the ridgeline, where it hovered in the cold winter air.

Men streamed into the gulch almost daily now as word of its richness made its way beyond the steep cliffs to the prospectors south and north of them. Jones kept track of the days by the newcomers, and by the news they brought. As November drew to an end, he began making plans to return so that he'd be at Rose's side when their baby was born. But there was such explosive excitement here that he delayed a little longer, although he knew he had enough money to buy a wagon and oxen, and even to have some capital left over.

Nearly every inch of land along Whitewood and Dead Wood Creeks had been claimed, and he felt compelled to remain on his site to protect it from jumpers. None of the claims had been properly registered, and posted in a newspaper as required, mainly because there was no newspaper. But Jones felt certain that shortcoming was about to change. There were roads now cut on each side of the creeks, and tents, dugouts, and cabins everywhere. There was talk that a sawmill would soon be needed to keep up with the building. Jones decided to remain a few weeks longer. He knew the baby was still a month away, and the longer he stayed, the fatter his purse grew.

In December, the prospectors set up the Lost Mining District for the Whitewood and Deadwood Gulches' claims. A man named William Lardner was elected to be the recorder, and each man paid him two dollars to register his claim. This accomplished, Jones finally felt as if he could safely leave his strike for a few months. He told his neighbor to the south of him, an old-timer named Frank Roderus who had been to California in '49 and Colorado in '59, of his plans. Frank agreed to keep an eye on his place while Jones was gone.

It was a bleak, wintry day when Jones paused at the ridge to look back into Dead Wood Gulch. Again he marveled at how swiftly things in his life changed. The gulch had become a bustling mining camp, the dead wood cleared and burned and the new growth mostly cleared as well, chopped down for sluice boxes, cabins, and bridges. The silent, pristine wilderness that he, Grove, One Stab, and a young granddaughter named Morning Snow Woman once knew was gone forever, replaced with the noisy, clangy, machine-made world of the whites.

Jones drew in a long sigh. Both worlds appealed to him. He was torn. He didn't know how he felt about it, but he was pretty certain how Rose would feel when she learned what was happening.

A daughter came into the world on January 22 with ten toes, ten fingers, and a healthy pair of lungs. Jones declared that the year 1876 was going to be a good one. He wanted to name her Alice. Rose leaned more toward Lakota customs, and drawing a bit from her own name, called her Winter Flower. In the end, they settled upon Alice Flower Jones, and not surprisingly, little Alice looked just like her mother: dark hair, dark eyes, olive skin. Not much of Jones had made its way into Alice, although it was still too early to know for certain. He thought he saw the potential for his own strong chin and straight nose. But only time would tell. For now, he was happy as a lark, and strutted about the camp circle like a rooster.

He stayed close to the Red Cloud Agency the next couple months, but he was anxious to be back at his claim. Finally, in early March Jones told Rose it was time to leave. She disapproved of their returning to the Black Hills, but he insisted that he had to check up on his claim, and that if he was going to start a freighting business, there was no better place to do it than in the boomtown bursting to life along Deadwood and Whitewood Creeks. In the end, Rose agreed to accompany him, saying that her place was by her husband's side. She spent the next few days packing up their household and making the rounds to all her friends and relatives, showing off little Alice one last time.

Jones and Carson Grove smoked a pipe together the morning he was to leave.

"I'll probably be out this fall to see what's been going on in *my* gulch," Grove said as they strolled along one of the pine-covered bluffs above the White River and paused to peer down at the Red Cloud Agency in one direction and Camp Robinson in the other.

"I don't know if I will still be there come fall, Mr. Grove. Rose isn't happy with the idea. If she has her way about it, we'll end up in Sidney, or maybe even Cheyenne."

Grove gave a chuckle. "She's taken with city life, is she?"

"Oh, a little, maybe. But that will wear thin after not too long. We both like the quiet of the plains, and the majesty of the mountains, and that might be one reason she doesn't want to return to the Black Hills. They are no longer peaceful, and certainly not the way she remembers them."

"Wherever you end up, drop me a note or something so me an' my missus will know where to find you."

"I'll do that."

As they started back to camp, Grove said, "You still carrying around that nugget, Nate?"

Jones reached into his heavy wool shirt and brought out the beaded bag that Rose had given him. A frown moved across Grove's face. Jones said, "You still think it carries some sort of curse?"

"I got a bad feeling about that thar thing, Nate. It ain't worth holding on to, and if it was mine I'd bury it someplace. But I can't tell you what to do with it."

"I've had it for months now and nothing bad has happened."

"Fontenelle had it only seconds, One Stab's wife held on to it a couple years, her son and his wife a few more years than she. You might be lucky and get away with it a dozen years. Or maybe you won't last a dozen months. The fact, plain and simple, is that everyone who has gotten hold of that thing and kept it has ended up dead."

Jones grinned. "Anybody ever tell you you're a superstitious old codger?"

Grove huffed. "Maybe I am, but at least these old bones are still walking around on top of God's green earth, not buried beneath it."

# TWENTY-FOUR

Jones looked the valley over, hardly recognizing the place. He tried to remember the once green and empty vista they had named Custer Park—one of the most beautiful of all the places they had discovered on the expedition. He tried to visualize it as it had been, but could not.

The streets of Custer City were a bottleneck of freight wagons, miners' mules, and hundreds of people. Beyond the main street at least four hundred miners' shacks filled the valley in a patchwork of more or less straight roads. Rose's mouth was a hard, stern line as Jones led them into town and dismounted near a noisy, hurdy-gurdy saloon.

"I'm going to get some information on what is happening up north, Rose. You and Alice wait here." She and the baby were attracting attention, and Rose was uneasy remaining alone, but someone had to stay with their belongings, which were stowed on the travois.

She dismounted, clutched little Alice in her arms, and stood near the dog as Jones stepped into the saloon.

Folks inside were dancing, and drinking, and having a merry time. Jones stepped up to the bar and ordered a beer. When the barkeep brought it over, Jones asked,

"Have you had any trouble with the military lately?"

He was a tall, hard, elderly man, with graying red hair, a gold tooth, and tobacco on his breath. "Not no more. They've given up trying to run us out, mister. These hills are wide open now, with ground being snatched up faster than the recorder can write down the names and collect his two bucks."

"What's happening up north?"

The man narrowed an eye, and there was a smoldering anger there. "Don't waste your time. It's here in Custer City where you will make your strikes, mister."

"Maybe—if there was any land left to claim."

"True, claim selling has been going great guns, but you can still get yourself one if you move quick. Take my word, this is where all the action will be. Why, Custer City is gonna be the hub of commerce for these Black Hills."

"But what about up north?"

The barkeep hesitated, then went on reluctantly, "Oh, there's some talk of gold up that way, but that's all it is— just talk. Some men get crazy at the word of another strike, leave their claims behind, and take off hither and yon."

"Is that what's happening here? Folks leaving Custer City for the strikes farther north?"

The man expertly spat a stream of tobacco juice into a cuspidor six feet away. "They'll be back, you wait and see. Right now everyone thinks that place, this Dead Wood Gulch, is the next El Dorado." He paused, then went on quickly, "Oh, it ain't hurt my business none. Them damn fools just don't know a good thing when they see it. They'll be back," he repeated, and Jones had the impression the man said it more to reassure himself than to edify a customer.

Rose was relieved to see him. "These people, they look at me strangely. They frighten me."

"They're just curious. They're mostly from the East and not used to seeing an Indian up close, that's all. Take the horses and dog north of town and wait for me. I want to look around for someone with more reliable information than I got inside that saloon.''

He walked with Rose down the street until he spied the recorder's office and went inside.

''Name, location, and two dollars,'' the man said without looking up from his ledger book, in which he was busily scribbling entries.

''I'm not here to register a claim.''

He stared at Jones with surprise, as if no one ever came into his office with any other sort of business. ''Is that right, young man? Well, then, what is it I can do for you?''

''I was interested in some news of the strikes up north and was wondering if you knew how it's going.''

''Like Sherman's march to the sea. There is a rush into those hills that's impossible to stop and shows no signs of slowing down. In fact, if you're thinking of going up there, you better have deep pockets. I hear all the claims worth owning are already taken up. Some people have begun to sell off parts of their claims to the newcomers, but they ain't cheap. And there's a big business in residential real estate as well. Town lots are going fast, fetching from twenty-five to five hundred dollars each, I hear. Folks are calling the place Deadwood, and it's taking on the shape of a real town. Already there are four or five little towns springing up with it along Whitewood and Deadwood Creeks.''

Jones was itching to be on his way. His claim was already staked out, but if the place was booming up like this fellow said, he'd have to hurry to protect his interests. Before he left he had one more question to ask. ''Has there been much trouble with the Sioux?''

The claims recorder only shook his head, giving Jones a tight frown. ''They're out there, all right. Every day we get news of a lone prospector, or even small companies of men being attacked and wiped out. But we haven't been able to draw a bead on the savages. They just strike without warning, then melt back into the forests.'' He made a derisive snort. ''Hell, the army can't even keep *us* out of their territory, let alone find the savages. The army is as helpless as a hobbled horse. General Crook has been through trying to keep the miners out and the Indians peaceful, but he's had little luck. Told us to just hold tight and sooner or later the government was going to work out a new treaty. In the meantime, men get killed.''

He wagged his head again and sighed at the futility of the situation. ''Gonna be a war, you know. Indians are nearly starving on the reservations—those that remain there, that is. The young and strong are fleeing back to their old ranges by the hundreds, and they are making big war talk. Crazy Horse and Sitting Bull are bringing the tribes together.'' He glanced up sharply and gave a narrow stare. ''You keep your eyes open and your rifle handy if you intend to venture out into those hills alone. That's the best bit of advice I can give you.''

''Thanks, I'll remember that.''

Jones met Rose at the edge of town. ''What did you learn, Nathan?''

''Deadwood is growing faster than anyone could have imagined, and we'd better get back to our claim quick.'' Without further delay, they started north along a new, wide road.

The skies had clouded over, and a heavy, wet snow began to fall. Deadwood was about seventy miles to the north, and Jones and Rose made ten that day, camping at a stream named Spring Creek. The weather cleared some the next day and they pushed on north, reaching the town of Hill City. Jones estimated there were fifty or sixty crude houses built along the creek, but many appeared empty. When he inquired of a prospector there, he learned that most of the population had abandoned Hill City for the big strikes up at Deadwood. Jones had come this way only a year earlier, and at that time there was hardly a trace that men had even set foot in the place. Since then an entire town had sprung up, and now was dying. He could only shake his head in amazement and push on.

They passed caravans of miners, all heading north.

Jones learned that the wide trace they were following was now known as the Deadwood Road, and it was a mighty busy place. Most everyone they met was friendly, yet they all gave Rose a cautious look, as if she was a one-woman war party all by herself. Just the same, one glance at Jones and they never said a word against her. Jones had started out tall, but now, with years of outdoor living under his belt, he'd broadened out in his shoulders and chest, and hardened in his face. Once, while bending over a pool of water to drink, he caught a reflection and spun about, startled, only to grin at himself as he realized the fierce countenance that had stared back at him from the water had been his very own. At times like that he'd sharpen his razor and scrape his face clean. Rose preferred him that way, but it was such a bother.

They made Deadwood Gulch two days later. The road brought them into it from the west, and when the valley finally opened up before them, Jones stopped, hardly believing his eyes. The entire length of the gulch had been stripped of its timber and hundreds of shacks jostled shoulder to shoulder along Whitewood and Deadwood Creeks. More cabins and tents climbed up the steep sides of the gulch, where roads had been carved out of the rocky ground. The first buildings they came to was a place all to itself called Elizabethtown, and it was only the beginning of a mile-long parade of shacks in various stages of construction. Where Elizabethtown ended, another took up the march.

Jones hardly knew where to begin to look for his own claim. Rose stuck close to his side, her eyes wide and wary. "There are so many people," she said quietly.

He scanned the opposite side of the creek where his claim lay. Then he saw the brown rocks high up the steep wall—too steep for anyone to cut a road in or construct a cabin on. With these as his bearings, he found the little cabin Grove had built, crowded now among the many newer cabins nearby, and something else. . . .

Jones drew up and yanked the Winchester from his saddle scabbard.

"What is it, Nathan?" Rose asked, catching his excitement.

"Claim jumpers. You stay here with the animals."

Jones started for his claim. When he crossed over old man Roderus's land a man Jones had never seen before stopped him with a shotgun. "Get offa my claim."

"Where is Roderus?"

"Roderus sold out to me. This is my land and you're on it. Get off."

Jones nodded his head at the next claim over. "That's my land, and those three jumpers are on *it*."

The man raised the barrel of his shotgun. "You sure?"

"I've got the paper to prove it."

Jumping another man's claim was serious business— shooting business—and this fellow wanted nothing to do with the problem. "Go on," he said, and hastily retreated behind a log and canvas shack that he called home.

The three men were a hundred feet away, working a sluice box they had built in the creek. Jones started along the gravelly creek bank. One of the men noticed Jones when he was a dozen or so paces off. He nudged his nearest partner, a tall, thin fellow with wispy gray hair. The gray head came about and the man sprang for a rifle leaning against the sluice gate.

Jones threw his Winchester to his shoulder and fired, splintering the rifle stock at the wrist. The man leaped back, fanning his hand. Jones worked the lever and put the nearest fellow in his sights. "You men are on my claim."

The rifle shot had echoed up and down the gulch. Prospectors from five or six nearby claims stopped working and looked over while men perched atop half-finished buildings in the fledgling town of Deadwood momentarily ceased their hammering and craned their necks.

"Who the hell are you, mister? This here is our claim," a big-bellied, ruddy-faced man with wild red hair growled.

Tall Gray glanced at his hand and said, "You nearly blowed it off!"

"You're lucky I'm in a generous mood. Now grab up your gear and march out of here."

The third man stared at Jones from beneath hooded eyes. He was a hard, compact man with a barrel chest and short legs. Of the three, only he wore a revolver. Jones measured them up. This fellow was the one to watch.

"I'm not going to argue the point with you, boys," Jones went on, keeping his rifle steady. "You're on my claim and I've got the paper to prove it. Now, I'm giving you five minutes to clear out."

By now a crowd was gathering, but Jones dared not shift his attention. Red Face said, "We've been working this site for nearly two months. Ain't nobody ever said we couldn't."

"Frank Roderus was keeping an eye on it while I was away."

"Don't know no Frank Roderus," the man wearing the revolver said. "Don't know you neither. But there are plenty of men here in Deadwood who know us."

"You have four minutes," Jones replied firmly.

They were slowly moving apart, and suddenly it was impossible to watch all three any longer. Jones had to bring this confrontation to an end right now or risk losing what little control he had. Then Red Face leaped behind the sluice box, Tall Gray dove into the pit they had been mining material from, and as Jones swung toward them the stocky fellow grabbed for his revolver.

Jones's rifle boomed. The revolver had just cleared leather when the Winchester's bullet knocked the man off his feet and laid him out dead on the gravelly bar along the creek. With the ringing of the shot still in his ears, Jones swiveled toward the hole. Tall Gray was curled up at the bottom of it, arms over his head, and Red Face was still out of sight behind the sluice box. For a long moment no one moved, then a man from the crowd came forward, carrying a shotgun.

"Drop that rifle, mister," he ordered.

Jones turned slowly. He didn't know this man. All he could figure was that this fellow also had an interest in his claim. "Who are you?"

"The name is General Dawson, and you can drop that rifle now, mister."

Dawson was not overly tall, with blond hair, a long beard that came down to the middle of his vest, and a new Stetson set at a jaunty angle. He didn't look like a claim jumper, and there wasn't the appearance of ruthlessness in his pale eyes that Jones had seen in the fellow laying dead by the sluice box. Just the same, there was determination fixed upon the general's face, and with that scattergun not six feet from Jones's chest, he laid his rifle upon the ground.

"Who are you? The law?" That was not likely, considering that this new gold rush camp of Deadwood was only a few months old and lawmen usually didn't show up so soon.

Dawson gave a short laugh. "About the nearest thing there is to law here in Deadwood," he said. "I'm the federal revenue collector."

There was some muffled laughter among the men in the crowd. Jones couldn't help himself, and he roared too, in spite of the shotgun staring him down.

Dawson grinned. "You find that funny?" he asked.

"Only a little. I find it more hypocritical." Jones glanced around at the rash of buildings springing from the narrow valley floor that only a few months earlier had supported virgin wilderness. "But I am not surprised to find our government Johnny-on-the-spot to collect its taxes, even though every one of us is here illegally. The government, who tells the Indians it's trying to shag us out, is the same government collecting taxes from this illegal town."

Dawson's grin widened. "It does make one wonder, doesn't it. Now, since I'm about the nearest thing there is to law in this *illegal* town, suppose you tell me why you killed that man."

"He drew down on me—and there are plenty of witnesses to back up my story."

"Yeah," someone called, "but it was you who brought the trouble to their claim."

Tall Gray and Red Face had emerged from cover. Red Face glowered like a lump of burning coal and said, "That's right. He come in here waving that rifle and saying we was jumping his claim."

"Is that true?" Dawson asked.

"It is."

"You say this is your claim?"

"It is, and I can prove it."

Just then William Lardner, the recorder, appeared, and he said, "Good to see you again, Mr. Jones."

"Lardner!" Jones said with relief. "Dawson, here's the man who can verify my story."

"Well?" Dawson drawled, shifting his view to the recorder.

"Mr. Jones was one of the first men to register a claim with me, General. In fact, he was one of the first men to find gold in Deadwood Gulch. He was here before I arrived."

Dawson said to Jones, "And this claim is the one you've registered?"

Jones took the water-stained paper in his hunting bag and passed it over to Dawson.

"Well, I reckon that settles it." He looked at Red Face and Tall Gray. "Looks like you boys were working another man's claim all along."

"There weren't nobody around when we got here," Tall Gray complained.

Dawson said, "I suggest the next time check with the recorder before you begin to work a piece of ground, Mr. Swenson. You and Mr. Blakely better get your tools together and find yourself another spot."

"Ain't no other spots left," Red Face, the one Dawson called Blakely, growled. "They're all taken up. Only thing left for us is to work for another man."

"That's *your* problem, Mr. Blakely," Dawson said with the icy compassion typical of government revenuers.

The crowd lost interest once the problem had been settled. Rose came through the crowd, clutching little Alice, and stood near Jones. Dawson tipped his hat.

"Ma'am," he said, then to Jones, "Your wife?"

He nodded. "My wife and child."

"Sioux?"

"Lakota," Jones corrected.

Dawson appeared a bit confused that a distinction existed, but he smiled handsomely at her and said, "Pleased to meet you, ma'am."

Blakely and Swenson gathered up their tools and said, "What about Canfield?"

"You can come back for him. Bury him up Whitewood Gulch with the others." Dawson frowned. "Getting to be quite a crowd up there."

Blakely glared at Jones, then at Rose and the baby. "You ain't heard the last of this, mister. You, your squaw, and your half-breed kid better stay out of my way."

"We don't need any of your threats, Mr. Blakely," Dawson admonished.

Rose spent the rest of the day diligently cleaning the cabin, which Swenson and Blakely had left in total disarray after tearing through it while collecting their gear. That night, with a blaze going in the fire pit, their blankets spread across the rope bed, and a buffalo skin on the dirt floor where Alice lay, cooing and grinning toothlessly as Rose shook a rattle near her nose, Jones took his battered journal from the saddlebags, unwrapped its protective oil-skin covering, and opened it up on the crude table.

"You know, Rose, I haven't hardly looked at this for almost a year."

She knew the journal existed, of course, but Jones had never told her much about it, or what it contained. "It's where I keep my thoughts and record important events," he said when she inquired.

"Ah," she said with apparent understanding. "It is your winter count."

He grinned. "You might call it that."

"Are you going to make the talking marks in it tonight?"

He ran a hand over the leather cover. "I suppose I

ought to bring it up to date,'' he said wistfully, ''but so much has happened I hardly know where to begin.'' What he meant to say was that somehow he had lost interest in keeping it up. But he felt he had begun something important, and that it should be continued. ''Yes,'' he said, ''I shall work on it tonight.''

Two hours later, with Alice sleeping peacefully, Rose looked over his shoulder. ''You have done much work, Nathan.''

''Yes, but I have much left to do.''

''That is good,'' she said.

He gave her a wry grin. ''Oh, how so?''

''A man with work to do is a contented man. A man who sits all day with his hands folded, and goes to bed early, is a man whose family goes hungry.''

Jones laughed. ''Is that a bit of Lakota wisdom?''

She smiled prettily. ''It is a saying among the women.''

''Well, sounds like a wise proverb to me.''

Her smile faded, replaced with a look of concern. ''We are back here now, my husband. Are you going to take the yellow rocks from the ground?''

''You don't want me to prospect anymore, do you?''

''You must do what you must, if we are to live in your world. But this digging in the ground, this struggle with other men who wish to take the yellow rock away from you, this I do not understand. It makes me . . . uneasy.''

''Well, if it makes you feel any better, it makes me uneasy too. Shall I sell the claim?''

''Then you would buy the wagon, and the cattle to pull it?''

''Yes. But we would remain here in Deadwood for a while. This place is sprouting like prairie flowers after a spring rain, and here is the place to build our business—at least until the people run off after the next big strike and the town goes bust. It happens all the time, and I've no doubt that ten years from now no one will even remember that a boomtown named Deadwood ever existed!''

# TWENTY-FIVE

Jones's claim, which stretched from rimrock to rimrock, was cut up by three streets: Sherman Street, Main Street, and far up the north side of the gulch, Williams Street. And it was hemmed in by Gold Street and Wall Street on his east and west side. As Jones strolled through the burgeoning town site the next day, it became apparent that those early claims, of which his was one, were not only being worked for the gold they might hold, but were being sold off in huge chunks to men interested in a different sort of gold—the kind that comes from the engines of commerce and the ring of a cash drawer!

Word spread that Jones had rescued his claim from the three jumpers, who had been reluctant to part with even one square foot of their good fortune. Now, suddenly, men whose eyes burned with visions of the future were descending upon him like locusts. What Jones thought would be a simple job of advertising his claim and snagging a prospective buyer was turning into a juggling act just trying to keep the offers to buy business lots from burying him. By the end of the day he'd sold lots to men named Ayres, Wardman, and Bullock, and he had a dozen other offers to consider. And he still held control over a large hunk of gold-rich property!

"Selling off has turned out to be more complicated than I ever imagined," he told Rose later that day after they had eaten their supper.

"What will you do?" she asked him as little Alice suckled in her arms.

"Go out and sell some more lots, I suppose," he replied, gazing at the bag of gold coins that he'd brought home with him. The sack reminded him of the little bag he wore around his neck, the *Tukan*, that Rose had given him. He laughed and felt in his shirt for it. "Mr. Grove tried to tell me this would bring us bad luck. Well, if this is bad look, my dear, then bring on more!"

Rose didn't laugh. "Carson Grove said that? Why should he say such a thing?"

"I don't know. Superstition, I suspect. He said that everyone who ever owned it has died. I say it's just coincidence."

Whatever she might have thought of that she kept to herself, but her dark eyes grew distant with some thought that had overtaken her and ruined her mood. Jones thought it must have been the mention of the death of her mother and father that had silenced her.

"I'm sorry, Rose." He shoved the bag back inside his shirt. "I didn't mean to upset you."

She looked down at Alice, rocked the child gently, and began to sing a soft song that reminded him of a chant he'd once heard among some Lakota women the day a hunter had been carried into the camp circle after a bear mauling. It unnerved him, and he went outside to smoke a pipe of tobacco and watch the evening shadows lengthen up the side of Deadwood Gulch.

As the days passed, more and more freight wagons arrived in Deadwood, carrying everything imaginable, from kegs of whiskey to bolts of canvas and barrels of nails. But the most curious cargo to arrive were the wagonloads of girls. Frail sisters, some called them. Others, who were not of a mind to mince words, just called them whores. Whatever their title, they were swarming into town almost as fast as the men whose gold they were after. They took up residence in crude shacks west of Deadwood and east of Elizabethtown in a section that soon was known only as the "badlands."

Saloons seemed to take to the Deadwood soil better than any other businesses, for they sprung up the fastest and became the most numerous. Next in line were the theaters, and in some cases only a fine line separated the two. The Langrishe Theater was by far the finest, presenting legitimate drama. From there it was all downhill: hurdy-gurdies, dance halls, burlesque houses, and simple saloons with a stage in one corner where young ladies demonstrated many ingenious and tantalizing ways of wiggling out of their dresses.

Jones sold off most of his holdings, but when it came to the actual claim site, and the cabin Carson Grove had built, he balked. He told Rose that they were worth more than speculators were willing to pay, and besides, they needed a place to live until he could have a house built for them. In truth, the gold bug still had its claws dug deep into his hide, and he couldn't bear parting with the claim.

Of all that he earned, he was careful to put half of every dollar in a steel box; Jones considered half of the claim Carson Grove's, and he intended for the old man to get his full share. He retained a single lot up on Williams Street, above the Black Hills Pioneer News building, where he intended to build Rose and himself a house someday.

Deadwood was booming. It had acquired city officials, who were scouting around for a man to appoint as sheriff. The Indian trouble became a plague of biblical proportions and soon bounties were being issued for Indians— dead or alive. Rose stayed glued to Jones's side whenever they were on the streets, and never ventured out alone. She had taken to wearing cotton dresses, fashionable sunbonnets, and leather shoes . . . in spite of how they pinched her feet. But beneath all these trappings of the white world, there was no hiding the Sioux blood that coursed through her veins.

Jones purchased a freight wagon and a team of oxen and immediately went scouting out business. It wasn't long before he had steady work, hauling freight up from Custer City.

A few weeks later, Ro Kinsey stepped out the front door of Nuttall and Mann's Saloon No. 10 and leaned against the wall and put a match to the new cigar he'd just bought. It looked like rain again. It had been raining almost constantly for the last week and both Whitewood and Deadwood Creek were a roiling torrent of water.

Rainy weather depressed Ro Kinsey. He blew a cloud of smoke up at the cloudy spring sky. Before him lay the muddy track of Main Street, with its constant clattering parade of ox teams and horses. The crack of a bullwhacker's whip and the cusses aimed at one of the animals were as much a part of these hills now as the soft murmur of the wind and the shriek of the hawk had once been.

Across the street stood a row of half-built clapboard, log, and canvas structures, and behind them the angry Whitewood Creek, its banks lined with tents and crude cabins. A couple doors down to his left an army of carpenters were crawling over the frame skeleton of the Belle Union Theater, busily sawing wood and driving nails. Not far beyond that was the cluster of flimsy ''cribs''—prostitutes' quarters—of the badlands. The girls there were doing a thriving business, one that made the freighting business pale—or blush, it might be said—in comparison. In any event, Ro Kinsey couldn't help but envy all the money being made on that end of town. He wondered if it might not be time to get out of the freighting business and into something else. He eyed a new saloon being built down the street.

The road ran east, past Elizabethtown, heading out of Dead Wood Gulch toward Crook City. He watched the traffic rumbling past for a few minutes, only mildly interested in it. Bradley Sink stepped out of the saloon, filled the air with the stink of a beer belch, and suddenly gave Kinsey a sharp nudge in the ribs. "Look there, Ro."

Kinsey had just spied the shapely figure of one of the badlands girls, and he was in the middle of stripping her naked in his imagination when Sink's elbow interrupted him. "What?" he barked, irritated.

Sink pointed at a freighter just passing by. "Look who's taken to bullwhacking."

"Jones!" Kinsey hissed.

"And his squaw."

Ro had not forgotten how Jones had weaseled into his carefully planned card game back in Sidney, or how he'd managed to conveniently put Sink out of the picture. He'd not forgotten the money lost, nor the humiliation.

"Reckon he's taken to living in these parts?" Sink asked.

"I don't know, but I intend to find out." Just then a gray-haired man passing by on the boardwalk said, "There's that bastard Jones."

"The sonuvabitch!" his red-faced partner said.

"You know that man?" Kinsey asked.

"*Know* him?" the red-faced man growled. "He run us off our claim. Says it was his. We put months of back-breaking work into it, but he had a paper. A lousy paper is all. Now we got nothing but day wages at another man's diggings."

"He lives here in Deadwood, you say?"

"Him and that Sioux squaw and their half-breed kid."

"A kid too?" Ro found himself grinning. "By the way, my name is Kinsey, Ro Kinsey. This is my partner, Brad Sink."

"Jim Blakely. And my friend, Swenson."

"Well, Mr. Blakely, Mr. Swenson, I'd like to hear more about this fellow who ran you off your claim. It just so happens he cheated me too, back in Sidney."

"He did?" Blakely's face turned several shades of deeper crimson. "The sonuvabitch!"

"And he doctored my whiskey and left me nearly dead," Sink put in.

Kinsey pursed his lips thoughtfully. "You know, maybe it's time Mr. Jones starts getting back a little of what he deals out. Come on, boys, let me buy you a drink so as we can discuss this matter a little more." Kinsey herded them all back inside the saloon.

Later, with the low afternoon sun hidden behind black storm clouds and a steady rain turning the already muddy streets into wheel-sucking bogs, Kinsey, Sink, Swenson, and Blakely scuttled up Main Street to the corner of Main and Gold and ducked under a porch. Their dripping hat brims drooped and their clothes were drenched and sticking to their skin.

"There," Swenson said, pointing a long finger toward the steep canyon wall across the gulch. "On the other side of the creek. That cabin used to be our place."

Kinsey peered at the dim shape of the cabin through the slanting rain. Darkness had settled into the gulch with the gathering of the storm. All that he could make out was the light showing through the single window and the familiar outline of a freight wagon parked alongside it. There appeared to be a crude corral built against the standing side of the gulch that climbed toward a pile of brown rocks a little to the right. Kinsey peered hard through the rain. Inside the rails of the corral stood a dozen or so oxen, their heads down, their rear ends turned toward the driving rain.

"He's got himself a nice herd, don't he?" Kinsey said. "Must have cost him a bundle. Be a shame if they spooked or something; you know how cattle can get in weather like this." He looked at the storm-darkened sky. There was a flash inside the clouds, and a moment later a low rumble rolled up the gulch. Along with the rain, a cold fog clung to the rim of the gulch and spilled gray, wispy tendrils over the edges in places. "Tonight, when it is good and dark, I say we pay Mr. Jones a visit."

•   •   •

"Ah-goo, goo, goo. Ah-goo, goo, goo. Ah-goo, goo, goo."

A giggle!

Jones laughed where he lay upon the blankets spread over the rope bed. An arm's length above his head two pudgy legs and two pudgy arms flailed the air as if by their very own effort they were keeping their owner afloat.

"Did you hear her, Rose? She giggled."

Rose was working on her mending in the light from a single oil lamp and the occasional flash of lightning through the window. She glanced over and watched Jones suspending their daughter straight overhead, his big hands completely engulfing the infant's chest. "She thinks her father is acting silly."

Beneath the table, the dog yawned and watched the antics a moment before laying its big head back upon its paws.

"Ah-goo, goo, goo," Jones resumed. Alice giggled, then drooled all over him. Rose laughed. The dog hitched a disinterested eye in his direction. Jones sat up and placed the child on a buffalo skin rug and sleeved the drool from his forehead.

"You're lucky it did not come from the other end," Rose teased.

"Alice wouldn't do that to me. I'm her father!"

"She has done it to me."

Jones leaned over and confronted his daughter with a stern face. "Would you pee on your father?"

As if she had understood, Alice Flower Jones grinned at him and giggled.

"A father gets no respect." He stood and crossed across the little room, then pulled back a chair and sat across from Rose. "She's a smart kid."

"It must be the Lakota blood in her," Rose observed, holding back a smile as she busily worked at mending a pair of his trousers. She was quite handy with the white's way of sewing.

"Must be," he agreed. "No doubt she got her good looks from you as well, my dear."

Rose only smiled. After a few moments of quiet contemplation, she said, "Why have you not sold this ground, as you told me you would?"

That caught him off guard. He stammered, then said, "Well, no one wants to pay my price."

"Do you not have much gold from the land you already sold?"

"Well . . . yes."

"Then why must you get so much more for this last piece?"

"Well . . . it's just the way the whites do business. You try to make as much money as you can. Some call it horse trading."

Rose glanced up from her work and looked at him curiously. "We have only one horse. You will trade it?"

"No, of course not. It's simply an expression, that's all. Besides, if I sold this place now, where would we live?"

"We have the piece of land on Williams Street where you are having our house made. Could we not put up a lodge there until the house is made?"

Jones gave a short laugh. "You know all the trouble there's been between the Lakota and the whites: the raids on prospectors, the price that's been placed on the Indians—" He saw her wince, and didn't complete the thought. "For us to put up a tipi in town would be like raising a lightning rod on a stormy night like this."

"Lightning rod?"

"Er . . . it's an iron pole that men place on top of their houses."

She looked at him blankly. "It keeps the lightning from striking them?"

She didn't quite understand the comparison he was making. There was still so much of the white man's world to teach her. He was about to go into greater detail, hoping it would divert the conversation from his reluctance to sell the last portion of his claim, when all at once the dog turned its head toward the closed door and gave a low rumble deep in its throat.

Jones and Rose exchanged glances. The dog was on its feet now, teeth bared, ears flattened. Jones listened, but all he could hear was the storm raging outside.

"What is it, boy?"

Just then there was a rapid knock upon the door.

"Wonder who that is in this weather." Jones opened the door and saw the figure of a stoutly built man, enshrouded in a black, dripping mackintosh.

"General Dawson! What in heaven's name are you doing out on a night like this?" Jones stepped back to let the man inside. The dog sniffed at Dawson's soaked and muddied pant leg, then went back to Rose's side.

"Evening, Mr. Jones, Mrs. Jones," Dawson said, wringing the water from his beard as Jones closed the door behind him. He glanced at Alice and grinned. "The baby sure is growing. Won't be long before she's walking."

"That's when our work will start." Jones laughed.

"I've a niece back East named Estelline. She's a few years older than Alice there, but she wasn't much bigger than that the last time I saw her. She's becoming quite the young lady—or so I hear from the letters my sister sends."

"Some coffee? We've got some hot."

"Sure, if it's no bother."

Rose put her mending away and set out two cups. The men took the table and she moved her work to the bed and laid Alice beside her.

"Thank you." Dawson sipped the strong coffee with relish. "Devil of a storm, isn't it."

"I've been keeping my eye on the creek."

"It's on the rise. I suspect that creek might cause us real trouble if we get many more of these gully-washers."

For a tax collector, Dawson was a likable man who had many friends in town. Jones had enjoyed the few conversations he'd had with the ex-general, who'd earned his rank during the War of the Rebellion. Dawson was intelligent and well educated, but could talk to a man on any level without sounding highfalutin.

Dawson noticed the exquisitely beaded pouch that Jones was wearing about his neck, and inquired as to its content.

"The Lakota call it a *Tukan*. It's sort of a personal icon that is supposed to bring good luck." Jones took the horseshoe-shaped nugget from the little bag and showed it to Dawson.

"I don't think I've ever seen a gold nugget shaped quite like that. Did Rose find it?"

"As a matter of fact, it was found right here at Dead Wood Gulch many years ago, by a trapper named Pierre Fontenelle. Rose's grandfather got it from Fontenelle." What with all the Indian problems the hills had been experiencing, Jones thought it wise not to go into the details of *how* One Stab had acquired the nugget from Fontenelle. "It's been handed down, you see."

"Interesting" was all Dawson said, returning the nugget to Jones.

Jones put it away. "So, what brings you by, General Dawson?"

"A lack of common sense, I should think." He laughed, then said more soberly, "Actually, I was visiting with Homer Colebanes, who, as you know, holds the claim a short ways up the creek from yours."

"I know Colebanes."

"I'm getting together a list of men who'd be willing to help out if the town should need them. You might call it a reserve of deputies. I've been all up and down this gulch today, and have of list of five men who'd be willing to help out. I could of had a lot more, but I'm being selective. Only want good, fair-minded men, you see. Colebanes said he would help out, and suggested I stop by and ask you, Mr. Jones. He thought you might be interested in seeing law and order upheld in this boomtown."

Dawson glanced at Rose, and Jones knew what exactly he was driving at. "I'd like to help out, General, but with my new freighting business just getting started, I'm spending a lot of time out of town."

"I understand that. Putting your name on the list will

in no way encumber you, Mr. Jones. I don't suspect we'll ever find ourselves in a situation where we will need to call up all our reserve deputies at the same time.''

''I'll give it some thought, General. You don't need an answer tonight, do you?''

''No, of course not. I'll just—''

Suddenly the dog was back on its feet, face turned toward the back wall of the cabin, lips curled back in that ferocious snarl. The low, warning growl had returned.

''What is it?'' Dawson asked.

''He must have heard something outside.''

''I'm surprised he can hear anything with this storm raging.''

''He heard you just before you knocked.''

A bolt of lightning flashed and the cabin momentarily filled with sharp shadows . . . and something else. The crack of a revolver sharp report so perfectly blended with the crash of thunder that it would have been missed completely if the men hadn't already been made wary by the dog.

''That sounded like a gunshot,'' Dawson said.

Jones dove for the door. Driving rain obscured everything beyond fifty feet in any direction. The creek was a roiling torrent, the sky a black, boiling cauldron. Jones heard a second shot behind him. Wheeling around, he stared into the darkness at the canyon wall a few hundred feet away. The ground beneath his feet began to tremble.

Dawson was suddenly at his side, shouting above the wind. ''That was definitely a shot!''

''It came from out back, by the corral,'' Jones yelled.

''What's that sound?'' Dawson asked.

''I'm not sure. . . .''

Another shot boomed in the night, and for an instant a streak of orange flame stabbed into the rain-swept blackness.

''Over there!'' Dawson said, pointing.

The low tremble beneath their feet had swelled to a rumble. Frantically, Jones searched his brain for the meaning of it.

Dawson yanked his Colt from under the raincoat and ran outside in the direction of the shot. Jones followed.

Suddenly he had it. "Wait!" he yelled, grabbing Dawson's sleeve. At that moment a bolt of lightning sent shadows ricocheting across the gulch, and in that jagged, blinding instant, Jones knew that he had been right. Dawson saw it too, and stopped dead in his tracks.

Jones leaped aside, dragging the general with him against the side of the cabin as the entire herd of oxen that had been penned up in the corral came stampeding past them, pinning them to the wall.

It was at that very moment that Rose happened to step outside.

# TWENTY-SIX

Jones stared in helpless horror as the thundering herd swept Rose away into the storm, taking their blind terror down along the creek, trampling tents, people, and anything else that got in their way.

"Rose!" Jones cried, charging out into the night, with Dawson leaping out in the other direction. As Jones searched the ground for his wife, he was vaguely aware of the general's revolver barking in the distance. He staggered blindly across the pools of mud, cold rain streaming down his face, calling her name and fighting down the mad panic that reached an iron fist into his throat.

And then, in a flash of lightning, he spied the crumpled pile of white cotton.

"Rose!" he cried again, dropping to his knees and side, gathering her up out of the mud, small and limp in his arms. Dawson was at his side, his revolver still in hand.

"There were at least three of them," he said. "I think I winged one of them." Dawson pushed the cabin door open for Jones, then closed the storm out behind him and took little Alice up in his arms as Jones placed Rose on the bed.

"How is she?"

"I . . . I don't know." He wiped the mud and blood from her face, saw the gash a hoof had made, then felt her pulse. "I just don't know."

Dawson lifted her eyelid and studied her eye a moment. "Dilated pupil. I've seen plenty of this in the war. She's in shock, maybe even a concussion to the brain. She's got a broken leg too—that's plain enough—and who knows what else."

"What can I do?" Jones said, fighting the panic. He felt helpless. This was not something he had ever had to deal with before.

Dawson however, had had some experience in these matters. "Bundle her in a blanket, build up a fire, and try to stop the bleeding. It's only a shallow face wound, and those kinds always bleed pretty fierce, but they're usually not as bad as they look. It's the injuries that we can't see that worry me. You keep her warm. I know a prospector who was a surgeon during the war. I'll go find him and bring him here."

"Hurry," Jones said, taking little Alice from him.

"I'll be back as soon as I can," Dawson said, plunging out into the storm.

"Stop fidgeting or I'm gonna hurt you more!" Swenson declared angrily.

"Here, bite on this," Blakely said, shoving the handle of a butcher knife between Kinsey's teeth.

"Hold him down again," Swenson said. With a quick glance at Sink, standing near the tent-flap, he added, "And I can use some help from you as well, Mr. Sink."

"What you want me to do?"

"Keep your partner from squirming, else I'm liable to run these tweezers clean through his bacon."

Kinsey spit out the knife. "Just get it over with."

"Hold him tight." Swenson stuck the tweezers into the open wound and fished around until he touched the bullet. Kinsey groaned, rocking his head on the ground, where they had him stretched out. The rain pelted the canvas tent and dripped in on them from a dozen different places. The ground was more mud than dirt, and the coal oil lamp flickered and smoked so badly, Swenson could hardly see what he was doing.

"I think I found it."

"Just get it done with, dammit!" Kinsey moaned, his face glistening from the sweat pouring off it.

"Oops, almost had it."

"Oh, shit, get it over with."

"Hold still. You made me lose it," Swenson snapped, then perched himself on Kinsey's squirming legs and tried again.

Swenson stuck the tool deeper into Kinsey's side. Kinsey howled and cussed and thrashed like a man possessed of a demon, then fell back exhausted.

Swenson held the lead ball up to the feeble light. "Thirty-six caliber, I'd judge it."

Blakely and Sink let go of Kinsey. He lay there heaving great gulps of air. Swenson poured some whiskey into the wound. Kinsey roared out again at the new pain and snatched the bottle away from him.

"You hurt me enough for one night. This whiskey will do me more good inside my belly than inside that bullet hole."

"Never claimed to be a doctor, Kinsey. If you didn't catch that slug in the first place, I wouldn't of had to dig it outta your hide. Remind me next time not to go along with any more of your lame plans. We could have all gotten ourselves killed."

"I didn't hear no complaints when I come up with it. Besides, you had your own grudge against Jones, just like we did." Kinsey took a long pull at the bottle and lay back down.

"Sure we did. Only no one never figured he'd hear us, let alone start shooting."

"What did you expect him to do?" Blakely growled. "Slap us on the backs and tell us what a good job we done driving off his animals?"

Swenson frowned. "I reckon we had it coming."

"Coming?" Kinsey roared. "Hell, Jones is the one what had it coming. Up until now I've just been teasing him. But now that he went and put a slug in me, it changes everything. Jones is gonna pay. He's gonna pay real good."

"What you got in mind?" Sink asked eagerly.

"Don't know yet, but it looks like until I'm healed over, I'm gonna have me some time on my hands to figure out something appropriate." His glance shifted from Blakely to Swenson. "You in with me?"

Swenson wasn't sure, but Blakely spoke up at once. "Count me in, Kinsey. I figure I still got a score to settle on account of him running us off our claim."

Kinsey's narrow glare came back and settled upon Swenson. "Well?"

He grimaced. "When you get your plan worked out, I'll let you know if I'm in or out."

"Fair enough. Now, slap a bandage on that hole. It burns like hell, and I've got some serious drinking ahead of me if I intend to ever quench them flames."

Willard Darnell had been a surgeon with the 114th Pennsylvania Zouaves, but after the war's end, prospecting for gold had infected him with a vengeance, and he'd been on the edge of financial disaster ever since. Too late for either the California or Colorado gold rushes, Darnell had jumped at a chance to strike it rich in the Black Hills. But like so many gold seekers before him, all he found was barren ground. His hopes dashed, Darnell took to regular counseling with a whiskey bottle, and that was all that kept him going.

General Dawson located Darnell in a saloon on Main Street, half drunk after one of his many sessions. A walk in the rain sobered him up some, and when they got to Jones's cabin, a half a pot of coffee brought him up to where he understood the nature of the emergency. By this time the night was nearly spent and half the town knew what had happened. Men were already out rounding up the scattered oxen to prevent any more damage.

Once apprised of the situation, Darnell called on long-unused skills and did a decent job of setting Rose's broken leg with the limited resources he had available to him. He stitched the gash on her face and verified that nothing else was broken, although he had no way of knowing what damage she might have suffered internally. She appeared strong, with only the broken leg and a mild concussion to show for the ordeal. By the time dawn arrived, Rose was resting comfortably and alert.

"You know, if this had been eleven or twelve years ago, I'd have probably amputated that leg, young lady," Darnell told her. "Lucky for you you weren't in my regiment." He chuckled.

General Dawson yawned and said he thought it was time to get on home. Little Alice was fussing. She was hungry, and Jones carefully laid the infant in Rose's arms.

"I think we ought to be leaving now," Dawson told Darnell.

"Oh, yes, of course." Darnell smiled past his gray, wiry beard, and his blue eyes seemed to sparkle when he added, "I'll be around later to see how you're doing, Mrs. Jones."

The rain had stopped falling sometime during the night. A chill damp was in the air and the gulch was still in deep shadows, while the trees along its rim gleamed a deep pine green in the bright light of the morning sun. The creek nearby boiled angrily with the added water it was receiving from the surrounding hills, its roar nearly drowning out the chirp of a nearby bird and the rat-a-tat of a woodpecker that drifted down through the dripping forests. Outside, Jones took both their hands and gave them a heartfelt shake. "I can't tell you how much I appreciate what you have done for us."

"A young lass like that will pull through just fine," Darnell assured Jones. "Her bone will knit up quickly and she'll be up and about in a few weeks. You wait and see."

General Dawson said, "See you around, Jones. If you need anything, don't hesitate to ask."

"Thanks, General."

As the two men started toward town in the gray light of morning, Jones said suddenly, "General Dawson!"

Dawson turned back.

"If you get word on who did this to us, I'd appreciate your letting me know."

"I will, Mr. Jones."

"Oh, I almost forgot. You can put my name down on that list of yours."

Dawson grinned. "I'll do that. Good-bye, Mr. Jones."

Jones went back inside the cabin and pulled a chair close to the bed. "Darnell says you will be up and around in a few weeks, Rose."

"He is a doctor?"

"He was during the war. He seemed to know what to do."

She touched the bandage that covered half her face. "He used the white man medicine?"

"It's the only kind he knows. As far as your face goes, it was grain alcohol and stitches . . . like Mr. Grove fixed One Stab." He looked at her leg, bound up tight between two wooden splints. "Now you and Mr. Grove can compare broken legs. He had one, you know. It happened on the expedition just before General Custer discovered your people."

"Why should I wish to do such a thing?" she asked, confused.

Jones laughed, partly from her innocence of the white world and its odd expressions, and partly out of sheer relief that she was going to be all right. Alice began to fuss. Jones took her from Rose, patted her back until she burped, then laid her back in his wife's arms. "I'm going out and see how many of our animals I can round up. A few were brought in last night by some men down the gulch, but over half of them are still missing."

Jones spent the morning searching the gulch for his oxen. Some men offered to help, but others ran him off their claims and told him to pack up his Indian wife and half-breed kid and leave Deadwood. Jones found the oxen grazing as far as two miles down the creek. Others he discovered at the bottom of prospectors' pits that pock-marked the landscape; one had a broken neck and was already dead. Two had broken legs and had to be shot. Of the fourteen head that had been corralled behind his cabin the night before, he recovered eight.

Jones drove them back to the corral, then surveyed the enclosure to make sure it was secure. Whoever had done this to him had simply slipped the rails out of their posts. Jones went around it with a hammer and nails and made certain the corral would not be so easily disassembled if another attempt should be made. Then he noted something on the ground and began lifting stones away. Just beneath them was a broad red stain, as if blood had been washed there by the rain. Dawson had hit one of them after all.

Jones noticed a man crossing the footbridge over the roiling Whitewood Creek and coming up the slope toward him. He was tall, well built, wearing a dark coat, and carrying a basket. His head was hatless, and his long face wore an even longer beard and mustache, with no side whiskers. As he drew nearer, Jones judged him to be in his late forties to early fifties. The black beard was streaked with gray, and in spite of the friendly smile, there was an intense burning in the man's gray eyes.

Jones met him near the cabin. "Can I help you?" he asked, wary of any strangers after the night's calamity.

"You are Mr. Nathaniel Jones?"

"I am."

The man stuck out a big, hard hand and gave him a warm shake. "I heard of your misfortune last night, sir, and I thought I'd stop in and see if I can be of help. I've brought you and your wife a basket of warm food."

"I appreciate that, sir. But I don't believe I know you."

"I just arrived from Kentucky the other day with Captain Gardner's freight train. I've got a job working on the Boulder Ditch. My name is Henry Smith. Reverend Henry Smith."

"A preacher? Well, I reckon Deadwood attracts all sorts of folks."

Preacher Smith smiled. "I've come not to mine gold, sir; I've come to mine for men's souls."

Jones nodded his head. "A place like Deadwood is in short supply of sky pilots, Reverend Smith. You should have no trouble making your strike here. Won't you come in?"

"Only for a few minutes. I need to get to my new job."

Jones glanced at the sky. "It looks like it's going to be another day like yesterday, Preacher Smith. I don't suspect there will be much work done on that ditch today."

Smith grinned. "Why, I do some of my best work on days like this, huddled inside a tentful of lost souls, waiting for the weather to clear. Nothing like having an audience with no place to escape to."

Spring in the Black Hills brought fierce thunderstorms, and that afternoon the skies darkened and rain began to pour again. While Rose and Alice slept, Jones paced the little cabin, keeping one eye on the rising creek and another on the corral. The cabin leaked in more places than Jones could count, or could keep up with in his scattered bean cans. He concentrated his efforts on keeping the streaming water from falling on either Rose or Alice as they slept. The dog found refuge under the table.

As evening came, Jones checked the loads in his Winchester, fed Rose a hot dinner, then took the dog outside with him and crawled up into the freight wagon, which he had covered with a canvas tarp. It was only marginally wetter inside the wagon than it had been inside the cabin, he decided as he settled down beneath the tarp. But here, at least, he had an open sight on the corral. If they came back, he'd be waiting for them.

Lightning ripped the churning sky and thunder crashed all around, rumbling and shaking the gulch like the insides of an iron foundry. If anything, the storm was worse than it had been the night before. Jones lay on his stomach watching the corral and the low-headed animals, and sometime during his watch, lack of sleep caught up with him.

The dog's barking awoke him in the early morning. All around him raged the tempest, now accompanied by a buffeting wind that rocked the wagon on its springs. At first Jones thought the villains had returned to finish the job they had started the night before, but a glance at the corral told him that the animals were still huddled together.

Through the slanting rain and flashing lightning, Jones could see nothing out of place. "What is it, boy?" The freight wagon rocked from side to side, and then one violent shudder seemed to cause it to skid a few feet on the muddy bank. . . .

*There was no mud where he had parked it! Only stones!*

Something thumbed heavily into the freighter's side, lifting the wagon momentarily at a steep angle before releasing it. As the freighter crashed back down on all four wheels, Jones scrambled to the open tailgate. A jagged bolt of white electricity revealed water swirling up to the axle of the wagon—and churning at the corner of the cabin, chewing away its foundation.

The creek had overflowed its banks!

The rending of wood, like the cry of a banshee, brought his head around as the cabin's roof suddenly sagged in one corner. Instantly, Jones leaped from the wagon, landing in water nearly to his knees. The current tugged him off his feet and he grabbed for a wheel rim, catching it before the raging creek swept him away. Jones steadied himself, gained footing, and leaning into the swift water, crab-walked to the edge of the cabin, where he managed a fingerhold in the gaping chinks between the logs. The crashing thunder, the barking dog, the roar of water all around him was a nightmare he hoped to wake from. But he wasn't dreaming.

All at once the freighter tipped on its side. Jones heard the dog squeal from inside, and the next moment the current was tumbling the huge wagon down the gulch.

Fighting against the water's relentless pull, Jones struggled toward the cabin door, finally got there, and began to work the latch. The door burst inward with a rush of water, and the current thrust him through it and instantly flooded the little building.

It was black as pitch inside until a blue-white bolt exploded nearby. Bobbing chairs attacked him, the table was swept up and wedged in the open doorway as if the river gods intended to keep him inside, pots and cups bumped into him almost teasingly, and papers and clothing swirled past as if relishing a ride upon the torrents raging outside.

As the blinding light faded, he caught a glimpse of Rose sitting upon the bed, back pressed against the wall of the cabin, Alice clutched tightly in her arms.

Jones waded through the maelstrom and grabbed her up into his arms. As he turned back, another flash showed him the door. He kicked the table aside and, bracing himself to face the deadly current, plunged out the door into the raging water.

In a tent not far away, Ro Kinsey lay awake listening to the storm crashing around him and the relentless rain pelting the canvas overhead. Nearby he could hear the snoring of the three other men, but that obnoxious sound was mostly buried beneath the barrage of the weather as it slammed into the gulch from every direction. The bullet wound in his side ached like a burning branding iron pressed against his flesh; but it wasn't the wound that kept him awake, nor was it the storm boiling overhead.

It was a deep, seething hatred that kept his mind scurrying around, seeking some avenue to have his revenge on the man who had put the bullet in him. In the last day and a half he had considered and rejected a dozen carefully worked out plans. But now, as his fevered brain churned the problem over and over, he hit upon an idea.

For the next hour he examined it from all angles, and in the end a grim smile worked its way across his face in the darkness. Yes, that would work for the meddler! Methodically, he went over all the details, and finding no flaws in it, he finally put his thoughts to rest and closed his eyes with immense satisfaction.

So long as the whites hated the Indians, and the Indians

hated the whites, he could work the scheme until he was a rich man—he could work it forever!

With the morning near, and the storm finally subsiding, Ro Kinsey tucked the plan safely away, knowing finally how he would deal with Nathaniel Jones once and for all.

# TWENTY-SEVEN

"Mr. Jones!" a voice cried out, echoing up the valley on a damp morning breeze. "Mr. Jones! Mrs. Jones! Can you hear me?"

"Good Lord!" another voice exclaimed. "Where is the cabin?"

"You don't reckon they were washed away with it, do you?"

"I pray not, General."

As if coming out of a drugged sleep, Jones rolled his head groggily and arched his back. He couldn't remember at first where he was, or even how he had gotten there. He ached all over; as if he had fallen asleep upon a pile of rocks. And then it all came back to him.

He glanced quickly around. He was inside the little toolshed he'd built back near the wall of the gulch. The ache in his back had come from the rough log wall of the shed, and the deadness in his arms was from the weight of Rose and Alice. They were both still asleep, and he had held them all night while he'd kept watch on the rising water.

In a flash of memory so vivid that it made him shiver, he recalled the struggle against the raging torrents as he had carried his family out of the doomed cabin. How he'd nearly lost his footing and had narrowly escaped being swept away with the flotsam as the gulch was being scoured clean by the all-devouring water. How, as he'd climbed to high ground with the water receding from his waist to his knees, its hold on him lessening, the storm had taken over, driving him back with its wind and rain. How somehow he had managed to overcome its violence too. Standing on higher ground, he'd seen the creek rising, as if with a will of its own, and a desire to consume him and his family.

In the howling gale, Jones had sought refuge in the only place left on his claim, the toolshed. He'd had no idea how high the creek could rise, but if the water did make it to the shed, he'd have to carry his family farther up the steep side of the gulch . . . perhaps even as high as the brown rocks! But the water hadn't risen much higher than the cabin for the rest of the night. He'd stayed awake to make sure it didn't, and he'd watched their home slowly being disassembled, being washed away piece by piece.

It was only after the storm had ceased in the early hours of the morning that Jones had permitted himself to finally fall asleep.

"Mr. Jones? Can you hear me?" echoed the voice again.

Jones gently laid Rose upon the damp floor of the tool-shed and stood in the doorway, shielding his eyes from the morning glare. It must have been late. He stepped stiffly outside and waved an arm. "General! I'm over here."

General Dawson and Preacher Smith were staring at the rock foundation, all that remained of the cabin. They whirled about at his call, then rushed up the slope toward him.

"Are you all right, Jones? Your wife and child?" General Dawson asked.

"They're both in there. We just made it out of the cabin before the creek washed it away."

"Praise God," Preacher Smith said. "You are one of the lucky ones."

"We've been all up and down this gulch, and everything within fifty feet of the bank of that creek is gone. At least a dozen men are missing, and hundreds lost everything."

"We lost almost everything," Jones said. He looked at the corral, where his oxen still stood. "At least my animals were on high ground."

"We found your freighter down the gulch . . . what is left of it," Smith told him. "The whole gulch is in shambles."

"Was my dog with it? He was in the freighter when it was washed away."

"Dog?" Dawson shook his head. "Didn't see any dog."

Jones frowned heavily and shook his head. "He was a good animal. If it wasn't for him, I'd have been washed away with the freighter, and Rose and Alice with the cabin."

Dawson said, "Nothing but splinters left of the freighter. Can't see how anything could have lived through that kind of destruction."

"We ought to find someplace dry to move your wife to," Smith suggested.

"Bring Rose and Alice up into my cabin. They can rest there until you find a place to stay. She ought to be kept warm so her injuries will heal proper."

"Thanks. I appreciate your offer, General Dawson."

Later that day Jones returned to his claim and surveyed the damage. Nothing was left of the cabin or the tools that had been left against its wall. But everything above the washed-out site was untouched, including the corrals and a prospect hole he'd been working before the disaster struck. Kicking around the rocks where the cabin had stood, he found some utensils and dishes and other belongings—bits and pieces of his life, scattered about. That was all. He had hoped to find his journal, which he always kept wrapped tightly in oilskin and tucked away behind the rocks near the fire pit. But it was gone—like everything else. He searched for the cash box, where he had kept Carson Grove's share of the claim—it had been buried beneath a stone in the floor. He did not find it.

Disheartened, he sat on a rock and looked around. All his prosperity had been washed away in a single night. There was nothing left. No, that wasn't true. He still had Rose and Alice, thank God. And the cattle. And he still owned the claim. So it hadn't been a complete loss.

Jones wished he had a smoke, but his pipe and tobacco had gone the way of the rest of his possessions. He glanced up at the brown rocks hanging over the edge of the gulch. Sunlight warmed them, drying the land. The gulch was steaming, like some tropical jungle. There was not a cloud in sight. How quickly things change, he mused; how fleeting the plans of man.

*Hell, now you're getting morose, Jones!*

He stood abruptly. He had things to do, and sitting around being gloomy and philosophical was never going to get them done! First off, he and Rose would need a place to live. He could rebuild the cabin, or start to work on the house he intended to build up on Williams Street, but either option, he knew, would take weeks, if not longer. No, he needed something quickly.

Jones strode back to the toolshed and dragged out the tipi he and Rose had lived in the first months of their marriage. Setting it up in Deadwood would be like asking a bully to throw a fist at him, but right now he didn't care. They needed a place to live, and he saw no other choice. He cleared a spot near the toolshed, well up from the creek, which had mostly returned to its banks, and then climbed to the ridge above his claim to scout out young, straight trees that would serve as lodgepoles. The search took him far from town, for most of the young wood nearby had already been chopped down by prospectors and builders.

Among the Lakota, setting up the lodge was strictly a woman's chore, but Jones had watched Rose do it often enough that within an hour he had the tipi standing straight and taut, and had already drawn a few curious onlookers.

"What are you gonna do with that thing?" one interested prospector asked, coming over cautiously, as though there might be some danger in the painted-skin dwelling.

"Live in it," Jones told him straight out, daring the man to make a remark about that. He didn't. He only shook his head and took a turn around the oddity, as if it were some strange critter he had discovered alongside the road.

As Jones stood there in the gathering dusk, admiring his handiwork, he heard a bark. Turning, he saw the dog limping up the creek.

"Dog!" he declared, going to the bedraggled beast and giving him a big hug. The dog licked Jones's face and followed him haltingly into the tipi. He seemed at once contented to be home and curled up and began licking his paw. Jones examined the leg. It wasn't broken.

Jones went into town and bought blankets and supplies on credit. The store was nearly sold out, as the flood had devastated all the settlements along the creek, and even some up toward Main Street, where the valley floor was more level and not so high above the normal flow of the creek. It was dark when he returned to the tipi, lit a lamp, built a fire, fed himself and the dog, spread the blankets on the ground, and prepared a pallet for Rose. Then he walked back into town to General Dawson's little cabin.

"I have us a place to stay, Rose," he told his wife, who appeared quite comfortable where she was.

"I have heard already," she replied.

Dawson grinned. "Word's all over town about you setting up that tipi. Some men are getting quite a kick out of it; others are thinking it was in mighty poor taste, considering all the Indian trouble we've been having."

"Poor taste or not, it's where we will live until I get some money in my pockets and a new cabin built. Anyone who has any problems with that is welcome to come by and pay me a visit.'' Jones patted the revolver on his hip, making his meaning clear. Then he carried Rose back to their claim. Dawson went with them, carrying little Alice and a basket of food that Preacher Smith had dropped by earlier.

Smith, Jones heard later, had been jumping like a frog on a hot griddle that day, seeing to the needs of as many victims of the flood as he could on his limited funds and the small amount of time he had away from his job digging the Boulder Ditch. Jones was determined to pay the man back for his kindness when he was able, but not having any hard cash at the moment, all he could do was offer encouragement to him for his good work.

The month of May came and went. Rose was walking around almost as good as new. Darnell, true to his word, had stopped by the tipi almost every day to check up on his patient. Jones thought that Rose's injury had probably done Darnell more good than his medical skills had done in healing her. He got a job working a claim for a man named Saunders, stopped drinking, and set up a part-time medical practice on the side, seeing to the oversupply of injuries that always plagued a boomtown. And considering the lack of medical doctors in Deadwood, Darnell was kept as busy saving lives as Preacher Smith was saving souls.

Jones worked his claim, rebuilding his finances. He bought another freight wagon as soon as he was able, and it didn't take long for him to get steady work making the Deadwood-to-Custer haul.

''I'll build that house up on Williams Street soon, Rose,'' he told his wife one evening as she prepared dinner. He detected a frown. Rose had come home to the tipi, and all was right in her world again. But Jones had told her over and over that they could not remain here, that someday he would build them a house and the tipi would have to go back into storage.

''Then will you sell this claim?'' she asked him.

He looked away without answering her, and Rose did

not press the issue, but went back to her cooking. It was always like this when she asked him about selling out. But this claim had supplied them both with so much that Jones was finding it harder and harder to keep his promise.

The wound in his side had healed, but still hurt—a constant, dull reminder that he had a score to settle with Nathaniel Jones. And settle it he would. Kinsey took a wicked pride in boasting that he hardly ever forgave, and that he *never* forgot. But he was in no hurry. He knew what he would do, and how he would do it, and in the meantime he was satisfied to stir the smoldering coals of anger the people of Deadwood were feeling toward Jones and his Sioux wife.

Ro had quit the freighting business and bought a business near the badlands that he called the Paradise Saloon. The money for this endeavor had come mysteriously into his hands, but no one in Deadwood ever asked how he'd suddenly acquired the cash and gold to start a business.

"It's a damn insult to this town, that man sitting up there on his claim living as those savages do. It ain't even a proper tent like you live in, Ralph," Ro was complaining one day in early June to one of his regular customers. "It's one of them damned tipis. Ain't we already got enough trouble with them savages without Jones rubbing our noses in it?"

Ralph Haggenback was already half drunk, and he couldn't have agreed with Kinsey more. "Someday someone will do somethin' 'bout that," he slurred, accepting a refill of his whiskey glass.

It was the reaction Ro had been skillfully trying to draw out from the man, as he had done in the past with anyone willing to listen to what he had to say.

The Indian trouble *had* escalated dramatically. It wasn't even considered safe to stroll into the forest that still covered some of the northern slope of Deadwood Gulch along Williams Street, where men of newly acquired wealth were beginning to build pretty cottages. Everyone was up in arms over the attacks on lone parties of prospectors, and the bounty increased on any Indian head brought in.

Ro thought that was hilarious, because it fit so well with his own plans . . . just so long as it wasn't *his* head that some lucky prospector brought in. As he had suspected that night a month earlier, burning with fever and hatred, and as he and his partners had discovered later when they had tried it out a couple times, anyone could slip into a breechclout, don a few feathers, and streak vermilion on their faces. Leave some moccasin footprints to be spotted later and a few arrows lying about. That was all the folks of Deadwood needed to convince them that the savages had struck again. In a surprise attack, or in the darkness of night, no one would know the difference . . . no one except perhaps another Indian.

Wild Bill Hickok came to Deadwood in the middle of June. Word that he was on his way was heralded far and wide before the famous gunfighter ever arrived. A mail rider from Custer City carried the word north, a day ahead of him, and folks clambered into town from around the district to witness the event.

When Wild Bill arrived, it was a sore disappointment to those who had hoped it would be with high style and perhaps some fancy shooting. Jones knew of Wild Bill only through his reputation as a lawman, gunfighter, and circus performer. Just the same, he, like the other citizens of Deadwood, had expected—or at least hoped for—something more.

Wild Bill arrived drunk, riding in the back of a freighter among a goodly stock of barreled whiskey. No doubt he had freely sampled the wares on the long trip up from Cheyenne. He came in on a wagon train with his buddies the Utter brothers and about two dozen whores. Among the celebrities who arrived that day was Jane Cannary, and Jones couldn't tell which of them was more drunk, Jane or Bill. It must have been Calamity Jane, he decided, for Bill still had enough wit about him to duck out of her way when she came staggering around one of the wagons.

"Bill! You sonuvabitch, where the hell did you get off to now?" Jane bellowed.

Bill and Charlie and Steve Utter had ducked into the nearest open door, which just happened to be Nuttall and Mann's Saloon No. 10.

Someone among the wagon train called out, "Leave it be, Jane. You lost out this time. Bill went and got hisself married."

A couple of the bullwhackers laughed, as if Bill's recent marriage to Agnes Lake, the owner of Lake Circus and an accomplished high-wire aerialist, had been a common joke among the teamsters. Jane growled, kicked aside a road apple, and made her way for one of the nearby saloons. Fortunately for Bill, it wasn't Saloon No. 10.

And that was it. The eagerly awaited arrival of Deadwood's first famous visitor was over, and the freighters began unloading their cargo.

Bill was disheveled, drunk, and in a surly mood—and who wouldn't have been, with an impassioned hellion like Calamity Jane after him. He got even drunker that afternoon, and later in the evening set up a tent with his two partners near the Whitewood Creek and spent a day or two panning for gold. But the prospecting didn't last long before Bill went back to the line of work he knew best—cards. It was rumored about town that Bill never did have any intentions of panning for gold. Some said he meant from the start to pan it out of the prospectors' pockets at the poker table. Others, fearing law and order would someday arrive to spoil the good times, suspected that Bill was in town to clean up Deadwood, just as he had Abilene.

Jones had no idea what had brought Wild Bill to Deadwood, but a few days later, when he saw a photograph of his new bride, who was ten years his senior, he thought he might have a handle on Bill's motives. Bill's tent was near Jones's claim, and the next Sunday morning, as Jones and Rose were about to go into town and hear Reverend Smith preach, the famous gunman strolled over and introduced himself.

Bill was a mild-looking man with almost boyish features and a quiet voice. He wore his hair long and his mustache full. His handshake was strong, his laugh quick and genuine; smiling seemed to come easy to Wild Bill, and it at once put you at ease with him, but there was ever that flinty wariness in his eyes which reminded you that this man was a killer.

He'd brushed his black frock coat before coming a-visiting, and was stone sober—for the moment. His manners were impeccable, and he tipped his black Stetson when Rose emerged from the tipi.

"My wife, Rose," Jones said, introducing her to him. "This is Mr. Hickok, the famous lawman."

"A pleasure, ma'am," Bill said, smiling. "You are Sioux, are you not?"

Rose nodded her head.

"I got to know many of your people while scouting for General Custer. Strong and brave warriors. They have my respect."

Rose merely smiled, but Jones said, "I rode with Custer myself, on his expedition to these Black Hills in '74."

"Did you now?" Bill said, suddenly interested. "Were you a soldier?"

"No, I was a correspondent. Actually, I worked with Mr. Donaldson, one of the expedition's botanists."

"Donaldson . . . Donaldson?" he repeated as if searching his memory. "Ah, yes, I recall reading some of Mr. Donaldson's newspaper reports. He had a nice way with words. Very entertaining."

Jones grinned. "I wrote most of it. Donaldson only went over them briefly and added a comment of his own here and there. He was far more interested in collecting plants than in penning reports."

"Really? Then I congratulate *you,* Mr. Jones. Oh, by the way, I hear that General Custer is even at this moment back in the field chasing down Chief Sitting Bull."

"Is he? I haven't been keeping up with events outside of Deadwood."

Bill smiled. "It will probably be another stunning victory for Custer. I've never met a man like him. Only fellow I know who manages to get himself into so many tight places and still come out smelling like ladies' sachet.'' Bill glanced at the tipi, then gave a short laugh. ''You've got nerve, Mr. Jones. I'll give you that much.''

''We haven't had many problems with it, yet. People either grin or scowl, but so far that's all. We can live with that.''

''I'm new in Deadwood, Mr. Jones, and already I've heard about you and your infamous accommodations. There are some people in this town who would like to do you harm.''

''I suspect that is so.''

Bill looked him up and down, then nodded his head as his view paused momentarily on the revolver at Jones's side. ''And I suspect you are able to handle problems when they come. Well, I'm out visiting my neighbors this morning, Mr. Jones. I reckon I'll go over and knock on McClintock's door next.''

''Rose and I were just on our way into town to hear Preacher Smith give his Sunday sermon. You're welcome to join us, Mr. Hickok.''

Wild Bill laughed and shook his head. ''I don't think church services are for me, Mr. Jones, but thank you for the invitation.'' He took out a silver watch and glanced at it. ''Besides, I have an appointment with a couple gents and a deck of cards in twenty minutes. Good day to you two.''

''Good-bye, Mr. Hickok,'' Jones said as the tall gunfighter strolled off toward John McClintock's cabin.

Jones saw Wild Bill a few times after that, but that was the first and last time he ever spoke to the man.

That next afternoon, Monday, June 26, Jones was making arrangements with Grant Hanaby to haul a cargo of general merchandise from the railroad at Sidney for Hanaby's new mercantile store when a rider pounded up Deadwood's street on a lathered horse.

''Custer's dead! And his brave Seventh Cavalry too!

They were all annihilated by the Sioux and Cheyenne on a river called the Little Bighorn.''

The news galvanized Deadwood. Prospectors chafing for some revenge of their own stopped working, speeches were made on saloon doorsteps, and liquor was passed around. Discontent spread like cholera, and Ro Kinsey saw an opportunity in it.

''I knew Custer. Drove a supply wagon for him back in '74, and I'll say this much—no finer man ever lived!'' Kinsey proclaimed to the milling mob that had gathered in the street outside his Paradise Saloon. ''It's always hard to learn that a man you rode with, a man you admired, a man like General Custer who only wanted to open up the West and make it a safe place for white men to live and work, is murdered in the prime of life by a bunch of thieving savages!''

''They've killed men all throughout this district,'' Swenson added. ''I've known two or three of them myself.''

Kinsey held back a grin. He'd known more than two or three. And many of the other men in the crowd had friends who'd died at the hands of the roving bands of Sioux, and that only helped fan the flames Kinsey was sparking to life.

''What can we do about it?'' Kinsey demanded. ''I'd say we're nearly helpless if the United States Cavalry can't even take care of the problem.''

''The problem is, they're all over the place. Like vermin,'' someone said.

''Yeah,'' another man added, ''it ain't even safe for a fellow to sneak off to take a healthy crap no more.''

A ripple of laughter made its way through the rabble, but the truth of the statement was blatantly clear to every man there.

''There's got to be something we can do. This problem has been going on for just too long now,'' one of the prospectors called out.

''There's already a fifty-dollar bounty out for every Sioux scalp brought in, and believe you me, I've had my eyes open. I can use some of that money,'' someone else shouted.

Kinsey had the crowd moving in the direction he wanted, and decided to have some fun. ''Settle down, boys, and let me talk. Everything you've said is true. This whole thing has gotten out of hand.''

Their roar of approval was a sweet serenade to his leathery heart. ''And I'll tell you what's galling me the most right now. It's that disgusting thing setting across the way there, right on our own doorstep.'' Ro thrust out an accusing finger at Jones and Rose's tipi. ''It ain't bad enough we got Injuns creeping around out of sight— we've got 'em living right here in town! Right under our noses. And what are we doing about it? Not a damn thing!''

He glared them down with a fiery stare which at that moment would have put even the most accomplished hellfire-and-brimstone preacher to shame. ''You say you've been looking for a scalp to collect on the bounty? Well, there is one right over there, waiting to be collected! Now, what are we going to do about that?''

Some of the men in the crowd were friends of Jones and Rose's. They spoke out their objections, but by now it was like spitting in the wind, and one by one they walked away in disgust.

''Hey, Moss, what's happening over there?'' General Dawson asked one of the prospectors who had been among those who had left the mob.

Moss looked back over his shoulder at Kinsey and the audience he had snagged into his evil plan. ''That troublemaker is talking them men into a frenzy, and it's that nice young man over yonder that they are scheming against. I wanted to be no part of it.''

''What young man?'' Dawson inquired.

''That Mr. Jones and his little Indian wife, that's who.''

''What has Kinsey got against Jones?''

''Nothing, I reckon. It's that Sioux wife of his that Kinsey is talkin' against.''

''Rose?'' Dawson frowned. ''The men are worked up

over the news of Custer's defeat, that's all. They'll settle down in a couple days.''

''Yeah, sure they will, General, but before they do someone could get hurt real bad.''

''I suppose you're right, Moss. I ought to go talk to them before they do something they will regret later. In the meantime, I saw Jones up the way at Grant Hanaby's new store. Go tell him what's happening here.''

Dawson crossed the street and slipped into the crowd. He listened to the men's heated words a few moments, then stepped up on a packing crate and said, ''Listen up, men. Before you run off and do something crazy, stop and think about it. Sure, we've got Indian trouble here in Deadwood, but Rose Jones isn't causing any of it. Neither is Nathaniel. If you boys are all fired up to do some Indian fighting, I'm sure the commanding officers down at Fort Laramie or Camp Robinson would be happy to sign you up.''

''Sounds like somethin' a government revenuer would say,'' one of the men shouted at him. ''Well, we don't let the government do our fighting for us, or make decisions for us neither.'' It was plain the man had sampled too much of Ro Kinsey's free whiskey.

Kinsey said, ''I don't think we want to hear the words of no government man right now, General Dawson. If you know what's good for you, you'll get out of our way.''

Someone from the crowd pitched a clump of manure at Dawson, then another, until the general backed down and removed himself from their line of fire.

''What are we waiting for, boys?'' Kinsey shouted. ''Let's tear that lice-ridden tipi to the ground!''

Grabbing up whatever they could get their hands on, they started for Jones's claim. Some carried guns, but most had only clubs and bare fists. They numbered about thirty men, and as they swarmed toward the creek, Ro let another man take the lead and found some excuse to remain at the rear. The gang made their way over the bridge onto Jones's claim.

Suddenly Jones appeared at his door with a rifle and the mob drew up.

One of the men said challengingly, "You intend to use that Winchester, Jones, or just stand there waving it around?"

"Get off my claim . . . all of you!"

"You might get off a shot or two, but after that you're a dead man."

"And so will some of you be," Jones warned.

A man named McCall pushed his way to the front of the mob and declared, "Yesterday General Custer and a whole lot of good men were slaughtered by those savages. We've put up with the Sioux among us long enough. But no more. We're gonna rid the Sioux vermin from these hills, and the housecleaning starts right here with that squaw you got inside there. And after we're finished with her, we'll tear down this filthy abomination you've set up for all to see. It's a blot on this town and we'll not put up with it any longer!"

Just then General Dawson showed up, carrying his shotgun. "There will be more than just a couple of you boys picking buckshot from your hides if you don't break this up now and go home."

McCall gave Dawson an icy stare. "Why don't you stay out of this, Mr. Tax Collector. It's gonna be a bloody afternoon, but it doesn't need to be any of *your* blood spilled."

"I've seen blood before, Mr. McCall. Seen it spilled all up and down the Southern states. Spilled my fair share of some of it. The prospect of seeing a little more here and now, mine included, isn't something that will turn me back from seeing justice done."

"We've given you fair warning," McCall shouted. The mob pressed close behind him. "Let's pull that tent down!"

A shot rang out behind them. Wild Bill Hickok was walking slowly toward them, a brace of pearl-handled Colts in his fist. He wore a long black frock coat and a black hat from beneath which his long hair spilled out.

He stopped a dozen paces off and stared the mob down.

Neither Jones's Winchester nor Dawson's shotgun had daunted these men one bit, but here was Wild Bill with only a pair of Colts and every eye was wide. Breaths had caught in suddenly tight throats and at once the angry murmuring ceased, so that the sighing of the wind was the only sound to be heard.

Bill said, "I'm downright peeved with you men! Don't you know I had me a long, hard night, and here it is barely one o'clock in the afternoon and you went and woke me out of a sound sleep. I'm gonna be working late tonight again, and I need my rest. Now, suppose you tell me what all this falderal is about before I get seriously angry."

The men stood there in stone silence, none daring to be the first to speak.

Bill hitched a revolver to the right and fired. A stick splintered and went flying from the hand of the man who was holding it.

"I'm a bit riled, boys. Someone talk to me or I'll start shooting hats off you gents. And when I'm awakened out of a sound sleep like now, my eyesight isn't too good." Bill took deliberate aim at a fellow near the edge of the crowd.

"It ain't nothing, Mr. Hickok. We ... we was just having a little fun, that's all. We'll go on our way now, sir."

Bill lowered his revolver and grinned. "Well, I'm not one to hold it against a man when he drinks a little too much and gets to feeling lively. You boys just keep it down to a low roar and take your frolicking over to the other side of town so I can get some rest. All right?"

The fire went out of their anger and the mob broke up and headed back to town—at a rather quick pace. When they had left, Bill looked across the gravelly ground at Jones and Dawson, grinned, gave them a salute with one of his revolvers, and turned back toward his tent.

Jones let go of a long breath. "That was a close one."

Dawson looked at him. "You know, with things being the way they are, I'd consider moving my wife and child out of this here town, at least for a little while. And it wouldn't hurt to buy yourself a plain canvas tent, either.''

Jones nodded his head. ''You know, General, you might just have a point there.''

Dawson grinned. ''Well, I think the fight has been scared out of them, at least for a day or two. By then, who knows.''

''I've just contracted with Mr. Hanaby to bring up a load of supplies from Sidney. It might not be a bad idea if Rose and Alice come along with me on the trip.''

''That sounds like a very *good* idea, Mr. Jones.''

# TWENTY-EIGHT

Kinsey, still smarting from his defeat the day before, looked out the window of his saloon in time to see Jones's ox-drawn freight wagon rumbling past on the street outside. He hurried out the door as the wagon, Jones, Rose, Alice, and the big dog rolled out of town. Across the creek, the tipi was gone. "Is he leaving Deadwood?" Kinsey wondered out loud.

"Leaving? Not likely," Blakely said, sticking his florid face out the door. "I heard that Hanaby hired him to bring up a load from Sidney for that new mercantile store of his."

"They took down the tipi," Kinsey said.

Blakely glanced across the way. "So they did. Well, maybe they don't intend to stay when they get back."

"Or maybe they just need a place to live while on the road," Swenson observed, stepping out into the warm sunlight.

Kinsey's fists balled at his side and a flash of anger drew his face into a scowl. "He can't do that!"

They looked at him curiously. Swenson grinned and said, "Can't do what, Ro?"

"Leave Deadwood."

Blakely was getting bored with the matter and stepped back into the saloon, saying, "Well, he's doing it, Ro, and I can't see as there is anything you can do to stop him." He dropped into his chair and snatched up his beer mug.

Sink, as usual, was drunk and grinning stupidly. "At least the pain-in-the-ass is out of your hair now, Ro."

"He ain't outta my hair yet. I got a score to settle with him, and he won't be *outta my hair* until it's done!" Kinsey shot a quick glance at the few men in the saloon. This early in the day, the Paradise Saloon was never crowded. Just the same, he lowered his voice and said, "It's time we take a razor to our faces again, boys."

Swenson grumbled. "You mean you want us to dress up like a damn savage again?"

"What are you complaining about?"

"I've got better things to do than to go out whooping and hollering and acting like a wild Injun."

"Our little masquerade has done you real good, Swenson. You've got gold dust in your pocket and drinks on the house, and I ain't heard you complaining about having to work too hard anymore."

Swenson grimaced and looked away.

"All of you have profited nicely off of our "Indian" raids. Now, we are going to pull it off again, and I don't want to hear no complaining. So get your faces scraped and your Injun Joe costumes out of hiding. It's a long trail between here and Sidney, and somewhere along the way, Mr. Jones is going to have himself some serious Indian trouble."

Little Alice was bundled up in a wool blanket against the evening chill, quiet and content to be held as the family sat around the campfire outside the tipi.

They were three days on the road to Sidney. The Black Hills were behind them, and ahead lay the long drive through rolling grasslands before they reached the pine bluffs, and then Camp Robinson beyond. Jones intended to keep well east of the military camp, for he would be

hauling Hanaby's supplies into an illegal town filled with
illegal prospectors, and by law, the army still had an ob-
ligation to keep him out of the Sioux territory, even
though it had pretty much ceased hauling people out of
the Black Hills. Jones didn't want to risk drawing attention to himself and having his wagon and team confiscated
on the return trip. He planned instead to take the eastern
route, which ran near the trading post on Bordeaux Creek
where he and Rose had purchased the ponies for One Stab
the year before.

Jones lit his pipe with a twig from the fire and blew a
cloud of smoke into the ceiling of stars over their heads.
The moon, being but a thin sickle and low on the horizon,
took very little away from their celestial glory. Now and
then a bat would dart after an insect, and in the distance
could be heard the lonely sound of a coyote.

"You know, Rose," he began after considering a few
moments how he would introduce the subject, "we had
us a close call in town."

She looked up from the baby and waited for him to
continue.

At least she could agree, he thought, finding her qui-
etness a stumbling block to what he wanted to say. "I've
been thinking—maybe it would be a good thing if you
went to live with your cousins for a few months. Just until
all the hard feelings in Deadwood over Custer's demise
pass and the Lakota raids on the prospectors stop."

"Will they ever stop? Will I ever be accepted into your
world, Nathan?" she asked.

"Certainly, Rose. In time the problems will all be
worked out—once the government and the Lakota comes
up with a new treaty."

She merely looked at him, and he wished to hell he
knew what she was thinking.

"I mean, this can't go on forever. Maybe, for a while
at least, you and Alice will be safer on the reservation."

"Your hair will be like the snow on many hills before
the problems of our peoples end, my husband. Is it better
for me to stay on the reservation, where the Lakota face

starvation because your government cannot supply the food it has promised? The Great Spirit is angry because the whites have entered his hunting grounds,'' she said with quiet resolution. ''There will never be peace until the Lakota are driven out of the land and all the braves are put to sleep beneath the grass of these hills.''

Jones frowned and puffed his pipe thoughtfully. ''I wish I could tell you that you were mistaken, my dear, but unfortunately, you are probably right.''

''Why is it you wish to return to Deadwood?'' she asked sensibly. ''There are many other places to go.''

He briefly grinned. ''You mean, 'west'?'' he asked, recalling the ambiguous remark Carson Grove once made in a Bismarck saloon, a long time ago.

''There is much land to the west. Someplace in it, we can make a home where men do not kill you because you live in a Lakota lodge . . . or marry a Lakota woman.''

He watched the crackling fire and the bright sparks rose on the updraft of warm air.

''It is the gold that draws you back,'' she said finally, and with stinging accuracy.

''We've had a string of bad luck, that's all,'' he said, sidestepping the accusation. ''It will get better.''

''Perhaps Carson Grove speaks the truth about the *Tukan*,'' she said softly.

''If you believe that, Rose, I'll throw it away this very moment. As far as I'm concerned, it has no magic, good or bad. I keep it out of sentimentality, and for no other reason.'' Jones stood and knocked the ashes from his pipe. ''I need to check up on the cattle and see that they are bedded down.'' He threw a saddle atop his mount and a few minutes later rode out into the night.

Jones didn't mind being alone, and he enjoyed driving a freight wagon, but it was times like these when he welcomed being part of a big caravan, if for no other reason than that the big outfits brought along night herders who did nothing but ride great circles around the lowing cattle, keeping them together and secure during the night with their gentle voices and soothing songs. Handling both the jobs of herder at night and driver during the day left little time for sleep. On trips like this, Jones usually got by on naps snatched here and there while in the saddle or on the driver's seat as the oxen tugged the heavy freight wagon on its slow way. And slow it was; unless spooked, cattle had only one speed. But to their credit, they were steady and reliable pullers, something that could not always be said for mules.

The road to Sidney crossed a hundred miles of what seemed like endless grass rolling away in every direction across the undulating landscape. After the grass, there came a thick stand of pine trees that eventually ended at the pine bluffs and the White River. The Sioux called it the ''dark forest.'' Jones liked its beauty and stark contrast to the gumbo prairies he was entering now.

They were four days out, with the prairie lying before them and the dark smudge of the Black Hills finally gone from the horizon behind them, when Jones spied the four Indians on horseback about a mile off, watching them.

''Wonder who they are,'' he said, pointing the distant warriors out to Rose. Jones generally did not fear the Sioux. He'd lived among them long enough to be known by most, and speaking the language and having a Lakota wife along was good insurance for anyone planning to cross Indian territory these dangerous days.

Rose studied them as they urged their horses into motion and started down one of the grass ridges. ''I do not know,'' she answered with a note of puzzlement.

Hearing the uncertainty in her voice, Jones regarded her. ''They *are* Lakota, aren't they?''

She shaded her eyes with her hand and studied the riders a moment. ''They do not ride like Lakota warriors.''

A tingle worked its way up Jones's spine as Rose's tone became more than just a little concerned.

''Cheyenne? Crow?''

Rose looked at him, confusion showing on her face. ''They do not ride like any Indians I have ever known.''

As they drew nearer, Jones could see this fact as well. "Then who are they?"

"I do not know, but they have rifles. I do not like the look of this, Nathan."

The riders were closing the distance quickly. He cracked his whip over the ear of the lead oxen to urge a bit more speed out of the beasts. But they only plodded on, stubbornly ignoring the whip or Jones's barrage of insults.

"Take Alice and yourself into the back of the wagon, Rose," he snapped, handing her his rifle after she'd clambered over the seat. Rose shifted the baby in her arms and took the weapon.

"Stay low and out of sight while I talk to them. It might be something as simple as too much whiskey last night."

"They do not ride like drunk Indians either, Nathan. They do not ride like Indians at all. They ride like the white man."

Jones knew that Rose was right. He'd seen enough Lakota horsemen to recognize how they sat a pony.

"Just stay out of sight, Rose."

She scrambled under the tarp with Alice and the dog as Jones tried futilely to urge more speed out of his beasts.

"He's making a run for it, Ro!" Bradley Sink shouted as they galloped across the grass.

Ro only laughed. Jones, he thought with amusement, stood a better chance of making snowballs on the islands of the Caribbean than he did outrunning their swift horses. He glanced at his partners. Sink and Swenson were galloping off to his right, both of them scrawny and pale-skinned, dressed only in buckskin leggings and breech-clouts. But hardly anyone ever notices that in the heat of an attack, so long as there is plenty of whooping and yelling. All terrified victims ever see are the feathers, paint, and naked chests. Even Blakely, riding on Ro's left, although meatier than the others, made for a passable Indian at a distance. His naturally flushed face helped hide other obvious discrepancies, mainly the hairy chest. The

solution to that problem, it turned out, had been simple—
the thick black thatch hardly showed beneath the porcu-
pine quill vest and the half dozen loops of colored glass
beads that he donned whenever they planned a raid.

Plunging down into a swale, the riders momentarily lost
sight of the freighter. When they crested the next hillock,
the wagon was much closer, and Kinsey saw that Rose
was no longer on the driver's seat with Jones.

*Little good that will do, putting the squaw into the
wagon for safety,* Ro said to himself. He couldn't risk
leaving anyone alive to finger him later.

Then they were almost upon the freighter, whooping
wildly and firing their rifles. Jones drew his revolver, returning the attack, but the range was still too far. Kinsey
stopped his horse and placed the rifle to his shoulder as
a small grin worked its way across his face. "You've had
this coming for a long time, Jones. I told you once I don't
forget—I get even!" He squinted along the barrel and his
finger tightened on the trigger. The .44-40 bucked against
his shoulder.

Jones lurched back, the reins slipping from his fingers.
He teetered a moment on the edge of the freighter's seat,
then took the long fall to the ground and lay there unmoving.

At that same moment all the gunfire finally spooked the
oxen, and displaying a rare show of excitement, they
broke into a run, carrying the driverless freighter along.
Where the road curved, the frightened animals took it into
their heads to barrel on straight ahead, across the rolling
grasslands. For a hundred yards the freighter bounced and
swayed until the terrain slanted steeply. Then gravity and
the freighter's top-heaviness took over. As it bounded up
over one rolling hill the freighter balanced momentarily
on two wheels. By that time there was only one direction
left for the wagon to go. Succumbing to gravity's relentless pull, it toppled in slow motion, crashing to the ground
and tumbling side over side three times before coming to
a rest in a cloud of rising dust.

They pulled in their horses and circled around the fallen body. Bradley Sink hopped off his horse and rolled Jones over.

"Alive or dead?" Ro demanded.

Sink put an ear to Jones's heart. "Alive . . . I think."

"He won't be for long." Ro glanced at Blakely. "Ride over yonder and check out the wagon. Can't see how anyone could have survived that tumble, but if she did, put a couple arrows into her. Got to make it look authentic."

"What should I do with him?" Sink asked.

"Take his scalp. That should answer any questions about who's responsible for this. Damned Sioux attacked again, it looks like," he said grinning. "Even killed one of their own this time."

Sink grinned wickedly as he pulled his skinning knife from his waistband, took a fistful of Jones's hair. "Hey, what's this?" Sink said.

"Here, hand that up to me."

Sink cut the leather thong and pulled the small, beaded pouch from around Jones's neck.

Ro dumped the horseshoe-shaped gold nugget into his palm. "Hmm, that's a right unusual piece, if I do say so myself." Then he recalled the card game back in Sidney where he had vowed his revenge on Jones. He remembered this beaded pouch, and Jones saying something about its being his lucky charm.

*It wasn't so lucky for you after all,* Ro thought, putting the nugget back into the pouch and hiding it away in the bag that he wore as part of his costume. "Go on now and get that scalping over with so we can haul our asses outta here before someone comes along."

To the Lakota, Crazy Horse was a mighty war chief, one of the great generals of the Battle of the Little Bighorn. He had led his people brilliantly against Custer and had won a glorious victory for the Sioux, Cheyenne, and Arapaho. After the battle, the Indians went in many different directions, knowing full well that the vengeance of

the United States military was about to be unleashed
against them.

After staying low and watchful for several days, Crazy
Horse had led his small band south toward the place of
his youth, the land he loved best, which lay near Beaver
Creek in the pine ridges of the western corner of what
had become Nebraska. But Crazy Horse recognized no
state boundaries. It was his land, all of it, and encouraged
by the victory at Little Bighorn—or what the Lakota
called the Greasy Grass River—Crazy Horse was determined to take all of this land back from the white man.

"Why do we sneak across our own lands like the fox
creeps at night into a camp, Crazy Horse?" One That
Kills in a Hard Place complained. "We have won a great
victory. We ought to send up a great signal fire to announce to the Lakota throughout the land that we have
returned, and will now drive the white man out before
us."

Crazy Horse glanced at the young warrior, then shook
his head. "You are still but a pup. You act rashly, One
That Kills in a Hard Place. To announce our presence now
would only bring the White Father's armies down upon
us. At the Greasy Grass we were many. Here we are
few."

"A man fights strongest when he fights in his own
home. Now we are home! I will kill a hundred white with
but a single arrow, for the Great Spirit fights with us."

Crazy Horse looked away from the boasting warrior
and studied the rising ground ahead, ever wary, ever on
the lookout for the line of blue coats. Somewhere, they
were out there—somewhere nearby, he was certain. After
the battle, Sitting Bull took a band of warriors north, into
Canada, while other chiefs headed west and east. As a
single force, they were mighty, but now, fragmented and
scattered, they were weak. And Crazy Horse knew that
the soldiers of the Father in Washington were hunting
them down.

One That Kills in a Hard Place slowed his pony and

dropped back a few paces, coming alongside a huge warrior named Hump. "He fears the whites still, Hump! We should be riding swift, like brother eagle, not creeping as a mouse afraid of the cat!"

"Crazy Horse knows what he is doing. Remember how he led us against the Long-Haired Chief at the Greasy Grass River. If he wishes to move with caution, then so be it."

One That Kills in a Hard Place gave a scornful sneer and glanced around at the other warriors, fourteen in all. Were they all content to slink on their bellies back to their women and lodges? Many looked weary, and some bore the wounds of the battle. Most just wanted to go home. In his mind he called them all old men. They had tasted blood, and now were sated. He had tasted it, and craved more. One That Kills in a Hard Place hated the white man with a fire that burned hotter than in the others. He withdrew a few paces and rode alone, sulking under a warm, late morning sun as they rode west, keeping well north of the Red Cloud Agency and Camp Robinson.

In the distance a gunshot echoed faintly. Crazy Horse drew up and listened. A second and then a third rifle shot reached them from beyond the rise of land. Crazy Horse tapped his heels against the flanks of his pony, and the others followed. One That Kills in a Hard Place hoped to find the blue soldiers beyond the rise, but when they crested it and Crazy Horse brought them all to a halt, he was disappointed to discover that it was only a small band of warriors attacking a white man's big-wheeled wagon.

"There is something wrong here, my brothers," Crazy Horse said after watching the scene unfold below them a few moments.

"What is the matter with those riders?" Running Bull inquired.

"They ride like children, afraid to let their ponies run free like the wind," Hump observed.

Crazy Horse frowned. "No, my brothers. They ride like the white man. Come!" He urged his horse forward. Below him he watched the driver fall from the seat of his big wagon and the cattle bolt and carry it wildly away.

Blakely had started toward the wrecked freight wagon when he happened to look across the wide prairie to his left. Instantly he reined about and drove his heels into the horse.

"Ro!" he shouted, bringing the horse to a sharp halt. "Over there!"

Kinsey and Sink looked up, and Kinsey roared, "Oh, shit! Let's get the hell outta here, boys!" And leaping to their saddles, they spurred their animals into a gallop.

Crazy Horse ordered some of his warriors to pursue the fleeing men while he and four others rode down to the body laying beside the road.

"Hump," he said as they leaped to the ground. "Look in the wagon. He might have been carrying food or weapons. Then cut those cows loose. We will take them with us and feast tonight!"

As the big warrior rode away, Crazy Horse, Smiling Rabbit, Crooked Bear Tooth, Slow Water That Sings, and One That Kills in a Hard Place approached the body. The hoofprints around it were those of shod horses. That confirmed the war chief's suspicions: These were not Indians, but white men posing as Indians.

Crooked Bear Tooth turned the white man over.

One That Kills in a Hard Place gave out a cry of delight, and drawing his butcher knife, fell upon Jones to finish the job the white men had left undone.

With the swiftness of a cat, Crazy Horse grabbed his arm and pulled the young warrior back. "No!"

"I must have his hair! This is he who took the woman, Morning Snow Woman, from me!"

"I know him as well, and you will not take his scalp."

"But he is dead!" One That Kills in a Hard Place protested.

"Then we will bury him as the whites do for their dead," Crazy Horse shot back, his voice hard and impatient.

Slow Water That Sings touched the place at Jones's neck that throbs, and his eyes compressed slightly.

"I am owed this man's scalp, Crazy Horse," One That Kills in a Hard Place countered, addressing the great chief in a familiar manner that some would have called disrespectful.

Crazy Horse's knife leaped from his waistband and the point pressed into One That Kills in a Hard Place's throat. "Back away from him, buck, or you will join the ghosts of your ancestors before the sun stands overhead. We will bury Iron Left Hand with the respect accorded a kinsman. I do not want to hear another word of objection from you, or you will join him in the hole and together you two can work out your differences in the silence of the cold earth!"

Slow Water That Sings lifted his head from Jones's breast and said, "Don't be too swift to dig that hole yet, brother. This white man still breathes."

Crazy Horse wheeled around and examined Jones closely. Past all the blood, he saw that the scalping had not gone beyond the first cut above the brow. The rest of the blood came from a bullet hole below Jones's neck and a little to the left. Lifting him slightly, Crazy Horse felt the sticky warmth on the back of his shirt.

"It passed through him."

Smiling Rabbit said, "The blood flows, it does not spurt. That is a good sign."

"Yes," Crazy Horse said.

Crooked Bear Tooth frowned as he looked into his chief's face. "But tell me, brother, what is this man to you that we should treat him as a kinsman? He is white, and on our land."

"He is the son of Carson Grove. Carson Grove was married to my mother's sister. Therefore, I call him kinsman. He is also joined to our sister, Morning Snow Woman."

With clear understanding of the matter now, Crooked Bear Tooth nodded his head. "We will do what we can for him."

Crazy Horse looked up then and saw Hump walking toward them carrying the limp figure of a woman in his big arms.

"Morning Snow Woman!" One That Kills in a Hard Place said, startled as Hump laid her gently upon the grass next to Jones.

# TWENTY-NINE

"Why would the whites dress like Indians and kill their own people?" Smiling Rabbit wondered out loud later that night as they sat around a campfire.

None of his companions could answer that.

Crazy Horse's father had been a medicine man, and he understood the secret way enough to mix a poultice to place upon Jones's wounds. He also prepared a tea that he hoped would help Morning Snow Woman, but her wounds, although not life-threatening like Jones's, were far more difficult to treat.

"There is no understanding the ways of the white man," a warrior called Broken Stick said, coming into the light of the fire.

It had been a day of many events. After driving off the make-believe Indians and discovering that Jones was still alive, they had made two travois from the tipi poles they'd found inside the wrecked wagon and carried Jones and Morning Snow Woman several miles to the south, where a small stand of trees crowded together near a creek. A camp was made so that they could tend to the two injured people without fear of being seen by any army patrol that might have been passing by. Now, late into the night, they

sat around the fire, talking of the mysterious behavior of
the four white men and watching Crazy Horse prepare his
medicine. They had butchered an oxen and their stomachs
were full, but their hearts were heavy . . . each man, from
time to time, couldn't help but steal a glance at the small,
lifeless bundle wrapped tightly in a blanket nearby.

Morning Snow Woman had regained consciousness
during the trip, but her mind seemed lost in the terror of
the attack. Although a close examination revealed that she
had broken no bones, oddly, she could not move. She just
lay upon the travois, staring up at the burning sun. Later,
they prepared a blanket on a bed of last year's leaves and
laid her next to Jones. Out of the respect given a warrior,
Crazy Horse placed Jones's weapon nearby him. Still
Morning Snow Woman did not move. She remained as
like the dead . . . except for the tears that seeped continually from her dark eyes, over her cheeks, and across that
livid, newly healed scar.

While the warriors discussed the matter, One That Kills
in a Hard Place moved off a little distance and sat brooding, his eyes fixed on the two forms stretched out upon
the ground.

The next morning they buried baby Alice on a hillside
near the creek where bright sunshine warmed the grass.
Morning Snow Woman could only watch as the men sang
the mourning song for her baby. Crazy Horse fed her
some of his healing tea and attended to Jones's wound,
changing the poultice and examining the hole in his chest,
satisfied that the puffy skin showed no signs of infection.

"How long are we going to remain here nursing these
two like women?" One that Kills in a Hard Place demanded after another full day and night had passed.

"I will stay until Jones and our sister are well enough
to leave," Crazy Horse told him. Then, raising his voice
for the others to hear, he added, "Any of you bucks can
leave if you wish. No man needs to remain with me."

No one spoke, even though a deep longing for home
and wives tugged their hearts westward.

One That Kills in a Hard Place strode away, and as his anger and hatred of Jones grew, a plan to rid himself of the interloper and woman-stealer took shape.

That afternoon Jones opened his eyes for the first time and saw Rose beside him, apparently asleep. Glancing around, he was momentarily startled by the sight of so many Indians camped about him. He remembered the attack . . . but these were not his attackers, he quickly realized. A warrior suddenly appeared beside him and hunkered down.

"You have come back from your death sleep, Iron Left Hand."

Jones's lips were parched, his throat tight as shrunken leather, but he managed to say, "Crazy Horse."

The war chief offered him a drink of water, which eased the tightness some. "What are you doing here?" Jones asked.

"We heard the shooting, saw the attack."

Jones was vaguely aware of a deep pain in his chest and his labored breathing. There was an odd tingling about his scalp as well, and he gently lifted a hand to examine it.

Crazy Horse grinned. "They were scalping you when we showed up and drove them off."

It all came back clearly now. "They weren't Indians?"

"No, they were white."

"Why?"

Crazy Horse shrugged his shoulders. "Who can know the ways of the whites. Even their own do not understand them."

Jones's eyes leaped to the war chief's face, then to his wife. "Is she all right? And Alice!"

"Morning Snow Woman is hurt in a way I do not understand. She suffered no wound that I can find, yet she speaks not, moves not." He grimaced, then went on, "The little one has gone to be with the ghosts of her ancestors. We sang the mourning song for her, because your wife could not do it."

For a moment he could not speak. "Alice? Dead?" he

said finally, fighting back the tears. "Does Rose know?"

"Rose?"

"Mountain Rose. It's the name Morning Snow Woman took for herself when we were married."

Crazy Horse nodded his head. "Yes, Mountain Rose knows."

The weight of this awful news crushed his spirit. Crazy Horse left him alone with his grief, and Jones lost track of the hours, but sometime later he looked over at his wife and said softly, "Rose? Do you hear me, Rose?"

She did not stir; her eyes were fixed upon the patches of sky visible through the layers of leaves and limbs overhead. Every so often she would blink, and that was all.

Jones kept talking to her, and in a little while Rose's eyes had shifted his way, even though her head had not.

He reached out and took her hand. "I know you can hear me, Rose. I'm here, and we'll get through this together." He thought he felt a faint squeeze from her fingers . . . but then, he couldn't be sure.

Once, when she was a little girl, Mountain Rose had had a frightening vision. She had awoken in the middle of the night—but not fully. Her mind was alert, her eyes able to search the shadowy darkness in the faint moonlight that came through the skins of the lodge, but that was all. Try as she might, she could not move. Old Man Sleep had lodged within her, taunting her to break his spell, refusing to flee into the night as he should have. Somehow Mountain Rose had understood that if she could make a sound, it would frighten Old Man Sleep and he would flee. Yet her throat had refused to answer the command of her brain, and mute, she lay there helplessly.

She remembered the supreme effort of concentration it had taken to will her hand to move. There was a clay pot of water by her pallet, and that had been her goal. If she could only tip that pot over, the sound of its falling would break the trance and she'd be fully awake and free of Old Man Sleep. . . .

And so it was now. Rose's brain was alert, and so filled

with grief for her little Alice that she felt she must die. But she knew she would not. Other women of the camp circle had lost children and had lived through the wrenching despair. But they had been able to keen the mourning song, and wrap their arms about the dead infant before committing its lifeless body to the grave. In this, at least, and in the embraces of those who'd mourned with her, there had been some solace.

But this . . . this horrifying paralysis; it made the tragedy that much harder to bear.

Her thought went back again to that frightening childhood night when she had only half awoken. Through the strength of her will, she had managed to drag herself from that nightmare—and, Rose was determined, she'd cast off this evil as well.

*Rose . . . Rose . . . Rose . . .* the soft voice echoed inside her head. At first she did not understand the meaning of it, but as the sun moved slowly across the sky, her thoughts cleared. It was *Nathan* calling to her. But was he calling from the dead or from the living? The living, she decided finally; she was certain of it. Her eyes slid sideways and there, at the very edge of her view, was her husband. Hurt, as she was, but alive.

*Did he know about Alice?*

If only there were some way to comfort him . . .

Her hand felt suddenly warmer, and in some unexplainable way it lifted an edge of the heavy grief from her heart.

*Night now?* When had the sun set? Had she dozed?

No, only her angle of view had changed. She was now looking at the dark blanket upon which her head rested. She had rotated her head to the left, and there was Nathan, asleep.

*She had turned her head!*

A small ray of light broke through the black clouds of grief. She had driven Old Man Sleep from her head and neck! It was only a matter of time now, she knew. Relishing this victory, Rose looked around. Night was near, for the shadows had lengthened and the patches of blue through the trees overhead had shrunk as darkness gathered in the leaves and branches. Nathan lay to her left, asleep. To her right was the campfire, where warriors sat about, talking amongst themselves. Nearby was Nathan's saddle, his rifle and revolver between them.

Footsteps stopped right behind her, but Rose could not see who it was standing there. When the man spoke, the voice was faintly familiar, but it was only after Crazy Horse stepped within her line of sight that she knew.

"Your head moves. This is an improvement, sister. Can you speak yet?"

Rose slowly shook her head.

Crazy Horse sat beside her. "No matter. That too will come back to you. The medicine is working, sister. Soon you and Iron Left Hand will be well. Here, I have brought you some tea." He lifted her head gently and put the bark cup to her mouth. When he took it away, he said, "I will make some thin stew for you now. It will give strength to your bones and muscles." The war chief went back to the others, and in a few moments several of the men came around and gave her encouraging words.

As night came on, Rose struggled with Old Man Sleep again and managed to drive him from her hands and feet. Arms and legs yet remained his captive, but now she knew the method, and his defeat was certain. Even her voice was poised to return, but for the moment, she knew, she must be patient.

Earlier that day, One That Kills in a Hard Place strolled alone into the trees. The wood of the cottonwood tree is soft, but a gnarled root, long exposed to the air and weather, can be tough as flint. After a short search, he found exactly what he needed and went immediately to work with his knife, removing a long sliver of the wood. Upon examining it, he decided the piece would do nicely and settled down in a patch of sunlight and began whittling the sliver into a thin needle, retaining a heavier portion of it for a stout handle.

He worked slowly, watching the grain so that he didn't

accidentally split the wood, careful not to weaken the needle as he carved a taper down to a sharp point. Then he
burnished it, hardening it further, with the flat side of his
blade.

When he'd finished, he had fashioned a tapering probe
the length of his forearm, half of it a handle so that he
could keep a strong grip on it. The Lakota knew of many
ways to kill a man. One That Kills in a Hard Place would
have preferred plunging his knife into Jones's heart and
seeing his blood flow freely. But Crazy Horse had forbid
harming the white man, so instead he would have to resort
to stealth. It would have to be tonight, before the white
interloper gained much more strength, for it must appear
as if his wound had killed Jones. That way no suspicion
would ever fall upon him, and that way too, he might still
woo Morning Snow Woman onto his sleeping pallet.

Standing, he examined the needle one more time, then
experimentally, he put the point gently into his ear and
wondered briefly what pain a man might feel as it was
driven into his brain. Perhaps it would be wise to muffle
Jones the instant he plunged it in. Yes, that's what he
would do. He would cover Jones's mouth with a hand and
with a single powerful thrust, plunge the tough, thin needle into his brain. He would die instantly and there would
be little blood to point to the method of his murder.

"The white man does not appear well," One That Kills
in a Hard Place commented to Hump later that evening
as they ate roasted oxen.

Hump gave him an odd look. "He grows stronger by
the hour. He will be walking about in a day or two."

The jealous warrior only smiled faintly. "I should be
very surprised by that."

Smiling Rabbit took a bowl of thinned stew to Morning
Rose and fed her until she wanted no more. "There is
movement in her hands and a little in her arms," he told
the warriors when he returned. "Tomorrow she might
even speak, if the Great Spirit continues to touch her
body."

Crooked Bear Tooth said, "It is Crazy Horse's medicine that knits her body back together."

They debated which was more important, the Great Spirit's healing hand or their war chief's strong medicine. One That Kills in a Hard Place insisted again that Jones was looking worse, and wondered if he would live out the night. The others laughed and told him it was wishful thinking on his part. The matter passed and the topic of conversation turned to the subject of the vision quests that each had had. One That Kills in a Hard Place took this opportunity to go off by himself to finalize his plans. If he was going to kill Jones, it would have to be tonight, for by tomorrow the white man would be strong enough that no one would believe his death had come as a result of the bullet wound.

It was dusk when Ro and his gang rode back into Deadwood. Ro headed straight for his saloon to check up on business. He had left it in the hands of a man named Sean Hannifin. Hannifin had owned a saloon in Sioux City before coming west with the rush, and like most of the "Hillers," had gone bust. So he fell back into the line of work he knew best—managing a saloon—and he did it very well. Hannifin's know-how and honesty left Ro with plenty of time on his hands to do what *he* did best . . . warming a chair at the gaming table.

"Any trouble while I was away?" Ro asked, filling a mug of beer to rinse down the trail dust.

"No trouble, Mr. Kinsey," Hannifin declared, polishing a whiskey glass with a towel. "The receipts are back in your office. I kept them locked in the desk drawer like you told me to. Did you catch many fish?"

Kinsey grinned. "Most enjoyable expedition I've had in years, Hannifin. Caught a couple big ones, and we ate 'em with relish too. Might just do it again next week, now that I got someone like you to take care of the place while I'm gone." He went to his office, a cramped cubbyhole at the back of the building that doubled as a storage room, and counted the money Hannifin had taken in while he was away.

Later, emerging into the smoky barroom, he spied a game just getting under way. Wild Bill Hickok was at the table. Kinsey had heard that Hickok was a fair hand at cards, and he'd been itching to see just how fair he really was.

"Might I join you men?" he asked.

Hickok had taken a chair against the wall. He glanced up, considering Kinsey with hard, unflinching eyes. Then his mustache gave a hitch as a small smile flashed across his face. "There's one chair left. It's okay by me if it's okay by you boys."

It didn't matter to the two other men, and Kinsey dropped into the chair and laid out the stack of gold coins that he'd brought with him from the back room. He wished he had Sink sitting across the table from him; they had worked together long enough to ensure that one or the other would walk away from the table carrying most of the gold. But he wasn't worried. There was more than one way to skin a cat, and he prided himself in being an expert cat skinner.

As the evening wore on, it became apparent that Hickok's reputation was based on more than just talk and smoke. The cards went back and forth, and Kinsey's stack of gold coins grew and diminished—but mostly diminished. The other men were having trouble too. Only Hickok's pile seemed to be regularly growing higher.

In the course of the long evening, Kinsey managed to hold back a king and a ten. Now, if he could only remain in the game long enough, the right cards were bound to fall into his hands, and with some artful shuffling, he'd be able to raise the ante and win back all of his losses and then some.

Sink and Blakely dropped by the saloon, helped themselves to a beer, and drifted on over to watch the game. Kinsey would have preferred they had stayed away. When it was going badly for him, he wanted no witnesses. When he was winning, that was a different story.

After a while, Sink and Blakely got bored watching and started their own game at a different table, which was just fine by Kinsey. His money was running low, but he was sticking it out, slowly growing to hate the placid smile that remained plastered across Hickok's face.

"Well, boys, looks like Lady Luck has smiled through my window one more time," Hickok said after a particularly profitable hand that nearly broke Kinsey.

One of the fellows threw up his hands. "Well, I got busted by the best, at least," he announced, and gathered together his few remaining coins.

"You boys in for another hand?" Hickok inquired of Kinsey and a gent named Keplatch.

"Deal 'em around, Hickok," Kinsey growled, counting his money. He had only enough left for one more play, and he intended to make it count.

Hickok tossed the cards into three piles and each man anted up a double eagle. Kinsey's hopes brightened when he sorted the cards. Two kings, a ten, a deuce, and an eight.

On the first round of betting, Hickok pushed the pot to Kinsey's limit. Kinsey saw the bet—but just barely. Keplatch raised. Pushing everything he had into the pot, Kinsey was still short.

"Looks like you're out of the game, friend," Hickok said amiably.

With the ten and king that he already had hidden away, this hand was a sure winner. It was only a simple matter of swapping out the cards in his hand for the ones tucked under his vest. "Hold up," Kinsey said, his mind racing. He dug inside his pocket and came up with the small, beaded pouch he had taken from Jones. "I got this," he said, quickly shaking the horseshoe-shaped gold nugget into his hand. "Look at the size of that thing. It's got to be worth enough to cover the raise."

Bill took it up and studied it admiringly. "That's a right unusual hunk of mineral, Kinsey. Wouldn't mind owning this myself. Make a dandy watch fob."

"Well?" Kinsey demanded. "Will you accept it?"

"I will, providing Mr. Keplatch agrees."

"It's my lucky charm," Kinsey said, steeling Jones's comment.

Keplatch examined the nugget with equal admiration. "Lucky, you say? Sure, I'll allow it—and I intend to *own* it just as soon as this hand is played out."

Kinsey dropped the nugget back into the pouch, and he set atop the pile of coins. The hand was played out with a gentleman's agreement to freeze any further additions to the pot. Kinsey called for two cards, and taking a huge chance, he managed the switch—but just barely.

Hickok's eyes flicked up, nearly throwing Kinsey into a panic, but then his view returned to studying the cards in his hand. Keplatch was staring at the center of the table, a trancelike expression on his face.

Kinsey began breathing again. Hickok laid his cards flat and covered them with a hand and said, "The moment of truth, boys. What do you have, Mr. Keplatch."

"Two pair. Queens over eights."

Hickok grinned slightly. "Full house. Tens and sixes," he said, flipping over his cards. "And you, Mr. Kinsey?" Bill's voice held an edge that sounded oddly playful. "Let's see if that nugget brought you the luck you needed."

Kinsey said, "If it did, it's about time. I've spent the night losing smartly to the two of you." He turned over the kings and tens. "Well, well, look at that. A full house too, and it's a mite taller than yours is, Bill." Kinsey reached for the pile of gold.

In a heartbeat Hickok sprang to his feet and snapped a revolver from his holster. Kinsey's hands reached for the ceiling as he scrambled out of the chair.

"Don't shoot!"

The revolver roared, wood splintered, and playing cards went flying. Bill stepped around the table and fired again, tearing a hole in the floor at the tip of Kinsey's right boot.

"What the hell—!" Kinsey yelped, leaping back.

Bill fired a third bullet, skinning the toe of Kinsey's left boot.

Kinsey high-stepped out of the way and danced backward. Bill drew his second revolver and, left-handed, stitched a row of bullet holes into the floor, driving Kinsey against the bar.

"Your luck *has* changed," Hickok said, eyes glinting with a cold calm that made Kinsey shiver.

"I don't know what you're talking about," Kinsey stammered.

"Don't you? Unbutton your vest." Bill took deliberate aim. "Do it now, or I'll do it for you." The revolver steadied on the top button.

Kinsey's hands shook so badly he could hardly push the buttons out of their holes fast enough. When he reached the third one, two playing cards slipped out and fell to the floor.

Bill's voice hardened. "I generally kill card cheats, but seeing as tomorrow is the Fourth of July, I'm in a generous mood." Without warning Bill's revolver swung out and raked across Kinsey's head.

He staggered, caught himself momentarily on the bar, then slumped to the floor, unconscious.

Bill holstered his weapons. "It's been a long, profitable night, gentlemen," he said to no one in particular. He studied the beaded pouch a moment, and a thin, satisfied smile spread across his face as he tucked it into his vest pocket. "Reckon I found me a new lucky charm."

Hickok casually collected his winnings, put them into a canvas sack, and strolled out the door and into the night.

# THIRTY

Old Man Sleep had settled heavily upon her chest, but with supreme effort, Rose had willed him to leave her legs and arms. It had been a wearisome struggle, but one that she was certain she would win. Already feeling had returned to her feet and hands, and if she tried real hard, she was able to force a bit of movement in her shoulders as well. Rose was determined that by morning, she'd have her limbs back, and then it would be only a short matter to chase the old man out for good.

What drove Rose on more than anything was her need to stand over her daughter's grave and grieve aloud for the infant . . . and for something else which she had not even told Nathan about.

*Nathan.* How weak and helpless he looked in his sleep beside her. Crazy Horse had honored him by placing his weapons nearby, as he would have done for a Lakota warrior. Like Rose, Nathan was struggling with healing and with his grief, she knew, although he had not spoken of it to her that afternoon. He had talked to her for hours, as if he had known that she could hear and understand him. She had desperately wanted to answer him, but Old Man

Sleep's spell had silenced her throat. Once he was driven out, then her voice too would come back.

Rose ceased momentarily from her effort, relaxing her arms and legs. The struggle made her weary. She could not afford to stop; still, a bit of rest might help, and relenting some, she allowed her heavy eyelids to come together.

A faint sound brought Rose instantly alert. She had lived her whole life in the wilderness, and her senses were keenly attuned to its constant small sounds. But this one was somehow different. . . .

*There it was again*—the soft step of a foot upon the decaying remains of last year's leaves. It made Rose recall the time when, as a little girl, she and a playmate had tried to sneak up behind her father while he had been sharpening an iron arrowhead on a stone in the door of their lodge. He had caught them, of course, for a warrior is always alert.

The soft whisper of leaves might have been caused by the breeze, but Rose thought not. A sense of something standing right behind her head made her blood run cold. She held her breath, not daring to reveal that she was aware of its presence. The sound of breathing, which would have been imperceptible to an untrained ear, came clearly to her now.

Through cracked eyelids she saw a dark form separate from the deeper darkness of the trees and step around them. A man! He moved quietly to her husband's side, then with extreme care, lowered to his haunches. In that moment, Rose saw his face.

*One That Kills in a Hard Place!*

And she saw something else too. A long, slender needle momentarily caught an edge of moonlight before it disappeared in the darkness alongside Jones's head.

Rose tried to move her arm, but at that moment Old Man Sleep fell upon her with all his horrifying, suffocating weight.

● ● ●

He had waited until the camp was quiet; then, stealing away, One That Kills in a Hard Place crept out into the forest to retrieve the needle. He waited at a place where he could see Jones and Rose. A full hour passed. Everyone was asleep. He stood and moved silently toward his victim.

He paused a few feet from Rose, and seeing no signs of movement, eased into the clearing. For a moment he knew, he would have to be exposed—though the deed would only take an instant. The moon was no more than a thin sliver of light, but to an eye adjusted to darkness it would be enough to see by. That couldn't be helped.

With the long needle in his hand, he lowered to Jones's side. All was yet quiet in the camp. Swiftly, One That Kills in a Hard Place positioned the needle at Jones's ear, lining it up precisely so that a single, powerful thrust would propel it deep into the brain of this man whom he hated. His attention was focused on this alone; there could be no mistake. It had to work perfectly the first time, for he would have no second chance.

He drew a deep breath as his grip tightened upon the deadly needle. His palm came firmly down over Jones's mouth. Instantly the man beneath him was awake. One That Kills in a Hard Place pressed down even harder, and at the same moment the needle started forward. . . .

The silence of the night was broken by a sound he had heard once before—the four metallic clicks of a revolver being cocked!

*Wakan Tanka!* his brain screamed as he looked up into the barrel of Jones's revolver, and the quivering hand that held it!

The barrel bloomed before his eyes with a blinding orange flame—he never heard the deafening roar—as his brain exploded and the top of his head peeled back like the lid on a can of beans.

The camp came instantly awake and warriors leaped to their feet and grabbed up weapons, ready for whatever had befallen them in their sleep. The thunder of the revolver, which she had only just managed to take from the holster that Crazy Horse had lain between Nathan and herself, had frightened Old Man Sleep, and as he now fled her body Rose sat up.

"Nathan!" Her voice was like the rasp of a file. Dropping the revolver and pulling herself to his side, she turned his face toward her.

"What is happening?" Jones asked, confused.

They were surrounded by Lakota warriors. "It is One That Kills in a Hard Place," Hump said, seeing the body sprawled a few feet away.

Crazy Horse knelt beside the half-decapitated man and frowned as he removed the killing needle from his lifeless fingers, at once understanding.

"He would have killed Nathan," she told him.

The war chief nodded his head gravely. "Much hatred burned within him." He glanced at the needle. "But this is not the way of a Lakota. A Lakota looks an enemy in the eye when he kills him. He does not sneak in the dark as the Arikara do." He flung the needle into the night. "Your voice has returned, sister. I am happy to hear it."

"Old Man Sleep kept me hostage. But I have finally defeated him."

Crazy Horse glanced at Jones, but when he spoke his words were meant for Rose. "The spirits are powerful, yet they have little strength against that which binds a man and a woman together."

Being a rawboned boomtown in the midst of hostile Indian territory, Deadwood celebrated the Fourth Of July with all the gusto of a convict given an early parole. Prospectors came in from the hills, freight men parked their wagons, and shopkeepers closed their doors.

The saloons and cribs in the badlands were doing a brisk business, and from all quarters came the crackle of firecrackers, the whoosh of skyrockets, and the boom of salutes. There was a parade down Main Street and lots of whiskey to be had as everyone waited for a fireworks display some of the businessmen had promised for later, after the sun had set.

Wild Bill Hickok had been corralled by a bunch of admirers and coaxed into a shooting show. Having spent some time on the stage with Buffalo Bill Cody in Chicago, and understanding a little about the circus as well, Bill knew how to please crowds. He pointed out a scraggly cottonwood tree near his tent that had somehow managed to escape the woodsman's ax, and drawing both of his pearl-handled Colt revolvers at once, began trimming the twigs off one of the branches.

Twelve shots rang out as fast as he could thumb the hammers, and when he had finished, that branch was as slick-naked as a prospector's pick handle! The shooting drew men from every part of town to see what was happening. To please them, Bill reloaded and did the trick all over again. There were those in the crowd who wondered how Bill always managed to keep a straight face when he claimed he never had a flair for showmanship, and that that was why he'd left circus life.

Later that day, as men gathered around a makeshift flagpole, General Dawson gave a stirring speech on freedom. He recited the Declaration Of Independence to them, and afterward he read a letter that he had composed and intended to send to Congress. It was a request to that "honorable body" to effect a speedy resolution of the Indian problem by terminating the Indians' title to the Black Hills and immediately opening the area up to settlement by the white man. The men cheered him wildly and promptly lined up to put their names to the document in support of Dawson's plan.

Blakely was one of the first to sign Dawson's petition. Afterward, he wandered from one celebration to the next, finally ending up at the Paradise Saloon.

"Where's the boss?" he asked the busy barkeep.

Reaching for a mug and sticking it under the tap, Hannifin hooked a thumb over his shoulder at the door to the back room. "Back there."

Blakely was already feeling his liquor, but he helped himself to a glass of whiskey from Kinsey's bar just the same and took it with him.

"Should have seen ol' Wild Bill putting on a show for the boys! That man knows how to handle a six-shooter all right," Blakely announced, coming through the door.

Ro was at his desk, his back to the door, and Sink had stretched himself out atop some barrels of whiskey, where he was reading a copy of Frank Leslie's *Illustrated Newspaper*. Sink glanced up and made a warning face, but it was too late.

Kinsey swung about, hatred burning in his eyes. "I don't want to hear nothin' good about that sonuvabitch Hickok!" The left side of Kinsey's face was colored with a dark purple bruise, and his eye had swollen shut.

Blakely retreated a few steps and said, "Sorry, Ro. I wasn't thinking." It was plain why Kinsey had hid himself away back here and was not out celebrating the Fourth with the rest of the town—he looked horrible. But Blakely wasn't about to tell him that now.

Kinsey turned away again and drummed his fingers on the desk. "I'm gonna get that man," he growled.

"What? Wild Bill?" Blakely said with a note of derision in his voice.

Kinsey looked over. "Yes, Wild Bill. Who the hell else would I be talking about?"

Blakely laughed. "I just seen him do some pretty fancy shooting, Ro. You'd never stand a chance against him."

"Not me, stupid! But there's got to be someone who'd take that gunman on—for the right amount of money."

"I don't know of any man here in town dumb enough to go up against Wild Bill."

Kinsey frowned. "Unfortunately, neither do I."

"I do."

They both looked at Sink who had lowered the newspaper and was grinning at them.

"Who?" they asked at the same time.

"He was one of them who went to burn Jones out last week. Got to talking with him later and come to learn he's got some kind of grudge against Hickok. He's a hothead and talks real tough when drunk, though not so much so when sober. A few drinks . . . a few bucks in his pocket''—Sink shrugged his shoulders—''who knows, he just might do it for you.''

''Who is this man?''

''Can't remember his name, but I know his face. I'll look him up and bring him by to see you.''

A few days later Sink showed up at the saloon, appropriated two beers, and wove his way across the crowded barroom floor to the door to Kinsey's office.

''Yeah, come in,'' Kinsey shouted at the quick knock.

Sink and another man stepped through, shutting the door behind them.

Kinsey was peering into a mirror. The purple bruise had faded considerably, and his eye was no longer swollen shut. ''What is it?'' he said, glancing from Sink to the stranger.

''This here is the man I told you about the other day, Ro.''

Kinsey's voice lost some of its belligerence. ''Oh, yeah. What's your name?''

''McCall.''

''You got some beef with Hickok, do you?''

''Lost my money to him. What's it to you?''

Kinsey pointed to the ugly mark on his face. ''I owe this to Hickok, that's what.''

McCall laughed. ''Heard about that.''

Anger flared in Ro's dark eyes. ''The whole town has heard. And that's something else I got against Hickok.''

''So, what do you want with me?''

Ro looked the man up and down. ''How much money did you lose to Hickok?''

''Three hundred and some change. All that I had, which makes it a lot.''

''You pretty fair with a gun?''

''Not particularly. I know how to use one, if that's what you mean.''

''How badly do you hate Hickok?''

McCall shrugged his shoulders. ''I don't particularly hate him at all.''

Kinsey shot Sink a burning stare. "Why the hell did you bring him here?"

Sink stammered, but before he could get a word out, McCall said, "Don't have to hate a man to want to get even. I'll kill Hickok for you, if that's what you want. Only . . ." McCall let the word hang, irritatingly.

Ro glanced back at the man. "Only what?"

"Only, it's got to be done the way I want it done. I'll have five hundred dollars for the job, and if I get caught, Mr. Kinsey, you will see to it that I'm let go. Otherwise, the whole town will know who arranged it."

Kinsey didn't like having terms dictated to him like that, but then, how many men was he going to find who were willing to go up against the famous Wild Bill Hickok? Kinsey slowly nodded his head. "I'll need a little time to get the money together."

"I got plenty of time."

"Half the money in advance, the other half once Hickok is put in the ground."

"I can live with that."

When they had gone, Kinsey turned back to the mirror and gently probed the puffy skin with a finger. Then, for the first time since his run-in with Hickok, he laughed.

On August 2, Carl Mann, part owner of Nuttall and Mann's Saloon No. 10, was having a friendly game of poker with a couple friends. Captain Massie, a retired riverboat captain, sat with his back to the wall, smoking a fat cigar and laughing in a deep, rolling rumble as he told Mann and the city marshal, Con Stapleton, a humorous story from his riverboating days. All at once Massie looked up and saw Wild Bill Hickok standing there.

"Got room for one more?"

Massie kicked back a vacant chair. "For you, Bill, we'll make room!" he said with the same rumbling laughter with which he had just ended his yarn.

"I'd prefer your seat, Captain," Bill said.

Massie chuckled. "I'd give you this seat in a heartbeat,

Bill, except it has become somewhat lucky for me. You see, I'm finally winning."

Mann and Stapleton grinned. Con Stapleton said, "You're gettin' jumpy as a mare in heat, Bill. Come and join us."

For only the first or second time in his career, Wild Bill Hickok took a seat in a public place without putting his back against a wall where he could keep an eye on all that was happening around him. The game went on, and shortly Bill's wariness faded into the background and that odd tingling at the back of his neck was lost to the concentration he was giving the card game.

Jack McCall strolled into the saloon a few minutes later. He was nervous and bought himself a beer but didn't drink it as he inched his way toward the table where Wild Bill was playing cards. With a shaking hand, he set the beer on a nearby table. Massie was laughing again as he dealt out some cards to the three other men.

McCall moved closer, his heart thumping like a bass drum and the sweat beading up on his face in the August heat. He was so close now he could see the cards in Hickok's hands: two pair, aces and eights.

McCall eased the .45 from his waistband and then, as Massie laid his cards down on the table and the others followed in their turn, swiftly drew back the hammer, put the muzzle to Hickok's head, and pulled the trigger.

The revolver boomed in the hot, still air, and Hickok lurched forward. The bullet passed through Wild Bill's head and lodged in Captain Massie's arm.

McCall leaped out the door crying, "I did it! I killed that sonuvabitch Hickok!" There was too much excitement in the saloon for anyone to go after McCall right then.

"My God!" Mann cried, jumping to his feet.

"Get a doctor!" someone else shouted.

Con Stapleton turned Bill over and grimaced. "Too late for a doctor."

Massie rolled his head, groaning as his shirtsleeve blossomed with a crimson stain.

Men from around town crowded into the saloon. General Dawson was one of the first, along with Hickok's buddy Charlie Utter. They laid the famous gunfighter on the floor while some of the men rushed out to apprehend the murderer.

"Bill!" Charlie groaned, his glazed eyes hardly believing what they saw. They had been friends a long time.

"Someone find us something to carry him out on," Dawson said. "A couple planks will do to get him to the undertaker." He looked down at the body. Hickok's forehead had been partly blown away, and brains were splattered all over the place. Something caught Dawson's eye then, and he reached into Hickok's vest pocket and withdrew a small, beaded pouch.

"Charlie, where did Mr. Hickok get this?"

Utter glanced over. "Bill won it in a card game. Said it was gonna be his new lucky charm."

"Won it? From whom?"

"Hell, I can't remember. . . ." Then he said, "No, wait, I do remember. It was that card cheat, Ro Kinsey. I remember now, because Bill nearly killed the man."

"Hmm. I wonder how Kinsey came by it. I know who the owner of this was, and it wasn't Kinsey. Mind if I hold on to it for a while?"

"I don't care—and Bill sure ain't gonna need it now, either."

General Dawson shoved the pouch into his pocket, then helped load Hickok onto a pine board and carry him out.

McCall was captured a little while later in a nearby theater and hauled before a judge appointed from among the men, since there was no official judge in town. Ro Kinsey, knowing that his neck was on the line as well as McCall's, managed to get a handful of his friends appointed to the jury, and after a hasty trial, McCall was found innocent on the basis of his claim that Hickok had murdered his brother a few years back.

He was released with the warning that he'd better leave Deadwood immediately, for Hickok had lots of friends in town. McCall was in complete agreement, but he had some unfinished business to see to first.

That night Kinsey slipped into the alley opposite Lee Street, where a crude set of stairs headed up the steep incline of the gulch to Williams Street above. Miners' shacks stood about in this secluded place, which was mostly dark now. When Kinsey saw McCall coming, he signaled to him, then moved into the deeper shadows of one of the cabins. A bright moon showed the porch of the cabin a few yards up the valley's side, but its light could not reach down into the shadows of the alley.

"You got it?" McCall demanded, his nerves stretched thin.

Kinsey shoved a wad of paper money into McCall's hand. As McCall stepped into a small patch of moonlight a few feet away to count it, Kinsey said softly, "I wasn't sure about you in the beginning, McCall, but you done all right."

"Not sure about *me*?" He laughed. "When my neck was about to be stretched, I was kinda worried you wouldn't hold up *your* end of the deal."

"My neck was on the line too."

"You better believe it. I'd have sung like a canary if they had put a rope around me." The bills rustled in his fingers. "It's all here."

"Two-fifty, like I promised you. You do good work, McCall. If I ever need another 'Hickok' murdered, I'll look you up."

McCall laughed. "No thanks. One Hickok in a lifetime is all a man needs. I best be out of here before one of his pards puts a bullet through my head. So long, Kinsey." McCall shoved the money into his coat pocket and started away, then turned back. "Why did you want Hickok dead so badly, Kinsey?"

"It's a motto that I live by: I don't let no one cross me and get away with it. Simple as that."

"Remind me never to get crossways with you." He grinned, then skipped up the steps to Williams Street and disappeared into the night.

"And don't you forget it," Kinsey said softly, listening to McCall's footsteps fading away. He was about to leave when he happened to look up. Where the moonlight fell upon a pane of window glass, the long, bearded face of Preacher Smith stared out at him. The window was half opened. It would have been impossible for Smith not to have heard Kinsey and McCall's words. "Damn!" Kinsey hissed softly, ducking his head and hurrying out of the alley.

# THIRTY-ONE

Nathaniel Jones stood over the little grave, peering down at it with Rose at his side. The month that had passed had pretty much healed the wound in his chest, but the hurt in his heart, he knew, would never heal over——not completely.

Crazy Horse and a few of the braves had remained with Jones and Rose as they both struggled to regain their strength. Rose had come a long way; all that remained of the horrible accident was a slight limp. Many of the warriors had returned to their homes and families, and those who had remained were preparing to leave now.

"*Wakan Tanka* has smiled upon you both, brother, sister," Crazy Horse said, leading his pony over to where they stood. "You are strong again. This is good."

"It is good," Jones agreed. "He has given me the strength to find those men who did this to us, who murdered our child. But it was you who stayed by our side and fed us and cared for us when we could not take care of ourselves. I'll not forget that."

"What is it you will do now?" the war chief asked.

"Find them. I don't know who they are, but I did not

have many friends in Deadwood, and if I haven't missed my guess, I will find them there.''

"Alone? You are still healing, brother, and there were four of them.''

Jones made a wry grin. "I'd invite you along to help, Crazy Horse.''

The Indian laughed. "If so, you would be inviting the lightning from out of the sky into your lodge with you. I would bring even more trouble than you already face. And anyway, I must return home with my brothers. I have been away too long.''

"There, you see? I reckon it is just me alone. But I'll make out.''

Crazy Horse nodded his head gravely. "Yes, I think you will. I have watched you grow from that day we first met—the day Carson Grove thought he could fool Crazy Horse with his lie.''

Jones was stunned. "You mean you knew?''

Crazy Horse swung up onto his pony. "I know when a man speaks words of truth. I see it in his eyes. You speak true words, Iron Left Hand. Carson Grove, he *often* speaks true words.''

"Why did you go along with the story?''

"Carson Grove is a good friend. If it was important to him for me to believe you were his adopted son, then so be it. But that is past. I have made up my own mind about you, Iron Left Hand. I call you brother.'' Crazy Horse reached down from the pony and clasped Jones's forearm in friendship.

"Crazy Horse. I ask one more favor of you.''

"What is it?''

"Take Rose back with you. I was foolish to have brought her to Deadwood in the first place. Now, with what I need to do, it would be better if she was not around.''

"No, my husband. I will go with you.''

Jones took her gently by the shoulders and looked into her face. It was battered and scarred from the crude stitches that Willard Darnell had made after the stampede—the first time he had almost lost her. But to him, it was still lovely, and he loved her more now than when they had married. In her marred face he saw the young Indian maiden called Morning Snow Woman, making soup with the women in One Stab's hunting camp. It seemed like another world. Indeed, it was another world: the end of the Lakota way and the beginning of the white way.

"You must go with Crazy Horse. Stay with your family so that I won't have to worry about you. When I am finished, I will come for you."

"No, you will not come back from this. I will bury a husband next, and then . . ." She hesitated before finishing the sentence. "Then our child will have no father."

"Our child?" His eyes narrowed. "What are you saying?"

"I carry your child, Nathan."

The news hit him like a pile driver. He pulled Rose to him and held her tight. When he finally released her he said, "I will return, I promise."

Crazy Horse said, "I will bring Mountain Rose to her cousins at the Red Cloud Agency."

"Thank you."

They mounted up, and as the Indians rode away, Jones swung onto his horse, watching, until Rose receded into the distance.

The trip back to Deadwood took him over a week. It hurt terribly to ride, so he made his way slowly at first, stopping often. After a few days, the pain in his chest lessened to bearable levels, but the going was still at a snail's pace.

In the two months that he had been away, Deadwood had doubled in size—or so it appeared to Jones as he viewed the boomtown from the head of the long, sweeping road that descended into the gulch. Urging his horse forward, he came to the sprawling outskirts of Elizabethtown, then passed the shacks of the growing Chinese section, and the cribs of the badlands. He reined up at a fork in the road. To his left was Sherman Street; what was left of his claim was down that way. Straight ahead was Main Street, and although Jones's first inclination was to check out his holdings, he decided instead to find General Dawson.

Dawson wasn't at home, but it didn't take Jones long to track him down at Nuttall and Mann's Saloon No. 10.

"Mr. Jones! My God, I'm happy to see you!" Dawson came across the saloon's floor and clasped his hand heartily. "Let me buy you a beer!" He hauled him to the bar and when the beer came, Dawson said, "There were rumors flying that you and Rose had been butchered by the Sioux. Your freighter was found on the road to Sidney, but other than the dead dog, there was no trace of you, although there were plenty of Indian pony hoofprints."

"We were bushwhacked," Jones said.

Dawson shook his head. "And you having yourself an Indian wife. You'd think they would have let you pass through safely. How is Rose, and the baby?"

Jones peered into his beer mug. "Rose is all right."

"Well, we have been having our share of misery with them damned savages. They went and killed poor Preacher Smith last Sunday as he was going to Crook City to hold a meeting."

"Smith?" Jones was stunned. "How?"

"Bushwhacked him, just like they did to you."

"Did you catch them?"

"No, but we will."

John McClintock had just stepped into the saloon, and hearing Dawson's words, he said, "I don't think it was Indians, General. My feeling is that it was white men dressed up like Indians—and I'm not alone on that."

"Ridiculous. What white man would do such a thing? And for what reason?"

McClintock only shrugged his shoulders. "I can't answer that, General."

"It was white men who jumped us," Jones said.

Dawson stared at him. "You can't be serious. They found Sioux arrows stuck in your wagon!"

"Just the same, it wasn't the Sioux who waylaid us. They were white, I'll swear to it. That's why I'm back here now."

"You think it was someone from Deadwood?"

"I have to start looking somewhere. I was hoping you might be able to give me a lead, seeing as you know most everyone in town."

Dawson was still too shocked by the notion that white men had attacked Jones to speak right away. He glanced at McClintock, who was wearing an "I told you so" smirk, then back at Jones. "I can't help you, Mr. Jones. I still think the whole notion is preposterous."

"If you hear anything, I'd appreciate it if you'd let me know." Jones set the mug back on the bar and walked out onto Main Street, then down to his claim to see what, if anything, was left of the place after his absence.

As Jones was leaving Saloon No. 10, across the street Blakely was about to enter the Gem Variety Theater for the afternoon show. He glanced over and stopped all at once, the color draining from his face as if he had seen a ghost. Then, as reality flooded back, his cheeks suddenly burned several shades redder than usual. "Jones!" he growled to himself.

*Was it possible?* For a fleeting instant he marveled at the man's tenacity for life, but then a thought began to gnaw at his gut. *If it was possible that Jones had survived after all, maybe it was also possible he knew who had attacked him. Could Jones point the accusing finger at the four of them?*

Blakely didn't see how that could be possible. They had been disguised. But if a man could survive all that Jones had gone through, well, then anything was possible.

Forgetting that the show was about to start, and that it featured girls who wore little to cover their charms, Blakely wheeled away and hurried back to the Paradise Saloon.

He burst through the back door. Kinsey glanced up

from his desk and said, "Ain't you learned how to knock yet?"

"We got trouble, Ro," Blakely said, gasping to catch his breath.

Kinsey rocked back in his chair and stared at the winded man. "What are you talking about?"

"It's Jones. He's back."

"Jones?" A sudden anger clouded Kinsey's face, and he exploded from his chair. "Jones is dead! What the hell are you talking about?"

"If he's dead, then we have an even bigger problem, because I just seen his ghost leaving Nuttall and Mann's."

"It's impossible."

"That's what I thought at first, but it's true."

Kinsey was speechless for a moment, then said, "I'd be more inclined to believe that that nosy preacher had come back from the dead. Or even Wild Bill with half his brains blown out. But Jones? Jones was a nobody."

"Well, that *nobody* is walking the streets of Deadwood, and if I don't miss my guess, he's looking for the men who ambushed him on the Sidney road."

Kinsey scowled, still not believing it. "Show me."

They crossed over to Sherman Street, and as they started down toward the creek Blakely grabbed Kinsey's shirtsleeve and pointed. "There. Jones made straight for his claim."

The cigar drooped in Kinsey's lips. "Who would have believed it," he said, amazed, and then with sudden resolution he growled, "Round up the boys, Blakely. It's time we bury Mr. Jones in a grave so deep he won't never crawl out of again."

The day after Rose was returned to her family, an old mountain man rode into the agency. He moved in among the scattered clusters of tipis that made up much of the Red Cloud Agency, halting his sorrel to study the clan markings painted on the skins of the lodges. Spying what he was searching for, he tapped his horse into motion and came upon fifteen lodges set in a circle, doors facing east.

He inquired of a young boy there, and upon getting the answer he sought, swung stiffly to the ground and, taking his heavy rifle with him as he walked over to one of the lodges.

"Mountain Rose?" he called.

In a moment Rose's face appeared in the oval of the tipi's door. "Mr. Grove," she said, surprised, but with a hint of relief in her voice at the same time. She stepped out into the sunlight, and Grove saw the thick scar running down her cheek.

"I heard, Rose. Heard about little Alice, too. I am sorry for you and Nate."

Tears came to her eyes, and she wiped them away. "She is with the ancestors now."

"That is true, but them what's left are sure enough suffering." Grove frowned. "News travels fast among the Lakota. Word is you was brought back by Crazy Horse, and then he skedaddled before the soldiers could nab him. Heard too that Nate wasn't with you. What happened?"

Rose told him the whole story, and when she had finished, Carson Grove snorted and shook his head. "He went back by hisself. Damn! That man is bound to get hisself kilt."

"What do you mean?"

"I mean he's going up agin' a whole town practically. If four of 'em took the trouble to waylay you along the trail, then I'll wager there are a lot more what stayed back, but still would like to see Nate put outta the way."

Rose told Grove about the attack on their home, and how Hickok had stepped in to help.

"How many days since he started out for Deadwood?"

"Eight."

"Well, that settles it," he said. "Looks like I'm a-gonna have to go to Deadwood and fetch him from the fire again." Grove hefted the long Sharps rifle into the crook of his arm and shoved a moccasin into the stirrup. "I'm gettin' too old for this sort of thing, Rose. A man my age ought to be sittin' back and enjoying life, not gallivantin' all over creation keepin' brash young men from getting their blamed fool heads blow'd off." He settled onto the saddle with a grunt.

"I'm going with you."

Grove looked down at her. "Oh no you ain't, young lady."

Jones kicked at a loose rock in what remained of the foundation where their cabin had stood before the spring floods ripped it away. The corrals farther up the sloping side of the claim were still there; they were in need of repair, of course, but what did it matter—he had no oxen to put in them. He went to the toolshed where he, Rose, and Alice had passed the night waiting for the floodwaters to recede. The door hung open, and as he'd expected, the building had been stripped clean of all his tools.

Looking around, he realized that he had nothing left—nothing but his horse and his revolver. Not even a pipe and tobacco to smoke!

Footsteps crunched on the gravel behind him. Jones turned. General Dawson gave him a thin smile and glanced around.

"Planning to work it again?"

Jones shook his head. "Just thought I'd look the place over one last time."

"You going to sell out?"

"I haven't decided."

"Plenty of buyers in town would be happy to give you almost anything you ask. Deadwood is booming, and it doesn't look like it is going to end anytime soon. This town has got gold in its blood, Mr. Jones."

"I've sort of lost interest in it."

"Where is Rose?"

"With her people. I didn't want her coming back here."

"And the baby?"

Jones glanced away. "Alice died in the attack. She's buried out there." He inclined his head to the south. "Somewhere on the Nebraska plains. And a year from now, the place will be lost and forgotten. Just a part of that vast grassland where once there was only the buffalo, and the Sioux.''

Dawson winced. ''I know there is nothing that a man can say, except I'm sorry. You still think it was white men who did it to you?''

Jones looked back at him, a fire burning suddenly in his eyes. ''I know it was, General. Don't try to tell me otherwise.''

''I wasn't going to. In fact, after you left I remembered something. That's why I came here.''

''What?''

''Hickok was murdered last month.''

That was unexpected news. ''I hadn't heard. But I guess it shouldn't surprise me too much. Men like Hickok who live by the gun usually have short lives.''

''He was back-shot. By a coward named Jack McCall. But that's not what I came here to tell you, Mr. Jones. When Hickok died, he had this in his vest pocket.'' Dawson dropped the beaded pouch into Jones's hand.

Jones stared at it. ''But how . . .'' He was confused. ''It was taken from me after we were attacked. Was Hickok one of them?''

''No. I asked Hickok's buddy Charlie Utter about it. Charlie said that Hickok took that off a fellow in a card game. Hickok called it his 'good luck charm.' ''

Jones's fist balled tight, clenching the pouch and feeling the hard lump of gold within it. ''Good luck? It is turning out to be anything but that. Who did Hickok take it off of?''

Dawson grimaced. ''It was Ro Kinsey.''

''Kinsey?''

''I didn't want to believe it at first. Then I remembered that it was Kinsey who instigated that trouble here on your claim before you and Rose went off to Sidney. Well, then it all made sense.''

Jones's face changed, hard lines of determination deepening in it as his hand went to the .44 on his hip. The revolver came out smoothly. He checked the loads and then, snapping the loading gate closed, shoved it back into the holster and started into town.

"What are you going to do?" Dawson called after him.

"Settle up with Kinsey—like I should have years ago."

"He's got friends who will stand with him," Dawson said, but Jones never turned back. "You'll end up dead," he added, this time in a low voice, for Jones had already crossed the creek and was angling for the Paradise Saloon.

Dawson stood there a moment, regretting what he knew must now be Jones's fate. With a frown, he shoved his hands into his trouser pockets, and he was about to leave when a gravelly voice behind his left ear growled, "Who are you?"

Bradley Sink sucked the suds off the top of his beer mug as he leaned against the wall of the saloon, near the front window, looking out of it onto Main Street. Blakely had jumped the gun, he thought. Maybe Jones hadn't died out on that lonely road as they had thought, and somehow he had lived, and now he was back in Deadwood. So what? Sink couldn't see what the big deal was all about. Jones still had a gold claim here, didn't he? Where else would the man go once he had healed up?

Sink grinned as he recalled the scalping he had nearly given Jones. He was curious to see how that had healed over. He took a long pull at the beer, then sleeved the foam from his mouth and glanced back out the window. It was a big waste of time as far as he was concerned. Kinsey was acting hysterical, like Blakely, and Sink resented being the lackey sent out to keep an eye on things. If Blakely was so damned sure that Jones was going to come looking for them, *he* should be the one standing here and wasting his time staring out the window!

He took another drink. As he lowered the mug and looked back at the traffic on Main Street, his arm stopped. He squinted hard at the wavy, sand-cast glass, then stepped to the batwing doors and stared over the top of them. Could it be? Nathaniel Jones was coming up the street, the determination in his strides unmistakable.

It probably meant nothing, but . . . Jones angled across the street, heading straight for the Paradise Saloon. Sink set the beer aside. "Jones is coming!" he said, bursting through the back door.

Kinsey peered out into the saloon, then swiftly shut the door. "He's here," he said to Blakely and Swenson. "Quick, get out of sight. Remember what I told you, and for God's sake, don't start shooting until I'm out of the way." Kinsey cast a quick look at Sink. "Get behind those boxes with the others."

They dove for cover, and as the storeroom became deathly silent, Kinsey wiped his sweating palms on his vest, glanced at himself in the mirror by his desk, pushed a nervous hand through his tangled hair, and sat down to wait.

# THIRTY-TWO

Jones pushed through the batwing doors and glanced around the saloon. It took a moment for his eyes to adjust to the dim light inside the long building, and when they did, he didn't see Kinsey. He went to the bar, his eyes in constant motion, probing the shadowy corners and taking in every face there. Some were familiar to him, others weren't. No one took particular notice of him.

"Where is Kinsey?" He kept his voice neutral so as not to draw attention to himself. If Kinsey wasn't expecting him, so much the better.

Hannifin inclined his head in the direction of the rear of the saloon and the closed door. "In back."

Jones started toward it.

"Usually when it's shut, that means Mr. Kinsey don't want no visitors."

Jones ignored him and stepped on through. Kinsey glanced up from his desk and slowly removed the cigar from his mouth.

"Mr. Jones?" Kinsey said with a note of surprise. "Perhaps I ought to put up a sign that says 'Knock.' It seems a common courtesy that no one in these parts understands." He grinned. "What is it you want?"

The room, although it took up the entire back area of the saloon, wasn't overly large, and the boxes and casks stacked about made it seem cramped. There was a cleared corner where Kinsey had his desk. A window onto the alley let in light. The sun at this hour threw a bright beam into the storeroom and glanced off a stack of barrels labeled "Whiskey."

Jones reached back and threw the door latch.

"Fixing to stay a while, are you?"

"Have you ever taken the time to study how an Indian rides a pony?"

"That's a curious question, Mr. Jones. No, I have not."

"Maybe you should . . . especially if you want to impersonate one."

"Whatever are you talking about?" Kinsey's easy tone was tinged with strain.

Jones opened his hand. The beaded pouch fell out and dangled by the leather thong. Kinsey's face blanched. Jones knew he had the right man. "This was taken from me by the men who tried to murder me on the Sidney road."

"I heard it was Indians that attacked your freight wagon."

"They were supposed to *look* like Indians, but they rode their horses like white men." At that moment Jones caught a glimpse of his image in the mirror behind Kinsey's desk. It was the first time he'd seen himself since the near scalping, and he was stunned by the ugly, pinkish scar that encircled his head below his hairline like a fat earthworm. "They did this to me," he said, the anger exploding in his voice as he jabbed a finger at his head. "They murdered my child and tried to do the same to my wife."

"You saying it was me? You have no right busting in here and accusing me of that," Kinsey shot back. "You haven't a shred of proof, and there ain't a court in the world that will convict me." As he spoke, Kinsey eased his way out from behind the desk. He halted in the middle of the floor and then unexpectedly grinned at Jones like a circus clown.

Jones didn't know what to make of this until the flicker of a shadow, cast by the strong sunlight, moved against the back wall. He had been set up. . . .

He drew his revolver, leaping aside. At the same instant two men moved out of cover, their guns exploding, filling the tiny room with a deafening blast and clouds of gray smoke.

Jones hit the floor, rolling behind a wooden crate. The recent wound in his chest sent needles of fire up through his neck and arms. The pain was nearly overpowering, but he couldn't allow it to stop him now.

The gunfire stopped and from somewhere in the smoky room a man said, "Did we get him?"

"Go look," Kinsey's voice roared, "and hurry it up!"

Jones heard the footsteps. They stopped near the pile of crates. He brought his revolver up. Suddenly he was looking up into the wide, stunned eyes of a man he had never seen before; then he pulled the trigger and the face vanished in the bloom of gun smoke. Jones edged along the back side of a tower of wooden boxes.

"God! He blow'd Swenson's head off!" someone—not Kinsey—exclaimed. Men from the saloon began to pound on the locked door.

More shots rang out. Jones ducked, not knowing where they were coming from. He heard among the ear-shattering reports the sound of breaking glass. The shooting kept him pinned down, and when it suddenly ceased and he stepped around the barricade, the last of them was diving out the window.

Jones hefted a leg over the windowsill. A gunshot from the alley drove him back inside. Behind him, men were beating harder on the door. There was a squall of splintering wood as the jamb began to give way. Jones glanced out the window again. This time the alley was empty. He folded himself through it and plunged after them.

Turning a corner, he spied one of them turning another

corner down the street and disappearing among the cribs and saloons of the badlands.

A shot from a rooftop tore flying splinters from the corner of the building by his cheek. Jones fired, missed, and leaped behind a rain barrel as three more shots drilled holes into it. The barrel spouted fountains. Jones lost sight of the man on the roof, and he still hadn't seen where the other two were hiding. Quickly he ejected the spent shells from his Colt and reloaded.

Across town, General Dawson had been startled by the rough voice behind him. He'd turned and stared at the old man on a line-back mare, dressed in buckskins, face half hidden behind a wild beard, long gray hair flowing to his shoulders from beneath a battered hat. There was a narrow, impatient look about his eyes as he stared at Dawson. Across his saddle rested a long Sharps rifle.

"Don't jest stand there with your mouth catchin' flies, mister. I asked you a question."

Dawson recovered almost at once. "Who's asking?" he asked tersely. Then he saw the second rider. "Rose!" His view leaped between the Indian girl and the old mountain man, and suddenly he understood. "I'm a friend of Mr. Jones," Dawson said. "Rose can tell you."

"Well, maybe yes, and maybe no. You still didn't answer my question, mister: What are you doing on this claim?"

"I came with some information for Mr. Jones."

Grove cast his view around the claim site. "Well, I don't see him around nowhere."

"He was here a few minutes ago."

"Where is my husband now, General Dawson?"

"He's gone after them, Rose."

"After who?" Grove demanded.

"The men who attacked him on the road to Sidney." Dawson looked at Rose. "The men who killed your little girl."

"How many are there?"

Dawson's sympathetic view lingered a moment on Rose before he looked back at Grove. "I don't know. The leader is a fellow named Ro Kinsey, and he has two or three men who tag along with him. Could be four all together, or even more."

"Kinsey!" Grove's snort ruffled the hairs of his beard. "I warned Nate that man was poison. Nate went alone, did he?"

"Yes."

"When?"

"He left here only a couple minutes ago. I suspect he was heading for the Paradise Saloon. Ro Kinsey owns it."

They heard the muffled gunshots from the heart of Deadwood. Grove glanced at the rows of wooden buildings across the creek. "Damnation! I'm a-gettin' too old for this sort of foolishness." He handed his reins over to Rose and slid out of the saddle.

"I'm going with you."

"No you ain't, young lady," Grove barked as he started into town as fast as his old legs would carry him.

Rose watched him a moment, frowning, then swung off her saddle too, thrusting the reins into General Dawson's hands.

Grove didn't see Rose angled off along Sherman Street. He had pointed himself in a different direction. At Main Street a crowd had gathered along the boardwalks and in shop doors. He wheeled to a stop. Scattered gunfire had started farther down the street, in the badlands, and the prudent folks were keeping well back. They had seen gun battles raging in the streets of Deadwood before, and more than one curious onlooker had found himself a permanent resident of the burgeoning graveyard up Whitewood Gulch.

Grove dropped Big 50's loading lever to check that there was a live shell in the chamber, and started down the street.

In another part of town, Nathaniel Jones crouched near the ground behind a leaky water barrel. From around the corners of two nearby buildings, Kinsey and Blakely were systematically punching holes in its oaken staves, and as the water drained lower, some of their slugs had begun to drill clear through both sides of it. Jones was hunkered down as low as he could get, and soon he'd have to make a break, for the water inside the barrel would no longer protect him from their bullets.

Somewhere overhead, Sink had set up a crossfire. Jones could only fleetingly catch a glimpse of him as he darted from behind a cupola, fired twice, then ducked back. Sink kept up a steady barrage, but Jones managed to snap off a shot toward the roof in return. Then a bullet tore though a barrel stave and burned a furrow along his right shoulder.

Jones rolled out from behind the barrel, his revolver cracking as fast as he could thumb the hammer. Leaping to his feet, he took three long strides and dove behind a privy a few dozen feet away. A second later a half dozen bullet holes splintered in the back boards, searching him out. Jones hunkered down, reloading his gun from the dwindling supply on his holster belt. He examined the searing pain in his shoulder. There was lots of blood, but little damage.

Glancing around, he could see no way out of this trap. Behind him, the gulch rose steeply to Williams Street, fifty feet above. He might scramble up it, but his back would be exposed to their bullets. The alleyway in front would put him in the clear line of fire too, like standing in a shooting gallery, he thought wryly. Between the two choices, the hillside offered marginal protection from Kinsey and Blakely, but opened him wide up to Sink's gunfire from his high vantage point atop the building.

Jones had no choice. He couldn't stay where he was. Crawling to the edge of the structure, he weighed his chances and then, aiming a deadly hail of fire at the rooftop cupola protecting Sink, sprang from cover and scrambled up the side of the hill.

Jones's heart battered his ribs as he fought the pain in

his shoulder, his chest, and his searing lungs, clawing up the slope like a monkey one step ahead of a leopard. The rocky slope was full of rubble from the construction overhead on Williams Street—but there was not a shred of cover anywhere.

A chunk of rock near his right hand exploded, sending blinding shards of stone into his eyes and face. Jones pulled back, lost his grip, and in a small landslide of loose rubble slid back down to the alleyway. His eyes cleared as he came to a stop. Shaking his head, he sat up, and there at the edge of the roof across the way stood Bradley Sink.

"I got him, Ro!" Sink shouted to his partner. "He's sitting here like a duck in a barrel!"

"Finish him off" came the command from somewhere beyond Jones's view.

A slanting grin came to Sink's face as he leveled his revolver at Jones.

A cannonlike boom suddenly echoed among the buildings, and at that same instant Sink was mule-kicked off the edge of the building. He flipped over and landed in a heap at Jones's feet.

The sound of that report was like an old voice speaking to him. He'd have recognized it anywhere. *Carson Grove!* He pressed up against the backside of a bordello and fed the last of his bullets into the revolver. With Sink out of the way, Jones scooted behind buildings and caught a glimpse of a blue shirtsleeve disappearing around a corner. Blakely and Kinsey were sprinting down the alley toward Main Street by the time he went after them. They wheeled and fired. Jones threw himself into a shallow doorway. He peeked around. A gunshot drove him back.

Then from somewhere far off, Carson Grove's big Sharps boomed again. Blakely flipped out into the mouth of the alley and sprawled in the dirt. Jones left his cover and ran to the body in time to see Kinsey dart into Saloon No. 10 down the street. Up the street, Carson Grove was shoving a .50-caliber cartridge into the chamber of his heavy rifle. Grove raised a hand and gave Jones a wave.

Jones spun and retraced his steps, hurrying along the rear of the buildings until he was at the back door of Nuttall and Mann's. The door hung open, and he slipped into a darkened storage room and made his way through it to the barroom. A dozen men crowded the front windows, peering hard into the street. Kinsey was not among them. There was nowhere in the narrow building for Kinsey to hide . . . and then Jones realized the truth. Kinsey had only passed through the place, and had left the back door open on his way out.

Jones raced to the alley and glanced along it. There was only one way Kinsey could have gone without Jones having seen him, and he started that way now.

Kinsey felt the first real pangs of panic when the big Sharps rifle boomed and Blakely cartwheeled into the alleyway. Seeing the puff of white smoke up the street, and the old buffalo hunter, Kinsey suddenly realized that he was now alone in this battle, that Jones had reinforcements. Not liking the odds, he decided it was time to break off the confrontation and find his way out of town as quickly as possible. He would lay low until he could regroup his forces and come back and finish the job he had started.

Nuttall and Mann's seemed the likeliest place to throw the hounds off his scent, and ducking inside, he shoved past the crowd there, burst through a back door, and then ran out the rear door into the alley. It was momentarily deserted. Starting east, he found himself once again among the cribs of the badlands, and then the tiny shacks of Chinatown.

Kinsey wheeled to a stop at a narrow footpath between two buildings, and was about to turn left and make his way into the hills when he saw something that instantly changed his plans. A woman had started up the path from Main Street below. Kinsey pressed against the back of the building as her footsteps grew louder. Grinning at his good fortune, he listened to the sound of her approach, timed his move, then reached around and grabbed Rose.

She struggled at first, but went rigid when the muzzle of his revolver touched her temple.

Jones pounded along the alley, the old wound like a clenched fist in his chest, the new one like a red-hot iron lying on his shoulder. He managed to ignore both pains as he drew up among the shacks of Chinatown, suddenly realizing that he might have lost Kinsey. He glanced around and listened, but the pounding of blood in his ears had deadened all other sounds as he started to move again, slower this time, watchful.

He had just passed a narrow way between two buildings when a voice turned him instantly around.

"Drop the gun, Jones," Kinsey's low growl reached out to him from the shadows. At the same time two forms separated from the darker shape of a couple planks of lumber leaning there. "I said drop it!" Kinsey barked again, stepping out into the open and pressing the muzzle of his revolver harder against Rose's head.

Rose gritted her teeth against the pain, her eyes wide with fear. There was a tight, determined grin on Ro Kinsey's face. "I'll spread her brains all over this alley if that gun don't hit the ground in five seconds!"

Jones eased down and set the gun on the ground.

"That's better."

"Let Rose go. It's me you want."

"You got that wrong. It's both of you. And then, when the time is right, I'll take care of that old man too. Nobody crosses Ro Kinsey and gets away with it, whether it be a famous gunfighter, a nosy preacher, or a nobody like you, Jones."

"Hickok and Smith. You had them both killed?"

"Considering you won't be around to tell anyone, yeah, I had them killed, or did it myself. And they weren't the first."

"You killed our child," Rose said.

"That wasn't in the plan, but it don't matter now anyway."

"It mattered much to me and my husband."

Kinsey gave a short laugh and pointed the revolver at Jones. "I suppose it might matter . . . to you. But don't worry none, because if you believe in the hereafter, her father is about to arrive. And you won't be far behind him."

Kinsey's finger whitened on the trigger. Rose's hand came out of the pouch at her waist and she drove the short skinning knife deep into his side. He gave a startled cry and flinched. The revolver exploded. Rose broke from his grip, her sharp nails raking his eyes.

Jones dove to the ground, grabbed up the revolver, thumbed the hammer and fired. Kinsey staggered back against a wall, eyes huge with shock. Jones fired again, slamming him harder into the building. A third bullet nailed him to the side. Again, and again until the hammer dropped upon a spent shell. Kinsey's eyes remained wide and staring as he slipped to the ground, leaving a bloody smear along the side of the building.

Rose was at Jones's side, her body quivering as he drew her close to him and held her tight. People began to show up, peeking cautiously around the corners at first, then gathering around them.

Carson Grove shoved his way through them, peered down at Kinsey, then glared at Rose. "I thought I told you to stay put, young lady."

"My place is at my husband's side."

"Neither one of you should be here," Jones said. "But I'm glad you are. How'd you know I'd be needing your help?"

"It's a long story, Nate." Grove shot a narrow look at Rose. "It's all about womenfolk who don't know how to take no for an answer." Grove slung Big 50 over his shoulder and grinned past the forest of white whiskers encircling his face. "Come on, let's get out of here."

It was nearly dusk when Jones, Rose, and Carson Grove brought their horses to a stop at the brown rocks overlooking the boomtown of Deadwood. Rough wooden buildings filled the narrow gulch from east to west as far as their eyes could see from this high vantage point. Shadows were beginning to gather in the valley, darkening the streets where a few hours before Jones and Rose had almost lost their lives.

Rose reached out and took her husband's hand. "You regret leaving?"

Jones had been looking at the rocky site of his claim . . . his *ex*-claim. He had signed it over to Willard Darnell, the down-on-his-luck army doctor who had set Rose's broken leg and cared for her after the cattle stampede.

"No, I do not regret it, Rose. I was just thinking how much it has changed since I first laid eyes on the gulch, when we brought you and One Stab here after that bear attack. Remember?"

"I remember. Much has changed. For both of us."

He looked at her and smiled. "I reckon it has. It's time we find us somewhere to make a new start. Someplace where we can raise that baby you're carrying. In peace."

"I will like that."

Grove leaned forward in his saddle and peered at the hillside upon which they had halted their horses. "I look around me, Nate, and all I see is the dead looking back. It was right here, right where we are standing, that Fontenelle found that gold nugget, and it was just a few feet beyond that he died. Since then, how many others? This here would be fitting ground for a boneyard."

Jones suddenly remembered the pouch and took it from his pocket. The horseshoe-shaped lump of gold fell heavily onto his palm. "You were right all along, Mr. Grove: It has brought nothing but bad luck." He looked at his wife. Rose nodded her head, understanding what he had to do. Jones dropped the nugget.

"It's finally back where it belongs, and I hope it stays put this time." Carson Grove snorted.

Jones and Rose turned their horses from the brown rocks and started away. Carson Grove nudged his horse after them.

"Where you figuring' on heading, Nate?" he asked.

"West."

"That leaves it wide open."

"Wide open is the way I prefer it right now, Mr. Grove."

"Mind if me and the missus ride along?"

Jones grinned over his shoulder at the old man. "Be our pleasure, Mr. Grove."